Russ L. Howard Library for House of Howard Publishing

The King of Three Bloods:

Book One: The Sire Sheaf
Book Two: The Frightful Dance
Book Three: Witan Jewell
Book Four: The Isle of Ilkchild
Book Five: The Bok of Syr Folk
Book Six: The King-Queen
Book Seven: The Scynscatha
Book Eight: Brekka
Book Nine: El Yid
Book Ten: The Evil Ennead
Book Eleven: Rebirth of the Elven-Gods

TheKingofThreeBloods.com

Visit the author on Facebook:

TheKingofThreeBloods.com/fb

THE
EVIL ENNEAD
BOOK TEN:

THE KING OF THREE BLOODS

RUSS L. HOWARD

ACKNOWLEDGMENTS

I EXTEND MY GRATITUDE TO PAULA Riggs whose tireless editing spanned seven years, much of which required her to endure my corny jokes, and to her husband Carl who had to endure the many blood drenched battle scenes in the book. Much appreciated help came from Jeff Day in preserving my sanity through dealing with my hated computer and for computer and technical assistance above and beyond waking hours. Particular thanks to Susie Stokes for her exquisite artistic talents and formatting despite her own busy schedule, and she, too, gave endless hours of technical direction. I give praise to my beloved wife whose constant feed-back and aide has always inspired me, and to my son, Adam, who gave continuous encouragement and deeply thought out opinions when asked. I thank my many children and my devoted friends who repeatedly asked, "Is it done yet?" Unto them I say, "Here it is."

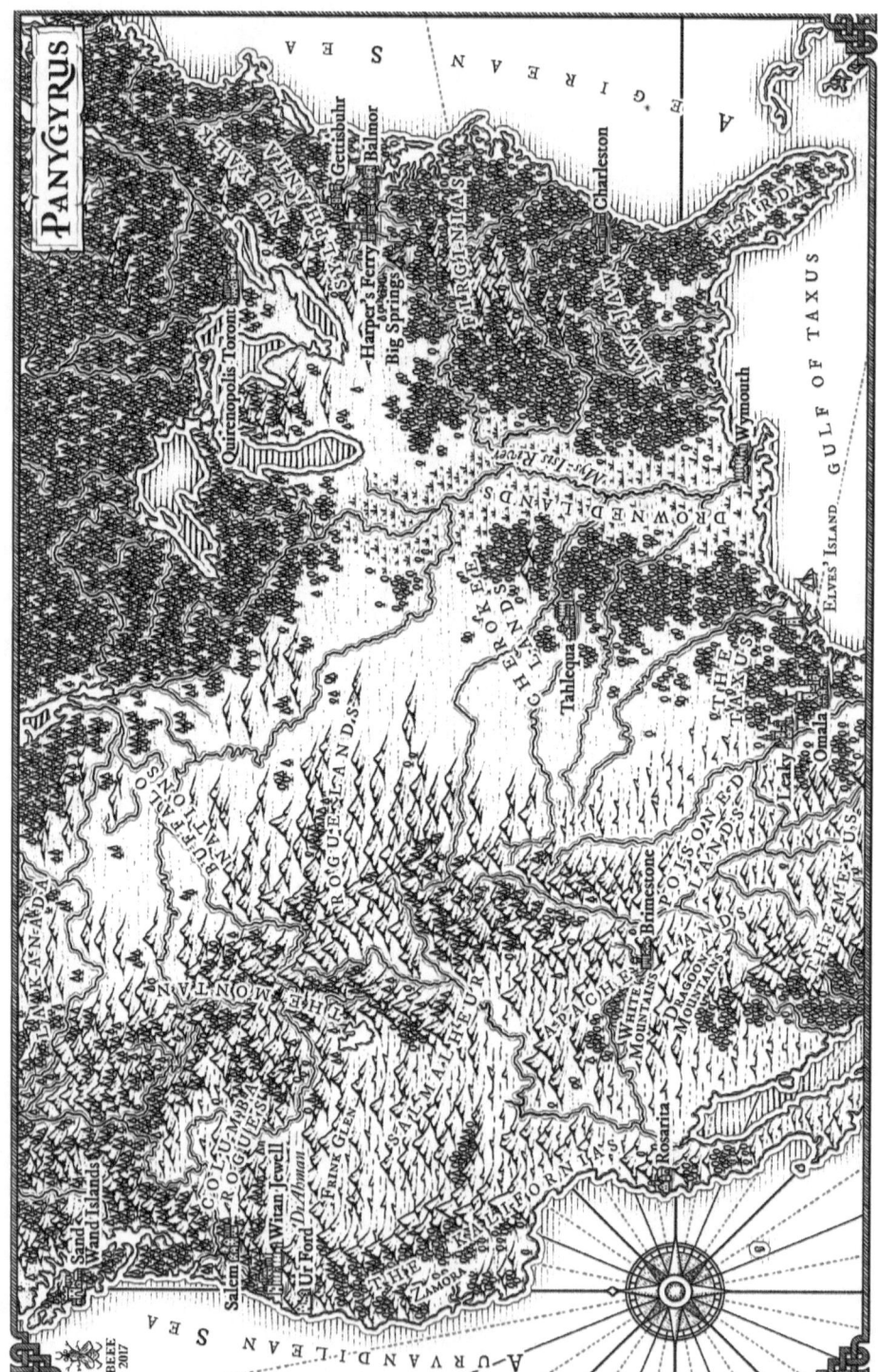

The Lands of Flight

A. Va Gedura
B. Mt. Hrumburg
C. Ur Ford
D. Abandon
E. Maiden's Head
F. Charly's Harbor
G. Table Rock Settlement
H. Hrusburg
I. Witan Jewell
J. Black Top
K. Namen Jewell
L. Eugene Zonga
M. Salem
N. The Sisters
O. Irmansul
P. Mt. Hereward/Yourlokes
Q. DiAhman
R. Mt. Leofric
S. Crater of the Elk Spirit
T. Klamath Lake
U. Forr Rock
V. Buzzards Run

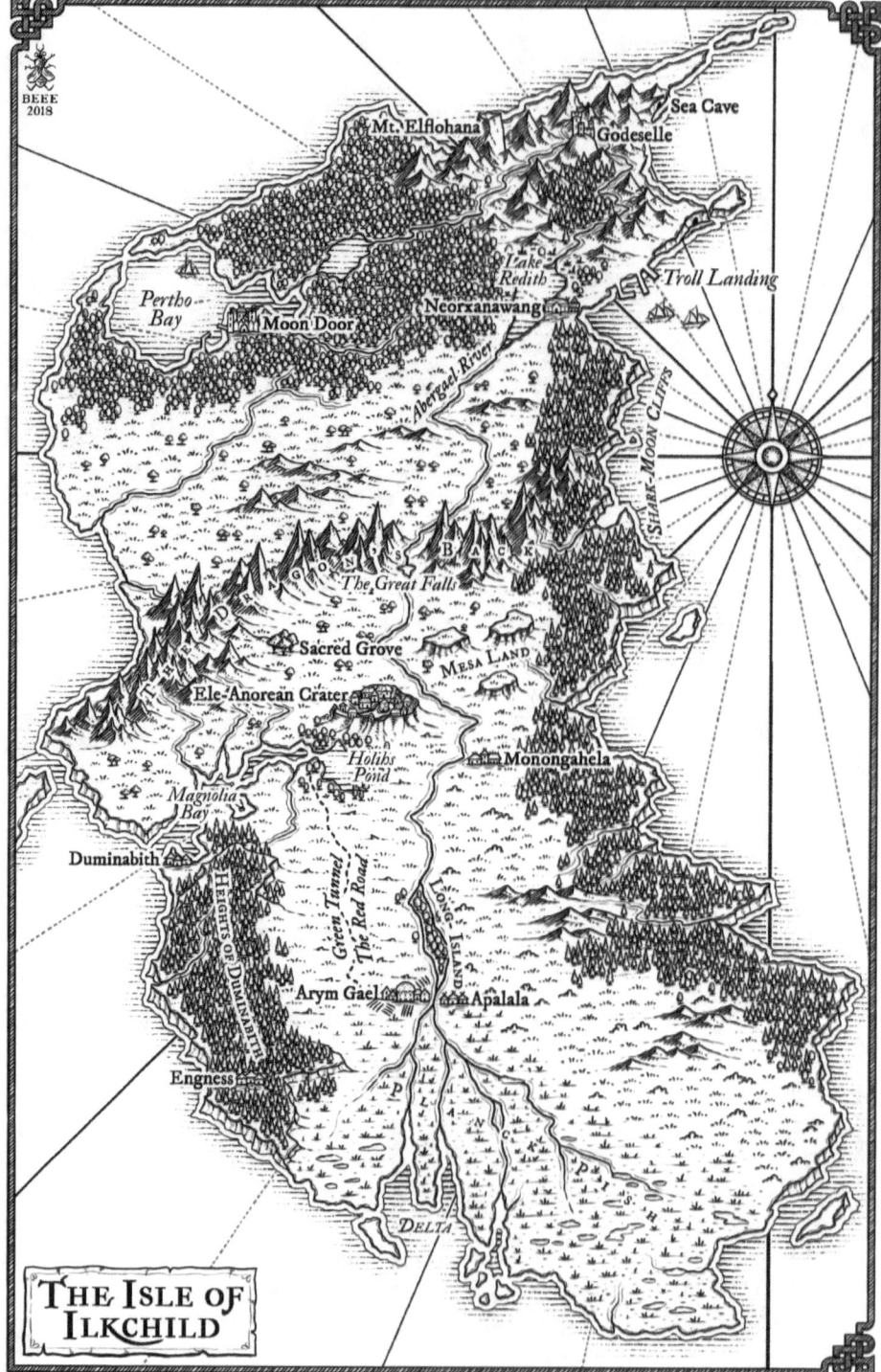

THE ISLE OF ILKCHILD

TABLE OF CONTENTS

CHAPTER 1 :

THE LAMENTATIONS OF KANARUS

ARUNDEL'S JOURNAL: IN THE YEAR *604 H.S.O. counting from the death Hrus-Syr-Os and the flight of the great falcon into the sun, we are fiercely locked in mortal combat with the emperor and his evil minions within his own lands. It appears to be the End War. The evil Ennead have murdered Wilona Saga-Jah-El-Ea, wife of Kanarus the Half-King, and they have dealt some very deadly blows to our forces. We shall not cease to call upon our gods for victory, for it is here we shall both crash and burn or like the fanisk bird rise from the ashes of our past and become victorious over our eternal enemy, the Pitters.*

"Great Ev-Rhett's Ghost," Arundel shouted. "Almighty All Father, seest thou what they have done to thy daughter? By the gods, this is Baldur's sister they've slain. For this, they will surely incur the wrath of the gods and feel the fury of Thor's rage."

Kanarus jumped from his horse with a scream of gut-wrenching anguish that made all the horses nearby to rear up in fright. A sight Sur

Sceaf had never before witnessed. He steadied even his own mount. Kanarus' breast had heaved so mightily that the rings of his chain-mail snapped and sprinkled on the ground before him. He threw down his white plumed helm and ran down the hill, threw himself to the earth and carefully cradled Wilona's head in his left arm. He laid face down upon the earth, throwing dust upon his golden head of hair as he cried out repeatedly, "Wilona, Wilona, Wilona, why art thou stolen from me? Why has the black faery come for you of all people? No second grief can ever touch me as deep so long as I live."

Freyxus leapt from her mount, took her golden takin fleece, and ran to comfort Kanarus. She laid the fleece over him and placed her hand upon his back, and wept mightily. Brekka's hand maids, Ynys and Wyth ran down the hill, covered Wilona's head with their scarves and reverently carried it back to their tent.

Kanarus held his hand up to Freyxus and said, "There is no comfort to be had here, Elf Maiden. Just burn me alive." The Half-King lifted his dust covered head up and looked at Sur Sceaf, "I beg you, Lord Sur Sceaf, build me a fiery byre right here. Melt away my sorrowful heart and let the flames send my spirit straightway into Wilona's white arms. I cannot live without her. I cannot live. Please, Almighty Norn Sisters, send me from mortal labor to refreshment. Let me join my wife in the halls of Valhalla. Let the celestial barge of Ullr take me away from this place of wrath and doom."

After a long silence, Freyxus and Verushka led Kanarus off the field and up to Sur Sceaf where his mount was being held by Uffa. Once again the Half-King collapsed in grief to the ground. Ruhm watched in deep sorrow as the evening sun beat down mercilessly with its last fierce red beams on the opening battle scene. Lord Sur Sceaf's face was riddled with mirrored pain for Kanarus. His attention was then drawn to Brekka hiding several knives in her sleeves, on and about her body--as Kanarus and the Apaches often do--where they were so cunningly disguised.

Oh no! What is she planning on doing? As if by some internally choreographed cue, Brekka held the iridium interior of her shield up to the last blazing rays of the sun. Ruhm saw her place her right hand in the center of it and watched the metal transmute into something that looked like quicksilver on a mirror's surface. She swept the beam of light coming from it like a flaming sword over the gawking, guffawing commissars. An instant later screams of agony came from atop the fortress wall. Her shield sliced its emitting ray at what appeared to be many times the brightness of the sun, so hot that some of the rocks on the turret exploded.

Commissars ran off the wall with smoking hoods. The emperor fled with Katus clinging to his sleeve. The top branches of the dead oak tree burned with flames that sent the carrion birds skyward in a dark cloud. Only Sanangrar was unaffected and continued to stare on, having had the benefit of a shielded -turret to block the rays of Brekka's shield.

Having achieved her purpose, Brekka lowered her shield and swung it behind her. In Ruhm's eyes she looked as fierce and as beautiful as a golden tigress as she circled her white buffalo. Her molten mane of hair, where it escaped her helm, shone bright in the evening sunlight. She raised her hand into the hold-fast sign for her lady knights and cried aloud, "Holy Night of the Mothers! I swear by hair and breast of Mother Freya and Mother Holle that I shall avenge Wilona's death. Evil must come, but woe unto those by whom it comes."

With little warning Brekka commanded her twelvers, and Spanix fyrd, "Do not leave Lord Arundel's side. I have an appointment to keep, and I swear by woon, there will be blood on those nine scarecrows tonight beginning with Sanangrar."

Incensed, she scowled at Sanangrar still standing atop the wall, took out her golden arrow and fired it randomly as if taking no thought or bother to even aim. It flew straight like a shaft of golden light, then darted, looped, and curved like a swallow in flight, zeroed in on Sanangrar and entered his skull right between the eyes. Sanangrar grabbed his face and dropped backwards, dead. The Syr Folk hosts cheered. The rest of the Pitters did not return along the wall. Awestruck, Ruhm had to consider what sort of Herewardi witchcraft could direct an arrow of death with that much accuracy, for the likes of such was never known among his people.

Suddenly, Brekka charged up the ramp on Ma-Za-Ma, shaking her spear in one hand. Instantly the cheers turned to cries of surprise and horror before silence fell like a heavy blanket. Ruhm felt to follow, but she did not beckon, and it could not have been any more painful to have one's heart torn out by its roots. It was as if she had leaped across an impassable abyss, and he could not follow to protect.

He was so distraught, he asked for permission to follow. "My lord, may I accompany her?"

Lord Arundel, too, looked to the king and exclaimed, "And I too, Father?"

Sur Sceaf looked them square on, "Suffer her to do this alone, so that all prophecy may be fulfilled."

Ruhm said, "Prophecy be damned…" before he trailed off in silence.

The shadow of evening began creeped up the bastion wall as the sun took its nightly journey down into the Underworld. The Pitters had not expected any such play. Their guards had left the wall once Brekka had beamed them with her elven shield, and Sanangrar's surprise death had drawn their attention away from closing the gates.

Without warning or announcement of intent, Brekka hurled her spear through the chest of one of the priests by the altar and slew the other with her two-bladed battle axe in the passing, before launching Ma-Za-Ma through the gates, swinging her axe like the black faery.

Ruhm's heart grew sick as the iron doors immediately closed after her with a loud *clunk,* like the heavy lid of a sepulcher. There she was, buried alive in a rat pit. Visions of them swarming over her wracked his soul to the core.

His mind twisted in horror, and his heart was overwhelmed with prayers for her welfare. He feared the same fate awaited her as had befallen Wilona Saga-Jah-El-Ea. *My god, that which I feared the most is come to pass. Her recklessness has finally become fatal. She has passed through the door of death from which there can be no return.*

Lord Arundel was beside himself with fear for his sister, whereas Lord Sur Sceaf remained calm and resolved, though his eyes burned with anguish. It was all Ruhm could do to keep from going after her, despite Sur Sceaf's refusal. His stomach churned and his wits failed him. Spitzer pawed and churned up the ground beneath his feet, unsure at the leg signals his master was generating. Ruhm could not imagine what was happening to the woman he so loved at that moment. Any such thought was too crushing to even allow. The entire hosts seemed to be shared in his torment.

To kindle a flame of hope, he rehearsed in his mind past battle scenes in which he had watched her engage the enemy like the tigress she always was, only to emerge with the victory in her teeth, but this appeared to be nothing less than suicide brought on by her grief over Wilona's beheading.

He glanced down at Kanarus, who was bowed in grief and still receiving comfort from the battle maidens. His friend appeared to have regained some modicum of composure, for he looked up from the ground at Sur Sceaf, and choked out, "My king, the gods do try me in their crucible. I have sinned in losing the lives of my faithful warriors in not being eternally vigilant. I broke the vows of a ring lord to protect my warriors. And I tempted the gods by offering them that which was dearest to me, thinking it would be my life they took, not my wife's. Instead they called payment on my boast." Kanarus smote upon his chest and looked up to the heavens as he cried out, "Forgive me All Father, but why, why didst thou not take me in her stead? I put on the green for thy sake. Why didst thou not take me and receive me as thy offering in her place?"

Sur Sceaf had a look of sincere compassion on his face as he looked upon the tormented White Apache. "Kanarus, Son of Ilker, the gods love you as a son and lay no charge at your feet. I know there is no comfort to be found in this moment, but in the name of Wilona's son, Anghrus, do not throw your life away on the Pitters' spears. Stay in the mind of a commander for your king's sake and for your people's sake. Be a brave heratoga unto your people this day. The line of our fathers back to the beginning is counting on you. Deal these demons the calculated death blows they deserve. By Almighty Sky-Clad Freya, you know Wilona would wish it so."

Talburt, Kanarus' new third in command, ran up to Kanarus and said, "My lord, it is enough you have suffered. I speak for all your men. From this day on we will all don the green with the same vow as yours, and follow our green knight to the other side of Hell to avenge your faery-queen. But to carry out that vow we need you here to lead us. Let's make them pay in full double measure for this abomination." Talburt raised his right hand to signal Kanarus' troops. All the Kaninchens under their yellow rabbit banner shouted in unison, "So mote it be." As the cries echoed over the assemblage, all eyes fastened on Sur Sceaf, but no commands came from either the high king or his son, the battle tactician, Lord Arundel.

Kanarus bawled aloud, making Ruhm feel like joining him for the fate which must surely now await Brekka. All, save for Kanarus and the tortured souls hanging from the bastion walls in the crow cages, sank into expectant silence. Every soldier, as far as Ruhm could see, sat bereaved. The painful knot in his throat threatened to suffocate him. Had not Kanarus told him the night before that he heard the cry of the black faery, the summoning call of Herewardi royals to their death? Suddenly, Ruhm found he was drowning in beliefs that were alien to his upbringing. Before, he would have dismissed these supernatural phenomena as coincidence, but now he was forced to give them some credence, for they were unfolding before his very eyes.

The cloud of grief that hung over the armies was shattered as Hrolwylf, the silver harrier, charged through the ranks on horseback. He was road weary, with torn, blood-soaked shirt, but as excited as a homing pigeon returning home to its loft. Within earshot of Ruhm, he delivered the message to Sur Sceaf, "My lord and king! Great news! Il-Alim has defeated the Pitter zonga of Charleston, collected great treasures, and the legions are fleeing in retreat back into Flar-Dah. He has assigned the new leadership in Charleston to General Messen and instructed them in self-government as you advised. Captain Juan is heading out to strike the legion's supply trains ahead of them, and Degataga has joined him to wolf-pack the Pitters as they retreat." The harrier paused to take breath. "Alim has sent me to ask if you wish him to pursue the legions to death."

"Tis well, Hrolwylf," Sur Sceaf said. "Rest, eat, get your wounds tended to, and we'll send another harrier to Il-Alim's harrier waiting in Winchester to relay the message along the harrier lines." Sur Sceaf turned to Uffa. "Write that I instruct Alim to carry on in cryptic mode, until we can address his needs properly with cavalry and troops. Order him to hold at Charleston and not to engage in any more major conflicts until we have first secured this zonga. Then bid our harrier to run the message by way of the Shenandoah Pike so as to avoid the rat packs still running loose."

Kanarus rose up out of the dust with eyes of fire and rage. His mount was brought to him by Uffa before he rode off to fulfill Sur Sceaf's order. Still a bit unsteady on his feet, Kanarus mounted and as he did so, his men began beating their shields with their swords and repeatedly shouted, "Kanarus, Kanarus, Kanarus," in a passion Ruhm had never seen before. The very walls of the zonga seemed to quake. Ruhm held back tears of relief to see his friend had arisen from abject grief to battle rage and readiness.

But hour after agonizing hour passed with no sign of anyone on the walls, and only torturous silence coming from the black iron gates as darkness began to envelope the Ea-Urth. The very air hung with death, oppressive heat, pesky mosquitos, and anguish of heart such as he had never known. He yearned for Brekka. His heart twisted and panted for her. *Where is my beloved? Will I ever bring her home again? God, I love that woman, but she is the damnedest and most constant source of torment to my soul I've ever known.*

Now, Ruhm chastised himself for not having gone after Brekka, and in the coming darkness, thoughts of horror were fearfully compounded. How could I have let her go it alone? It was all very shocking and happened all too suddenly for me to reason the best course of action. But she so strongly hates my mantling her with my protection? If I ran to her aid, it would have been the timber that broke the mule's back. All the same, in hindsight I would have done it anyway. I'd prefer to die with her to than live with this agony of not knowing what fate is befalling her behind those dark walls. Wait, there is one thing I can do.

Glancing around, he noticed Sur Sceaf had ridden over to confer with his blood brother, Mendaka; the peer of the gods in counsel on a strategy. Ruhm waited until Sur Sceaf acknowledged him and then said, "My lord, it is dark enough now, the Jokers are cave scouts and can lead us to the hidden passage. Shall I take a detachment and lead an internal attack on the fortress? Perchance to rescue Brekka?"

Sur Sceaf shook his head. "No, your cavalrymen will not be any good at ground warfare, or should I say, underground warfare?"

"Not as good as your fyrd, but certainly up to the task. I, more than anyone, bear the most desire to free Brekka."

Sur Sheaf nodded an acknowledgement, "Better you should take Starkwulf, Russell, and Ev-Rhett, and their twelvers than your horsemen. Pray Charly Duke's hidden passage is real, and if so, go through the caves. Once you get inside, do not fight for anything but the front gates. Get them open and there won't be a Pitter left to stand against a wall in the morning. May Baldur speed you before it is too late."

Ruhm was elated. Perhaps now he could rescue his beloved. "It shall be done, my lord."

As Ruhm rode off to fetch the cave scouts, he looked up to see the dead tree at the gate entrance. The fire in the branches had long cooled, but the tree endured. It was eerily lit by sconces of light along the bastion wall, and the tree was now loaded with sleeping vultures so thick the branches were weighed down and seemed to ooze with blood. Unless his eyes were playing tricks on him, he saw dark ethereal forms moving on and about it.

The Herewardi were right in their assessment. This truly was a tree of terror.

Lord Arundel took his place in the line of commanders, having had Wyth and Ynys take the head of Wilona to Kanarus' tent as prescribed by holy ritual so as to sing her spirit a safe journey through the Underworld where the chariots of the Idisi would swing low to carry her safely up to Valhalla. Once in the Hall of Heroes and the Hall of Freya she would feast with them and the gods and goddesses in the evening, and take up their far flung battles throughout the galaxies during the day.

Sensing the somber mood, Redelfis and Yellow Horse remained near and silent. Kanarus was heart sore and weary; his eyes still red from weeping. However, he had regained enough composure to sit mounted on the other side of Sur Sceaf. Arundel's heart not only ached for his cousin warrior, Kanarus, kinsman of his mother, but it also wrenched and tightened like a wet knot for Brekka. Sadness seemed to multiply sadness.

Since she was a toddler herding flocks of geese on the farm, his relationship with his sister ran ever so deep. Hunts with her in the night woods, the encounter with the grizzly in Glide Garth, and the hunt of the grass beast all came flooding back in his memory, as well as the many fun days together at Ele-Anor-Ness learning the tree magic and bee magic together from his beloved wife and bee mother, the queen Zschamillah. When Brekka was five winters, she had already began to press him to teach her the skills of a warrior. When he finally yielded, he found that the linden shield was taller than she was, and the arrows were a full ell's length long and would have served her tiny hands better as a spear than an arrow. Over the years he and Ilkchild had taught Brekka to be an accomplished sword master, how to use a long bow, how to swim, how to fight with staves, how to memorize the sacred codes, and always stood as her advocate whenever needed. Her mother, Lana the Quailor, did not like the way the twig was being bent, especially since Brekka took to the warrior spirit as if it were her in-born nature. He remembered the time he had to explain to his near-mother, Lana that his Herewardi ancestor, Ullr the shield maker and weapons smith so loved Adelonda, a Quailor girl, that he became baptized into the Sea of Christ and joined the Quailor, whereupon the Quailor renamed him Hollar and called him Ludwig. After several years he returned to many of his Herewardi ways and took Redith to wife, and was to take Lila to wife when he was slain defending Salem.

Brekka, of all Arundel's kin, was the dearest to his heart. She was as much a daughter to him as she was a sister. Always he had had to defend her right to be what she was, a lady-warrior, but this impulsive behavior was the part of her being a lady knight that he hated more than anything else. Repeatedly, during their training sessions, he had tried his best to temper her reckless disregard of logical consequences. But he knew that her capriciousness was what also endeared her to him and gave her such power to confuse his heart and to destroy her enemies.

The black leghorn cock crowed from its stone monolith, apparently, due to all the torch and lamp light it mistook for dawn. It was a false harbinger for daybreak, which would not come any time soon. This was to be a long and dark night in Syr Folk history.

Soon the stark night sky grew its star marks. Crickets began to chirp, and swifts darted above, with their singing of a melancholy night song. At his father's direction, Arundel brought the armies of Kanarus, Ruhm's cavalry, and the dog soldiers to the fore. He just sat mounted, staring on at those iron gates and willing them to open with all the energy of his heart. Still they remained tightly shut and locked as if welded. Only the horrible demonic creatures on the gate stared back through the dark at him, their red eyes mocking his agony and frustration.

At a signal from Sur Sceaf, Arundel had the horn of Heimdal brought out to blast twelve times in the deepening twilight for Wilona's passing from the underworld over the Rainbow Bridge and into the realms of the Holy Idisi. Her soul having been weighed on the feather scale and having been found to be in perfect balance with the Forty-Four Laws, she was excused by the gods from labor to refreshment. At the first resonant tone of the horn, red, orange, yellow, green, blue, indigo, and violet lights rose into mist from within the Big Springs, causing all the Syr Folk armies to marvel. It was told by the old ones, that when great love exists between man and woman, that their offspring are given to hearing elven song and speech, and some few to understanding it. In the mist, Arundel heard harmonious voices, exultant hymns, but did not know whether it was by ear or thought. As he looked around, it seemed that for the most part, the troops were oblivious to the songs he was hearing, perhaps because they remained on the edge of human hearing, just as the speech of the gods was beyond the ability of the vast majority of human ears to hear.

As Arundel stared at the multicolored, shimmering display in the lap of the Big Springs, Redelfis, also hearing the hymns, leaned from the saddle to whisper only to him, "A goddess has died here today. The elven voices declare it so."

Yellow Horse murmured reverently, "Wilona was the whitest woman I ever saw. She was definitely of the fair elven race I have heard of in tales of the folk-mouth. No doubt, she is destined to take her seat in the councils of the gods from whence she came."

Arundel was terrified that this, too, might be the fate of his sister. No matter how glorious the Halls of Valhalla or Freya would surely be, he did not wish to part from her. No matter how composed Kanarus managed to appear, his torment was like riding with a rusty sword embedded in his heart. Arundel's heart drew into the tight knot of grief once again. He could not imagine the torture of losing one of his wives as Kanarus had done this day, but he knew he could not bear a life without seeing the smile of his dear sister that had so often greeted him with such cheer in the mornings, and remained his steadfast ally throughout life. Only the agony of his father and Ruhm could surpass his own. He swallowed his fears and vowed to rescue her. And if it were necessary to scale that wall, he would find a way to do so—or by the gods die trying!

At the final blast of Heimdal's heraldic horn, the ethereal lights ceased over the waters, and darkness closed back in again. The snorting *heorrr* of the mute swans reverberated across the springs. Carrying a torch, Ruhm and his motley crew of hillbilly boys rode along the line of commanders down the hill where the ballooners floated their colorful, well-lit air ships to the rendezvous point near the giant sycamores where the springs angle east. Under the billowing canopy of the sycamores waited Starkwulf and Va-Eyra, the thunder twins—Ev-Rhett and Russell, and the two twelvers with a mule loaded with torches, lamps, and cave gear.

Ruhm quickly introduced the Jokers. Having freshly come from stave fighting, the boys were smeared with dirt, and they were attired in little more than canvas nickers and moccasins. In the torch light their deeply tanned skin still glistened with sweat.

After greeting Ruhm with a "Waes Hael," Starkwulf addressed the boys. "Hail, Lazy Jokers, General Lee is in charge of this expedition." He paused to nod in the direction of the twelvers. "Russell and Ev-Rhett will be giving us military backup with their troops, and as for me and my wife, we are able to blend perfectly in any environment. Therefore, if we do find a way into the bastion, we will go first, so as not to be detected. If I ascertain it is safe, we will summon you. Now tell me, which one of you is going to show us the hidden passage way?"

"All of us," the boys chimed in unison.

Ruhm rubbed his lip with the back of his fist. "Well, Charly we don't need you all. Just one guide will do."

"Beggin your pardon, sir," Charly said with uplifted brow. "It's all of us or none of us. We Lazy Jokers have pledged an oath ever since we went into the dead lands that—"

"What! I thought no Hickoryan, and certainly no Pitter, dared to venture into the dolmans of the dead."

Charly pulled a piece of tan cloth from his pants pocket. "Here, read this. I copied the etching on the stone of one of the dolman's on my shirt when Leroy and I were looking for heathen gold. We didn't fear any ghosts or haints."

Ruhm took the scrap and saw that the letters were runic. "I cannot read this. It seems to be an ancient script of some sort."

Starkwulf reached out his hand. "Let me take a look." After a moment he nodded. "You are correct, Ruhm. It is Herewardi runic. It says, 'The swans will sing when the crows are silenced.'"

"What the hell does that mean?" Ruhm asked impatiently.

Va-Eyra replied, "It means that the Herewardi culture will sing when the Pitter crows have all been put to the death. It is a holy writ born of old." She paused to smile at the boys. "And by the way, we Herewardi do not use the term dead lands to refer to the kings' heights. This is the sacred land of the revered kings of old.

Charly appeared a bit flustered. "Beg pardon, ma'am, we done knew them kings was buried there, but folks hereabouts always called it the dead lands."

Garth, the tall redhead, spoke up, "That's why most of our folks are afraid to come here. It's so scary that even if a sheep wandered in there, we just let it be all by itself. Most times they come home, though, I heard tell one came back with long twisted horns; which was a very strange thing because it had no horns when it went in.

"Well, it was when we first went into the De—Kings' Heights and saw this here writing we took to be magic, we figured that if it protected the sleeping kings, it would protect us. Since most of our kinsmen fear magic and might think the heathen writing would open the portal to all the evils that befell the heathen kings, like the dragon sickness, we took that oath that I was telling you about, that we would never tell anyone what we saw or heard or found except we all six be agreed. From that time on it's been all for one and one for all. Kept us alive in all our mischiefs we've wrought on the Pitters, stealing their supplies and selling them on the ghost market, as we have done up to this day."

Leroy shot Charly a side long look. "Ain't ju forgot something?"

Cincinnatus nodded vigorously. "Don't forget how it protected us when we were almost eaten by some of them moth men."

Starkwulf and Va exchanged looks. "Something you said there troubles me Charly," Starkwulf asked urgently. "What do you mean by moth men?"

"I can explain," Leroy said, "We all went down the sink hole." He looked at a freckle-faced youth with a sash that bore the figure of a joker reclining with a straw to his mouth on it. "Steff here had the only torch and was leading us through a giant cavern with ceilings higher than you can throw a rock."

Garth the redhead, interjected, "That's when we found that chamber filled with those boxes of boom sticks."

Ev-Rhett interjected, "You found explosives?"

"Yeah," Leroy said, "we all grabbed a stick, and then when we got home Garth wanted to be the one to keep them. His father said they were evil magic sticks, threw them on a bonfire. Blew the hell out of his pig sty. Killed six pigs and damn near made his mule insane. Whoa, Garth, was your father ever pissed at us."

The boys all laughed and started crowding each other with their horses.

"Stay on track boys and let Leroy finish the tale," Russell said as his twelver assembled in a tight phalanx behind him, "we're pressed for time, so make it quick."

"Well," Leroy said, "It was right after we found the magic boom sticks that we heard a dragon groaning and screaming like a monster inside one of the caverns. We went to investigate it down a narrow cliff along the wall, when Steff stepped on a sharp rock and hurled the only torch we had over the ledge. There we all were, stuck in the dark and hung up on a cliff wall as high as a tree. We were figurin what to do when down below we saw this dim light. Then we saw it came from doors that opened straight out of the walls. All of a sudden, this here creature came sauntering out like a winged demon. Looked like half-man, half-moth. The moth man crouched down and one of them dark hooded men came out the door and climbed up on its back. Next thing we knew, they were flying past us so fast we felt the wind from its wings swish over our faces."

Steff, the boy wearing the green sash with the Joker ensign on it riding across his naked chest, interrupted, "Man, were we terrified. After the doors closed up we stayed up on that ledge for more'n hour, talkin bout how we had heard of people losing sheep and how folks were having their livestock ripped apart by a monster wingin down out of the sky like a falcon."

Ev-Rhett said, "Maybe a bear or a wolf?"

Cincinnatus rushed to add, "No! Not at all. People here abouts know the difference. It had to be this moth man killing the sheep and goats and if'n we didn't get outta there, we were likely to be his next supper."

Leroy jumped back in, "We was feeling our way back down the cliff, slowly like, when a roar took us by surprise. There before us came a dragon out of its lair to beat all hell, with billowing fire, and smoke as it roared by. Same as a big ass rollin log on fire."

"T'weren't no dragon," Charly objected, "I tell you, it was a giant roach with two mouths of fire and smoke trailing it. It just ate the dust as it grazed."

"All I know," Cincinnatus blurted out, "was when I saw the fire and smoke we all darted along the ledge and scurried out that sink hole faster than a fox with its tail on fire."

Steff laughed. "And Charly was a runnin so fast he fell down three times. Somersaulted like a pinwheel."

They guffawed and poked each other teasingly.

Charly glared at them, "That was cuz I heard that moth man give out its witch cry."

Steff said, "It weren't no witch cry. It was more like a goat scream."

It was obvious to Ruhm that Starkwulf was busy trying to figure out what they might have seen, and Ruhm had no frame of reference either. Besides it didn't matter, he only wanted to be in the caverns; to hell with the monsters, roaches, dragons, or moth men. Brekka was his only concern and, if he had to, he would march through hell to find her. He had to save her or die in the attempt. He had seen with his own eyes how Pitters had pulled the captives tongues out and forced them into those bloody crow cages to live their last days in agony. He had seen the faces of the mutilated women and couldn't bear that happening to his Brekka. Time was working against them finding her unharmed.

There was supposed to be a full-moon tonight, but either smoke or clouds had blotted it out, leaving only a shadow moon. Perhaps the Herewardi gods were giving them cover. Ruhm squeezed his sword hilt, heard the sound of steel on leather as he realized in his impatience he had unconsciously sought to unsheathe it. He glanced at Starkwulf before reluctantly agreeing that all the boys could accompany them.

Ruhm said, "Time to extinguish our torch and switch to lamplight."

He nodded to Va-Eyra, who lit each one and began passing them out to each boy.

Ruhm ordered, "Put them on dim. Just turn the shutters on their sides."

"Lead on, Charly!" Starkwulf said. "We'll have a look at this roach-dragon and the moth man you fellows claim you saw."

They rode for no more than five or ten minutes through tall cattails in the marshlands bordering the Big Springs. To the right, the dark silhouette of the sacred mound reminded Ruhm of a pregnant woman's belly in full bloom. It rose perhaps three plow lengths to its top.

Charly called a halt. "We won't need any horses anymore." He pointed with his walking stick. "Just up that hill in the sumac grove, and in there's the sink hole. It'll drop us right into the quarry first, and then we cross straight over to a small rock formation by the quarry wall, afore weaseling our way through a narrow passage into the gigantic caverns."

At Ruhm's orders they dismounted, quickly strung out a ground line, tied down their horses, and followed on Charly's heels.

Russell looked at the horses being tied out in the open. "I hate to leave my horse here in this open marshland with no guards."

Cincinnatus declared, "I know. Those Herewardi horses are like sunbeams. Whiter'n snow and swifter'n wind, all bedizened with red tackle. Beautiful sight. Damned pity, if those moth men took to feasting on'm. Way I heared it they rip an animal to sunder, rake it with their claws and lap up the blood 'for it even dies."

Ev-Rhett said, "You needn't worry Russell. If the horses see something coming they will break line and run for home."

While the others were still securing their horses, Starkwulf inquired "Charly, while we're waiting for the others to join us, I'm curious about how you boys discovered this sink hole."

"We were just hound huntin one night for coons and got the bright idea to go on a treasure hunt. We'd been talkin of all the heathen gold to be found in them grave barrows to the south, but weren't no one dared go onto the mound. Brought our hounds, cuz we heard there were mere-wolves and wights that defended the barrows of the king-race, when all of a sudden, we came upon all these huge square cracks, just over there." He pointed to a flat area barely visible in the lamplight below them. "There were twelve squares squeezing out this crazy light in the night, like crushed lightning bugs on a chessboard, and each square was twenty foot by twenty foot. The next day we came back to see what they looked like in the light of day. Thinking what if we had awakened the heathen kings from their graves? What if their wights arose and pursued us to our deaths? You can't even see them squares in the daylight less'n you're right smack dab on top of them, but we found them alright. All you see then is a thin straight line in the grass. That's when Leroy threw down our bottle of brandy on a stone henge as an offering to the gods for protection from the mere-wolves, but we didn't know that's why he threw the bottle. I grabbed Leroy by the scruff of his shirt and we were asking him why he threw away our only booze when we spotted a Pitter rat patrol riding out of the cattails across the marshes. Ran for the only cover we could see hereabouts, that there sumac grove. That's when we 'scovered the sink hole. First we's afraid to go down and explore. We peaked over the edge and saw the Pitters were comin closer. So we went down the hole to hide anyway. We ended up sliding down this long tunnel only to see it come out at the bottom of the quarry. By Joa, I'm tellin you, it goes right down to the foundations of the earth."

Leroy interrupted, "Those squares can open too. I think they're doors. I figure it's how they let loose lots of them moth men all at once. People hereabouts be sayin they done seen night swarms of them moth men darkening the skies thicker than a swarm of june bugs."

Ruhm said anxiously, "If that happens we'll deal with it. Right now we need to get there as quick as possible."

With Ruhm and Charly in the lead they scurried up the hill in the subdued lamplight that distorted everything into eerie shadows and silhouettes. They finally reached the sumac grove, which was one of many coppices of thickets. They pried through the thicket opening and squeezed through the tangled branches. Sure enough in the midst of the grove was a gaping mouth to a large sink hole. Ruhm tweaked the shutters on his lamp just enough to see that the hole angled down a slide to the north. "I can see why this was a good place to hide."

Ruhm lifted his lamp and opened it for more light. The passageway was steeply angled and had been created by water wearing away the rock and dirt until the plug at the bottom burst to form a chute taller than the average man and as wide as two men.

Charly whispered, "It's best to sit down and slide. Once we hit the bottom we'll have to put out the lanterns. When we first slid down there, we saw a hole on the opposite side of the quarry which we later blocked off with a fence of stones so that only we would know how to get in. Best let me go in first."

Leroy said, "Good idea. Don't want you crushing nobody."

Charlie punched him in the chest. "Smart ass!" Then dropped down through the sink hole and disappeared. Ruhm waited as each member of their party dropped through the chute. Just as Russell was preparing to enter the hole, his golden amulet snagged on a protruding branch or root that nearly strangled him under his weight.

Before Ruhm could help, Ev-Rhett came to his rescue. After freeing him, he warned, "This is a bad omen, brother. I told you not to choose an amulet bearing the tiwaz rune of Tyr. You know it represents the north star. Didn't you remember the wizard wheelursun said choosing that rune always means you will be called upon by the gods to make a sacrifice on behalf of others." Ev-Rhett squeezed his brother's arms tight. "Be careful, I don't want to lose you, brother. Maybe you should not join us tonight?"

Russell tucked the gilded amulet back inside his shirt. "I'll be alright, just a little clumsy." The Twins slid down one after the other.

Ruhm estimated they slid a good fifty feet before the passage spread into a vaulted chamber. They exited into the quarry surrounding the bastion. Ruhm dusted himself off and ordered them to extinguish their lamps. Once the lamps were shuttered, Ruhm saw that Va-Eyra's silver armor still shone even in the dark. "Va. Do you have anything to cover the sheen of your armor?"

"I have my neck scarf."

Starkwulf helped her cover herself in the back, tucking the scarf in her back where she was unable to reach. "I've always told you, you shine above everyone else."

She chortled an amused laugh.

The opening into the quarry itself admitted no more than one person at a time. With Charly in the lead, followed by Ruhm, they moved stealthily in double file across the expanse, taking great care not to dislodge any stones. The sconces from the bastion walls emitted a faint glow by which they could see the ground before them. When they reached the other side of the quarry, Charly led them through the maze of rocks, which concealed a narrow entrance. Everyone, especially Charly and Va-Eyra had to squeeze through.

Once inside, Ruhm was astonished to see a massive cavern system spread out before them lit by some eerie source of light, just as the boys had described; Caverns as wide as three dragoons long and as high as one could hurl a stone. It took considerable time for everyone to squeeze through and begin to gather into a phalanx.

Va-Eyra glanced up at the imposing ceiling. "Black and blue hell, what in the name of the gods could hold up a vault this high?"

Ruhm noted that the ceiling gave the appearance of having been finely carved and chiseled.

Leroy said, "Well, as you see by them there long skinny poles full of lightning bugs, Miss Va-Eyra, that there are tree size limestone mushrooms holding the ceiling up."

Ruhm waited till the last of the twelvers joined the phalanx, then asked Charly, "Where to from here?"

Charly whispered back, "See that first column there with an arrow painted on it. Right after that, we bump into the underground stream and turn left."

Ruhm ordered the lanterns to be unshuttered. As the light reached into the far chambers, he realized this was a far more elaborate system than he had expected or could have ever imagined. One route through the caverns was lit. The side chambers were all darker than night. To the south of the first column ran a crystal clear stream disappearing into the dark distance. Some of the caverns had been left the way nature had formed them, while others simply had been altered, presumably the work of the Amerikan giants, for, just like the citadel, the Pitters had simply used what had been left from the giants.

"Charly, have you ever followed this underground stream to its end?"

Charly shook his head. "It's hard to tell. We thought we found its end once, only to discover it flows again on a lower level of caverns. I'm telling you this place is kinda like an enormous honeycomb. There are underground lakes and streams to be found everywhere. But we were never able to find an end to the caverns."

Starkwulf toed the hard compressed surface. "Well, it has to go somewhere because this looks like a road." He hoed the hard surface with the heel of his boot. "See it's compacted."

Ruhm lowered his lantern to study the packed limestone surface. Upon closer inspection, he noticed what looked like ruts from very wide wagon wheels.

Starkwulf said, "Look to the sides of the road. Those are human foot prints, obviously, made by someone wearing the jackboots the Pitters favor."

Va-Eyra pointed to the stream. "This is likely where they get their water."

Charly nodded. "Yes'm, that's right, because no Pitter will dare to go near the Big Springs. My uncle told me when they were building this bastion that a Pitter commissar was attacked by a swan and drowned in the pools. Took him by the foot and carried him down to a watery death. And worse than that, they ain't ever found that body. Ever since, the Pitters fear the wight's, water nymphs, and mere-wulfs that haunt the pools and the mound."

Steff said, "You mean Old Uncle Jess, the chicken farmer told you that? He worked here?"

Charly said, "Didn't have much of a choice. He couldn't pay his tithe and was forced into a labor camp."

Ruhm felt energized. "If this is where they get their water then that means this road must lead to a way into the bastion." *And a road to where my beloved is being held.*

Starkwulf asked Charly, "Where'd you see the dragon and the doors?"

Charly said, "Just about two plough lengths up ahead if we follow the stream." The boys all had a confirming look of fear in their faces and turned from their japery to hyper-vigilance, even with two twelvers of seasoned warriors standing at the ready.

"Let's press on," Ruhm ordered. "Time's passing."

The creaking of leather and the faint jangling of chainmail echoed off the walls like the sound of blowing autumn leaves. Beneath their feet the dust rose and settled on their boots and moccasins like ashes from a bonfire.

After considerable walking along the twisting stream for what seemed like four or five minutes, passing entrances to other caverns on their left, they came to a fork of two gigantic tunnels branching out to the right and Charly said, "We stay to the right near the stream. About a plough's length straight through that large tunnel and we'll be there."

Ev-Rhett asked, "Where's the other fork go?"

Charly said, "To a huge chamber filled with quarries, lakes, and sink-holes that run to the center of the earth." After two hundred paces, Charly whispered, "Get ready! We're almost there."

Just as they rounded the corner past a large column of limestone, Leroy blurted out, "There's the dragon. Look to it! It's huddled straight ahead and looks to be asleep."

Cincinnatus said with pressured speech, "If it's asleep we mustn't waken it!"

Ruhm called a halt. The boys had described it well. Indeed, this 'Roach' looked like some giant insect with prominent bulging eyes; perfectly still, lying asleep in the cavern dust, or perhaps in a state of hibernation of some sort.

After a moment's inspection, Starkwulf said, "I do not think the thing is living." He cocked his head to get a better look then said, "Ruhm, I believe this is a machine of some sort. It has the stark appearance of being fashioned of metal."

Charly and the other Jokers looked at one another. One of them laughed nervously. Cincinnatus said, "Ain't no metal I know of can move as fast as a horse and spit out fire and smoke."

Ruhm was amazed at the sheer size of it. Even if Starkwulf was right, only giants could have molded such a large piece of machinery. He pondered what they were walking into. "Let's look closer."

Ruhm signaled for everyone to pull their swords and to proceed cautiously. The twelvers went into their stealth mode.

Starkwulf pointed. "See, those are wheels on it, not legs. If it were a dragon or a roach it would have legs. Wheels means man made it."

The Jokers nodded their heads as if forced to agree.

As they drew nearer still, Ruhm saw that the top of the wheel was four feet above his head. Cautiously, he jabbed his sword at the wheel. It bounced back. "Pronk," he said. "I'll be damned; the wheel is made out of pronk."

"What's that?" Steff asked.

"It's a bouncy extract made from fig trees that the Ele-Anoreans discovered."

Charly shrugged his shoulders at the Jokers. Cincinnatus prodded him to keep moving.

By this time the two twelvers were stretched out to measure its full length, spaced out from hand to hand.

"It's a machine of some sort, alright," Russell added.

Ev-Rhett interjected, "This is all looking way too familiar. I saw similar things in the underworld of gloomulah. Brekka said they are the earth eaters made by the Amerikans."

An intrusive image of Brekka hit Ruhm's heart like the impact of a burning star. He had to shake his head just to get the thought of her out of it. He told himself, *She's alive. She's got to be alive. Must stay focused.* He had to find her before it was too late. Before the emperor slew her or devised some unthinkable defilement of her.

Starkwulf said, "Machines that eat the earth. Well, boys that explains your dragon, but I can't think of what your moth man might be."

Ruhm ordered the swords to be re-sheathed. "Speaking of moth men, where are those doors they came out of?"

Charly said, "Just keep following the stream, and the doors can't be more than another plow length ahead."

The smell of lime dust stirred by their feet grew progressively stronger. The cement smell and dust coated their nostrils. Ruhm stifled a sneeze and snorted to clear his nostrils.

Suddenly, Charly held up a hand, halting their progress. Ahead about ten paces was a towering wall of rock. Built into that was a square doorway wide enough and tall enough to allow two men on horses to ride through with room to spare. The doors gave the appearance of being painted grey metal and stood flush with the ground.

Ruhm, Starkwulf, Va-Eyra, and Charly moved cautiously towards the doors until they stood directly in front of them.

Charly turned and pointed to the opposite wall. "See, that is the ledge where we were hung up on when Steph threw down his lamp."

"So you didn't try to open them?" Starkwulf asked.

"Hell no! Like I said, we was as scared as all get out. Nearly pissed ourselves."

Cautiously, Starkwulf felt around with his hands, pushing at the doors in different directions. They didn't move. "No knobs, no handles, no hinges. All I see is these big round colored rivets driven into the rock surface to hold the door. So how do the Pitters open them?"

Va-Eyra remarked, "But those rivets are only on one side of the door."

Ruhm said, "Well, what about that strip of metal above the door. What's that for? It almost looks like there are numbers on it."

Russell and Ev-Rhett joined them. "I know what this is," they said in unison.

Then Russell added, "We saw doors like these in the citadel of the Poisoned Lands. Those aren't rivets; if you press them, the doors open and close without touching."

Ev-Rhett said. "Just press those buttons."

Ruhm walked over and pressed the top rivet. Only to jump back when the doors started to part.

Va-Eyra said, "Look above the doors! The metal strip has the number three lit up."

When the doors fully opened, a small square room appeared.

As the others crowded closer, Ruhm said, "This is one of those riding rooms, like in the citadel we were told about. I am sure the first level must be the bastion level."

Ev-Rhett said, "In the citadel, there were forty levels." He peered up at the numbers on the metal strip. "Looks like this has only twenty levels. You know when we were in the citadel, they lit the underground just like this. The hags in the citadel said they have a wheel in the stream that produces the light we are seeing. I'll bet they have just such a wheel here as well if we were to look."

Russell explained, "The way this room moves is, you stand in the room, press the number of the level you want to go to and the room lifts you just like a bucket in a well and you are carried to the level you pressed."

Va said, "Damned if I'm going to get into some magic room. Hard to tell where you'd end up. Maybe Niflheim or Hell."

Starkwulf said, "Well, my dear, the twins have ridden in them and they assure us its safe."

Ruhm said, "If this is level three, does that mean there are two more below us or two more above us?"

Ev said, "I'm pretty sure it's like the citadel, there are two more above us and seventeen below."

Ruhm thought for a moment before blurting out. "The first level must be the floor of the Bastion."

Starkwulf interjected. "Our way inside."

"That's where they will be holding Brekka." Ruhm said, "That's where we go. How do we make the room go?"

"Problem is," Ev-Rhett said as he walked into the small room, "we can only get there ten or twelve at a time."

Russell added, "Our compatriots may already be engaging the enemy above. In any case they'll be distracted enough that we may be able to get all of us there before we're even detected."

Russell said, "Yes, but what of the moth man and the chambers below this?"

"My only concern is Brekka and opening that front gate," Ruhm said as he contemplated Russell's warning. "To hell with the moth men and anything below the surface. Leave the monsters for another day. I only want Brekka."

"As do we all, Ruhm," Va-Eyra said. "But we must have a plan."

Starkwulf nodded. "As I said before, this calls for cryptic exploration first. Va and I will go in crypsis, just the two of us. When the doors open, we will assess the feasibility of an incursion and report back."

CHAPTER 2 :
THE VIRGIN SACRIFICE

I T HAD BEEN THREE HOURS ON the water clock since Ruhm departed for the caverns. In the meantime Sur Sceaf had summoned his commanders for a final briefing. He explained the heightened preparations for battle in the event that Ruhm and the others were able to find a way to open the gates. While they waited for a signal from Ruhm, Sur Sceaf had the troops and horses fed on a rotational basis.

Long Swan stood and read aloud the revised plan crafted by Sur Sceaf and Lord Arundel. Sur Sceaf then led the discussions on the target sequences of taking the large landing, securing the altar in anticipation of Ruhm's forces securing the gates and then the gate house which the Hickoryan merchants declared was just inside the wall to the right as one enters. Kanarus had insisted that he and the green knights be given the assignment to clear the inner court of the bastion before the main surge of troops.

Sur Sceaf asked, "Are there any amendments to the plan?" He waited. "Hearing none, we shall proceed as written."

Bonfires were maintained on and near the ramp and also along any roads leading into Big Springs. To prevent flanking movements and rat pack attacks, he had strengthened the guards at all access points. Zrael and the Wyrm-Kats were positioned near the ballooners next to the pools of the Big Springs. At his command the wyrm kats would attempt to climb the ramp. He also had Brekka's twenty six faery-hounds of war brought to him by the longbeard boys, Fairbeard and Forkbeard, sons of his dear friend, Elfbeard. These hounds were personally bred by Brekka to be gentle and pliable to friend, but fierce and deadly to foe. Additionally, she bred them white with red ears so as to be seen by day or by night during pitched conflicts. Pitters feared these eager dogs of war. Setting loose the hounds made any conflict easier, as they were as fierce as dire-wolves or the Cerulean Beaucerons, which they would also employ.

Before the lineup of commanders took up their stations, Talks-As-He-Walks strolled with a sprig of burning sage and a turtle rattle to invoke the blessings and protection of the thunder beings on Brekka, and Ruhm's forces. He was soon joined by the Mufsiks and the buffalo nations in a dance to invoke the thunder beings assistance in Brekka's victory over death. Sur Sceaf prayed to his own gods in his heart and hoped the thunder beings were attending.

With Arundel's assistance, he anticipated as many negative elements and sensitive spots in their plan as the two of them could imagine, but there was nothing they could do about that ingenious narrow ramp leading to the landing. Wide at the bottom, but narrowing at the top, it constrained their forces into a tight funnel where the enemy could hold them off indefinitely.

At Long Swan's suggestion, Sur Sceaf signed for the long bowmen to come to the fore. These archers could draw a sixty-eight inch long bow of ninety to a hundred and ten pound draw. All bows sported bowstrings of silk and flax, and their deadly wolf-arrows could pierce the thickest of armor. Even though the Pitters had the high ground, the long bow archers would be able to easily clean the Pitter archers from the walls of the bastion, and the Pitter archers could never reach them with the flimsy Pitter bows they had. Each Syr Folk archer would be supplied with sheaves of twenty-two arrows which got constant replenishment from the attendant green beetles.

Sur Sceaf went over everything in his mind one final time. If possible, the wyrm kats would create the first distraction followed by the war-hounds. The archers, under Hrolwylf's command would be essential in giving cover to Kanarus and his Green Knights flushing the landing while he and his twelver, and Heimdal secured the altar and the exterior of the gates. The lady knights would focus solely on freeing Brekka and providing her with her mount and reinvesting her with blade, helm, and shield. This was to be the battle before the battle, and the siege of the fortress would follow with the Syr Folk hosts under Lord Arundel.

Uffa said, "My lord, Siwel the Chartreusean gave me a potion. He said it was to be administered to Brekka and would act as a tonic to fully revive her from any trauma she may have undergone. She won't feel the pain and will still remain alert."

Sur Sceaf's gratitude for the synergy between the chartreusean medicine men, the Syr Folk healers and Quailor doctors was boundless. Their combined skills rendered their medicine ten-fold more effective. "Deliver it to Freyxus, and tell her to follow Siwel's instructions."

The green beetle hastened over to Freyxus. Sur Sceaf signaled for the balloon master, Jake the Blue, to launch one of his balloons over the bastion to scout the activity and preparations in the inside of the walls, a place they designated as the inner court. He also signed for Jake's ballooner to signal at the first sign of Ruhm, Starkwulf or Va-Eyra. Additionally, he instructed Jake to have the entire ballooner force to be ready for deployment.

He signed for Kanarus and his twelver along with the faery-hounds standing to the ready, so as to prepare to sweep the ramp clean for a full-bore attack on the bastion by Arundel's elite fyrds.

Sur Sceaf and Arundel sat mounted beside the array of commanders, the dog soldiers and Kanarus, who were to make the quickest strike. Uffa moved up from his customary station directly behind Sur Sceaf to say, "My lord, there is a signal coming from the scouting balloon."

Sur Sceaf glanced at the balloon that was halfway between the spring and the bastion. Sure enough the ballooner was signaling with his lantern that archers had appeared on the bastion parapet. He also signaled that archers were running the length of the bastion walls.

"Uffa, signal the ballooners to pull back beyond arrow's reach."

Uffa unhooked his lantern, quickly lit it and sent the signal. The archers were now visible atop the bastion and, as Sur Sceaf watched, drew back their bows and fired at the balloon. The balloon appeared unharmed as it continued to rise and retreat. The archers ceased, but remained atop the parapet.

He had just turned to Arundel to order the start of the Syr Haka, when he was interrupted by the distinct *thunk* of the iron gates opening, followed by the grinding and creaking of the mechanism swinging the heavy doors wide. He prayed it was Ruhm. But instead of Ruhm opening the gates and relieving the agony of his heart, the commissars followed by a multitude of priests and legionnaire guards came parading out in front of them like a proud murder of crows.

Sur Sceaf signaled for the fyrds to get their archers at the ready, but decided not to deploy them for fear of what the Pitters might do to Brekka. Instead, he chose to wait until he knew what the enemy was about. As they sang their hymns to Angrar, one by one the priests placed their blazing torches all about the altar of Angrar and by the tree of terror. At a signal from the cantor, the priests began a low droning chant in honor of Angrar.

When they were finished, a priest bearing the Pitter banner of the broken sahle cross placed it in a holder between the tree and the altar. Sur Sceaf struggled to see in the twilight dim of the torches the words written upon the banner. It came to him slowly. Written in the hated Pitter religious tongue, 'V*estigia Nulla Restrosum,*' which simply meant, 'Never Retreat.' The tongue had originally been venerated but became an abomination in the mouth of the Pitters.

He expected the gates to close again, but when they didn't, he commanded, "Dog Soldiers and Green Knights, get ready and at my command, we charge in."

Mendaka, Going Snake, Chise, White Moose, and Kanarus all signed they were ready. Talks-As-He-Walks continued to stroll back and forth along the line of commanders, burning sage and invoking the aid of the Thunder Beings and the spirit of Tah-Tonka.

Sur Sceaf took a tighter grip on the reins, planted his feet firmly in the stirrups, and pulled his helm snug. Just as he was about to give the charge command, bugles sounded from the altar. The priests bowed themselves low to the earth in the direction of the gates. His heart beat faster and his blood raced through his veins.

An instant later the emperor Hryre Seath appeared in a purple robe holding a ruby-eyed bat staff which was known as the spear of Hormah. He appeared in the opening where he stood for a moment before strutting in front of his banner. The emperor remained silent, scanning the Syr Folk. In his other hand he bore a pink rose.

Arundel said, "I think he's singling you out, Fa.

Indeed, Sur Sceaf had the distinct feeling the bastard was challenging him.

"Is this the Hryre Seath, the mighty emperor that has shaken all the tribes across the whole of Panygyrus?" It gave Sur Sceaf the impression of a gangly purple crane with his spindly limbs, staccato steps, and his long thin neck and prominent Adam's apple. "The bastard reminds me of a crane with a fish stuck in his craw."

Mendaka said, "And a female crane at that."

Sur Sceaf thought it was a laughable image, but at this moment this comical character bore the power of life and death over his daughter. Sur Sceaf signed for the flag of Panygyrus to be unfurled. The beautiful flag was red at the bottom, white in the middle, and displayed the sigil of the confederation in a golden feathered-serpent against the background of the three tiers of red, white, and blue.

The emperor raised the spear high and shouted in a voice that was surprisingly high-pitched, "Herewardi, sons of whores, turn your ears to me and hear your fate, which I decree in the name of Angrar. We have captured the witch, and we know her to be the true seed of the woman. We have examined her and found her to be a virgin, as was the prophecy. Our sorcerer, Katus, can feel the evil power that emanates through this Witch. Hryre Seath paused as though for effect. "Here is what I think of your virgin." He bit the end off the pink rose in a symbolic gesture that he planned on ending her life.

"I'd give anything to gut that fish right now," Lord Arundel declared.

"Patience my son, he'll get his due soon enough. If all goes as planned, we'll stuff a fish down his throat too big for that skinny neck to swallow."

After a few more beats of silence, the emperor continued, "A virgin-witch is a very fitting sacrifice for our great god, Angrar, whose wrath you shall soon feel in full measure. For, after he drinks her blood, he shall drink yours. You should know this altar at the knees of this old tree has long been saturated with the blood and tears of sacrificial victims from your Herewardi ranks and those rebels defiant of our holy ways. When this witch entered our realm, she brought sickness upon us and into our midst. So, also, we may kill her that we shall all be healed by her blood. Then we shall kill the rest of you as was prophesied by our high priest, the Skull Worm, who shall perform the necessary sacrifices and ministrations with the grand seer Katus presiding."

Going Snake came before Sur Sceaf with White Moose and his Mufsiks. "My king, we cannot allow for this. I can't endure her death. She's like a sister to me. Please, may we charge now?"

"I share your pain, Going Snake, every muscle in my body is screaming 'charge,' but the wisdom of my heart tells me not yet." Sur Sceaf took a deep sigh before explaining further. "If we charge now, the bastards would simply murder her, but if we wait as the ur fyr directs me, the opportune moment will come to free her. It is also possible that Ruhm will breach the bastion in time to save her or to create a diversion for us so we can save her."

Sur Sceaf knew very well that there could be little time to waste. If the Pitters' pattern held true, their rituals were always conducted so as to invoke an emotional response to incite the enemy into a premature and unplanned response; to do that they would kill Brekka slowly and with the maximum horror. Above all, she was the greatest trophy they had ever possessed, the supreme tribute to Angrar. Through this ritual she would be sealed to Hryre Seath as a slave for all eternity. Hryre would not rush it, but savor every moment.

"But my lord," Chise implored, "I respect your reasoning as always. The great spirit informs me that if we charge now, we can get in those gates."

"The great spirit directs you aright and is not in contradiction to the Ur Fyr, but your eagerness blinds you to the appropriate moment. Bear with me, my apache brother. Hold back your war rage for now."

"If that is your order," Chise said incessantly, twisting the reins of his mount and muscling his horse back into line. "But you understand, the apache way is to always favor action over inaction. Giving the enemy unrelenting hell is the only way we know how to fight."

Possible ways to free Brekka raced through Sur Sceaf's mind. Not daring to divert his eyes from the horror above, he raised his hand for all to hold fast.

"None of us need to fret, King Sur Sceaf," White Moose said. "The knives of my Mufsiks are slaying the Pitters even now as we wait. That is the sickness of which they speak. The Mufsiks sent the curse from Quirenopolis to Albany, and it is spreading. The curse will soon overtake all of the Pitters from one end of the land to the other."

White Moose's comments barely registered with Sur Sceaf, nor could he be bothered to tease out their meaning, with his daughter in such a precarious predicament. He wanted only to save Brekka. His mind wouldn't entertain anything else. He knew Hryre Seath's sole focused intent was to slay her. It was as if he and the emperor were met on some high tight rope to see which one would get knocked off first. Either he could save his daughter, or Hryre Seath could plunge her unto her death.

"My lord," Arundel said, "what is needed right now is some sort of distraction to delay the start of the ritual blood-letting and to give Ruhm more time to find his way into the bastion, but what?"

"I have a plan--"

Another intrusive bugle blast sounded above.

Kanarus exclaimed, "By Thor's hammer, look!"

A collective gasp went up from the Syr Folk.

Sur Sceaf was horrified to see a group of nine black cowled cone-headed priests gathering near the altar, three of whom bore brazen bowls, and four who held Ma-Za-Ma. One bore Skull Worm's personal ensign, and another carried a large bulky bag. Four of the priests tugged at the ropes to lead the white buffalo out to the roots of the dead tree. Another priest led the blind Katus, who shuffled out to his usual position at the north of the altar, where he leaned on his staff and the altar alternately for support.

Several heavy ropes were securely fastened around the bull's neck and head so as to stabilize him. The bull staggered as if it had been drugged. The priest with the large bulky black bag sat it down. From the bag protruded the hilt of Brekka's wave blade and her golden shield. A slight wisp of white feathers indicated her helm was also contained in it. He walked up the three steps of the altar and placed Brekka's helm, wave-blade, and golden shield on and about the altar like they were jewels of offering to their heinous god, Angrar, whose blood lust had not been sated in the past five hundred years of the Pitter Reign of Terror over the main land of Panygyrus.

The proud beast snorted its disapproval, and thrust its head from side to side tossing priests who dared venture too near. The Skull Worm, with his personal ensign of a skull with a worm crawling out of the eye socket was the officiating officer in the ritual.

The Skull Worm stepped forward at the front of the bull. With a wave of his hands he directed the four priests to stretch the ropes taunt. With the bull thus safely restrained, the Skull Worm grabbed Ma-Za-Ma by his horns. The buffalo bellowed so loudly the sound reverberated through the ground and rippled on the surface of the Big Springs. The Skull Worm twisted the bull's neck, locking one horn under his arm, then took Brekka's wave blade from an assisting priest, raised the blade and sliced through the white buffalo's throat. The mighty beast fell to the ground while the priests hurriedly clustered around and caught the gushing blood in brazen bowls.

The dog soldiers let out a collective gasp, and the multitude of the Syr Folk mumbled their disapproval aloud. Sur Sceaf saw Mendaka look down at the ground and shake his head.

As the first bowl was filling with bull's blood, the Skull Worm walked out in front of the large white carcass, laid Brekka's sword on the altar and shouted, "Listen you tribes of red men, you children of the woods, plains, deserts, and mountains. This day I have slain all your hopes along with your ungodly beliefs, that you may know that there is but one god and Angrar is his name. We shall cut your lands and bleed you as we have bled this mighty beast, for Angrar has purposed to give us the earth, that we might rule over all people as both the superior and chosen race. It is part of our divine destiny as given by the dark elves."

The priests chorused, "There is one god, and Angrar is his name! There is one god, and Angrar is his name! There is one god and Angrar is his name. And Katus is his true messenger."

A priest stepped forward to hand the Skull Worm a ceremonial vulture-feathered crop. The Skull Worm took the crop, dipped the feathers in the bowl of buffalo blood, and splattered the blood three times against the tree of terror.

Sensing the tension that was mounting in his troops, Sur Sceaf feared that maybe some young bucks like Chise and Zoot might take it upon themselves to act recklessly. But as he glanced at the lady knights, he took note that the buffalo's keeper, Talks-As-He-Walks, remained as calm as a summer day, and this gave him some comfort, for Talk Walk was very close to the gods and knew their intent.

Sur Sceaf knew the fate of the Syr Folk would be determined by what he decided. Despite his fears for his beloved daughter, he had to trust in the Ur Fyr to reveal the proper moment to strike, a second too early and all would be lost.

The Skull Worm handed the vulture crop back to the priest in exchange for the wave blade. With two expert sawing slices he gutted the bull. The priests ripped out the offal, and then caught the heart in a basin.

The two priests presented the basin to Katus, who lifted out the heart and pronounced a curse upon it before returning it to the bowl. Next the two priests presented the basin to the Skull Worm, who also removed the heart and held it above his head. Dripping blood, it shone crimson in the torchlight, and blood trickled down the Skull Worm's hands and into his sleeves.

"We dedicate the heart of the red man to Angrar." After placing it back in the brazen basin, he carried it to the tree, and laid it on the knees of the dead oak, and intoned the one god. The assembled priests clapped and shouted their approval.

When the celebration died down, the Skull Worm raised his blood-drenched hands. "You people of the Syr Folk Confederation, look to this dead oak. The Herewardi once flourished and dominated here in this very land. Like this oak they once spread their branches wide, dispersing their heresy of heathen gods, their obscene hieros gamos marriage practices, and foolish concepts of liberty for all races. But as you now behold, their oak is dead. Thus shall your fate be on the morrow, for you have dared to stir the wrath of Angrar."

Sur Sceaf signed for the troops to initiate one stanza of the syr haka in answer. A roar went up from the troops, and thundering shields beat out a threatening rhythm. The syr haka was nearing its end when four black-hooded priests came out of the gates carrying a ceremonial litter draped in black cloth bearing the mark of Seath on it etched in white.

Lying on the litter was a young naked blond boy of unknown tribe. The priests set the litter on its legs, and then placed the child on the altar as if he were a lamb. The boy offered up a feeble struggle, but was bound both hand and foot and could scarcely move. Katus felt blindly for the child's chest. Raising his voice, he intoned, "Almighty Angrar, I implore you to feel the beat of this son of an infidel's heart, which we shall soon cut out of his chest and present to you as our offering and warning to those who dare resist thy will."

The Syr Folk went silent with shock. Sur Sceaf braced himself for the blood-letting. Next to him both Arundel and Kanarus stiffened as though ready to charge, but no blades were raised. Instead the priests picked up the litter and carried it back into the bastion.

Sur Sceaf looked up at the dead tree once again. It was casting its ghostly shadows all over the fortress walls. Suddenly, he remembered the time Redith had pointed out how a dead tree had more life in it than a living tree. A tiny flame of hope grew in his chest, only to be extinguished when the four priests returned, this time with a mummy-like figure wrapped tight in white muslin as though prepared for burial. The mummy was placed upon the altar next to the man-child, where it lay stiff and still. Clearly dead!

Sur Sceaf's breath caught in his throat. *Could it be? Is that my daughter already dead?* He did not know why, but he felt no premonition of such.

Katus fumbled forward, feeling for the altar until he laid his hand upon the mummy. "Almighty Angrar, we dedicate the enslavement of the soul of this white witch to your service."

The blood drained from Sur Sceaf's head, and he reeled in raw agony in the saddle. A scream rose in his throat which he barely managed to contain. *Odhin, I beseech you. Is this all my fault? Did I somehow miss the ur fyr's promptings?*

Ary screamed. "By Baldur, they've murdered Sis."

Kanarus cried, "No, no, that mummy has no head. See the muslin at the neck is bloody. I tell you, Lord Arundel, that is clearly the body of my wife, and it appears they ran her through with a spear by the blood stain on her belly. For this desecration I swear eternal vengeance. Now I charge you, my king not to restrain me. I will not suffer them to bring further profanity to the body of my beloved wife."

Although he hated to acknowledge it, Sur Sceaf felt a certain relief that it was not Brekka. At the same time, he gained a greater appreciation for Kanarus' suffering.

"Lord Kanarus, we will do all in our power to prevent that from happening, but know this, I am bound by the gods to follow the ur fyr. Please, as the head of Syrdom, I beseech you to trust me in this."

Sur Sceaf now understood the emerging pattern. "The next time they will bring Brekka out as their offering. They're drawing this all out for maximum effect. We must not give them the satisfaction of pandering to their rituals."

Arundel said, "But Fa--"

Kanarus belted out, "Look! That has to be Brekka they're carrying out now!"

Sur Sceaf now knew for a surety it was Brekka, for his heart leapt within him and told him it was so. His beloved daughter was tightly wrapped in white swaddling, like Wilona's mummy, but with the addition of some sort of strange red rope that crisscrossed over the muslin like netting binding a seagoing sun fish.

She was summarily laid alongside the man-child and the other mummy, face up. Sur Sceaf decided it was time to institute his first plan. He whispered to Uffa, who took a message to Zrael that it was time for the wyrm kats to find a way up the ramp.

Lord Arundel exclaimed, "Look, Fa, she's wriggling. She's still alive!"

Kanarus added, "She's fighting to the last. Just like I know Wilona did."

"My lord, this may be your last chance to save your daughter!" Chise cried out.

"Not yet, Chise! Not yet!"

The young chief threw the turtle rattle to the ground in utter frustration.

Talks-As-He-Walks picked up the rattle. "Fear not, Chise, Brekka is thrice burned, and she always emerges from the fire more pure than ever. Remember she is the white buffalo woman, the adopted daughter of the red man. Take heart young chief, this is the dawn and re-birth of the red man you are witnessing. Nothing good is born without blood and pain." Talks-As-He-Walks raised his hand as if to entertain no more argument. "You do not know the power of waiting for the right moment, but you will learn. For you are the blood of the great and wise chief, Mangas, and the likes of you cannot be found in any of the other tribes. Long have the red men waited for you to take up our spear."

Sur Sceaf waited anxiously for the prompting of the ur fyr, only to hear the pounding of his own heart. He scanned the shadows to the right of the ramp where the torch light did not reach, looking for any sign of movement from the wyrm kats. But so far he saw only dense shadows.

According to what the Lazy Jokers had told them, the entrance of the bastion was nearby, and Ruhm could possibly be coming out of there. If so, he would signal him to attack and free Brekka, followed by a full scale attack.

Lord Arundel said, "My lord, something is happening. Time has run out."

Sur Sceaf looked between the altar and the tree to see that Hryre Seath had the Hormah spear. Sur Sceaf's guts twisted in him. Hryre Seath lifted the bat staff high once again. The Skull Worm bowed deep to his emperor before approaching the altar. An attendant priest handed him a black obsidian knife such as they often employ in ritual killings.

The Skull Worm pronounced, "And now, under the holy rites of the dark elves, we have bound the witch in muslin and netted her in the intestines of the white woman. I shall kill the witch; and by crushing her skull destroy the power of the Herewardi forever from the earth. But first we blot out the light of her body, that she may not see to work her evil in the earth anymore, and hang her upon the tree of death for all to watch how slow and agonizing her death shall be."

Everything in Sur Sceaf screamed in protest. His muscles tensed. He forced himself into inaction. He sensed Arundel was on the edge of losing control, and stretched his arm before Arundel to hold him back.

The Skull Worm raised his sharp knife and stabbed down into Brekka's eye. Brekka yelled out in anger, and thrashed against her bindings. The muslin over her face spread out red. The Skull Worm stretched his arms out wide as they shook in some kind of devilish ecstatic release like quaking leaves. With outstretched arms, he placed his hand in Brekka's blood and held it up for all to see.

"Behold" he shouted, exposing the red palm of his hand, "The blood of the virgin. And now we suspend her as the fool she is from the hanging tree."

The priests held their hands together prayerfully, palm to palm, and said three times, "There is one god and Angrar is his name!"

Subsequently, two black-clad priests rushed over to tie Brekka's left foot with a silver citriodoran rope and then tied the right leg crossing over the left in a square angle forming the number four, the sacred number of the Herewardi. Sur Sceaf clenched his jaw at this act of mockery. With great ceremony, they threw the rope high up over a large branch. With all hands on the rope, the two priests raised her upside down until her body was dangling three feet above the ground, with the red blood-soaked muslin dripping on the roots of the tree.

As she hung there wiggling and struggling like a worm on a hook, Sur Sceaf's heart went out to his beloved girl. He wept internally. *Oh Brekka, my Brekka, daughter of my heart, how I wish I could exchange places with you at this moment, but alas, the norns have woven this.* But even still, no prompt came from the Ur Fyr.

A great rumble arose out of the earth, and then the very foundations of the bastion shook.

Kanarus said, "It is the horned god, Tyranus. He is angered by all this."

But Hryre Seath shouted, "As you see and feel by the quaking earth, Angrar is most pleased with our sacrifice."

The priests shouted in sinister glee.

The emperor moved over close to the dangling cocooned body of Brekka. With his dark mitre pointing up into the leafless vulture-filled branches of the tree, he shouted out, "I did not spare my own sister, La Papessa, who thought to take my place and supplant me, like you, Witch. You," he pointed to the cross legged-dangling body, "are in our holy tongue, the *Vagina Dentata* that Katus prophesied would come to devour our lands. You have seen all that I have built, and have come down to swallow my throne and altar up for yourself. But the church of Angrar endures forever: made new by the spilling of your blood."

An exultant cheer rose from the priests.

"Katus prophesied that La Papessa was a foreshadowing of this witch. My parents, the emperor Kittim and his wife Roma, thought to favor La Papessa with my hand in marriage. But I will never share a throne or my kingdom with anyone else. I didn't even spare my sister-wife, for the dark elves promised me I could get greater power by slaying her and holding all her power in her brain. For this cause I remain celibate. Neither shall I spare this Herewardi witch, who thought to emasculate us all. Yes, witch, we heard of your works in Leakey, where you sent thousands of my loyal subjects into the underworld to become sodomites in the next life. For this, you shall pay dirty damned dearly."

Again a mighty cheer went up from the priests

"Here in my hand," Hryre Seath said, as he lifted what looked like a stone ball from a bag that hung from his side, "I now hold the brains of La Papessa, mixed in lime to harden them. With the brain of La Papessa, I shall smash the skull of this Herewardi witch and mix her brains the same way. Thus Angrar has favored me on the right, and on the left; and I shall rule the day with the brains of my enemies in each hand that all may know, I am the center and the Favored One of Angrar. I am the anointed whom all shall come to worship." He walked back and forth, displaying his trophy with a sinister smile so wide it could even be seen by the Syr Folk at so great a distance.

Sweat dripped from the palms of Sur Sceaf's hand, and his heart fell with the anguish of not being able to go to his daughter's aid. He heard the still small voice of the Ur Fyr saying, *Hold fast. The time is not yet come.*

CHAPTER 3 :

A GOOD CAT DESERVES A GOOD RAT

ATOP THE RAMP BY THE altar of Angrar, the armed warrior-priests exulted in their most prized captured possession, Brekka. They hit their spears against their shields whilst shouting "All Praise Angrar!"

The landing easily held the five hundred warrior monks, and could have held four times that many had they wanted. Hryre Seath now had the choicest jewel of Herewardom in his possession, Brekka, to do with as he saw fit. While the others celebrated, the emperor continued to rant and rave in ecstatic delight, his voice growing more and more shrill as he boasted that he would ultimately feast on her flesh and sharpen his teeth on the bones of a virgin.

Exultant, he raised his arms and looked directly in the direction of Sur Sceaf. "Hear me, you sheep lords, now is the great day of my power when my greatest enemy, the seed of the woman, is caught within my coils forever, from which none can deliver. As you witness, the squirming bitch's heathen gods could not protect her against the power of Angrar invested in me, and she is now under my thumb. By the sacred ritual, the she-fiend has been made half-blind with the sacred knife of Kittim, for she had given her sight to a vain cause. Soon she shall die slowly here. We will disembowel her at the ennead tree, and will bring about the end of her lustful people. You shall now witness how Angrar shall restore my empire back to me in its fullness."

He turned to take a few steps to the tree where he lifted the spear of Hormah and tormented Brekka with jabbing pricks in the shoulders and back to further her torment. Once again, he raised his voice to a shout.

"Fools, to think that a woman could ever defeat me! You Syr Folk shall be scattered like swarms of bees before the mighty wings of Angrar this very night. For in my wrath, I shall release the ravenous gyrlocks, and open the gates of Hellheim, and let slip the bone-crushing tyfons upon you."

Sur Sceaf gritted his teeth, knowing what cruel satisfaction Hryre Seath was taking in all this. He uttered audibly, "That damned freak! What evil does this mad man purpose to send upon us now?"

Brandishing the now-bloodied spear of Hormah, the emperor finished with a flourish. "Vicar of Rattus Maximus-- Commissar Skull Worm-- commence the final preparations. Sacrifice this man-child, the spawn of Hickoryan traitors, and let his parents watch from their crow cages. Thereby we shall open the portal to Angrar, sacrifice the woman, and have this witch spiritually bound to me for all eternity."

The Skull Worm bowed, and with his bloody hands presented the blade of Kittim to Katus. The blind seer raised his hand over the knife of Hryre's Seath's Emperor-Father and proclaimed, "Blood of the virgin bind victory to thee, now and through all eternity."

The Skull Worm retrieved the blade and kissed the cold stone knife.

As the chant in praise of Angrar began, Sur Sceaf could scarce contain himself, shifting in his saddle, until White Thunder snorted his protest.

Heimdal inquired, "Shall I blast, my lord?"

"By the gods, not yet, Heimdal." The terrifying thought came to Sur Sceaf that this was the fruition of his dark vision of the marring of Brekka that he had had in Front Royal. Despite the silence of the Ur Fyr, he knew that something had to happen, but no distraction was presenting itself in this patience trying moment.

"It is time! Ary, take my command. I'm going to offer myself in place of Brekka."

Looking shocked, Lord Arundel lodged his protest, "No, Fa, you--"

A sudden confusion and chaos gripped the Pitter warrior-monks. Breaking formation they shoved, pushed, and were running over one another, fleeing in panic and alarm, much as goats mob one another when a wolf explodes into their presence.

Sur Sceaf exclaimed, "Praise be Woon!"

"What's happening?" Kanarus asked,

Sur Sceaf grinned. "It's the Wyrm Kats. They are attacking."

Scratch let out a blood curdling scream, leaping through the air like a crazed cat, while Chloe and Mauser headed straight for Brekka. Scratch bounced off the altar with another scream and sliced Hryre Seath across the face with his extended claws. With a shrill of alarm the emperor stumbled to the ground. His Hormah Staff flew from his hand and slid over to the base of the dead tree. Scratch pursued the staff and snapped it in half with his powerful teeth.

While some priests fled, other more devout priests fought to get at Brekka, but Scratch and Mauser fought the attacking priests off with teeth and claws as Chloe tore at Brekka's bindings with her razor sharp teeth. In the rush to save themselves, the priests knocked Katus to the ground. Pushing and shoving, The Skull Worm helped Katus back to his feet. In the confusion the Skull Worm's mitre was trampled underfoot revealing his shaven tattooed head.

He screamed over the din, "Buglers have the archers give us cover!" At the same time most of the commissars ran to Hryre Seath's aid. With some difficulty they managed to gather him up. The emperor appeared dazed and in shock, his scratched face dripped with blood as they all but dragged him to the safety of the gates.

Sur Sceaf's attention was riveted to Brekka. With the assistance of the wyrm kats, Brekka struggled to free her head and arms from her bindings.

Ary exclaimed, "By Hangatyr, she lives! This tells me, Brekka is woon's anointed maiden."

"My king," Kanarus said, "I will put every one of those warrior-monks to the edge of my blades."

Sur Sceaf directed, "Clear the landing, I'll shield Brekka until her lady knights can mantle her, and I'll take the altar and gates."

Lord Arundel said, "Kanarus, once your green knights clear the landing, I'll bring the hosts of our armies in."

Kanarus straightened in the saddle, raised his sword and shouted, "Vengeance for Odhin's daughter!" He charged forward with his green knights following. Most of the monks turned toward this new threat, only to be attacked by the war hounds, allowing the green knights the chance to charge for the gates before they had time to close.

Sur Sceaf stayed focused on Brekka. Once one arm was freed, she reached for the small dirk she routinely concealed in her vambrace.

Before the wyrm kats could completely free her of all the intestines and swaddling, she swung her body back and forth until her momentum brought her in contact with the Skull Worm who was supporting Katus with one arm and scrunched over feeling for the mitre with the other. With a lightning like motion Brekka skillfully jabbed the stiletto into the vile commissar's jugular. The Skull Worm grabbed his throat with both hands, fell back with blood spurting from his neck and died writhing beneath Brekka on the knees of the ennead tree.

A loud cheer rose from the Syr Folk. At the same time Sur Sceaf heard the inner voice say, *'Now!'*

Sur Sceaf signed for his long bowmen to clear the bastion walls and keep them cleared, then he signed for the hound handlers to let loose the rest of the dogs of war. The hounds bolted down the promontory, across the road, and up the ramp howling and baying in a smoking pack of flesh tearing teeth. He turned to the lieutenant of Brekka's twelver, Freyxus, nodded, and then shouted, "Charge!"

Sur Sceaf dug his heels into White Thunder's flanks. He felt the surge of horse muscle beneath him as his mount reared up and then lunged forward, its steel-shod hooves eating the distance between the promontory and the ramp. At his order, Uffa remained behind while Heimdal followed with horn and sword at hand. Sur Sceaf's first concern was freeing Brekka from the few remaining monks determined to complete this sacrifice to Angrar, the only bridge to victory over the Syr Folk that they understood.

The wyrm-kats now had the scent of the enemy and were chasing, clawing, and biting at the terror stricken, fleeing priests, like terriers in a rat pit. Another wave of the Pitter bowmen returned atop the fortress and tried to loose, only to be driven back by the Syr Folk longbow men before they could even nock their arrows. Soon, the longbow men had cleared the bastion walls by raining down a pelting storm of their deadly wolf-arrows.

A monk sounded a re-grouping on his bugle, and the monks began to fall back into a defensive formation, while the constant swish of wolf-arrows above kept the Pitter archers from retaliating. Soon, Pitter shield walls were established on the landing in an effort to regain order and repel more Syr Folk attacks. At the same time the green knights were challenging the monks in a contest to see who would reach the gates first.

The ketten now surrounded Brekka, relentlously flailing at the charging priests. Sur Sceaf felt his heart swell with exhilaration as he and Heimdal raced over the landing where several of the war-hounds continued leaping and tearing into the retreating enemy mass. Behind him, his twelve kept pace, while Kanarus' green knights closed in on the gates, striking the priests with blades, tomahawks, and war clubs.

The Horn of Heimdal blew loud and long before Heimdal put his horn aside and joined Sur Sceaf in the melee. Once the lady knights under Freyxus' command pulled up beside Sur Sceaf with Brekka's mare, Cyncnus, in tow, they cut a swath through the melee to reach Brekka and the man child.

Sur Sceaf, the wyrm kats, and the faery-hounds struck the teeming priests with a ferocious vengeance unparalleled in any previous engagement, insomuch that chunks of flesh and blood rained through the air hitting their shields like a hail storm. The path now cleared, Freyxus rode swiftly to the altar with Cisne and Pata, who dismounted, and freed Brekka from all that was binding her save the cord from which she hanged. Pata and Cisne held Brekka up to keep her from falling to the ground as Freyxus with one swing of her saber cut the silver cord from the grip of the tree of terror. The other lady knights fought off the remaining three commissars and their monkish defenders with a fury, their labyruses cleaving rib cages and skulls like sausage grinders.

Together, Sur Sceaf and the wyrm kats, with the assistance of the lady knights dealt with the commissars from the other direction. When one dared turn and confront him with a spear, Sur Sceaf deflected the spear with his battle axe and hacked his head off like one severs a pig's head. He turned only briefly to make sure Brekka was safe, and saw her lady knights were getting her carefully to her feet. Freyxus removed the vial of Siwel's Chartreusean potion from her pouch, unsealed the top and bade Brekka drink the entire contents. Siwel had promised that this would energize even the near dead for six hours, and ward off any poisons or infections.

Brekka was finally in safe hands, surrounded by her devoted warriors, even though she stumbled a bit from her paralyzed leg. Pata took one of the strips of muslin and wrapped Brekka's wounded and bleeding eye with the makeshift bandage, which would have to do until Walter and the hospitalers arrived.

Brimhilde, the youngest lady knight of fifteen winters brought Brekka Cyncnus. While Cisne helped Brekka to mount, Brimhilde tossed Brekka's helm to Pata and then retrieved her liege's wave blade and shield from the altar.

Sur Sceaf splayed a charging Pitter. As he spun around he spied Verushka grabbing the blind Katus by his dark cowl. "Your appointment with death has come, Soul-Eater," she shouted triumphantly. "Let it be recorded by the lore master that you shall die by the hand of a virgin."

The blind seer slipped in the blood of the buffalo at the altar as he attempted to twist free from her awful grasp. But he was no match in strength to Verushka, who jerked him to herself, and leaning from her horse, slit his throat. Katus vainly attempted to gurgle out some dark curse before choking in his own blood. Verushka held him tight until she could thrust the same blade through his liver. Uttering a Herewardi curse in turn, she tossed him at the base of the altar of Angrar, where he lay twitching in a dark heap on the stairs. Several of the long-eared war-hounds ran up to lap up his blood, while two others violently shook his limbs with their teeth and ripped him asunder.

The priests backed towards the gates, defending themselves as best they could from the forest of blades and spears wielded by the green knights.

Sur Sceaf swiftly hurled a battle axe through a charging attacker and stood guard, completing the securing of the altar and the tree. He shouted to Brimhilde, "The boy! Rescue the boy on the altar!"

Brimhilde mounted the altar and untied the young child. To prevent the dogs from harming him, she wrapped her white swan scarf around his middle to cover his nakedness and to place her scent upon him. As Sur Sceaf kept a protective vigil, he could see the boy was still in shock. "Are your parents in the crow cages?"

The boy shook as if chilled. "No, my whole family was taken from Arden and killed atop the wall. We lived in Arden under the protection of Rhoda Eckstein. But when the Pitters came, they accused us of helping the rdokians." Brimhilde looked the boy square on and charged him. "Do not move. Keep this scarf if you value your life. Wait here by the altar until you see a young man dressed in green. His name is Uffa. Tell him to take you to Brekka's tent, and I will come for you. From now on you are my son. Tell Uffa Brimhilde orders it so. Do you understand what I'm telling you?"

The wide-eyed child nodded his head in stunned silence.

Sur Sceaf had waited until Brimhilde had taken proper care of the child. "Praise Baldur, Katus the cannibal did not get his supper!" He nodded his approval at her and signed to Heruwer to join him.

Heruwer swiftly rode over to him. "What is your request, my lord?"

"Your sole commission at this moment is to free those poor souls in the crow cages. Fetch the orchardists' ladders from Benders Wood. The hospitalers can direct you. Employ as many wagons and men as you require. But make all due haste."

"It shall be done, my lord. Where do you want them taken once rescued?"

"Have the hospitalers set up a special tent for them and see to their every need."

Heruwer signed for his twelver to follow and commenced freeing the captives from their crow cages.

"Today the crows will be gorged on Pitter flesh instead," Heimdal commented, a sense of satisfaction in his face.

With the southern part of the landing now secured by his twelver, Sur Sceaf turned his attention to the gates, where a rat pack of Pitters emerged. As he charged forth, he yelled for his twelver to accompany him. He caught a glance of Brekka swinging her blade, her lady knights in a turtle phalanx around her as she, too, wasting no time, rushed for the gate.

A huge rush of pride filled his heart. *She is such a magnificent manifestation of elf blood, a true elven queen.* With renewed determination he slashed through a multitude of Pitters, muscling an entry with his horse through the gates. The amassed legions of the emperor were assembled in full battle array within the courtyard. Sur Sceaf ordered Heimdal to blast a signal to summon the wyrm kats and war-hounds to his side. An instant later Scratch leaped and bounded to his side, followed by Mauser and Chloe, increasing the pushing and shoving at the now gorged gates.

Scratch grinned through bloody teeth. "We kill rats now. Me help Top Cat kill rats!" He said gleefully.

Sur Sceaf choked out a laugh. "We kill rats now, Scratch."

The kats and the war-hounds charged through the gates screeching, snarling, and growling with bared teeth. A bugle sounded retreat, and the Pitter legionnaires broke ranks at the sight, turned and fled into the interior. Sur Sceaf scanned every cluster of the cowled-priests, the majority of which were fleeing. He checked out every movement for Hryre Seath, but could not see where the priests had managed to secrete him.

Sur Sceaf surprised himself by entering the gate before the green knights, who had been battling for entrance but, then Kanarus and his men had a far greater fight, having met the first onslaught of the emperor's crack troops. Once beyond the gates, he and some of his Twelvers crisscrossed the courtyard, slaying the fleeing priests and legionnaires, but they still could not locate the emperor. The wyrm kats clawed at any Pitters they came upon, while Sur Sceaf waited for Kanarus and his green knights to make a safe entry.

Once they joined him, he glanced briefly back out the gate and saw Brekka in full command of her lady knights, cutting her way into the fleeing warrior monks like nothing had ever been inflicted upon her. He realized he could spend no more time searching for Hryre Seath. His first priority needed to be to immediately secure the asset of the gate house as Long Swan had instructed.

Next through the gates came Mendaka and his dog soldiers. Sur Sceaf yelled, "Mendaka, join me. Leave the legions for Kanarus to clean up. Place a detachment of your dog soldiers with Heimdal at the gate and follow me."

He shouted, "Heimdal, stand guard like a ram at this gate. Suffer no Pitters to pass or repass. Summon Lord Arundel. I must be off to the gate house to stop the gates from closing." Heimdal blasted long and hard for the fyrds to follow the green knights inside the gates.

The cheer of the elf-maidens went up behind Sur Sceaf as he, his twelver, and Mendaka's forces dashed through the courtyard to the right. Whirling his battle axe, he was nearly jolted from his saddle by the impact of the charging swarm of Pitter legionnaires. The Pitters seemed determined to protect the gate house at all costs. With Scratch in the lead, the wyrm kats lunged over the top of the cohorts and opened a pathway through them, utterly terrifying the superstitious legionnaires in the process.

Sur Sceaf commanded his horse with his legs, and the legionnaires were summarily trampled underfoot. Those who had not been slain had their throats torn out by the dogs. In his pent up rage, he employed his battle axe to wreak utter havoc on anyone within his range, sending streaks of red blood spraying over his snow-white horse. Screams of agony went up everywhere. War horses screamed and neighed as they trampled and kicked the surprised Pitters.

The smell of blood and carnage filled the night air as the sound of clashing shields, swords, shouts, yells, and screams bounced off the enclosed walls. Frightening shadows danced in the torchlight of the bastion. And still, Sur Sceaf pressed his steed to trample its way towards the gate house amidst the swinging blades and jutting pikes. Everywhere was the sound of alarm. Once again, White Thunder made swift work of any enemy underfoot. And the legionnaires broke into any space they could get just to flee those kicking hooves of steel and the terrifying cat cries.

Directly before him, Sur Sceaf spotted the stone room that housed the gate mechanisms directly before him. In the next instance, a pike grazed his shoulder with a sharp burning sensation. He looked down into the rat face of a snarling gate guard. With one swing of his axe he relieved the Pitter of the top of his head. Then, with a burst of speed he reached the door of the gate house just as the Pitter guards began to close it.

"Get us in Mauser!" Sur Sceaf shouted and pointed.

With a happy snarl, Mauser leapt over the heads of the guards, pushing their pikes out of his way as though they were stalks of corn, and sending terror into the scattering guards. He forced the closing door open with his legs. Sur Sceaf ducked beneath the lintel and shoved through with his war horse. Mendaka and the Ketten were right behind. Ahead, he spied a gateman attempting to roll the gate wheel closed. With his scramasax he swiftly hurled a death blow to another gateman's throat. Chains were rattling and the klunk of the gate's reversal was heard. The gigantic cogs ground and screeched, and the chains groaned with their load. With a mighty swing of his battle axe, Sur Sceaf severed the chain in the gate house, causing the remaining chain to whirl around the wheel and discharge its severed link, thus rendering the gate permanently open.

Sur Sceaf had the brief realization that this gate house would make the perfect command post, and was large enough to house his commanders with room left over to have an armory, and central place for supplies. Additionally, the landing would serve well for establishing the field hospital. From this point on he hoped to direct the sweeping of the labyrinth caverns.

Once, the surrounding area was secured and the interior court was purged of the enemy, he turned his attention to Ruhm's absence. Where were they?

An unexpected new attack took place outside the bastion during the night. As dawn broke it became clear that the enemy had managed to exit the caverns from an unknown position during the battles of the night from an unknown position. In all likelihood the legionnaires had numerous secret exits outside the bastion walls and were attempting a flanking maneuver, but found their retreat cut off by the immediate deployment of Syr Folk armies. Mounted on white thunder, Sur Sceaf exited the gate house into the enormous courtyard stretching at least fifty yards to the mountainous pyramid of earth and stone. He had been so preoccupied with securing the gate house and court yard at the ground level of caverns that he had not had a chance to thoroughly inspect the areas outside the walls. Now, as he stood scanning his surroundings, he realized that like the central rock pyramid which had a series of hidden doors in the tiered cuttings, that these same sort of hidden doors must exist outside the bastion as well. His study of the bastion from the kings' heights had revealed the doorways in the upper tiers, and that each tier had a series of cave entrances, which suggested a honeycomb labyrinth of caverns contained within the pyramid. He assumed these caverns also ran out beyond the bastion walls. He scanned the tiers to study the three hidden doors, so as to better uncover the hidden doors beyond the walls.

Turning his attention toward the gates on his left, the green knights were pursuing the retreating legionnaires who had been trapped outside the bastion's caverns in the night. Directly in front of the gates, the battle continued as Ary's fyrds forced their way into the melee where Brekka and her knights were engaging the warrior monks who now realized they had no way of defeating the Syr Folk beachhead, nor did they entertain any further hope of returning to their underground stronghold.

The Syr Folk were filled with battle fury and rage. Brekka had regained her full strength, thanks to Siwel's ingenious potion, and was slashing her way through the fleeing Pitters with her tight band of lady knights at her side. Though blinded in one eye, and from the looks of her bandage eye patch, still bleeding, she was no less fearsome in her engagements.

That's my girl! The image of Woon, she lives and is as full of spunk as ever!

Scratch, Mauser, and Chloe had done their job perfectly, producing bedlam, chaos, and terror as intended. Inside the fortress the chaos of the enemy was spreading. It was apparent from their chaotic response that the Pitters had not prepared for a defensive response in their own bastion and had failed to account for the possibility that the Syr Folk would prevail over the monsters of the night. The central command structure had broken down. Sur Sceaf couldn't imagine any commanding general allowing for this much confusion. But, perhaps, as his Fa had told him, "Break the spear of Hormah, and you break the spiritual power of the Pitters, for they believe it to be a talisman of invincibility. Now that the wyrm kats had broken it, the morale of the legions broke with it."

It was ironic that Scratch, one of the litter of ketten that Xelph had discovered in the sea cavern on the Isle of Ilkchild, had served as the instrument of the spear's destruction. His original intent had been to have all such creatures destroyed as an abomination, but when Xelph rescued the three tiny creatures twenty some years ago, the Ur Fyr prompted him to let them live. He considered this testimonial proof that following a righteous course always leads to victory.

Outside the gates the number of slain enemies was great, and the bodies of dead legionnaires littered the courtyard and had been stacked like cordwood along the corridor walls, so as not to interfere with circulation.

As some of the remaining interior legions slithered in retreat back around the mound, another group of priests, who appeared as if they wanted to escape in any way they could pressed for the gates. The wave of fleeing priests ran straight into Kanarus' and Brekka's knights. After a short battle, they were cut down like a scythe through barleycorn. What had propelled these priests to attempt escape rather than retreating as had the legions back within the mound baffled Sur Sceaf. Perhaps the command structure had broken down even more than he originally thought. It only heightened the mystery of what was going on inside the caverns.

From previous intelligence reports, he knew there were tens of thousands of Pitters in this bastion, some said perhaps upward of a hundred thousand. Surveying the area, he saw only remnants of the legions he had encountered when first he passed through the gates. Where were they? Kanarus and his men had stationed troops at both sides of the courtyard, and yet, the legions within were gradually disappearing.

The violent confrontations had ceased. *How have so many disappeared so quickly? And where have they all hidden? Was the speed of the plague somehow accelerating?* Before Sur Sceaf could come up with a reasonable conclusion, the sconces along the Bastion walls went out. Only a few torches burned to give them light in the dimly lit courtyard. Heimdall, ever in tune with the turn of events, blasted the six pips on his horn for those bearing torches to light them.

Determined not to let Hryre Seath escape justice, Sur Sceaf ordered Heimdall to summon Zrael and the wyrm kats as well as those under his immediate command-- his Twelvers, Mendaka, Going Snake, and their dog soldiers--then he rode to the center of the courtyard.

After his fyrd had reassembled, he declared, "I'm confident that Kanarus and Brekka can handle the courtyard. Especially with Lord Arundel's forces moving in. I have determined it would be wisest for us to scout to the right in an effort to locate Hryre Seath. I can't be certain, because of the confusion, but I believe I caught a glimpse of a cadre of priests hurrying him in that direction during the last alarm."

He ordered the Wyrm Kats to take the lead, as their vision was far greater than a man's. They moved away from the gate house, deeper into the corridor to the right, where they soon discovered half-dead Pitter hell-rats lining the galleries, lying in the grey limestone dust with bloody pink froth issuing from their mouths and noses, fully armored, but too lethargic to even fight. Such easy targets indicated that something besides battle damage had to be wrong with them.

As they proceeded farther, they began seeing non-combatants crumpled in the dust. Upon closer examination, many of the Pitter dead bore no wound marks at all. The deeper they rode into the bastion, the more puzzled Sur Sceaf grew. Something had happened in the dark of the night before. There was even a host of Pitter females, some indicating they had made a hasteful flight, as they were still dressed in night attire, lying dead next to the men. Worst of all were the dead and lifeless offspring still clinging to their mothers, with contorted and painful expressions on their faces.

He signed to halt. Looking as puzzled as Sur Sceaf, Mendaka declared, "This is no fortress. This is a tomb."

Chloe sidled to Sur Sceaf's side and purred, "These rats smell sour. Me no bite. Sick rats. Pssst!"

As Sur Sceaf watched the jerky snaps of Chloe's tail and contemplated her meaning, he suddenly understood the words of Chief White Moose. The Mufsiks had brought on this death-plague. But by what means? And though he heard White Moose declare the plague, he hadn't thought it would be so extensive.

Mendaka commented, "Look at these Pitter kits; it appears no one had cared to attend them. It almost looks like they've been cast out. Something is very wrong here, my lord. Something very dark has struck the enemy from within."

Sur Sceaf sighed. "If it's the same plague that I heard about in the northern campaign, it spreads like fire through their population. Sol-Om-On reported that the Pitters at Albany were actually slaying any in their midst that manifested signs of the plague and throwing them on fires, often before they were even dead. I suspect that's what we are witnessing here. They probably didn't have enough medicine to go around and also immunize their legions in the south lands so they sacrificed these."

"Shouldn't we avoid contact and burn these carcasses before it spreads to us?"

Sur Sceaf shook his head, "According to Sol-Om-On, the plague only affects those of rat's blood. But you are correct. For hygiene's sake, we must remove the carcasses and burn them.

He heard Heimdall blast his horn twice, which was the sign for the beetles, and the wagoneers to come in with the supplies. Then, there was a pause followed by three blasts for bringing in the hospitalers.

Mauser gave out a trilling purr, and pointed behind Sur Sceaf, "Pretty lady fire-cat comes."

Sur Sceaf turned to see Brekka and her lady knights approaching. Brekka rode up, angled her horse next to her father, and looked intently at him with her one good eye. "We've broke the Pitter resistance. Kanarus is mopping up."

She turned her attention to the Ketten now gathering around her. "Scratch, Chloe and Mauser, I want to commend you all on your excellent actions at the altar yesterday and you're fighting alongside me today." She smiled at Scratch. "You may not realize it, but when you bit Hryre Seath's spear in half, you broke the power of the enemy. Now the enemy is of a mind to leave."

Scratch lowered his chin and gazed up at her with adoring eyes. "For Pretty Lady Fire-Kat, Scratch break many spears."

Once again, she regarded Sur Sceaf. "Where to now, my king?"

"Hold by me for now."

"But, Fa, I am ready to fight."

"I know you are, as are we all. But, even the strongest warrior needs a breather. Despite the potion's healing effect, your wound is taking a toll. You can't possibly be rested enough now. And I'm ordering you to get that eye stitched as soon as Alf Hegele shows up at the gate house with a hospitaler wagon. After that, I want you to pitch your bed on one of the benches in the gate house and to get some rest."

Reluctantly, she sheathed her sword again and lifted her hand above her head, the signal for her lady knights to be at ease. Some of her knights dismounted, others took off their helms and shook down their long hair. Several of the dog soldiers went over to compare battle stories and offered their pemmican to the elf-maidens.

Sur Sceaf commanded, "Going Snake, would you see to it as soon as the beetles arrive that they carry my order to all ranks to start three hour rotations, rest their horses, and get a little shut-eye?"

"It shall be done, my lord."

Turning to Brekka, Sur Sceaf's heart melted for his daughter. "My dear, I haven't had time to talk with you, but you gave us a frightful scare when you entered these gates alone. I can only pray your antics were all prompted by the Ur Fyr. I know mine were."

"Of that you can be assured, Fa. People call me reckless, but I only act under the light of the Elf Fyr. I knew beyond doubt I had the protection of Odhin upon me." She withdrew the silver iridium necklace from beneath her swan-scarf. "A gift from Wilona."

"Freya's immortal necklace," he exclaimed. "Govannon spoke of it. Said it was made under dwarven advisement."

Sur Sceaf studied his daughter's face. The faery-glow still clung to her. Other than her wounded eye, she seemed remarkably untouched. Tilting Brekka's head with his hand, he lifted the patch bandage to examine her eye, fearing the worst. He was relieved to see the puckered gash was above her eye. Although horribly swollen, the eye itself appeared to be still intact and he was sure Siwel and Walter would come up with some healing balm for it.

"Can you see through that eye?"

"I'm sure it looks worse than it is. You know how head wounds bleed. It will need some stitching, but I think I will still be able to see."

"Since the death of Talking Stick," Going Snake interjected, "I've known the Pitters' cruelty, and I've never experienced such horrible grief as when they had you in their clutches. I fear I made a perfect nuisance of myself, my lady."

"You certainly did," Mendaka declared derisively. "The lord Sur Sceaf would have been in his rights to relieve you of your command."

"Forgive him Dak; he was only expressing what I was feeling, especially, after witnessing Wilona's cruel death."

Brekka smiled warmly at Going Snake before turning serious once again. "Father, I know now what Wilona meant when she said I would become her daughter this day."

Sur Sceaf frowned. "Perhaps you could explain that to me then."

"She had foreseen that I would be separated from her bowels, wrapped in her intestines. Don't you see, it has made me her daughter by proxy."

"I had already assumed that was the case. My dear."

Mendaka leaned in and said, "The thunder horse once told me, that it was ordained from your birth that you would be the daughter of the gods. From your mother came your tenderness, from your grand mother, Redith, came the guidance of the thunder beings, and from your father's bloodline you have inherited the favor of the herewardi gods. It only stands to reason your calling would be crowned by a rebirth through a daughter of those gods."

Mauser had drawn near Brekka and began stroking her calf and foot. Cyncnus snorted her disapproval. Brekka looked down and commanded, "Back Mauser, back!" As the smitten Wyrm-Kat slunk off to rejoin the other Ketten, Brekka said, "Does Mauser seem to be getting more frisky of late?"

"It's all the excitement of battle." Zrael said, "Fighting gets them pumped up with sexual energy. Just make him keep his bounds. Keep him in his place and there won't be a problem."

"Believe me I will. I've had a lot of practice over the years. Now, we've rested enough, let's finish this business, go ratting. I wish to avenge the blood of Mother Wilona."

Going Snake declared, "I second that suggestion. Let's give them hell."

The continuous din and clashing of shields in the distance caught Sur Sceaf's attention as he said, "I applaud your eagerness, but this situation calls for moving forward with extreme caution. We will soon have this courtyard all the way around the pyramidal cliffs under control, if not already. But the gods only know where the legions have gone, and we have no idea if they have booby-trapped the inner caverns or even if this is all an elaborate staged trap to lure us into an ambush. And what in the hell will we do if Hryre Seath lets more of those tyfons and gyrlocks slip?"

Kanarus and Eldritch rushed to the left of the courtyard, in pursuit of a fleeing Pitter rat-pack in the dark, their horses' hooves hammering out sharp blows against the stone floor. The sconces flickered, giving barely enough light to see by as they rapidly closed the distance between them and the men on foot. When Kanarus and Eldritch came within a spear's throw, the Pitters rounded a curve, disappearing entirely from sight. Anticipating the kill, they spurred their horses faster. They rounded the curve riding in hot pursuit only to discover an empty corridor ahead. The Pitters had disappeared.

Kanarus called an immediate halt, exclaiming, "That's the damnedest thing I ever saw. They were just there a moment ago." He looked from side to side, but everywhere he looked on the right and on the left was only solid walls of rock with piles of rock and stone every fifty feet or so. Kanarus gazed up at the smooth wall before him. Somehow these piles of rock against the wall had no logical reason for being there.

Eldritch turned his horse all the way around, dismounted, and said, "They can't have disappeared like that. It's got to be some sort of trick." He called for the torchbearer, and then felt along the wall in the flickering light. An instant later, he paused to peer closer, "Lord Kanarus, look at this!"

Kanarus dismounted and joined Eldritch, who was pointing at a straight line running up the wall about seven feet high, and then making a square turn. Kanarus was able to discern it was the outline of a very cleverly disguised door. After signing for the archers to be at the ready, he backed up a few steps before charging the door with his shoulder, only to bounce back. Looking chagrined, he rubbed his shoulder. "Well, I'm sure this is where they went in. But how did they get it to open and close so damned fast?"

Eldritch, who had continued to examine the rock face, indicated a small protuberance that appeared to be a small stone embedded in the limestone, "I think this must be the device for opening it."

Kanarus ran his fingers over the object which felt more like horn than stone, but he suspected it was neither. "I agree, this is almost certainly man made. Look, when you push on it, it yields." Using his thumb, he pushed it several times, but the door remained closed. "Well done Eldritch. This is most certainly a door, but they must be able to lock it from within. How do we follow, and should we? We have no idea what's beyond this barrier."

Kanarus walked over to his saddle bags, reached in and pulled out a piece of red ochre. He signed to his Silver harrier, "Report to Lord Sur Sceaf that we were pursuing Pitters who disappeared, seemingly, into the rock, and upon further examination have found a well-hidden locked door on the interior wall. We suspect there are more. The Pitters have sealed this entrance and likely the others as well. Tell him, we will search the walls for more of these doors and mark them all in red."

As the harrier goaded his horse away, Kanarus quickly drew a big red X over the door. "When we find and mark each door, I want guards posted at every one. Should the door open, the guards are to blow the alert signal on their hunter's horn. And keep in mind, if they can go in, they can come out."

CHAPTER 4:

THE DEMONS AND THE GATE HOUSE

S UR SCEAF DECIDED TO SET up the gate house as his temporary
command post because it was strategically located by the gates and
facing the pyramidal mound. Additionally, it was as Sur Spear's
Shepherd Hall at Witan Jewel with a dormitory housing the gate and
parapet guards at one end and a mercantile center at the other. The
Pitters also had rooms for storage of the guards' weapons and armor.

He had the wagoneers bring in pikes, swords, tomahawks, scramasaxes
and equipment to repair over which he placed one of his weapons masters,
Yfel-Slayer, son of Pyrsyrus by Sky-Wylf's hearth. Tutored personally by the
wizard Govannon, the young man was an artisan with weapons, armor and
utensils. Additionally, he requested the presence of Long Swan, Heimdall, and
Uffa. Young Alf Hagele and Rolf served as a go between for the hospitalers.

After Sur Sceaf received Kanarus' message from the silver harrier, he ordered
more torches lit. Stepping from the gate house, he looked up at the pyramid's
imposing walls. As shadows danced over the walls, it reminded him of the ant hills
constructed by the vicious fire ants down in the Taxus. The disappearance of the
great number of the legionnaires, and the doors discovered by Kanarus betokened
an entire fortress within a fortress, no doubt leading down into the chthonic realm
of Hryre Seath, a place where Katus' nightmarish rituals were likely conducted.

Mendaka and Going Snake came to stand at Sur Sceaf's side. They
had been helping the armorers unload the pikes from the wagon when
the harrier had arrived with the message from Kanarus.

Mendaka commented, "The Hickoryans merchants said that when this bastion was being built, the runaway slaves reported an entrance to a pit at the top into which you can toss a stone and never hear it hit bottom."

"That sounds like the deep hole Brekka described when she climbed the eastern mound, and scouted out the bastion from above."

Looking upward, Going Snake narrowed his gaze and weighed in, "The only way I can see we might get in is to scale those cliffs, but they could repel us if they saw us coming. And what were those storage tanks that Brekka discussed in the council fire used for? It can't be water because the merchants said they have ample resources for water within."

Sur Sceaf paddled his beard, "I don't know what their purpose is, but Sol-Om-On sent a report that the zonga at Albany had a large tank that exploded like a burning star when it caught flame." He paused for a moment, "You trigger a thought in me. Those tanks have to be serviced somehow. I doubt that they could do that climbing up and down those steep cliffs. This would suggest they have access somewhere up there."

Brekka, who had been resting on one of the benches inside, per Sur Sceaf's command, joined them. "Did I hear a mention of my name?"

Going Snake turned to smile at her. "We were just discussing the hole at the top of the pyramid you described. My father heard from a Hickoryan that it is a bottomless pit."

"I can easily believe that." She, too, scanned the cliff before them. "Although I am ready to slay anything that moves, the Ur Fyr fills my bosom with an awful foreboding, Fa. We could find out soon enough that we are sitting on a damned hornet's nest, and I'm damned sure it will soon be shades of the Poisoned Lands all over again. From the way it appears, this mound is a whole rabbit's warren of tunnels. The Pitters could mount a surprise attack from chust about anywhere. They know every aspect of this place, and we don't know the tenth of it, yet. This much I do know. When they carried me down to the tunnels below, they appeared to be endless. More so, even, than Gloomullah's nest. We need to be on high alert at all times."

"Your warning is well taken, we have learned never to underestimate them."

Sur Sceaf stared at the formidable cliffs that were just as much an enemy as the Pitters. "We have no real concept of what we're up against. As it stands, we'll have to find an alternative way into that mountain and flush them out one by one, inch by tedious inch, until there is not a damned Pitter left to piss against a wall."

Sur Sceaf had just dispatched Alph, the Quailor hospitaler to get Dr. Shanks to take another look at Brekka. He knew head wounds that got infected could have dire consequences, and he did not want to lose his beloved daughter for lack of care. To pre-occupy himself until Dr. Shanks arrived, he was counseling with White Moose about what role the Snow Men and the Mufsiks would play in the upcoming battle.

White Moose said, "The best role my men could play would be as shock troops."

Sur Sceaf assented.

Brekka raised her head off the pillow, "I agree, Fa. The Snow Men strike hard and fast."

"I welcome your comments, my dear, but once again you are supposed to be resting."

Sur Sceaf was about to resume his conversation with White Moose and the Mufsiks when Kanarus and Eldritch arrived with their men at the gate house. Upon entering, Kanarus saluted and signed 'mission accomplished'. "We marked thirty doors. Four of which were much wider, and appeared to be double doors eight foot each. We can think of no reason for them to be so big, unless it's to get the mounted legionnaires out as quickly as possible."

Eldritch declared, "On the eastern side of the mound we discovered many more bodies, untouched by battle."

White Moose said, "It is the Mufsiks' knives which slew them."

Seeing the concern in his face, Sur Sceaf said, "You need not worry, this sickness will not touch us. It does not affect man."

Eldritch related, "When I was a boy, there was a devastating plague which the shaman Red Knife said was brought to them by mice. I remember our dead lying in the dust much as we are seeing the Pitters here. Red Knife said the plague came out of the Poisoned Lands. He ordered us to burn the bodies, all of our caches of grain, and to move to the mountains. I am sure that is what saved us."

White Moose shook his head, "I told the king, and I told the flaming hair that the Mufsiks knives will not touch any but those of rat's blood. It will pass over us harmless as a dove to its water hole."

"Forgive me, White Moose, but I still cannot understand how this could be," Eldritch plied.

"The Mufsiks are our holy warriors." White Moose declared. "They are the bringers of death. So they fear naught. Let me explain it to you like this; our shaman, Straggle Claw, sent the Mufsiks out with a spirit-medicine on their knives. After they placed cuts across the cheeks on the Vardropi, the spirit medicine enters their bodies and then it takes some time to kill them. Before they are dead the spirit of death departs their lungs and then jumps from enemy to enemy through their breath. Once emitted from the lungs it becomes so deadly that it travels on the wind, until every last Vardropi and Pitter; man, woman, and child shall die from it. Once released, there is no calling back the hand of death. That's why they are the harbingers of death. They are Mufsiks."

"Pray tell," Eldritch said, "that still doesn't explain how their poison knives know how to distinguish Pitters and Vardropi from the rest of us."

White Moose sighed. "It is simple. Straggle Claw saw all the evil the Pitter and Vardropi had done to the red man in the snow lands, and it grieved his spirit so that he fasted many days and cut upon himself as he cried unto the manitous. Then he hung from his breasts in the sacred rites of the sun lodge, and finally, in his travail, he talked with the great horned manitou who heard his cries from the other world. The manitou held out his hand, and as Straggle Claw looked in the hand he saw a sick rat with pink froth oozing out its mouth. The manitou said, 'Find these rats and coat the knives of your holy men in their blood. Then take you nine Vardropi and peel their face with your knives and I shall release the angel of death upon the hosts of all Vardropi and Pitters so that he will slay only those of the Pitter and Vardropi blood.' It worked slower on the Vardropi, but as you see, much faster on the Pitters, once they were visited with the bad air, death hewed them down."

"Thank you for that clarification, White Moose," Eldritch bit his lips. "It eases my apprehension."

"Mine as well," Sur Sceaf acknowledged, "Thank you for the added information. You've answered a riddle for me. I wish your Mufsiks could use their spirit-medicine to get us in these doors."

White Moose said, "I will have them consult the manitou."

"I would be very grateful for that. What is for sure is that unexpected luck favored us in the capture of this fortress. It was not in our immediate calculations nor was it in that of the emperor. But what is sure, is we are not going to abandon this asset or our footing for the enemy to reclaim it. Sure, we have suffered great losses, but I fear they would have been far greater without our unexpected gaining of these inner courts."

Sur Sceaf made good use of the existing furnishings in the gate house; a long trestle table, oak chairs, and the dormitory with bench bunks upon which Brekka was attempting to rest. Her lady knights hovered over her, clucking like a flock of cedar waxwings around a nestling as they vied to attend her needs.

Seated at one end of the table with Heimdall in attendance, Sur Sceaf was discussing the battle plans with the first rotation. At the other end sat Long Swan who had been reviewing his log and had just returned quills and writing tablet to his scribe's leather case. There in the lamplight, Long Swan seemed like some heavenly being attired in his pure white hooded robe. Sur Sceaf considered him sent by the gods for the great support and counsel he had always proffered.

Just outside the entrance Uffa was busy sending the beetles on their numerous errands. He had just delivered a communication from Il-Alim that he was training the Young Prince Anghrus in crypsis. The gods had already witnessed to Sur Sceaf that Anghrus was to play a major role in the coming generation. Therefore, the Roufytrof had tasked all the great men of the land in training and educating the young prince in all the arts of war.

A plough length away to each side, against the western and eastern walls, the horse masters were busy finishing the corrals in the broad courtyard, while stable boys were feeding and watering the horses from one of the public cisterns spaced periodically along the mound wall. Grooms were assessing the horses' health and well-being, as farriers set up their smithies and examined the sureness of the shoes.

Dr. Walter Shanks had shown up with Siwel as Sur Sceaf and Long Swan were discussing the pros and cons of various approaches to securing the caverns in the safest way possible. Sur Sceaf was distracted by the struggle Dr. Walter Shanks was having with Brekka as he stitched her eye. She kept twisting around attempting to get her input into his strategizing.

"Fa, Ruhm suggested we take the secret cave in. Let me take my lady knights and go through the sink hole to the hidden passage in the quarry. We must press our advantage while we can. Let us call the terms of battle. Not them!"

Dr. Shanks sighed, "My lord, would you insist this young lady sits still while I'm stitching. It's like pinning a tail on a donkey with the way she moves."

Sur Sceaf stifled a laugh before he gave her a firm browbeating, "Sit still, Copper Locks. I won't entertain any more counsel from you until Dr. Shanks has finished, pronounced you whole and hale, and then I want you to take a long overdue nap."

She growled and pouted as Dr. Shanks revealed, "You are one lucky lady. The cut was clean and missed your eye altogether. There's no infection and I pronounce you ready to go when your father gives you sanction to do so."

Long Swan grinned. "Don't you know by now, Walter, she is Lady Luck? I've never seen anyone do the things she has done and live to tell."

One after another, wagons containing bags of beast stoppers, pikes, and sheaves of arrows arrived and were swiftly unloaded by the wagoneers then stowed neatly inside according to the plan of the weapons master, ready for quick access. Undertakers were in the courtyard loading up the fallen soldiers to take to the afore designated cemetery Garden of Heroes in Pikeside. At the same time, the hewers of wood and the haulers of water were instructed to dump a load of Pitter bodies in the quarry and then to burn the rest. If the Pitters had any means of seeing their dead being desecrated by the wild dogs and vultures feeding on their carcasses, it might be insult enough to perhaps rouse them out of the mound.

The lore master approached, and with a look of consternation on his face said, "My lord, it's been nigh seven hours, and it approaches the last watch. It troubles me that Starkwulf and Ruhm have not yet attended this counsel."

Brekka twisted her head as Walter was putting in the last stitch. "Ruhm has convinced Starkwulf to hear the Lazy Jokers out. They claim to know a hidden way into the caverns. Perhaps they have left on their own to find the way in."

Sur Sceaf shared the same concern. "I hope not. Unless the hidden passage leads into some sort of immense tunnel system, then perhaps they got lost. I can't help but fear some evil may have befallen them. Maybe they ran into Hryre Seath and his damned elite legions. One moment he was there and then wasn't. The emperor is like a gator that has headed for deep water. I am vigilant, methinks he is about to resurface any moment, and it troubles me that two of my commanders are off on an unsanctioned mission."

Long Swan suggested, "Perhaps we should send another party in through the sink hole in search of them. Or do you think that would be too risky?"

"No need, my lord, we are here." The mighty frame of Ruhm appeared through the door way.

Ruhm was followed by the Hickoryan Jokers and Russell with his twelver. Escorting them were White Moose and the Mufsiks. Heimdall or any of the other Horners would have announced their arrival.

Everyone gasped in surprise. "How ironic is it that just as we were discussing your fate you were at the door, as hail and hearty as when you left us."

Mendaka laughed. "They don't even look ruffled. Were you in the caverns?"

"We ran a brief reconnaissance. We were inside, alright. And have come with many tales to tell."

The Twelvers waited outside the gate house door while the Jokers, ignorant of protocol, crowded in, their voices tumbling over each other as they commented on the stockpiled weaponry.

Sur Sceaf sighed in relief. "I admit, we expected you much sooner than this. We were concerned that you had been gone for so long. Thank the gods, you are safe. You're just in time, we're working out a systematic way to flush these caverns and would be very interested in what you saw below."

"What happened to Brekka? Why is she laying in a hospital cot again?"

Brekka was stirred from her slumber by the voice of Ruhm. She sat up to make sure she was not dreaming and saw that the Lazy Jokers had crowded into the room. Her heart leapt. "Ruhm, is that you?"

The boys were startled by her voice and turned toward her. At the same time, with a shout of "Brekka!" Ruhm plowed his way through the Jokers to get to her. Kneeling in front of the bunk, he took her in his arms, nearly smothering her with the strength of his embrace.

"Thank God, you're still safe."

Her father chuckled, rose up, and declared with amusement in his voice. "I wish to send this meeting from labor to refreshment, and all of us will give these two some time together before we reconvene here in the morning."

As Sur Sceaf and Arundel herded the boys from the room, Ruhm pulled back and looked at her at arm's length. A look of dismay came over his handsome face. "Your eye! Your eye! Did Doctor Shanks say it's going to be alright?" He cupped her face tenderly in his battle calloused palms.

Her voice was a little throaty, "Only a stab to my head." Brekka reveled in his touch, heedless of the stabbing pain it was causing. "Skull Worm's knife nearly got my eye, though I still see. I hope it does not deface me. Walter said there is no infection."

"No, no, nothing could deface your beauty."

"Doctor Shanks did his best, but I fear there will be scarring."

"The stitching is as fine as any seamstress could have done on a piece of rare silk." Ruhm pulled out a pink lady's scarf from beneath his chest armor. Brekka was startled, because she had previously given him a white swan scarf as a token of her love for him, but she told herself it was probably his mother's. Out of his pocket he produced a curious small skin vial covered in green duck feather. After removing the cork, he poured some amber liquid over the delicate scarf, and then tenderly wiped her wound with the tingling potion.

"Brekka, this liquid is a powerful medicine made of eyebright and inula, the herb you call Woon's Spear, especially formulated to heal the eyes by a Cherokee mountain witch called Liza. It'll set your eye right in no time. It took my eyes from blind to full sight within a week." He paused as he poured more of the healing liquid over the scarf. "Now, I have to tell you, and this is all I'm going to say about it. What you did was so far more horrible than my worst nightmare could ever be. You have got to stop tugging my heart around. It can't take anymore. When I was told the tale of your bravery it was terrifying to me. Please, tell me what they did to you."

"To begin with, Father Odhin spoke in my heart and charged me by the ur fyr to be his offering. With the all father's promptings, I charged into the bastion with Ma-Za-Ma plowing through a host of Pitter legionnaires while I cut off heads, arms, and limbs in my passing. I managed to kill a host of the enemy before a wall of Pitter pikemen unsaddled me. A group of dark warrior monks bound me, and led me down the corridor of the courtyard to a hidden door that led down a narrow tunnel, past enormous glass rooms, chust like in the citadel. I could tell by the rooms I saw on the way in that this place was built by the Amerikans and predated the Pitters and maybe even the Herewardi when they dwelt here."

"Yes, I have seen rooms like that down below. Also hidden doors, most of which we could not open. We found a mechanical monstrosity that Russell called an 'earth-eater' like you saw in the Poisoned Lands. Did you see glowing tubes that looked like they were filled with lightning bugs?"

"I did," Brekka exclaimed. "The hags told us they were left over from the days of the Amerikans. There were several of them in this chamber where they laid me on a stone table and tied me to the four horns of what looked to me exactly like drawings of an altar of dark elves. I did my best to thwart their designs but they overpowered me by their sheer numbers."

"I wish I'd been there to sever their filthy rat paws from their bodies!"

"If those vile monks hadn't searched me for weapons, I would have bled them all. Truth is, they never found them all. They were too busy examining my virginity. The monks left, giving me hope that I might be able to escape my bonds, but they were soon replaced by the ennead of commissars and the blind seer, Katus. They mocked me and called me 'a squirming bitch in heat' and talked about all the delights they would take in offering me up as an unblemished sacrifice to Angrar."

"The rat-brained bastards obviously don't understand that human women do not go into heat." He took a deep breath before asking in a low tone, "Forgive me for being blunt, but did they defile you?"

"Praise Freya, that's one thing they didn't do, because their prophecy declared I had to be a virginal offering. But Katus did examine me again for proof. Starting with my head, he gradually felt down the length of my body until he got to my codpiece. He had it removed and then examined my nethers and declared me to be an intact virgin and the seed of the woman of prophecy. He exulted in my degradation and ordered me to be freed of bonds. But I didn't have a chance to attempt an escape before they swarmed over me with strips of swaddling that they wrapped about me like a mummy's shroud. Later, I learned they had used Wilona's intestines to further entwine me." Her voice broke, and she had to stop.

"By Christ and Thor, is there no deprivation they will not stoop to." He wiped a tear from her cheek with the silken scarf, she hadn't realized she was crying. "Surely your gods were with you."

It was the first time Ruhm had ever made respectful reference to the gods of Os-Gard, and it set a flicker of hope aflight in her heart. "I can still hear the vile insults they flung at me and feel the prying claws of that sycophant of the dark elves. But the worst was when they carried me out to that horrible altar on the landing where the Skull Worm stabbed me just above the eye. I'm sure he supposed he had made me a one eye. Then priests hanged me from the tree of terror. As I dangled helplessly, I suddenly heard the piercing cries of the wyrm kats and knew salvation was afoot. Sure enough, thanks to the kats and my sister knights, I am here before you while Katus and the Skull Worm are writhing in the vilest pits of queen hell."

"Thank god and the gods, I did not have to witness any of that, because the last few months have shown me I cannot live without you." Ruhm supported her head in his left hand as he once again dabbed the healing potion on her wound with the scarf in the other. "I thought you dead when I saw those damned gates close on you. It was like the jaws of hell had swallowed you up and I was powerless to help. I can't believe you got away with only this wound."

He pulled her head to his lips and planted a big smacking kiss where her hair parted on the crown. She realized what a void her life had been without him, and just how much she had missed his company and tender attentions. She was determined to never let him out of her arms again, come what may. She slowly drifted into sleep in his protecting arms.

It was nearly time for the meeting with Ruhm and the rest of the scouting party. Arundel, Redelfis and Long Swan had already arrived, and were partaking of the wine, bread and sheep cheese the stewards had provided.

Sur Sceaf walked out into the courtyard past the fire of a weapon-smith's bellows, and went off to relieve himself near a Pitter cesspit some seventy-five feet or so from the gate house. As he made his way along the sheared rock wall of the mound, he noticed approximately every fifty feet was a pile of recently dumped rocks stacked against the mound wall. He also noticed that every twenty-five feet three inch wide slits approximately six to eight feet tall had been cut into the rock face. As he placed his hand against one of the cracks, he felt the suck of air passing over his fingers. *Could this be an air shaft?* He wondered. He considered plugging these, but as his gaze travelled upward, he spied more slits on each tier all the way up to the seventh where *Brekka had seen the opening at the top.*

When he reached the cesspit, the foul odor made the hair in his nostrils curl with revulsion. After he waved the torch over the reeking pit to insure there were no surprises there, he took a satisfying piss. When he finished, he decided he would remove himself afar off from the foul odor of rat piss and turds and seek solitude somewhere in the shadows of the wall. He walked through the dimly lit corridor until he found a place near the corrals that was free of people moving about. He edged past some tool sheds, a few half-filled wagons, and one wagon still upon jacks with wheel it's off and a stand of scattered fruit.

Behind a mason's tent he leaned on some rough ashlars and prayed to the gods for guidance in hopes that they might reveal some way to crack the hard nut of the mound core and gain access into the enemy. Rumors from the locals were that the interior mound could not be penetrated, and that the Pitters had supplies and resources enough to last ten years, maybe longer.

As he lifted his arms in swan prayer, the nearby corralled horses began to stamp and snort as if a predator was near at hand. Despite the balmy night air, he felt cold, and began to shiver. He poised as taut as a bowstring. Suddenly he was covered in thick darkness and cold fingers ran over his skin. His knees buckled, and with no control over his muscles, he collapsed to the ground. He felt a force grip him from which he could not free himself. His tongue was bound no matter how hard he strove to speak while he desperately attempted to call for help. The forces of terror that lurked in the night gripped him and threatened to snuff out his very breath.

Three figures that were darker than night appeared before him, their eyes like blue flames in ice. He could not distinguish their faces, only those piercing cold blue, unblinking eyes out of realms unknown to man. He felt the frigid breath of death settle over his being as if a chill winter blast was blowing ice barbs through his bloodstream.

A sinister cracking voice rasped and hissed at him, "Sur Sceaf, blood of Os, your doom is now at hand. A power greater than you is about to devour you and suffocate all light out of this land. Your confederation, constitutionalism, and sovereignty shall crumble in a ruinous mess about your feet. And Mount Heredom shall never again rise to speak from the ancient dust, but once again return to be the haunt of ghosts and doleful creatures." Then the tallest of the three sinister creatures stepped forward to say in some forgotten tongue. '*Pidiu scal er in deru uuicsteti uunt piullan enti in demo sinde sigalos uuerdan.*'

Sur Sceaf's heart understood it was a pronounced curse and meant he would fall wounded without victory.

When he feared he must surely pass over into the realm of the dead, he beheld the caring face of Redith before him. He mustered all the strength of his soul and prayed even more fervently for deliverance, *Oh, Baldur, fairer than the sun to look upon, deliver me from these foul pale elves and their black spirits. Release me from the grip of the muspilli and make my runes stronger than their curses.*

A beam of light filled his head and immediately dispelled all darkness, as a voice spoke in his heart: *Sur Sceaf, my beloved, marked of Odhin art thou, I am with thee, even to the end. Fear not these children of darkness nor fret to set thy hand against Angrar. Go out this night with wolf-boldness to meet them. For what it is, it is not, and shall be.*

As the powers that bound him released their grip, the tall dark figure thrust out its boney black finger and rasped one last threat, prinnit mittilgart, before disappearing into a dark mist, and the darkness became less dark. He was given to understanding that it meant the death of middle earth or something equally evil.

As he felt his strength return to him, he rose from the ground and saw Long Swan in his white hood approaching. "My lord, are you ready to reconvene?"

Kanarus sat outside the gate house reading the letter sent by his son, Anghrus. The boy, now a young blood and already married was currently under the tutelage of Il-Alim and his cryptic warriors down near Charleston. Previously he had been traveling with Redangus while obtaining his proficiency at sea. The Roufytrof had singled the young prince out for a very special commission for which only a few were privy to. Kanarus was immensely proud of his son, the only offspring he had from he and Wilona. He served as a constant monument to the love that had once been between he and the boy's mother. He felt he may never overcome the grief of Wilona's death. He kept trying to see the positive side to his fate, but he nursed a secret anger at the norn sisters for depriving him of the greatest love he had ever known.

He wondered where Wilona was. Is she sailing through the stars on Ullr's celestial barge? Is she in the dark realms of hell or does she ride with the Desir in the heavens. Death is such an unassailable chasm between us. If love is a fruitful tree, death is like going into your garden to partake of its fruits only to find your favorite tree uprooted and nowhere to be found.

Only a deep dark pit lies where once trunk, flower, leaf, and fruit once stood. As my father told me. *'When all is lost, you must hold fast to what is left, for hope alone is the only salvation for those drowning in grief.'*

He took Anghrus' letter, placed it in his bosom pocket and rejoiced that he at least had a branch left from the tree of Wilona.

Long Swan's Log : My previous entry was interrupted, initially by Ruhm and the Jokers as the first of the exploratory party to return, and secondly, by a touching reunion between General Custus Ruhm Lee and the Lady Brekka. This forced us into refreshment, after which we reconvened an hour later to hear General Lee's report.

He states there are vast caverns to be accessed by the secret passage into the lower chambers and that the Lazy Jokers report a spiral road runs from bottom to top, and at one point the road parallels an underground river. I have determined it is the underground stream, the wizard river of old which our ancestors would visit by way of a cave near Thor's oak, which has now been blasphemed and twisted by the Pitters into a dead tree of terror.

The caverns are far more extensive than any of us ever imagined, and the exploratory party had to work their way through an absolute maze to get to a moving room, very much like the ones we found in the citadel that brought them to the surface. This was the first time we heard the Pitters had moving rooms here. Ruhm said the panel in the moving room indicates there are at least twenty levels below the courtyard. We have posed the question as to whether all the hidden doors are moving rooms or not. Ruhm said that both he and Starkwulf did not believe so.

Finally, he reported, all of the exploratory party came to the surface together in groups of twelve, which was all that the moving room could hold at one time, but when they arrived at the level of the courtyard, which was as high as this moving room could go, they split up to increase their chances of covering more territory. But when they split,

Ruhm and his party discovered only dead Pitters in the alley encircling the pyramid, untouched by weapons, and that a number of Herewardi white war horses were already corralled in the courtyard.

His first encounter was with Uffa, White Moose, and the Mufsiks, who confirmed that the Syr Folk had breached the fortress and his immediate request was, "I need to see Sur Sceaf right away." He was summarily led to the gate house where he awakened the Lady Brekka from her much needed slumber as they had had too little time to debrief one another before.

As I write this we still have no word of Starkwulf and Va-Eyra, who explored the other side of the fortress. The rays of the sun are streaming into the fortress, but they have not yet joined us. Concern is mounting. Sur Sceaf has sent out a twelver to search from the gate house into the left alley or corridor.

CHAPTER 5 :
THE BONE CRUSHER

WHILE THE OTHERS HAD GONE for food during refreshment, Sur Sceaf had gone to pray. Consequently, Long Swan insisted he now go out to the landing and partake of the repast prepared by hospitaler cooks, who, as part of their mission in this war, were tasked with providing sustenance for the patients and staff as well as any other Syr Folk as required. Ingenious as always, the cooks and servers had set up their kitchen wagons near the hospitaler tents and laid out the food and drink on trestle tables that were easily dismantled for transport.

Although reluctant to leave his command post, Sur Sceaf welcomed the opportunity because it also allowed him to visit the wounded in the hospitaler tents, now functioning at nearly full efficiency on the landing. As they approached the open gates, he spied Alf Hagele climbing into the driver's seat. He was acting in the capacity of a driver of one of the ambulance wagons transporting more severely injured to the secure medical facility in Bender's Woods.

Sur Sceaf had just greeted the gate guards when he heard a familiar voice calling out, "Surrey," his young blood name known only by family and the most intimate of friends. He whipped around to see Starkwulf and Va-Eyra with his Son Ev-Rhett and his twelver following. They approached with the usual swan salute.

"Wulfie, Sis, and Ev. So glad to have you back. I hope Ev didn't get you involved in exploring all the caverns. He's hard to get off a trail once he's on it."

Va smiled "We know how to keep him in line. Just like I had to keep you from disaster after disaster."

Ev protested, "If we had only known you had things under control here at the top, we could have scouted a lot farther. Me'n Russell are pretty sure those caverns lead all the way to the core of the Ea-Urth. I swear, Fa, we saw a great river, small streams and lakes, not to mention sink holes that probably go all the way to Muspelheim or the dread worm, Nidhaug's lair from the looks of it."

"It was with great relief we learned from some of Kanarus' troops that the Lady Brekka is safe," Starkwulf ventured.

Va-Eyra asked, "My lord, has Ruhm and his party arrived safely?"

"Thanks be to the gods, they are safe in the gate house."

With a twinkle in his eye, Long Swan added, "And likely to stay there, as Ruhm is glued to Brekka's bedside watching over her. He's clucking over her like an expectant hen over her brood."

Starkwulf said with a grin. "I'm glad to hear that. While we waited until the traveling room returned from taking the second group to the surface, we were attacked by a Pitter rat pack coming up the spiral road from below. T'were'nt much of an effort to dispatch them, seeing as the foot of death had nearly ground them into the dust."

"That is good, old friend," Sur Sceaf said with a smile. "I'm glad that no harm has befallen all of you. Long Swan and I were just on the way to get something to eat. Join us, and then we will adjourn to my command post at the gate house, so I can relate the alternatives we have come up with. I'm confidant you can help us with that."

Starkwulf pulled a face. "I pray to the gods, they're serving more than just sauerkraut and pork."

"I'm sure they'll have sausage and spaetzle as well."

Starkwulf frowned. "Truly, I've eaten insects and grubs that tasted better."

Sur Sceaf was delighted to find corned beef and cabbage was the main course. Ev'Rhett grabbed a plate and began heaping it with boiled potatoes. "I could eat the soles of my boots right now."

Despite Starkwulf's grumbling, he ate heartily and went back for seconds, washing it all down with several krugs of hard cider that had a tongue-tingling bite of winesap in it. After they had stretched their ribs to the limit, they headed back towards the gate house. Leading the way, Sur Sceaf motioned for Starkwulf to draw near so no one else could hear, and whispered, "I noticed in a cesspit on the south side of the fortress a large pile of manure. Some of the manure was horse, swine and rabbit, some was Pitter, but there was also a large pile of the blackest shit I've ever seen."

Starkwulf's eyes grew wide. "You mean like the color of shit from vampyr bats? Like we saw down in the mexus lands?"

"Yes, precisely, only on a larger scale with the individual stools as large as human stools." Sur Sceaf scowled in disgust at the memory.

"That would have to be some bat!"

"And that is not all. There were turds the size of enormous elephant dung in those piles. The gods only know what they came out of."

Starkwulf winced. "I hope we don't find out, but I fear we might before this is over."

Long Swan said, "Va, I am so glad you are here to make sure our brother cleans his plate like the old days when you had charge of our uncontrollable horde. I've been trying to get him to the table for nigh an hour."

As they approached the gate house, Russell ran up and slapped hands with Ev'Rhett. "I told you I'd be here first. What took you so long?"

Ev answered, "We encountered some stinkin' rat packs. What about you?"

"Easy as a summer morning, that is as long as we ignored the constant pining of Ruhm for Brekka."

While the Thunder Twins were busy one upping and flyting each other, Sur Sceaf, Starkwulf, and Va-Eyra entered the gate house. As soon as Ruhm spotted them he rose up and exclaimed, "Hurray! You finally made it. I was beginning to worry."

Ruhm and Starkwulf took each other in a royal embrace, which was repeated by Va-Eyra and Ruhm.

"Sorry to be late." Starkwulf said apologetically. "I had a slight interruption at the bottom of the moving room! We were compelled to slaughter a drift of half-dead demons. It all had us baffled as to how weak they were. Fortunately the Mufsiks explained to us that there walks a deadly plague amongst the Pitters, and it saps their strength before they fall from exhaustion."

Va-Eyra nodded. "I almost felt sorry for them. They could barely lift their swords. But I couldn't help wishing it was always that easy every time."

Brekka sat up. "I second that. Actually, Fa-Sis, White Moose claims that it will eventually take them all."

Sur Sceaf warned, "We would be most foolish to count on that. Remember there are probably Amerikan scientists in there, and they probably have concocted a remedy."

Starkwulf and Va removed their helms and took seats at the table. As Sur Sceaf pulled out his chair, he waved to the twins to enter. They were still joshing and teasing one another. Ruhm assisted Brekka to rise, and with an arm around her shoulder, like a protective husband, escorted her to the table.

Va, still in her silver armor, smiled indulgently at her. As she filled her krug from a pitcher of Wolf's Tooth Ale, her always sharp gaze inspected the contents of the gate house. She took one quick sip before jumping up to explore the contents of several hemp sacks in the armory.

"For Baldur's sake, Va," Starkwulf exclaimed. "What are you doing? Sit down."

Oblivious to her husband she reached down and picked up a haversack. "Here they are! These are the beast stoppers, aren't they?"

Sur Sceaf then turned to see what she was selecting. "Yes, beast stoppers. Why do you need those?"

She smiled. "Charly said that he and his father delivered pigs and horses to the Pitters for tithes and taxes in kine near here, and while they made their delivery, a door opened on the face of the cliff to receive the livestock. About a hundred paces away from the gate house. He swears, he spied a cleft in the walls wide enough for a person to pass through and swore he heard spine-chilling animal sounds he'd never heard before coming out of it. It reminded him of what old Farmer Sencindiver claimed he heard the night he lost over a hundred head of cattle. When he went out to explore, he saw only blood and offal on the ground, as if they had been eaten whole. Charly's father swore it had to be wolves, but the old man said there wasn't a wolf pack in the whole world large enough to do that kind of damage without leaving more carnage behind."

She looked at her husband and said, "Stop giving me your indulgent looks, Wulfie!" She paused momentarily to stare Starkwulf down.

Sur Sceaf remembered that look. Even though she was only ten years older than him, it had stopped him dead in his tracks on more than one occasion.

Starkwulf ignored her warning gaze. "You do realize the boys have vivid imaginations. Witness what they called a dragon turned out to be an earth eater machine left over from the Amerikans."

Va returned, "But what if this time they turn out to be right. There just may be something more monstrous in those caverns. You of all people should know that sometimes myth has root in reality."

Sur Sceaf almost choked on his ale. "I know better than to argue when you get that look on your face, Cat Queen. What bedevilment are you planning?"

Starkwulf winked at him as if to indicate he, too, was very familiar with that 'make it happen' look of hers as well.

Va-Eyra returned to her seat. Sur Sceaf recalled that when they were children, his father had said she was always like a sharply focused predator, and it wasn't a good idea to ever get in her way. Why else would she have chosen the jaguarundi as her totem animal? She was definitely one with those cats.

Va-Eyra returned to her seat and took another sip of ale before explaining with her usual airy determination. "After Charly marked the map, Ev-Rhett, Russell, and I have come up with a plan. With your permission, we will take the beast stoppers and torches and scan the side of the mound for possible air shafts that a man could pass through. If it's anything like the caverns below, this place is honeycombed with passages, which means the Pitters have to be getting air in the underground somehow. If we find the entry points, we can open the doors from within so that the fyrds can purge the caverns. I can't imagine the hidden entrance we explored earlier leads to every chamber of this immense bastion."

Sur Sceaf nodded. "Well, that confirms what I had already deduced. I saw air shafts, but they were all no more than three inches wide at most. Kanarus also mentioned seeing these slits. For a hole to be three foot wide, like you describe, it must be a means of feeding the beasts through. Kanarus attempted to shine a torch through the smaller slits, but all they could see was darkness beyond the light."

Ruhm interjected, "What would happen if we blocked the air slits up?"

Sur Sceaf answered, "That is a brilliant idea, but it is a daunting task that could take weeks which we don't have. Our immediate plan is to attack those doors today." Sur Sceaf turned to Uffa. "Fetch the lord Arundel. I want him in on this." He turned back to his sister. "Ary needs the information you've brought us."

Va-Eyra frowned. "You can talk all you want, but we better get started if we are to find the entry points before nightfall. I'm going to talk with the Lazy Jokers some more. I need clarification."

The gate house was nearly empty when Va returned to the table. At the far reaches of the dormitory, Brekka now sat with Ruhm along with Verushka, Freyxus and her hand maids, Wyth and Ynys. They were oblivious to the comings and goings and the continuous mischief-making of the Jokers. Showing no sign of fatigue, the boy jokers were still hanging around the armory like a business of ferrets, curiously handling weapons from the numerous sacks, crates, barrels and baskets while talking about plying them in battle.

While Ev'Rhett and Russell filled rucksacks with beast stoppers, Starkwulf assisted Va in donning her armor. "I understand why you're insisting you don't need me in this expedition, and I will honor your wishes, but promise me that if you do find some kind of entrance, you'll report back to us rather than explore it on your own."

Va settled her silver breast plate before tying her swan scarf around her neck. "I promise. Besides living with you is all the danger a woman needs."

He laughed before dipping his head to kiss her as he handed her a labrys he borrowed from Pata. "This should be enough metal to fend off any cave troll you might encounter."

Several of the Jokers immediately came over to examine the expertly crafted double-headed axe specifically designed to fit a woman's smaller hand and made from a light, but strong metal.

"Be careful, boys. It is razor sharp," she warned as she handed it to Charly for examination. Charly touched both points gingerly before nodding. "Glory be, this is the lightest metal I ever felt. One thing's for sure. This baby will get you comin' and goin'. Reminds me of a sickle Old Man Sencindiver once fashioned. It had a hickory snath and a grass cutting blade that he would peen and slide a whetstone over to make it cut sharper than a razor."

"Sure is pretty, too, with that emerald eye starin' right at ya," Leroy exclaimed. "Pro'bly has magic powers, I wager. Huh!"

Gingerly, Va took back the gleaming labrys and tucked it back into the especially designed holster that Starkwulf had in the meantime attached to her belt. "The magic is in the way a warrior uses it. These axes were made at Govannon's forge under his supervision and, like all his weaponry, infused with elven elixir and virgin's milk. The only thing older and stronger is royal blood."

Leroy's eyes were filled with excitement. "How 'bout takin' me along, so's I can see how you ply that wicked thing."

Charly glowered at his friend. "Hey, you egg-suckin dawg, that possum's on the stump, I'm the one who's gonna show them where the hole is. You ain't never seen it."

Before Leroy could protest, Va declared, "We don't have time for bickering. Leroy, you can carry the torches. Charly, you carry the beast stoppers, so that the twins and I will be free to defend us should the need arise."

"Here, you go, Charly," Russell said, handing him a bulky rucksack.

Charly immediately peeked in at the contents. "Wowee, I've heard stories about these things. Heard tell they're like boom sticks that give off green smoke that's s'posed to drop a dragon in its tracks. I bet those Pitter's'll run like a scalded haint when we hit 'em with this."

Ev'Rhett handed over the other rucksack while Leroy gathered up a bundle of torches and flints.

Just as they were about to set off, Sur Sceaf arrived with Long Swan and Mendaka. "Be careful, Sis," Surrey offered her. "Even though the ballooners report no signs of activity from the Pitters, it behooves us to be ever vigilant. If you see anything suspicious, come back immediately. Even though the emperor appears to be withdrawn and licking his wounds, who can know what devious devices he might spring on us. We're inside the gate, but he still has command of the caverns below. He is still master of his lair."

"Surrey's right, Va. Remember that the bastard has the capacity to call on the dark forces and their foul brood."

"Don't worry. Me and Leroy won't let anything bad happen to the queen," Charly exclaimed.

Va exchanged looks with Starkwulf who winked and said, "My dear, it seems like you're in good hands."

She grinned. "Okay, Charly, lead on. Show us to the spot you described next to the abattoir."

"Sure thing, Lady Queen, it's just right over there." He hefted the rucksacks to his back and led the way across the sunlit courtyard to the abattoir which was located a few yards from the door Kanarus had marked with an ochre X.

"Look how cleverly they've disguised that opening," Va pointed out.

"Even better than the doors in the Poisoned Lands," Ev said.

Va and Ev carefully examined every inch of the limestone surface of the wall for any irregularities that might indicate an air shaft.

They examined approximately thirty feet of wall, inch by inch before encountering a canvas shed used to store the abattoir's saws and blades. They were about to go around the shed when Russell noticed the rear canvas wall appeared to be fluttering in an otherwise windless afternoon.

Va-Eyra ordered the twins to drag it away from the wall. Behind it was the much sought after entryway, about the height of a man and of a width just narrow enough for a slender man to squeeze through.

"Hot damn, Charly, you were right!" Ev'Rhett exclaimed.

Va whispered, "Do you hear that?"

Russell said, "I don't hear anything."

Leroy declared, "I can't hear a lick cause of all the damn ruckus all of y'all are making. Sssh!"

Ev'Rhett said, "Get closer."

Va and Russell stepped closer to the cleft.

Ev whispered, "Listen. It sounds like the muffled groaning snorts of a bear or perhaps a boar."

Va frowned. "He's right. Something is in there and it doesn't sound human. We should find out what it is." She took a torch from Leroy's bundle. After it was lit, she squeezed into the cleft, and thrust the torch before her. "I can see scattered and splintered bones on the cave floor. And look at these walls here in this cleft; they're greasy looking."

Ev peered closer. "Probably a feeding shaft for whatever creature they keep in here." He pressed hard against her side. "What do you think? A way down?"

"Possibly, but I can't see well enough. It's too dark inside." She tried to squeeze through, but to no avail. Her armor, especially the breast cones wouldn't let her pass. "With my armor on I can't squeeze through here and I'm not inclined to remove it."

Russell said, "I'll do it, I'll go in. I'm the skinniest."

"I'll be damned if you are, young man. I've laid out bigger warriors than you before. If there are monsters inside, I don't want to be the one who has to explain to your Fa and your wives that you were eaten on my watch."

"But Fa-Sis," Ev'Rhett complained, "We just want to take a peek and get some point of reference. We've got our swords, we've got the beast stoppers, and believe me I've seen them drop the biggest of beasts on the plains of Makakka before. Besides we need this intelligence. It's our one chance to take the Pitters by surprise."

"Anyway," Russell and Ev said in unison, "only one of us needs to go in."

"Yes," Russell affirmed, "and that would be me."

Before Va could respond, Ev had stripped off his mail until he was naked from the waist up. After putting his shirt and mail to the side, he stuffed the map in his pants pocket. "It's settled. I'm going in. I have charcoal and the parchment Flammelf gave us. I'll make a good map so I can find my way back out."

"Bug shit!" Russell exclaimed. "Let me go, Ev. I see better in the dark than you. Remember that time we went on that coon hunt with those Hickoryan boys in Rippingale and you didn't make it back until morning."

"That's because you put me with Horace Green. That man was bad to drink and took the wrong trail while I was singing."

"It makes no difference; I was the first to call it. I get to go in."

"Shush! You got an evil omen today. Your amulet of Tyr caught on the entrance to the cave. That means the runes that were cut for you today will spell evil and I couldn't live without my brother."

Va reached into Leroy's sack and pulled out another torch. "Give us a good diagram, Ev. Record the lay of the caverns. And if you get injured, I'm going to kill you myself." She lit the fresh torch with her flint, and handed it to Ev. He thrust the torch through the crevice, sucked in his belly and squeezed through the crack as easy as a weasel.

Leroy exclaimed, "Man those two argue like a couple knee-babies."

Va stifled a laugh and Charly raised an eyebrow.

Ev sounded excited as he looked back out. "I can already see it's a big chamber. I'm standing on a narrow stairway ledge cut right into the wall that we could with a little difficulty send warriors down. And the air is sucking hard downward. It's got to be the way into the enemy's nest."

"Or the stairway to Hell," Va said.

Ev went silent. After an anxious wait, that seemed longer than it was, Russell whispered close to the slit, "Ev, you alright in there?"

"Did you hear that sound?" Ev's voice sounded muffled.

"Hear what?" Va asked as she pressed near the hole with Russell.

"Listen, there it is again." Ev said and then paused. "Sounds like a bull buffalo when it's been shot down in the dust. You know, heavy breathing." He paused. "There it is again."

Russell shouted, "I don't hear a damned thing. Probably just the wind sucking through the tunnel."

"This ain't no...Uh oh! What the hell? Shit! Russell get me the beast stoppers. Quickly!'"

"Why, what is it?"

Everything went absolutely silent. Ev would not answer when spoken to. Va looked at Russell who shook his head. Then slowly together they attempted to look into the chamber and only saw the torch light on the floor below and large shadows dancing against the opposite wall. Heavy breathing and a shuffling sound came from within. Without warning a thunderous roar reverberated from the chamber, followed by enormous sickle-sized claws on a hairy arm thrusting through the cleft that nearly snagged Russell before Va swiftly pulled him back.

Russell was shaken, "Shades of Hell! What was that?"

"I don't know what it was Russell. Maybe it was one of Loki's kin? Who can know what offspring the Alien God has begotten? What I do know is that it was big, hairy, and powerful. Look at those claw marks on the crevice. By Loki, what has happened to Ev'Rhett?"

"I'm going to have to go in for him." Russell went back to the dark hole. "I can see some light from the torch lying on the dirt." He shouted in. "Ev'Rhett, if you are in there, give us a sign or something, and I'll get you."

Another thunderous roar was followed by two sets of those steel hard, sickle-sized claws attempting to open the crevice, and then slicing as they pulled away.

Russell turned to Va with sheer terror written on his face. "I think he's dead, Va. By the Gods, I think my brother is dead!"

Just then Va heard a whip-poor-will whistle.

"He's alive," Russell shouted. "We've gotta get him out of there before that troll gets to him."

They drew near the tunnel again, but only close enough to listen. They could still hear the heavy breathing, snorts, and lots of shuffling sounds, as when a bull is unwillingly put in a narrow stall.

Va attempted to get a peek inside when a rock struck her breast plate and fell to the ground. "What was that?" She cried, and then looking to the ground saw the rock was wrapped in a sheet of vellum. She grabbed it and together she and Russell read the note on the map Ev'Rhett had written.

Va unfolded it. "It says, 'Carefully lower the beast stoppers in to me. Hiding in a dark alcove to the right of you. The beast can't see me. You ought to see it. It's a giant tro of some sort. Why I can't talk. Wind is sucking downward. If you throw a beast stopper I should be safe from breathing the fumes. But it's a damned sight better than being eaten alive by this monster. He can jump up here. So be careful and please hurry!"

Russell immediately set to stripping off his armor, grabbed the rucksack with beast stoppers in it, watched for the huge shadow to pass in the other direction, and then squeezed through the crevice. He swung the rucksack as best he could in the direction his brother had indicated.

Before Russell withdrew from the opening, Ev whispered from an alcove, "Over here, in the alcove. Toss me the bag and get the hell out of here."

Russell attempted to support himself and pass back through the hole when he screamed a horrific, "Owww!"

Va grabbed Russell by his arm to pull him out. "What is it? What happened? Are you hurt?"

"Oh gods that love me, it feels like my hand is being crushed between two boulders." In the background it sounded like blades were being raked furiously across the interior cavern walls."

Va and Charly held Russell tight as he was pulled downward and farther into the cavern. Suddenly, the tension released and the three of them fell back to the ground. Blood was spurting from Russell's left arm like a hose.

Va immediately sought to console Russell who writhed in agony and rolled over the ground. To her rear she heard shuffling, turned and saw Ev was squeezing his way out and choking from the green smoke coming through the hole.

He too appeared to have been injured. "By the gods, Russell, forgive me. It's bit your hand off. The bastard has bit your hand off. I knew there was evil intended for you this day. Why didn't you stay home? The runes spoke it. Once your tyr amulet was snagged, I knew it. Oh damn it, my brother, it hurts us. It hurts us." At the same time holding his own left hand and falling to the ground in shared pain with Russell.

Va quickly grabbed up the torch from where it had fallen, and said, "Rus, I love you, but we've got to get this seared to stop the bleeding." Russell screamed and writhed in pain.

"Leroy, hold his good arm." The Joker dropped the bag of torches before kneeling down to clasp his hands around Russell's uninjured arm.

"Now, Charly, take this torch and sit on his knees. Hold the flame as steady as you can and don't pull away, whatever you do."

Leroy's face was as ghost white as a haint, and his arm shuddered with sympathy. Sweat poured from his brow as he took up his position.

"Ready?" Va asked.

Leroy nodded. She grasped Rus' bleeding arm and swiftly plunged it into the flame. As it sizzled and seared, the smell of burned flesh filled the air. Rus fell back to the earth again in utter agony, his eyes alternately opening wide and then closing tightly.

"Oh damn it!" Ev'Rhett screamed, "I feel it Va, I feel it. Do something for him."

She took the scarf from around her neck and bound the wound so Russell wouldn't see the horror of his handless arm. "We're going to have to get to the hospitalers and get some aloe vera and honey on this right away."

Russell writhed and moaned in pain, and Ev mirrored all of his same agony. Both were gritting their teeth, their eyes rolling in pain as they pounded the ground with their other fist and rocked in mirrored misery together. She had heard, but never witnessed, that when one was hurt the other felt it, too. As far as she could see, Ev-Rhett had no visible injury.

Charly, too, was clearly shaken. "Is there anything else we can do for him, Ma'am?"

"As soon as I give Rus some poppy tears, you can help me get him up, and support him while we return to the gate house for proper treatment."

CHAPTER 6 :
THE WINGS OF DARKNESS UNFOLD

WORD HAD SPREAD QUICKLY THROUGH the bastion and on the promontory about the troll attack on Russell which resulted in the loss of a hand. Tensions ran high. The warriors sensed the terror they could soon be facing. New monsters meant more death. Va had accompanied the twins to the hospitaler tent, while Leroy was sent to the gate house to report to Sur Sceaf. As soon as he received the report, he closed the journal he had been updating and hurried off with Leroy to the hospitaler tent on the landing.

When he arrived, he found Dr. Shanks and Siwel bending over the table where Russell lay covered with a woolen blanket. Charly stood with Va and Starkwulf while Ev'Rhett held his brother's good hand.

As soon as Walter spotted him nearing the table, the doctor immediately declared in a reassuring tone, "I think he's going to make it, my lord, thanks to Queen Va-Eyra's speedy and expert cauterization."

Siwel added, "Let me reassure you, my lord. The net has told me so."

Charly frowned. "What is the net?"

Without looking up from the herbal potion he was administering to Russell from a tiny glass vial, Siwel responded, "You know, it's what the Herewardi call the Ur-Fyr, and the Quailor the Holy Spirit. Surely you Hickoryans have something similar?"

Charly thought for a moment. "I guess we do, only we call it a hunch."

Moving closer, Sur Sceaf laid a hand on his son's knee and gently squeezed. "Your deeds shall be sung by the bards in all the settlements of Herewardom. We're all very proud of you." He glanced at Ev. "Both of you."

Ev took a deep breath. "Honestly, Fa, you should have seen this Tro. It was hard to see the details because of the torchlight, but what I saw would make a grizzly look like a kitten."

Russell slurred, "Bigger'n a grass beast and …" His voice trailed off. Ev finished his sentence. "And a mountain of rippling beast flesh. It was taller than a giraffe and had teeth like hammers and fangs like the Shark Wyrm."

"I've been chewing on it," Ev-Rhett declared, "and come to think of it, the dang critter smelled like a Pitter cesspit and had him a roar that made the earth shake."

Sur Sceaf turned to Va. "Did you see it, Sis?"

She shook her head. "In all frankness, I didn't see it fully, but I saw its claw, and from the description of the twins, it sounds like Garm, the dog of hell."

"Fa Sis is…right. It's a corpse swallower. Saw …human bones all over…floors. Cracked skulls." He shuddered.

Starkwulf nodded. "In all likelihood, they are probably Hickoryan rebels who were fed to the beast."

Dr. Shanks shot him a warning look. "Enough! My patient needeth rest."

Ev spoke up, "I ain't leaving."

"Fine, but the others need to depart. Thou hast sufficient information for now. Come back in the morning."

Exhausted, Sur Sceaf had retired to his bed in the gate house shortly before midnight, confident that the guards he'd posted at all marked doors, the riding room, and the parapets would alert him to any danger. When he had checked on Brekka, she appeared to be in a gentle sleep, with her hand maids resting nearby.

He had just drifted off into a dream when high above the bastion, Cerulean ballooners floating overhead suddenly sounded their alarm with a droning blast of their ram horns. This was echoed by a warning from the trumpeters stationed on the parapets.

Sur Sceaf bolted upright from a deep slumber, jumped into his boots and grabbed his sword before running into the courtyard to assess and attend the alarm. Above him, on the pyramidal mound, there was what looked like black smoke roaring out of a great furnace, then he realized it was not smoke. Winged creatures hit the skies, pouring out of the top of the mound in great clouds and all but extinguishing the moonlight.

In the ample campfire lights it was easy to distinguish that these were black, unusually large creatures, the size of very tall men, with great dark wing spans and eerie shrieks that curdled the blood, sending chills up the back and neck.

Soon his ears were bombarded with high-pitched screeches like the echolocation emitted from swarms of bats he had heard down in the Taxus caverns. Out of the dark sky, legs emerged from beneath the umbrella-like wings amassing overhead and began ripping apart tents that were pitched in the courtyard, and snatching men into the air. Warriors were being dropped from great heights, their screams filling the air as they plunged to their deaths with awful crashing impacts, often injuring their compatriots below as well. A second wave of the flying wraiths poured out of the mound and descended on the hosts of Syr Folk inside the bastion where they scurried to enwrap the fleeing warriors in their deadly wings.

Some of the dark winged creatures bit and clawed at the men as Sur Sceaf strained to see what form they had. He grabbed a torch from the wall holder, and ran out into the fray. He signing for his fourteen year old Quailor beetle, Thund, who had just emerged from his tent to the left of the gate house. Strands of winged creatures filled the air until the sky went black, and the moon was entirely blotted out.

He turned back to tell Thund to sound a retreat to the forests, only to discover that in mere seconds one of the black wraiths had already descended and enwrapped Thund so securely in the cocoon of its wings that only the lad's head showed out the top. He could see in the torch light that the creature's hot-pink tongue was pumping its way down Thund's throat like a pulsating serpent. At the same time the creature was clamping its brutally large teeth over the boy's mouth as its wolfish fangs gorged over the helpless lad's cheeks. Though the boy struggled, there was no hope of Thund ever freeing himself through his own exertions.

Sur Sceaf drew his sword, and leaped with the bound of a blood-mad cat, and thrusted his blade into the beast's heart in one well-placed jab. The creature's steel-trap jaws snapped open, full of razor sharp teeth. Then with a loud suction sound it withdrew its long thick tongue from Thund's throat. Its eyes burned red with hell-fire as it let out a demonic screech. Its head writhed from side-to-side while its long tongue danced like a cobra in the fire light. The creature slowly shriveled like a bat caught by a torch flame while its wing tips stabbed into the ground for support as it collapsed before Sur Sceaf's feet with one final gurgling shriek. Sur Sceaf paused briefly to make sure it was dead, only to discover it resembled a large winged dog of a sort he had never encountered.

After confirmation that the black wraith was dead, Sur Sceaf turned to the lad, who was coughing and struggling to suck in air like a drowning man when first brought to the surface. His cheeks bore the severe lacerations of the fiend's fangs, but other than that, Thund's face was intact and would fully recover. At the moment he appeared to be in shock, his eyes dazed and his lower jaw hanging in disbelief. Sur Sceaf called his name, but at first the boy did not appear to hear him.

Finally, Thund said through a daze, "What...what are they?"

"Moth Men!" Sur Sceaf helped the boy to rise and waited for him to stabilize. "Stay by my side, lad. I'll have the trumpeters sound a retreat myself."

As the two of them moved up the stairs to the right of the gate house towards the parapet, they encountered the two trumpeters running down the stairs from the wall in fearful flight, with torch in one hand and trumpet in the other. Sur Sceaf stopped the silver-clad youths by placing his hand on the chest of the first one, thus ending their stampede for safety.

"Come with me," he ordered firmly, holding up his torch and giving them a stern look. "Sound the call for cover from the walls. We need to alert all the camps of this imminent danger."

The trumpeters gave a reluctant look, but then swiftly did an about face and headed back up the stairs in front of him. Once they were atop the bastion walls, Sur Sceaf hacked at any dog-bat-moth amidst the ever-present sound of flapping wings and bat-like signals bouncing all around them. As warriors fell from the sky, the trumpeters sounded the call for cover.

"Alright," Sur Sceaf said, glancing at Thund to make sure he was recovering. "Now the three of you find shelter as quick as you can. Go to the gate house, get inside, and close the door behind you. Stay there until I come."

As Sur Sceaf stood atop the bastion walls to get a better view of what was happening, his attention was immediately drawn to the Cerulean ballooners. Now easily visible in the moonlight, a pack of the same dark creatures were crawling over the surface of their balloons soon the demons commenced shredding the balloons with their sharp hooks and teeth while other demons bore off writhing, blood drenched warriors into the air. It was a brain-shattering scene straight out of Hellheim. One after another the balloons plummeted from the sky, and the skies rained Syr Folk blood in profusion.

Hearing the swishing of wings above him, he thrust his blade upward, and felt the impact of the steel striking a solid object which shuttered through his body. Sur Sceaf quickly retracted his blade in order to strike again, but with another eerie screech, the dark moth man spiraled down to its death over the parapet. He followed its fall only to see the balloon carriages smashing on the landing below, dashing the passengers to death on the hard rock surface like broken eggs. He winced over the losses and rage surged in him. Grabbing one of the trumpeters' signal flags they had left behind, Sur Sceaf signed for the archers to fire at will.

Soon, he delighted in hearing the hundreds of shrill screams piercing the air as many the huge black, bat-like creatures tumbled to the earth in crumpled heaps. One crashed, riddled with wolf-arrows. Surprisingly human-like fingers at the ends of the wings clenched and unclenched.

"Shades of the Amerikans, it is a were-bat. Not part dog, but part man and part bat."

He poked at the fallen man-bat with the tip of his sword. It twitched. Thick black thatches of fur covered its shoulders. Its wings were bony, leathery bat's wings. It had clutching feet, with dreadful thick talons and a hook over a hand at the end of each wing that in and of itself could be employed as a dagger. Worst of all was the face that was part human, with high forehead and protruding nose, but part bat with large pointed ears, demonic red eyes, and frightfully sharp teeth. The lolling tongue appeared to be a foot and a half in length. *This must be one of the trans-humans that the hags described to Brekka in the Poisoned Land.*

In anger and frustration, he called out, "Mighty Tyranus, Horned God of the Dark Clouds, show us how to destroy these devilish menaces."

As the heavy swooshing of wings could be heard below, Sur Sceaf looked over the edge of the fortress wall and saw one of the were-bat struggling to mount the sky with a beetle-green clad body in the talons of its feet. The boy was desperately wriggling to get free of its demonic hooks.

As it rose up parallel to where Sur Sceaf stood, the creature looked him straight on. Behind those burning-red eyes, he sensed a disquieting, malevolent intelligence with dark and sinister intent. He slashed at the creature's shoulder, partially severing one wing with his sword and rendering the demon incapable of further flight. As swiftly as he could, he grabbed the dangling wing and pulled the hissing creature over the wall. Its thrashing wings pummeled him upside the head like a fighting goose strikes. Sur Sceaf was blinded by blood and battle fury as its large pink tongue writhed in the air, worming towards him, and those sharp teeth opened like a bear's jaws for the kill.

He quickly drew back his blade and thrust the creature through the chest and twisted. A convulsive tremor vibrated through the beast's frame. It had somehow managed to capture Thund in those taloned feet once again. While the creature was screeching, Sur Sceaf quickly freed the young half-Quailor from its dagger like claws, and then with one swift slice severed the were-bat's head.

"As I was going to the gate house, I fainted, and the next thing I knew, I was in the air again."

"They're bound to have you for supper, my boy. This time, you stick with me."

Thund exclaimed wide-eyed, "I'll do anything to keep out of the clutches of those son of bitchen nachtschwarmers."

Suddenly, up high on one of the cliff walls, doors opened. Two red-clad priests stepped out holding torches high. Hryre Seath appeared, readily seen in the torchlight. On his bald head sat a new, ornate, purple conical mitre with gold embossing and bejeweled with precious rubies, exactly like the one they had confiscated by the altar. Indeed, the emperor was attired in his usual purple robes with a gold breast plate that shone like fire in the torch light.

As he stood there staring down, two bent, shriveled figures stepped out of the darkened interior and hobbled forward to stand on either side of the emperor in the circle of torchlight. One was an old man, while the other appeared to be a woman, who leaned heavily on a bamboo rod. Both wore robes of anemic blue that shimmered like glass.

Sur Sceaf thought, *Who are these two old cronies, and why are they shown such deference and respect by an emperor who disdains the company of anyone he does not consider an equal?*

Hryre Seath began speaking through a hollowed bull horn. Facing the gate house he bellowed, "Sur Sceaf of the Herewardi, the Iron Lord of Battle, you dared to think you could have victory over me ever since your voice broke through the silence of the Umpqua Forest." He laughed. "Now, is the great day of my terror when the forces of Angrar shall drain you of all your blood and deal you the same death we dealt your longfathers in the beginning of your reckoning of time. No longer need we fear the death plague of the seed of the woman, and now we unloose the fullness of the wrath of Angrar upon you and return death for death. I warn you, our flying gyrlocks shall devour you in your sleep before this night is over. And when we let slip the tyfons, the giant beasts will show you the hopelessness of your cause. This night, I shall cover the land with thick darkness and set the teeth of beasts upon you. Then I shall leave your armies in shreds and pieces scattered over the earth for the vultures to feast on as you did unto ours. Thus, will the Herewardi and the Syr Folk be blotted from the earth and be no more. And all middle-earth shall burn." He gave another diabolical laugh before disappearing into the cliff opening, followed by the shriveled old man and the tottering old woman, who had to be escorted by one of the priests.

No sooner had the doors closed than another door opened several tiers above, belching out another swarm of were-bats. At the same time, heavy dark smoke, so thick one could hardly see, oozed out of the slits along the cliffs. An acrid odor reminiscent of steaming vinegar stung Sur Sceaf's nostrils and eyes, and soon began muffling sound; like pillows over the ears.

The smoke filled the bastion and the valley with an oily fog that extinguished all the fires of torch and camp, leaving a most unsettling darkness and disorientation. It, too, was unlike any smoke or fog that Sur Sceaf had ever encountered, so unnatural in appearance and had such an unnatural smell that it had to be of supernatural origins.

He, like every other warrior, stood isolated and alone in the dark. First, he looked down through the rapidly thickening smoke and caught sight of what he thought were the movements of his archers entering the stairs leading to the parapet. With Thund glued to his side, he shifted his attention to the promontory and caught a fleeting glimpse of dark figures falling from the skies.

Not only from the skies, but also from the ground Thund pointed and yelled, "Look, do you see those huge dark trolls moving on the camps? They have the appearance of giant badgers or wolverines."

"That must be the beast that bastard emperor called a Tyfon. I suspect that's the same troll that robbed my son of his hand." He sucked in a sharp breath. Whatever they were, these monster trolls appeared to be muscular and hairy, just as the twins had described. They stormed on four legs at twenty feet tall from his perspective, and were cutting through his troops like a wild boar rips through a rice paddy.

Before the blackness had suffocated all light, he beheld his beloved son of Faechild's hearth, the much respected commander and shape-shifter, Widukind, lord of the spearmen, leading his hundred like a long forest of Herewardi spears against the bone-crushing cave trolls. When, at eight winters, Widdy defeated three young bloods at the same time in a fencing match, Long Swan prophesied that no iron could bite him, and none ever had, of either friend or foe. *But, what about the teeth and claws of these vicious and bloodthirsty monsters? What then?* thought Sur Sceaf.

To his great relief—Widdy and his men began to prevail against the tyfons. One-by-one, three massive beasts crashed to the ground, emitting such agonized screams and roars that it caused the other beasts to retreat before the thicket of sturdy Ash spears with bronze points dipped in deadly cobra-lance venom. Widdy had found the kill-spot on their soft underbellies, eventually felling them; at what great cost to Widukind's vaunted hundred, Sur Sceaf dared not calculate. Though a victory of sorts, it failed to stem the mighty night swarm of gyrlocks pouring out of the caverns above.

Throughout the night, attacks from the ravenous were-bat gyrlocks decimated the ranks of Sur Sceaf's men from one end of the armies to the other, and there was little retaliation to be had. But in the heavy, suffocating darkness, Sur Sceaf beheld the horned god, Tyranus, walk into the courtyard, and the earth trembled under his feet. Soon a swift breeze followed him, and the black shroud of smoke lifted from the blood-drenched lap of Big Springs. Once again the ambers of the campfires re-kindled. Gradually, some visibility returned. Archers could now see their targets more clearly, and pike men bravely impaled the giant trolls, and warriors hurled beast stoppers at them.

Sur Sceaf shouldered Thund down the stairs clogged with beetles and harriers who had intelligently sought out the safety of the stone walls. When he and Thund reached the gate house, he ordered the boy to stay inside while he ran to the gates to assess the damage in the courtyard and on the landing. He was particularly concerned that the gyrlocks had besieged the hospitaler tents. To his dismay he found the tents hanging in fragments from the poles, but to his relief, the patients, including Russell, were remarkably unaffected thanks to Rolf Hagele and the horned god's timely appearance.

According to Walter Shanks, Rolf Hagele had had enough presence of mind to fetch Brekka's war hounds from their kennels. It was a brilliant decision because the hounds used their fine-tuned noses to detect the attackers from the sky without having to see them. The dogs had dispatched their duties nobly, as attested by the many shredded and torn Gyrlock carcasses littering the landing. He could scarcely wait to relate to Hartmut and Meny Hagele the heroic account of their second son.

As the sinister smoke continued to dissipate, he saw that, despite the horrendously costly blackout, his men had managed to fight on through the darkness. Sprays of arrows continued to send black forms plummeting from the skies. Tyfon carcasses and his own fallen laid strewn across the landscape as testimony to the monstrous battle that had taken place in the suffocating heavy fog.

To Sur Sceaf's dismay, because of the gross darkness his men had unintentionally slain some of their own, as attested to by the Herewardi arrows in their bodies. The Pitters unexpected use of their unholy black fog threw a wrinkle into the battle plan, and now he and Arundel would have to re-strategize.

Going Snake galloped his horse up the ramp to the landing. "My lord, we've managed to halt the menace of the tyfons. We stopped them with Widukind's spearmen, the cobra-lance venom and the beast stoppers."

"Tis well, Going Snake. Spread the word for all the troops to pull back into heavily wooded areas. Tell the commanders it is my decree that only clear shots will be allowed in the future. Too many arrows have felled friends as well as fiends. These losses are great and grievous and are always the worst to bear."

It was about two hours before dawn during the third watch of the night. The land surrounding the bastion was littered with the mountainous hulks of the slain tyfons. The surviving gyrlocks flew off searching for easier prey in the countryside and foothills. Hospitalers were busy taking the more grievously wounded and mauled back to the landing. Chartrusean medical support staff were industriously clearing away the remnants of the ruined tents and erecting replacements.

Finally, after receiving reports, consulting with Lord Arundel, and getting ready for the next rotation, Sur Sceaf made time to visit his sons in Walter Shank's hospitaler tents. When he arrived, he spotted Walter carrying a bowl of hot water from the surgery tent into the newly raised recovery tent.

Everything seemed so orderly in the tent, and running smoothly. More pallets were crowded in. The tent was surprisingly hushed. Not at all like the hospital tents of former days. As he followed Dr. Shanks down the narrow center aisle, he spotted several attendant nurses he knew from Godeselle. "Walter, I commend you on your great work here. You have saved many lives with your efficiency and skill."

Walter sat the bowl down between Russell and Ev'Rhett. "For my part I thank thee, but these chartreusean nurses have been indispensable; and that banana green medicine man, Siwel, is a cornucopia of miracle medicines. As tired as thou lookest, thou couldst probably use the wasp-coc medicine he gave earlier. Made me as energetic as a March hare."

"No thanks, once I leave here, I'm going to get some rest. I just wanted to check on how Russell is doing."

"As thou canst see, he's chust down a few pallets sleeping beside his brother. I've never seen anything like it. Every pain Russell had, Ev'Rhett also had, and he wasn't pretending or empathizing. The pain was real. Therefore, I administered the same medication to both of them. It wondereth me how the two remained so connected all these years."

Sur Sceaf declared, "It's been that way since their infancy. If I ever needed to spank one the other would respond equally. No wonder they grew up to be such hellions. You could never correct one, without also punishing the innocent."

"I'm sure they planned it that way." Walter and Sur Sceaf stooped down near the twins. Sur Sceaf picked up a cloth, dipped it in the hot water and began bathing Russell's brow and arms.

Walter offered him a look of compassion, "An awful pity he lost his hand, but other than that, he should recover in a couple months. And thy wildcat of a daughter told us all how to do our jobs before she bolted out of here into the dark to fight again."

Sur Sceaf noticed Russell's eyes opening drowsily. "Oh, hi, Fa," he said in a dreamy voice, "The cursed beast got my hand."

Then Sur Sceaf saw Ev'Rhett, whose eyes were also half open, spoke in an equally drowsy voice, "I couldn't care less if the beasts eat us or not."

Walter put his hand on Sur Sceaf's arm, "They don't feel any pain or have any earthly concerns. They are in dreamland. They're both on the ship of poppy milk chust sailing through dreamland."

Sur Sceaf nodded that he understood. After Russell fell back to sleep, Sur Sceaf walked out of the medicine tent and proceeded across the landing, past the gates and sidestepped the congealed blood surrounding the altar. Without the light of the priest's torches the area around the tree of terror was especially dark. Standing under the skeletal branches of the once noble tree, he raised his arms to the heavens. *Oh Mighty Tyranus, God of the Dark Clouds, I give thanks for protecting and sparing the lives of my loved ones. All Father Woon, I thank thee for thy guidance. Oh Holy Freya, Mother of Heaven and Earth, please place special watch over my daughter, Brekka, that she might fulfill the measure of her creation and live to see her seed unto the fourth generation. Woon, protect my family--*

Suddenly, a deeply resonant voice from above his head interrupted his prayer. "Sur Sceaf, my loyal and beloved son, your faithful petitions have come up before the throne of Os-Gard. Now hear my words." The words stirred his heart and pierced him to the core. As he spun around, a tall figure surrounded by a brilliant veil of light stepped out from behind the tree.

The ancient white beard was dressed in a deep hooded, royal saxon-green cape with the luminous wake knots embroidered in shimmering gold on the brim of the hood. "The generation of Herewardi that lived during the glory of this tree have passed beyond the mould and ascended in the celestial bark of Ullr to enter their rest on high. But not far from here, they have left their most treasured memories in an ancient Hawthorn at Ili-Tor. There is where you will find the holy temple mound of Heredom. There shall your daughter preside as haeligewaecca."

"I know you Old Man, thou art the chief of the gods, thou art all-father Odhin, who once walked with me in the high desert when I first set out to fulfill my commission."

"Yes, Sur Sceaf, my son, you know me well, don't you!" He raised his arms to the square in the sign of the Swan and said, "This night will seem long to you, but it is not happening in the reckoning of time for men of the mould. Permit me to introduce some of your longfathers to you." Suddenly, the veil between them dispersed, allowing an even more resplendent glow to form around the all-father, so bright that his green cape now appeared whiter than bleached wool. In the brilliance greater than day light, two additional beings appeared beside the all-father on either side. Each gave the sign of the Swan and then one said, "I am Alfred," and the other said, "I am Hereward, king of the saxons."

Odhin smiled. "Sur Sceaf, my beloved, hear them. Alfred and Hereward are my trusted and proven sons. They will lead you in the path of truth and life, that you may establish a holy folk worthy of the visitation of the gods and elves, where faeries will bless the land, make your sons strong and your daughters beautiful, and increase the beauty and fertility of these lands tenfold, that Midgard may be returned to its paradisaical glory."

For what seemed like many hours, the three of them conversed with Sur Sceaf, as a man converses with his own children on points of kinship, kingship, government, and spirituality. Then Woon declared, "We will now take leave of you, our choice son, in whom we are well pleased. When we depart from you, you will be inundated with darkness, but know this, I have bestowed upon you the power to command the demons, the dark elves, and the Muspilli so that they may never do thee fatal harm again in thy generation, though they may buffet thee from time to time and seek to thwart thy progress, I shall put the fear of thee upon them for time and all eternity."

With that pronouncement the light swirled around the three heavenly beings who appeared to be consumed by a flash of lighting that shot skyward like a geyser with a large clap of thunder. An explosion of brilliant light covered the sky above. Stunned, and very weak from the meeting with woon, Sur Sceaf was lying upon the ground looking up into the dead branches of the tree of terror.

He sensed slowly pushed himself off the earth and got to his feet, he saw he was now some distance from the tree. He heard sinister laughter. There in the darkness of deep night he could make out three darker than night forms standing tall in black hooded robes on the knees of the tree. As he drew near them, he saw their pallid skin like the ashen grey of a corpse, black hands, and fierce icy-blue eyes.

He sensed the presence of sheer malevolent evil and fear ran up and down his spine. "Who are you?" He demanded.

They rasped out a sinister laugh.

"By all that is holy, in the name of almighty Woon, I command you to name yourselves!"

"We are the controlling gods of this world." The tallest of the three rasped, "Thy longfathers called us Scucca. But in thy tongue I am called Inquisitor." He nodded towards the second form, "This is Imperialist." He pointed to the third dark figure, "This is Terrorist. We have assumed many blasphemous names among the sons of men. We have existed since the beginning of worlds without number. We have power over the living and dead nations who worship us. Even the walls of death cannot contain us."

"What do you want?" Sur Sceaf demanded, loath to hear the answer, but suddenly infused with a sense of power and energy upon remembrance of Woon's pronouncement.

The Inquisitor laughed, "We are going to and fro in the earth to destroy the souls of men. The same as we have done in other worlds heretofore shaped. Thou mayest have triumphed over us, Sur Sceaf, and are now beyond our reach, but know thou this, there are yet many pockets in this land where we rule supreme with enough mendacity to plague thee and thy seed in the generations yet to come. We shall do everything in our power to thwart thy progress and the progress of thy confederation on the earth." He laughed again. "What a fool thou art to think any people are mature enough to endure a confederation, that different races and religions can actually be tolerant of one another.

"For there are lands even now beyond the seas of Aegir where we reign, and should any of thy seed not keep the forty-four laws, they shall be in our power and become swift prey to us, for us to work our deceptions and confusions upon; even as we did to the Amerikans, whom we deceived into giving up their confederation for a federal government, and their republic for a union, their gold for worthless paper money, and eventually, their liberties for security, their identity for globalism, until they were wholly within our power to grind in our mill of destruction as they cannibalized their rights away.

"In the dawning of thy race, we made Herewardi blood to flow in this land like wine. But we have reigned in blood and horror in many other lands as well, and our chief abode is in the center of the earth. We command far more than the Pitters. Few there are who can triumph over us. For we are the soul-eaters. We are the destroyers of the nations and worlds without number."

Sur Sceaf had had enough. "I know your names," he taunted, "and now I possess power to command you. Therefore, depart from me and this land! You have no right to be in Middle Earth, you workers of darkness and iniquity."

A crack of thunder rolled through the skies, and their dark forms began to crumble before him, then disassemble into a dark mist that slinked back into the earth.

CHAPTER 7 :
THE GARDEN OF HEROES

THE MORNING STAR, EARENDIL, WAS not seen in the darkened eastern sky, nor was it followed by the usual dawn light. Instead, a dull gloomy smoke filled the sky and bedecked the bastion and surrounding environs. At the same time the upper doors on the cliff walls opened to receive the returning swarms of were-bats. The horrible plague of vermin poured into the doors along the cliff, returning from their hellish night hunt, like swarming flies to a latrine.

Even with only a few hours of sleep, Sur Sceaf was surprisingly energized. His first concern was his family's well-being. While he was having breakfast at the cook tent, he sent Uffa to check on the twin commanders. After Uffa's swift return, he reported all were well, although Hrolwylf had sustained a wound to his foot, Arundel a slight cut to the face, Brekka only nursed her old wound, and she complained of Ruhm's hovering attention. For a young blood, Uffa was well skilled in knowing what information to report and to leave the superfluous out.

As Sur Sceaf walked out of the cook tent in the breaking light of dawn, he saw the undertakers were beginning to gently take up his fallen warriors, who lay strewn over the ground. Though their numbers were too numerous to count, he swiftly counted up to thirty dead tyfons and endless black were-bat carcasses. It was clear to him now that it most likely had been a tyfon that chomped off Russell's hand, but now the giant beasts lay lifeless, food for vultures, and those horrible winged demons were scattered like black rags across the landscape, with their bony frames of leathery wings twisted in various macabre poses. It was a chthonian scene from forty depths of hell. Warriors gathered them in great piles and set them to fire. Out of the piles of burning were-bat corpses a sour smoke arose like a menacing genie. This was an enemy that most armies could not have bested, but fortunately this time Widukind and Kanarus had managed to vanquish the giants. He shuddered to think there would likely be a repeat of this experience in the coming night. But the next time they would be better prepared. He wondered how many of those fierce beasts survived, because in the dark he had not seen their numbers nor where they went. *Are there still more below?* He and Arundel would now have to factor in the presence of these creatures in taking over control of the caverns.

Another obstacle he had contemplated just before sleep was why Hryre Seath and the rest of his troops were immune to the same plague that had taken so many of the other Pitters earlier. This was a riddle he needed to discuss with White Moose and the Mufsiks. He would be sure to inquire at the leadership meeting he had scheduled for eight on the sundial.

After assuring the fallen heroes were being properly attended to, he walked to the altar, the least populated area for his morning prayers. Flies filled the air, and vultures perched on the tree of terror in greater numbers than he had seen in a lifetime. One of the first things he had ordered was for Long Swan to re-sanctify the tree and the altar unto All-Father Woon, the healer of abomination. The sight of the dried blood staining the altar stirred him to anger. The senseless killing of the innocent sacrificial victims all those years evoked a white hot fury in him. He trembled at the thought that his daughter's blood had been mingled on those stones.

He felt to weep over his own fallen, smote his chest with his fist, and choked out an anguished cry. "So many of my brave warriors dead. It's all my fault. It's all my damned fault. When Arundel relayed Pomer's warning about these eaters from the stars, I made the mistake of thinking it was a Rdokian exaggeration, a mere tale of their mountain witches designed to warn them of the dangers of contact with Pitters."

By the altar he knelt and swore vengeance for Wilona and his fallen warriors. Today would be a sacral day of grief for all the fallen, a Herewardi tradition since the days of Elrus. With his own hands, he would help Brekka construct a dolman atop the Mound of Tor-Ili for her proxy mother, Wilona. There, they would lay her body and head together to rest until she came forth in the morning of the first resurrection to be joined by all her loved ones.

While his father, the High Lord Sur Sceaf, was at the altar for his morning prayers, Arundel waited at the gates with Brekka, Ruhm, and Kanarus. Starkwulf and Va-Eyra were meeting with Ilrundel and his troops in the valley of the springs. Though it was difficult in the hustle and bustle of morning activities, to find a place to meet in private, Going Snake had suggested they move to a recently emptied cluster of wagons and supply carts just off from the cook tent, left of the gates.

"My comrades in arms, I need your help," Ary called to his cadre of leaders. "We cannot afford to suffer the losses we underwent last night. So far we've been on the defensive. We've got to come up with a better solution for changing that. I've beaten my brains out trying to think of a way, but so far I have come up with nothing. Perhaps you all have hatched an idea or two? If so, now would be the time to let me know."

Kanarus patted a sorrel molly's neck. The mule, smaller and prettier than the other mules, let out a bray. "Cousin, I have given this much thought. I have but a few barrels of the shoot powder left, but I was thinking if we could get enough of it into the air shaft we could blast a hole in the walls big enough to march through."

Going Snake said, "That's a great idea. And I volunteer to plant it."

Ruhm thought for a moment before interjecting, "With all due respect, Lord Kanarus and Going Snake, I don't know that that would have much effect. We could blast in only to find they are sealed off at an even lower level. If we use all the shoot powder before we know where it's best applied, I'm thinking it would be a big mistake. Starkwulf and I came up from the third level, and everything below us was sealed off tighter than a frog's ass. This tells me that the first three levels are more or less service and supply caverns, and that the real heart of this ant colony lies much deeper. The numbers on the traveling room tend to support that. Also the Jokers told us they know of a cache of boom sticks. We just didn't have time to collect them. We've got to get to the bottom and come up. That's my theory, that they will least suspect an attack from below."

"I'm, with your plan Ruhm," Brekka said. "It's all too obvious to me that we need to grab those boom sticks and employ them on a cavern by cavern basis starting at the bottom."

As though agreeing, the molly brayed again.

Arundel frowned. "I don't like the enemy setting the terms of engagement. Fa has placed me in charge of the troops here on the surface. Kanarus, and you too, Ruhm, along with Starkwulf, are the most likely to lead the assault underground. Brekka, you and your lady knights should assist. Let's see what ideas Fa has come up with."

It was approaching seven thirty on the sundial when Sur Sceaf left the altar. He walked back to the gates where he was met by Heimdall and Uffa, and shortly thereafter was joined by Brekka, Arundel, Kanarus, Ruhm, and Going Snake, who appeared to have been huddled behind a cluster of wagons. As Mendaka emerged on horseback from the courtyard, Sur Sceaf commanded Heimdall to signal the trumpeters to blast for assembly.

Once the fyrds, dog soldiers, Hickoryan cavalry, and red nations were all assembled, on the landing, in the valley of the Big Springs, and on the promontory, Sur Sceaf returned to the altar and held his arms up for greeting and silence. When the buzz subsided, he addressed them with as much confidence as he could muster.

"Our losses come to us at great cost. I appoint today as a sacral day of grieving. We shall continue with burning the enemies on the bonfires. Then we shall bury our own dead, and build a dolman for Wilona the fair, that generations to come may pay tribute to for as long as these stones last. We shall gather the letters and journals of our fallen to send to their families and loved ones. Let us go down into the woods of pikeside to mourn and to bury our dead.

"We shall make for them a garden of heroes. It shall be a place of eternal memorial where the boys in grey, and red, and blue, and the nations of red men may all rest together until Woon, Christ, or the Thunder Beings call them up out of their graves at the end of times. But today we sing our grief-stricken dirges to our own gods. And for now, representatives of each tribe will bury their dead and record their names in the Book of the Dead as honored heroes to be celebrated in our annals forever more.

"Sadly, this will be but a brief respite, for tonight we must return here with torches and pikes, and should the giant beasts attack, we shall slay them with the beast stoppers and poison lances. We will station our archers so that we are all a safe distance from an arrow's shot. And we will raise bonfires throughout this land. If we must move about, it will be in tight, turtle-circle phalanxes, and we will fire our arrows at those demons until the ground is black and blanketed with their carcasses. When the legions march out of the ground, as I suppose they must, Arundel's phalanxes will be waiting for them. And when those giant beasts come out of the ground, we will be waiting for them with the beast stoppers. Remember, if the essence of the beast stopper blows upon you hold your breath for as long as you can, for its poison has a short persistence, and its killing power is in the inhaling of its essence. I go now to consult with your senior commanders who will issue more specific orders. But for now we shall pray each of us in our own way for the safe journey of the souls of our fallen into the other world. We will now honor the memory of our dead with silence and the twelve blasts from the lurs."

At the last deep throated blasts of the lurs, Sur Sceaf was startled by the cries of the warriors facing him, many pointing upward, and archers readying their bows. Sur Sceaf spun around and looked up at the bastion walls. Seeing nothing he lifted his gaze to the cliffs beyond. The large doors, high on the cliff walls, had slid open again. An instant later, Hryre Seath emerged atop a cliff wall with the same two aged figures attired in their deep blue robes, and a coven of handsomely cobalt blue uniformed dominikers, too far off to shoot with an arrow. At a gesture from the emperor, the door below opened. An instant later, three were-bat's came into view, clearly larger, and mahogany brown in color instead of the usual black like the attacking vampyrs of the night before. Clinging to their backs were commissars in orange robes, who wore what appeared to be saddle bags on their backs. As soon as the winged beasts took flight, another group of three appeared behind and likewise mounted to the sky.

Brekka grabbed Ruhm by an arm. Pulled her shield around and cried, "Ruhm, hold up my shield with me. Place your hand on the iridium side alongside mine." As they did this, they turned toward the third group of were-bats just taking to the air. As soon as the sun lined up with the shield, a spear of light formed that was twice the power of any beam Sur Sceaf had ever seen. The ray struck one were-bat after the other. The instant the beam struck the bats, the riders plummeted from the sky like wounded ducks on smoking wings, and people below scrambled to get out of their way. One by one commissars crumpled with sickening thuds, crashing to the earth on the landing between the gates and the altar.

Arundel said, "By Holy Tyranus, Sis, why didn't we do that before?"

Brekka took her hand from the shield. "I had no idea that when Ruhm joined his hand with mine it would multiply the power and the reach of the shield. It was chust something that came to my mind. It is even as Govannon instructed me, 'Silver follows gold, and when united, it doubles the brilliance'. I'm just starting to figure this out." She smiled and displayed the shield. "Don't you see Ruhm, I am silver, you are gold just as this shield. It doubles our power when we become one."

Sur Sceaf pondered Govannon's quote as he, Arundel, Brekka, and Ruhm ran to the fallen were-bats. Two of the commissars had died from the impact; the third was injured and unconscious. The saddle bags and their contents were strewn across the impacted area. As warriors trotted close with swords drawn, Sur Sceaf commanded, "Do that commissar no harm. We want to question him."

Arundel drew his attention away from the commissar and went to one of the were-bats. "All of their wings are singed to naught, but this one here is still alive." At the same time he stabbed at the crumpled, smoldering creature that flopped and twitched, but offered no fight. As Sur Sceaf took a step closer in order to study the dying were-bat, he discovered that these creatures, in addition to their coloring and size, looked very different from the black Vampyric Were-Bats, who had serpentine pink tongues, and mouths filled with rows of razor sharp teeth. "They don't look near as ugly or as malicious as the black ones." He reflected aloud.

"Indeed, they are almost handsome." Brekka remarked. "They have the melding of a man, a horse, and a bat. Maybe even some fox. If that's even possible?"

As others on the landing gathered around for a better look, Arundel declared in a disgusted tone, "All is possible with the dark science of the Amerikans. There is nothing they could imagine that they would not do."

From the corner of his eye, Sur Sceaf caught sight of the injured commissar attempting to move. He walked over and studied him. "Broken back and ribs, I suspect."

He reached down and retrieved the bag lying next to the commissar. Who awoke and croaked out, "Kill me, Sheep-Eater!"

Sur Sceaf said, "Not yet!" Before carrying the bag a little way off to examine the contents. Inside, he found numerous glass vials wrapped in cotton, as well as an object that looked like a sharp pin attached to the end of a vial-like chamber with a curious plunger mechanism inside.

Sur Sceaf returned to the crushed Pitter and said, "From the looks of it, you have a day, maybe a day and a half left to live in agonizing pain." He looked down into the beady brown eyes flashing pure hatred at him. "I can kill you, and put you out of this awful misery or..." He paused to point to Brekka, "This woman, shall have your balls on the end of her blade. Tell me what the contents of this bag are used for. And then, and only then, shall I kill you mercifully. What'll it be?"

The yellow teeth parted just enough to allow the Pitter to wheeze out, "Medicine. Medicine." He coughed, and blood ran down his chin in an ooey streak. "Medicine... that will stop... the sickness... of the seed of the woman and break the teeth of the vagina dentata witch once and for all."

Sur Sceaf looked at his compatriots with raised eyebrows. One by one they nodded that the Pitter spoke truth. Sur Sceaf agreed with them. "Who gives you this medicine?"

The commissar appeared torn between disclosure and pain.

At a nod from Sur Sceaf, Brekka stepped forward, slowly drew her blade and with a sly grin tapped his groin with the tip. "Speak truth now or face your next life as an eunuch."

Looking horrified, the Pitter hissed, "Vardrop and Ish."

Arundel looked over in dismay at Sur Sceaf, "Holy Tyranus, do you really think their gods are somewhere inside the caverns?"

Before Sur Sceaf could answer, Brekka exclaimed, "I know they are in there! It comes to me slowly, that the harridan, Gloomulah, mentioned she had companions, Doctors Vardrop and Ish, who had taken off with her research just before the collapse of the Amerikans. It makes sense that they are in there using the same science and dark knowledge that Gloomulah had. Obviously, they've found a remedy for the Mufsiks' plague and are sending out these demons to protect their legions in the South Lands from the ravages of the disease."

Arundel said, "Fortunately, those flying to the north won't get any satisfaction, because there are no enemies of consequence left in the North Lands."

Brekka said, "But if the medicine in those vials gets to their legions in the south, I fear this will lead to a greatly protracted war."

Sur Sceaf pondered the costs to Il-Alim and Ehira, but knew everything depended on flushing out this den of demons first. "Somehow, we must find the way into Hryre Seath. There's just got to be a way to sever this serpents head."

Brekka glanced up at the emperor who seemed unconcerned about the carnage below as Brekka had been unable to shoot down six of his messengers. With great ceremony, she lifted her blade in a mock salute, and then swiftly plunged it into the commissar's heart. His head swung back and he gasped and rattled for his last breath.

"He deserved a merciful death," she said as she wiped the blood from her sword with some limestone dust before re-sheathing it. "I suspect, Ish and Vardrop have their dark magic to draw upon just like Gloomulah did. If I've learned anything, it's that these Amerikans can all be killed, chust like any mortal man. But we've got to find a way into them."

CHAPTER 8 :
WERE-BATS AND WYRM-KATS

AFRENETIC FLOW OF ENERGY CAME out of Arundel as he explained, " Kanarus' men have searched the entire perimeter of the bastion and have marked a number of sealed doors, cleverly hidden along the walls. It is my belief we must use the boom-sticks to blow open as many of these doors as we can and breech this bastion from every angle. The more doors we open, the less capable they will be of defending themselves, and thereby they will be distracted from Father and Starkwulf seeking to infiltrate the lower floors."

"Hopefully, we will find more of the moving rooms through those doors, or at least stairways," Starkwulf said. "I couldn't get the moving room we found to go below level three, and there are at least 20 levels according to the numbers on its wall."

Brekka warned, "We need to take a double measure of caution. We don't know what's behind any of those doors. This all brings to mind the tunnels of Gloomulah, when we unleashed those damnable chimpanapes. And now we've seen that Vardrop and his Ennead are capable of every evil and more than Gloomulah. Let's do everything safely and accurately, and prepare ourselves in perfect phalanxes to meet whatever lies behind those doors."

Ary felt the cold chill of truth hidden in Brekka's prophetic warning.

"I think it would behoove us to act as soon as possible. Any time we waste could cost us dearly in lives and ground gained," said Kanarus.

"I'm for that," Brekka agreed.

Ary puzzled for a moment. "I'm not one for haste, but our greatest defense is surprise and speed at this moment. We can spare our men fighting with at least a portion of the monsters by throwing boomsticks and beast stoppers down the feeding shafts. Once the doors are breeched, Going Snake and I will remain on the surface to ensure we maintain what we have won above the ground."

Sur Sceaf spoke up. "Starkwulf and I will be taking our twelvers into the caverns as soon as we know a passage down. I think it best we wait until we have seen what is behind those secret doors before we resort to wandering around the caverns through the Lazy Joker's entrance. And when we do find a way in, Brekka and her lady knights will be needed as well. Afterall, for this purpose have the lady knights come into this world at this time, that the Seed of the Woman might fulfill her mission and defeat the empire once and for all."

"Give us some of those boomsticks, as well," Starkwulf said, "We may find there are more doors sealed down below than even on the surface. They may be of potent use to us. Sur Sceaf and I are well enough versed in how to utilize them."

Va Eyra broke her silence, "I want to point out that we who are going into the bowels of this bastion will be breathing the air down there. I for one do not want the gases of the beast-stoppers causing me to gasp for my last breath. The death they emit is never a pretty sight. I'd much rather die a shield-maiden's death with my sword in my hand, than choking on green smoke. Give us the beast-stoppers, and you who stay above use the boom-sticks and rubble to clear out the feeding shafts."

After using the boom-sticks to open the first hidden door along the bastion wall, they found another moving room. This one was able to travel to all the floors below. Sur Sceaf's expedition went all the way to the bottom floor. As guides, a number of the Lazy Jokers came along, having secretly explored many of the tunnels in the past. They led them through a tunnel marked with an arrow pointing up an incline. The walls narrowed into a smaller tunnel from which the air blasted acrid whiffs. The tightness of the tunnel forced them to go four men abreast. The ceiling now hung ten feet above them. After a walk of perhaps three hundred feet they came out into another chamber on a higher level.

Chloe hissed loud, the whiskers on her face were moving in synchronized twitches with her nose. The hair on her back rose up in a high bristle. She bared her teeth and assumed a crouching, stalking mode, ready to pounce at any moment, the tight sinews and muscles visible through her tawny fur. Scratch and Mauser responded the same. Chloe was quicker to pick up the scents, and the other ketten seemed to understand that she was the better gifted of the three.

Chloe said, with her nose still nervously twitching, "Smell of fly men." Her catlike voice swished in whispers off the large cavern walls. As she turned to look back, her highly reflective eyes shone like hot coals in the dusky light.

Starkwulf stroked Chloe's head. "Good job, Chloe." Then to the others added, "We're probably getting close to the were-bat camp and they're picking up the scent far better than we can."

Several booms were heard above, and then the sound of falling of rocks through dark holes at the other end of the chamber. Soon, five were-bats fell through the holes and crashed on the rocks beneath, dead. The large air shafts apparently ran all the way to the top and some of the were-bats must have been sleeping in them. Another boom shook the earth, followed by rocks and three black were-bat bodies fell through another shaft on tattered wings, indicating to Sur Sceaf that Ary had found some air shafts and was tossing explosives down them.

One of the were-bats moved feebly for a moment, and then lay still. More booms and more bodies, ten this time.

"I want a closer look at one of these freaks," Charly exclaimed as he started toward the body, only to be halted by Starkwulf's hand on his shoulder.

"Not a good idea to stand under falling objects, my lad. Best we stay clear of those holes. Boulders could easily be dislodged and come down on your head."

They spent an hour searching various dead-end tunnels before they found tunnels that bore a plaque of a man walking up an incline. They figured that it indicated the way up to another level of caverns. Verushka was making notes on a map. When she finished they moved on. Sur Sceaf wanted to investigate the were-bats at closer range, but a long time had passed on his water clock since they'd discovered the first sign of a man walking upward. He judged it to be about two hours after high dark. This was in the approximate range of time Ary said he would commence the heavy bombing. Because of the time lost in searching the labyrinth of feeder tunnels off the main tunnel, he felt more pressed to find Hryre Seath's bunker in hopes the Pitters would not suspect he was launching a pincer spearhead attack from below.

"We must locate the core. Let's keep moving up through the chambers, until we, with the help of Odhin, uncover the emperor's den. Everyone, light your torch! In the unlikely event that one of those winged demons survived, you don't want tongue, teeth, or talon to touch you, and as we discovered, the fire of the torches should be enough to keep them from molesting us."

Starkwulf passed Leroy a piece of fungal punk to light his torch, since Leroy had somehow lost his in one of the tunnels. "Pity we hadn't figured that the tunnels that angle upwards would lead out before we trudged through all those other tunnels," the lad grumbled.

"We did the best we could," Va-Eyra said. "This is, after all, our first time in this maze, and who would have ever guessed they were this extensive."

Soon, they were back in phalanx formation, with the wyrm-kats leading them through the chambers and tunnels upward, secure in their assumption that they were on their way to the emperor's chamber.

Sur Sceaf trusted in the kettens' senses being much sharper than their human senses. They stopped frequently to sniff the air and twist an ear at a particular sound or disturbance ahead. The ketten were proving to be an invaluable early warning system. Yet, with the many torches burning, the interior of the tunnels and chambers were now far more visible.

Each level was held up by massive mushroom shaped columns of limestone and, again, had an endless labyrinth of smaller tunnels running out from them like spokes on wheels. They stuck to following only the tunnels with an incline marker of the stick man. After they arrived on the fifth level, they discovered chamber after chamber of pronk storage barrels. Some stacked three high and perhaps fifty deep. The earth shook, but not as violently as before, so they studied the barrels for a moment.

"Probably fuel for their machines, or maybe food," Brekka suggested. "Whether for man or beast I know not, but they are at least similar to the ones we found in the citadel."

Charly declared, "Then they must be mighty hungry, 'cause there's so many."

Sur Sceaf nodded, and ordered the ketten to move on through the main tunnel marked with the image of the man following an incline upwards. After they came up the incline of the sixth level from the bottom, Chloe's tail was twisting back and forth like a hissing viper, and all three Kats were signing, "Danger," with a swift drawing of their clawed hands across their throats. Their eyes were wide and black.

Steff cried, "What stinks so bad?"

A sickening sweet stench filled the air. Va-Eyra and the lady knights took out their scarves to cover their noses and mouths. Sur Sceaf ordered the torches to be held up high. Before them was a large catacomb in the middle of a huge chamber littered with piles and stacks of what appeared to be black mud covering the entire chamber floor. The muck was everywhere except along the edges of the surrounding walls which were protected by a rock overhang.

"Well," Starkwulf scrunched his face from the stench and said, "whatever it is, we need to find out if we're to cross this chamber to the next passage inclining upward, and the sooner the better."

Charly pointed with his torch. "Look at that wall over there. It's got a feeding trough that starts here and runs long enough to feed at least two thousand head of cattle I'd say."

Va-Eyra clarified, her lips moving through the scarf. "Not likely cattle."

As they stepped out into the dark chamber, Leroy said, "What in blue blazes are all those piles? Looks like the blackest mud I've ever seen. Must be important. None of the other caverns had this cut away wall to keep you from stepping in that greasy slime."

Starkwulf took a few steps forward, looked up, and laughed. "Alas, son, that's not mud. Look up."

They held their torches high outside the overhang. Endless werebats hung upside down from the cavern ceiling.

"Shades of the colosseum," Freyxus exclaimed, "the beast wars are upon us." She threw back her long blond ringlets, drew her sword in her right hand, and Ruhm helped her with her shield. She held it through its handles with her left arm, while grasping her torch with the same hand to be ready. Her eyes stayed brightly fixed on Ruhm as he moved on.

Verushka pointed a finger. "This place has to be the demons' camp."

A few strange clicks pierced the air. Starkwulf let out, "Uh-Oh!"

This was followed by a chorus of screeches sounding throughout the caverns. The ceiling writhed with black bodies, like a dense herd of buffalo moving across the shadowy dark vault above them. This was followed by wraith-like shadows darting across the walls, and piercing bat signals bouncing everywhere. Dark forms filled the air. Beady red eyes flashed in the torchlight, and those long pink tongues dangled in the air from their sharp-toothed mouths like hundreds of serpents.

The were-bats tasted the air, and sent out their almost insect-like clicking sounds from every direction. It became very disorienting, and Sur Sceaf felt as though the clicks were echoing around inside of him, requiring a strong act of will to press on. Sight became the only sense that he could trust.

"Use your torches and swords, and work for the marked tunnel on the left." Seeing the reluctance of the others to move, he shouted, "Come on! Move your asses. The were-bats can't pursue us afoot. We have to get into the smaller tunnel."

Suddenly, the clicks multiplied exponentially, and the were-bats showed increasing agitation. With the ketten in the lead, everyone moved swiftly under the stone overhang. What they had only felt as a breeze until now became much stronger as they got to the tunnel entrance.

Freyxus, always the shepherdess, stopped, and turned around and returned to the rear in order to guard the lady knights. Ruhm joined her. The underground wind grew stronger, whipping Freyxus' hair like a strong gale from the sea. She wondered how such a powerful wind could possibly blow this far below ground--unless the earth was indeed hollow as she had once heard postulated. As they entered the tunnel, they saw a large metal box attached to the ceiling. There was a whirring sound coming from it, and it appeared to be sucking the air into it.

Just inside the entrance to the tunnel Sur Sceaf stopped with his sword to the ready, his eyes fixed above while urging the others to quickly move into the narrow tunnel. Brekka stopped next to him while the lady knights filed through. "Fa, may I take a shot at them with my shield?"

"Good idea. Make it brief. We've got to keep moving."

"Ruhm, would you assist me?"

Ruhm teased, "Always at your service, your highness."

Freyxus smiled. There was something starting to cook between Ruhm and Freyxus.

Brekka just looked at Ruhm with a scowl and ordered, "Smart ass, chust hold the torch up." She swung her shield from her back. "Hold your torch a little higher." She angled the shield until it caught the light, and then flashed the beam toward the ceiling. Wherever the beam struck a swath of were-bats fell to their deaths like flies under a candle flame.

At the same time Sur Sceaf caught sight of a flight of were-bats descending on Freyxus, who was bringing up the rear. She was attempting to fend them off with her sword, but getting overwhelmed. Ruhm quickly raced to her aid, swinging his sword wildly. Metal bit flesh, with a loud *clunk,* and a severed, hairy talon-covered foot hit the ground. This was followed by the most hellish of screams, the mixture of a panther and a woman's scream with cicada-like undertones following.

Starkwulf shredded the wing of one of the hell-fiends and fended off a vicious snap of its teeth with his shield. Dark wings wrapped around the shield. At the same time another were-bat struck Va-Eyra's shield where she held it over her head. Scratch had returned to the cavern from the tunnel. With a single pounce he sunk his teeth into the jugular of the were-bat menacing Va-Eyra. When the wings of the were-bat went limp, Scratch thrust the were-bat to one side with his powerful limbs, then sprang into the safety of the tunnel once more. As soon as everyone was gathered inside, the were-bats landed in profusion to crowd the entrance, but were reluctant to force any entry.

Steff asked wide-eyed, "What happens if they follow?"

Starkwulf declared, "These narrow tunnels are too difficult for them to navigate with their cumbersome wings."

"It's a waste of time to stir this cauldron of hell any further," Sur Sceaf belted out, "we need to keep focus on our mission to find Hryre Seath."

As they hurried along the tunnel floor away from the entrance, Sur Sceaf called a halt "Are there any injuries?"

There was a silence before Va-Eyra called out, "Only my pride."

Several booms followed in succession, the sound muffled by the close tunnel's walls. According to the time table worked out with Arundel, they had another good hour before they would run out of boom sticks.

"Let's take a break here in the safety of this tunnel. We don't know what lies ahead and we need to be refreshed." He leaned against the tunnel wall to chew on a piece of pemmican.

Va-Eyra could not resist scratching the kat's ears, she was so proud of them. Cooing she pulled Scratch's head into her bosom and rubbed his ears and back vigorously. "Good boy Scratch! Good kill!"

"Be careful Sis," Sur Sceaf warned. "These male kats are intact and are easily aroused and very difficult to turn off."

She removed her hand swiftly before giving Scratch a gentle nudge away. "Thanks for the warning. I could have used that advice a moment earlier."

Starkwulf grinned. "Most especially, around a woman of your exquisite beauty. My dear Cat-Queen." Still grinning, he patted her teasingly on the buttocks.

Seeing what he thought was a blush on his sister's face, Sur Sceaf joined Starkwulf in a laugh, then said, "But you can pet Chloe."

Scratch protested, "Not Chloe, Scratch like petting. Want more."

"Then you will have to get Chloe to pet you, Scratch," Sur Sceaf said as he studied the were-bats activities in the eerie light out the far entrance of the tunnel. "You know Zrael has told you not to touch female humans because of what it does to you."

Scratch let out a long "Grrrrh! Scratch like women." The cat paused for a moment, began to posture, but then took on a submissive stance and said, as though remembering, "Sur Sceaf Top Cat, he kill big bear." He began sniffing the tunnel ahead as if there had never been a problem.

Starkwulf shrugged his shoulders. "Cats! What did you expect?" Then changing the subject he inquired, "How do you suppose the Pitters capture the wind, like that, and pull it into that large box?"

"I have seen them at the citadel." Brekka told him. "Some draw the air from above and others blow out the air from below. It keeps the air from getting stale by circulating it. It's the same principle as a hand fan. Yiska said they call them fans."

Va-Eyra observed, "I think they use these tunnels as service tunnels, which tells me they may not have as much control over these were-bats as they would like us to think."

"What makes you say that, my dear?" Starkwulf asked.

"Isn't it obvious, they need these tunnels to safely approach the were-bats. Otherwise, I think the Pitters are as much a prey for eating as are we."

"You may have a point there, Sis," Sur Sceaf said, "but I saw Hryre Seath up top very close to them, and the commissars seemed to have total control over the ones they rode."

"Yes," Va said, "but that was the brown bats, not these black ones."

"An excellent point."

The were-bats still clustered at the tunnel entrance, sending out their bouncing clicks, but they did not enter.

Relieved, that he didn't have to worry about an attack from their rear, Sur Sceaf motioned them forward. As they progressed, the incline rapidly grew steeper. Oddly, there was what looked like a white pronk flume or pipe about two feet off the floor running the length of the tunnel. Cautiously, Sur Sceaf placed his hand on it, and heard some sort of alarm go off like the honking of a goose. This was followed by the feel of something surging through the flume beneath his palm.

Freyxus was still bringing up the rear like a shepherdess over her flock of sheep. She shouted up to them, "I saw a series of smaller tubes like this sticking out of the wall of the cavern over that long trough. Like some kind of feeding mechanism. I think the goose alarm is used to call them to feast. We should investigate."

"Freyxus, I'll send you, Ruhm, and Scratch back to ascertain what it is." Sur Sceaf declared, "The rest of us must keep moving to meet the timetable."

Ruhm said, "It shall be done, my lord. We will return shortly."

As Freyxus, Scratch, and Ruhm headed in the opposite direction, several more blasts followed from above. They raced up the tunnel until they became winded from the exertion. Sur Sceaf called for a rest.

As they headed back towards the entrance, Ruhm was expecting to take the lead, but Freyxus swiftly made it clear this was her mission by asserting herself to the fore. Instead of muscling his way past her as he would with any other junior officer, he found himself both amused and stirred by her exuberant self-confidence. Not for the first time, Ruhm found her long blond hair and sapphire blue eyes to be seductively alluring. No matter how much he had chastised himself about swiving women when his heart belonged only to Brekka, he still found himself very much aroused by Freyxus. There was a magnetic familiarity with her, as if they were somehow spirit bound to one another. Her beauty was intoxicating and her will indomitable, her intelligence unequaled. She had a bearing that was at once feminine and yet indescribably powerful. She was in possession of what the Herewardi termed the Faery-Fire.

Upon reaching the entrance they were once again overwhelmed at the wall of stench assailing their nostrils. Freyxus called a halt with a raised hand.

Scratch said, "Stinking bats. Filthy bats. We hates them! We do!"

"Time to put your scarf over your nose." Freyxus said. As Freyxus drew her swan scarf over her nose, she scoffed, "For heaven's sake, Ruhm, quit daydreaming and put your kerchief over your mouth."

"Not daydreaming. I was merely assessing the dangers of us going any farther."

"You needn't trouble yourself. I've already assessed the matter."

He grinned. "For someone as young as you, you sure act like you know it all."

She tossed her hair back. "That's because I do. Mother Freya has given me the heart of a vixen. I perceive even the semblance of danger before it arrives."

"Alright, Miss Smarty Fox, lead us to the trough." Even though she behaved as a vixen, as a warrior, she was as confidant as any man he knew.

Scratch hissed close to his ear, "Rurruhm like Freyxus."

Ruhm stepped a few feet away, embarrassed that even the kat had so easily discerned his overwhelming sexual attraction for Freyxus, but there was more there than just sexual attraction. She had a spiritual hold on him he could not account for. *Where in the cosmos is this coming from?*

Freyxus gave a flirtatious look at Ruhm as she teasingly shot back, "Freyxus likes Ruhm."

Ruhm's face grew warm. He quickly pulled up his kerchief. "Let's not forget what we were sent here to do."

She teased with dimpled grin. "I promise I won't hurt you, Ruhm. I would just soften you up for Brekka." She brazenly laughed.

Scratch stepped between them. "Freyxus like Top Cat Ruhm, so no hurt, no scratch Ruhm. Top Cat Ruhm. Him big man, head cat over horse men. Him gots sharp sabre."

Ruhm collected himself, coyly adjusted himself and declared openly, "It's true, I feel something Freyxus, but now is not the time to talk about such things. For one, there's absolutely nothing about the smell of bat-shit that turns me on, and secondly, we have a mission to complete." Without waiting for an answer, Ruhm took over the lead. Surprisingly, when they reached the mouth of the tunnel, they discovered the were-bats were still on the ground, but to their amazement, they were clustered at the other end of the chamber. Going unnoticed, they followed along under the overhang to where they had seen the empty feeding trough earlier. Even as they cautiously drew near it, the were-bats took no notice of their approach and only jostled each other for space at the feeding trough. The constant cicada-like clicking and lapping sounds as the beasts fed made it difficult to hear.

Scratch hissed, "Blood! Trough filled with blood." His tail twitched while his head darted from side to side.

Ruhm kept watch for any potential danger. Freyxus edged over to the lip of the trough. Approximately a foot away stood a black faced fiend crouched over on boney black wings, his pink serpentine tongue alternately swimming in the blood and drawing the red liquid into its teeth filled mouth as it dripped from his lips. Other were-bats were jostling down the line for their turn, and letting out protesting screams as their elbowing neighbors pushed and shoved.

Freyxus turned to Scratch. "Do you still smell blood, Scratch?"

Scratch was purring loudly. "Smell blood. Want me kill fly-man?"

"No Scratch. No kill. We tell Top Cat Sur Sceaf what we see," Freyxus said. She shifted her gaze back to Ruhm and said, "We better check."

"There's only one way to know for sure that it is blood." He started for the trough when she placed a hand on his chest and said, "Let me."

Once again, he found himself intrigued by her boldness. She was so much like Brekka, a woman of beauty, courage and strength, but he dare not allow himself to jeopardize his already tenuous relationship with Brekka. He did not understand Herewardi courtship practices and decided he would keep his approach to a Hickoryan style, a monogamous approach.

"Suit yourself, but be careful." Feeling a powerful urge to protect her, he slipped his saber from the scabbard and braced his feet.

Throwing an amused look, she withdrew her scramasax from her ankle sheath and carefully edged closer. Slowly, so as not to arouse attention, she leaned over the trough and dipped the blade in the liquid. Ruhm noticed that some of the bats that had drunk their fill had noticed them and were becoming progressively more agitated by their presence.

Scratch had also noticed the behavior of the bats and assumed a protective pounce pose. "Hurry, fly men want eat us."

Freyxus stepped back, drew the blade under her nose and sniffed. "It's blood. This smell is not a stranger to my blade. Same metallic odor." She held the blade close to Ruhm's nose. "Here, take a sniff."

She was right. The odor was unmistakable, evoking visceral memories of scenes of carnage. "Undoubtedly, it's blood. But for god's sake, whose?"

Cisne and Pata offered hunks of the blue sheep cheese to Sur Sceaf's Twelvers, who in turn offered the ladies strips of side meat from vendors in Front Royal. Meanwhile, Sur Sceaf consulted with Va, Starkwulf and Brekka.

"Thank the gods for Going Snake's ingenuity and brilliant use of the boom sticks the Pitters' attention is drawn to the surface."

Charly interjected, "I don't mean to toot my own horn, but all the times we was exploring this place, we never got this far, but we never got caught. I'm thinking not many are wont to come this deep anyways, but we always had to be careful around the riding rooms."

"Duly noted," Starkwulf answered. "And we are grateful for your service." Grinning, he turned to Va. "These boys remind me of when Chise and Zoot were boys in Copperopolis."

She nodded. "Certainly they are as precocious as Chise and Zoot were."

After approximately fifteen minutes, the company was refreshed and Sur Sceaf was ready to move on when Brekka cried out. "Here they are, Fa. Ruhm is returned."

He watched Ruhm and Freyxus returning. He had too many daughters to not know that smitten look on Freyxus' face. He glanced at Brekka, but could discern no disapproval.

Scratch came directly to him and hissed in an almost liquid sound close to his ear, "Blood."

Ruhm added, "My lord, the pipe is carrying blood to the trough, and those fiends are lapping it up like kittens. But what puzzles me is how did they keep it from coagulating?"

"That's a good question. The Quailor make a sausage from blood, but they whip it to keep it from coagulating," Sur Sceaf explained. "I don't have the answer, and I don't have the time to ponder the matter now. Come, let us move on up to the next level. Those "kittens" seem content enough feeding for now, and are liable to leave us alone on full bellies."

"Not kittens," Scratch half hissed. "Bad... Fly-Men. Blood lickers."

"That's right, Scratch," Va-Eyra confirmed. "They are not kittens,"

As they approached the seventh level from the bottom, a strong musty odor filled the air, like the smell of duff in a damp old broken log in the deep forest. The wyrm-kats were puzzled at first, then Chloe said, "Shroom garden." And Mauser said, "Rabbit."

After they walked another fifty yards through the tunnel, it opened into a large open chamber. Sur Sceaf whispered the command to halt. The chamber appeared to be man-made and was lined with hundreds of white rabbits, row upon row in viminal, wicker cages filling the oval room almost to bursting. Stone walkways crisscrossed the floor. Though Sur Sceaf searched for guards or workers, there were none he could see. Perhaps they came in shifts to attend the feeding.

"Everything looks safe, but keep your eyes peeled." He led the way down the center walkway. Interspersed with the cages were teeming hordes of mushrooms in large mounds of compost. He leaned down to feel the soft friable soil. "Straw, manure, and an earth mixture. How ingenious."

"Mushroom gardens," Verushka said. "Of course, they don't need sunlight, neither do the rabbits. But who are they for?"

Brekka knitted her eyebrows in a frown. "Well, methinks those were-bats must eat more than blood, but the mushrooms are probably for someone with a more refined palette. I'm thinking there must be a team of scientists here just like at the citadel. This has all the makings of an agrarian enterprise, an underground farm of sorts similar to the ones

Bufo oversaw in the citadel. Shades of Gloomulah! I prey they don't have any chapinapes."

"What is certain is that these beds are all well-tended like the ones at Ele-Anor-Ness," Sur Sceaf said. "It still befuddles me as to why we haven't run into any workers down here yet."

"Humans," Va-Eyra said, "are not wont to dwell underground unless compelled."

"But do they have a servant race like the grodor?" Brekka thought out loud. "It's crossed my mind several times. There is a lot I've seen here patterned after the underworld at the citadel, but enough different to make me know they were not sharing their intelligence."

"Workers, servants or slaves, they were probably all drawn to the blasts above," Starkwulf said. "We should press on with all due haste before the enemy has a chance at discovering us. The swifter we move the greater the element of surprise. Sever the serpents head before it has time to recoil and strike."

As they moved up the tunnel following the flume through the large rabbit chamber, Sur Sceaf twisted around, wrapped his hand around the knee-high pronk pipe and felt movement through it again. It had almost a pulsing motion. He was curious about what Scratch had said about the blood.

Brekka read his thoughts. "Fa, I could cut this pipe with my axe and cut off the blood supply to all those Were-Bats."

"I considered that, but the Were-Bats would only go in search of sustenance, and the damage they might do to the local populace would not be worth it to me. It would be unfair to the Hickoryans in this area."

"We could just barely prick the pipe with the tip of a blade. I want to see if it is supplying the blood to those vampyrs."

"Let's go for it." Sur Sceaf took the tip of his sword and punctured the flume. A fine red spray squirted out, spraying over his hand and forming a tiny puddle in the grey dust of the cave floor. "By the gods, all I can hope is that this is not human blood, because it is still quite warm to the touch." Steam rose from the rocks and dust the spray struck around Sur Sceaf's feet.

"Anything is possible with these Pitters," Starkwulf said. "Bastards of a bastard's spawn. They are all given to devilish works which they justify in the name of their perverse one god."

"Your theory proved right, Brekka," Sur Sceaf said, "The were-bats are being supplied with fresh blood so they will do the Pitters' bidding. Maybe it is as you say that they eat other things also, but I think this blood is a special treat to them. Probably keeps them returning here after foraging. The question that now troubles me is where does all this blood come from?"

"Fa," Brekka said as she placed a hand to the tunnel wall, "you're not *really* thinking its human blood, are you?"

"Couldn't say, but any obscenity and abomination is possible with these Hellheimers."

Va-Eyra kicked lightly at the flume. "Just follow the tube and it should take us right to the source and the answer to your question."

Leroy asked apprehensively, "Why would you want to do that?"

Va-Eyra answered, "Because we will not suffer such abominations to continue."

"What about going after the emperor that you were so damned dead set on getting to?"

"If we have to, we can divide our forces," Ruhm explained. "That's why Starkwulf is here."

With the ketten in the lead once again, they followed the tube up through the narrow tunnel to the eighth level. As they approached the tunnel exit, the odors and stench became close to unbearable. And sounds of horror filled the air. Monstrous squeals and screams. The were-kats' hackles were up high on their backs.

"What fiends of hell make such sounds?" Starkwulf said.

Several blasts shook the chamber they were in, reminding Sur Sceaf of the pressing of time. "I cannot guess what's making those sounds, but as always, stay vigilant," Sur Sceaf ordered, torch and shield in one hand, sword in the other. As they moved forward the stench increased.

"Wooh!" Va said, "I know that smell." Her nostrils flared and her face scrunched. "I smell piggy poo!"

Jumping up and down like a kid in a play pen, Scratch said, "Pigs! Pigs! Scratch catch piglettes! Scratch eat!"

The tails of the Wyrm-Kats were going wild with excitement. Sur Sceaf commanded in his most forceful tone, "No catch pigs!" Then, placing his hand on Scratch's chest, said, "Top Cat will look first." Scratch became submissive under his rebuke.

There was ample light on this level, so Sur Sceaf doused his torch in the thick dust and ordered the others to do the same. As soon as all torches were extinguished, he asked the ketten if they smelled humans."

Chloe, who had the most sensitive nose said, "Me smell dirty man."

Sur Sceaf carefully sidestepped the ketten in a swift fluid movement, and peered from the tunnel entrance into the next level. The area spread out far in the distance, resembling a livestock yard.

From where they were, he saw no humans or Pitters. He signed, "Proceed cautiously and quietly," before leading them into an area of vast pens of pigs, one after another, as far as the eye could see. And the eye could see far, because there were many bright lights of some unknown source all along the walls, on the ceiling, and on posts throughout this hellishly over-crowded stockyard where pigs were packed together like cigars in a box.

Then, to one side, he saw a large platform made of concrete with trees and plants in rectangular planters and long metal tables like a mess hall. Sur Sceaf signed, "Go cryptic." All but the Jokers ducked and went into stealth mode, crouching down along the corrals for cover. Ruhm motioned for the boys to copy his movements, which, to his astonishment, they accomplished like practiced warriors.

As they passed from one alley to the next, they came upon an area about ten man lengths in front of them where several aproned workers were engaged in the act of slaughtering hogs that hung squealing from clamping hooks, which ran through the tendons of the pigs back legs. Several men slit their throats, and then pushed them over the vats to bleed out. The blood was captured in the vats, and another man was pouring some form of powder into it, while yet another stirred it in.

As they crept through the stockyard, glutted rats prowled in great numbers over the fence rails. Sur Sceaf knocked a rat off his leg and whispered, "Those people don't look to be Pitters--shaven heads, ashen complexions, yes, but no tattoos, no rat teeth, no hair bristles. Can't be Pitters."

"Perhaps Hickoryans," Starkwulf said. "That would make them captive laborers pressed into involuntary servitude for the empire." He paused. "But over there, at the first mark on the medicine wheel, there stands your three overseers. They are definitely Pitters. See, spear in hand of one, other two busy writing."

"Not many guards for so many laborers," Va-Eyra whispered. "I count twenty laborers at most."

"Where could they escape to?" Starkwulf offered. "Below they would be eaten alive by the were-bats. Above, there are legions to deal with. Poor souls must have to live their lives without seeing the sun, nature, or birds in all this stench and gore and drudgery, day in and day out. And only those few token potted plants to remind them there is a green world and a blue sky somewhere above them. It's a living hell."

"So few plants, nothing like the wilds," Va-Eyra said. "It's grossly systemic, unnatural. And all these soul searing sounds! How would you like to spend your life wallowing in blood and shit all day long? No wonder the Pitters call their labor camps, their 'labor force.' You have to be *forced* to labor under conditions such as these."

Brekka moved closer to whisper, "Griselda once explained to me that the amerikans once did this. They called it 'corporate farming,' chust like the corporate mills, and mines in the north lands. But it must be four or five in the morning by now. Why would they still be working at this hour?"

Va pulled the scarf farther up over her nose. "This place probably runs three or four shifts. You know, how Muryh did when he was building the temple."

"Yes," Brekka said, "But that was a labor of love, and the workers were volunteers, and all received their fair wages so that none went away dissatisfied."

Sur Sceaf said, "Including those three nearest to us, I count eight guards or overseers. Can we take them without raising an alarm is the question? I want to interrogate those workers. They would likely know the shortest way to the den of the emperor."

"Sure enough!" Starkwulf pointed out. "See how all of their attention is drawn to the slaughtered pig carcasses every time they pass through those membranous veils. The overseers are marking their books. Let's creep up, and as soon as they turn their backs on us, we could charge. It should be easy in all this noise and activity. I mean, I don't even see but one with a weapon."

"You don't think it would be better to pith them with a needle or an awl then?" Brekka asked.

"I considered that, but we don't know what the response of the captive labor will be," Sur Sceaf said as several booms rumbled from above.

"It will be favorable," Starkwulf told him. "Better they should see us do it than do it in secret or they might get blamed. Back in the days when I had a bull's flare for battle, I freed many a labor camp, and always they embraced me as their deliverer."

Sur Sceaf said, "Let's get them. Brekka, you take Ruhm and the lady knights around the concrete platform to attack from the side. Hit the guards sitting at the table next to the vat, you know, the ones filling out forms for the laborers. Starkwulf and I with my twelver will assail them on the platform. If the laborers should rise up, you will have our back. You Jokers, stay here until it's all over."

Charly whispered, "But...but—I could club..."

"No argument, Charly."

The various factions dispersed and took up their positions, signing that they were ready. Sur Sceaf with Strarkwulf, Va-Eyra, and his twelver following two by two, crept up to the platform and watched momentarily. As the swine carcasses swinging on their hooks from above came up to what looked like some glassy strips of leather, it halted momentarily while the overseers inspected each one. Sometimes, they would turn it to one side and then the other and then wave for the laborer to move it along the overhead track.

As soon as the overseer with the spear turned his back, Sur Sceaf gave a whip-poor-will's call, and his compeers charged. He hacked the head off of the one with the weapon, went for the next who was just turning up from his book, and ran his sword through his throat, turned to the other only to see Va-Eyra had already run him through. Brekka, Ruhm, and Freyxus finished off the others. In less time than it takes to tie eight calves for branding, the overseers were all dead and bleeding on the sidewalks.

Gradually, as the word spread, all work came to a screeching halt.

The captives did not know what to do or expect. The ones within sight of the takeover just stared dumbfounded the thought crossed Sur Sceaf's mind that they might have some binding loyalty to the captors, like the Huskers and Dominikers, but, as they stared at him, their empty faces reflected they were just stunned and bone weary of endless labor. The light of life had all but been extinguished in them, and only their ox-like stares and dropped jaws greeted him.

Ruhm asked, "Are you Hickoryan?"

One of the laborers, a big lout, spoke up but mumbled it out, "We are."

With a nod from Sur Sceaf, Ruhm continued on. "We have come to set you captives free."

The Hickoryan workers looked at each other, but remained silent.

"My lord," Ruhm said, "look at their eyes. They appear to be drugged."

Although he understood their lethargy, Sur Sceaf grew impatient. Time was pressing. He needed to get these laborers to safety in case these ceilings began crumbling under the explosions above. "Stop the flow of that blood," he ordered in his command voice. "Cease the slaughter of those pigs, and get into that tunnel over there by those tables."

When the laborers hesitated, Brekka, Freyxus, and Verushka nudged them forward past a long alley of pens and into the tunnel ahead where they waited for further orders. Sur Sceaf sent his twelver lieutenant, Heruwer, ahead to reconnoiter the tunnels, while the rest of the twelvers scouted out a dormitory they discovered adjacent to the abattoir. Sur Sceaf darted his head through the veil of the abattoir, which he found to be composed of some see-through gossamer cloth that had the texture of smooth leather. Everywhere he looked, there were swine carcasses hanging, and the room itself was unseasonably cool. After a thorough visual examination of the area, he determined it was an ice house for storing the meat before it was cut and packed for use by the cooks, similar to a Herewardi abattoir.

It wasn't long before Horst Longchin, sub-lieutenant of the twelver, returned to report, "My lord, the dormitory has forty sleeping laborers. What is your wish? Shall we guard them here?"

"Bring them."

"But, my lord, won't they slow us down or even impede us?" Horst was a descendent of a Quailor, who had fought under Ludwig Hollar and his mother was the daughter of a mountain giant from the mount hood area where every one of their red haired race was a head taller than any other tribe of humans. Horst was strong enough to tear a person limb from limb, but was so gentle of nature that his aggressiveness only appeared in battle or amongst enemies. It was said he was the only man known to be able to control the wolf-rage of the beserker lurking within him and all those who had chosen the path of the shield biters took his counsel in ernest.

"I'd rather have them with us than behind us where they can raise the alarm. I'm waiting to find a box chamber where we can corral them while we complete our expedition. Tell everyone to light their torches again and continue following the stick figure signs. Stop when you reach Heruwer's position and follow his direction."

Horst hurried off to obey the orders and Starkwulf signaled Sur Sceaf with a loud whistle to hurry over to the edge of the cement dock.

Starkwulf was bent over some boxes. He looked up and said, "This is rat poison, my lord. If we add it to the vat, we can kill those demons and be done with the matter. Solves the problem of fighting them and keeps the Hickoryan folk safe, like you mentioned."

Sur Sceaf thought for a moment. "Once again, the inestimable Starkwulf comes through. Brilliant plan, Wulfie. Let's get it started."

Together the two took the several boxes of rat poison, laid it on the platform above the vat of hot blood, broke the cakes up finely and swept them into the vat and stirred them in with the long wooden paddles, which had been tossed aside by the workers. They repeated the process until they were sure there was enough poison to kill all the were-bats and then some.

Va-Eyra came up and said, "What on earth are you two doing?"

"Your brilliant husband found rat-poison. We're poisoning those damned were-bats and hoping it gets them all."

"Well, I don't know about brilliant. Once he almost poisoned me by putting too much ergot in the dwale. But I must admit I felt like a god for several days afterward."

Laughing, Sur Sceaf felt for the button that drained the vat, and the poison was soon racing to the famished were-bats below. "We've done all we can do here. Let us press on."

As they reached the tunnel, they found the twelvers herding the last of the sleepy laborers up the incline. Along with Starkwulf and Va-Eyra, Sur Sceaf found his way to the head of the caravan.

Brekka was talking to several of the wide-eyed laborers and explaining to them what the wyrm-kats were, and not to fear. She petted Chloe on the back to demonstrate their harmlessness to a friend.

"It is done," Sur Sceaf proclaimed to Brekka and the others, "praise the gods, we poisoned the bastards." He paused and took a deep breath. "Now that the were-bats are taken out of the equation, we can rest a lot easier. I assume that the powder they were pouring into the blood was some sort of drug and something that keeps them fairly subdued and also keeps the blood from coagulating. We simply added the poison to the mix."

Brekka said, "Fa, these captives were taken from labor camps when they were but tender children and brought here to work." Brekka's eyes filled with compassion. "They report that Angrar sends them the orders, and the Pitters make sure they do it. They raise pigs, chickens, rabbits, eggs, and mushrooms for the Pitters and the priests of Angrar. They live, work, and sleep here below ground and only go up for sun one hour one day a week."

With this intelligence, Sur Sceaf felt a driving compulsion to find the emperor and his vile priesthood and crush the serpent's head. After all, he had to assume this generational plague of Pitters would in all likelihood be wiped from the Ea-Urth. He was convinced the longer the Syr Folk stayed down here in the caverns the more the serpent's coils were wrapping around them. All he could think to say as he turned to the captives was, "How do we get to the emperor?"

Brekka repeated the question to the portly, lummox, who didn't look all that different from some of the oxen Sur Sceaf had plowed with in the fields of his youth, and whom he considered might even be as slow of wit. "Can you show us where Hryre Seath abides?"

The rotund man with ox eyes and a bloody, full length white apron covering his front, said, "I'll show you where the emperor lives. I'm glad you killed the Pitters. Our Dominicker friend, Tom Tom, taught us to hate Pitters and to resist our bondage."

"What name do you go by?" Sur Sceaf asked.

"Donny Laer. I was enslaved by the Pitters at nine years old. The bastards sent the rest of my family to other labor camps, and me underground to tend chickens, rabbits, and now hogs and drogs."

"Donny," Sur Sceaf said, as he rummaged through his backpack for some parchment to draw upon. "Please, what is the fastest way to get to the emperor?"

"Two more levels up," the ox of a man said. "I can show you. You won't need to sketch it. But I've only been there twice. Nice cozy place the emperor has, he and his favorite Dominikers and priests."

Sur Sceaf re-geared. Donny suddenly seemed more intelligent, and Sur Sceaf had to briefly chastise himself for pre-judging him as a dumb ox, for this had to be a place of throttled emotion and willed dumbness just to stay alive.

After warning everyone to go into stealth mode and be as quiet as possible, they followed Donny as he led them to a narrow opening cut into the right wall of the tunnel.

"This is a short cut to the next level." He pointed to a spiraling staircase.

Sur Sceaf exchanged looks with Starkwulf, who nodded. He nudged Donny quietly, "Lead on."

CHAPTER 9 :
THE SPIRAL STAIRWAY

AS DONNY LUMBERED UP A WINDING metal stairway ahead of him, the noise of his heavy step louder than that of a stalker, Sur Sceaf was not sure whether the pig odor was coming from Donny or if something even more foul and sickening laid ahead. The stairway ended at a gate on the next level. Donny opened the gate and led them into a broad limestone chamber much the same as the ones below.

Sur Sceaf called a halt and waited until the last of the laborers had entered. Ruhm and the Jokers brought up the rear. Ruhm secured the gate behind them. Sur Sceaf decided that before moving on, he needed to ask Donny what lay ahead. And besides, many of the laborers appeared to be flagging, like they were in sore need of a rest. In fact, many had already found places to sit against the walls and instantly fell asleep sitting up.

Frowning, Leroy glanced around before saying, "Beg pardon, Sur Sceaf, but I'm gettin' mighty confused here. First, you're in a yank to hurry, makin' us run through these tunnels like weasels chasing a rat, and now you're takin' your good ol' time, slow as a molasses in winter. Which is it?"

Sur Sceaf smiled at the boy. "You're right, Leroy, we are in a hurry, but we need to have a care for these poor souls, and besides, they have valuable information that we could glean from nowhere else. In fact, I suspect their knowledge of these caverns will put us leaps and bounds ahead of ourselves."

Scratch was suddenly agitated, his hackles up. Mauser and Chloe instantly assumed a pouncing position. "Scratch smell fly men here. No like! Kill Fly Men."

Brekka pointed. "Are those more were-bats on the ceiling?"

She flashed her shield up on the ceiling only to see a great stir moving like a wave across the ceiling. Something looked down at them like the heads of large foxes hanging upside-down and emerging from some sort of leather sacks.

"It's alright," Donny said as he placed his hand to force Brekka's shield down. "No need to disturb them."

"But there are were-bats up there," she exclaimed in a whisper.

"These are the fruit eaters," Donny explained. "Pitters call them drogs. They're only used to carry the commissars from place to place. Harmless and easy to command."

Va moved to the Kats' side. "Stand down, Scratch. These fly men no hurt Ketten or Top Cat and friends."

Scratch stared upward. "No trust Fly Men. Eat Blood."

"No, no, these Fly Men eat fruit. Friend Donny says they are safe."

The ketten relaxed somewhat, but still twitched and held their ears back, a sign they weren't fully convinced.

Donny bent down until he was eye-to-eye with Scratch. "Believe me, Scratch, these bats do not bite kats or people." Straightening, he said, "Now the ones below, the black ones with the long tongues, they're the ones who drink blood and bite kats and people. You have to be very careful around them. The Pitters call theme Gyrlocks. Even when we feed them pig flesh, they can be dangerous. See." He pulled what looked like a small flute out of his pocket. "We have to carry these when we feed them raw flesh. Else wise they would feed on us. But one blast from this whistle, and they flee back. Seems their ears are too sensitive. Otherwise, you have one hell of a mean Gyrlock to fight off. Then they're all teeth, tongues, and talons."

He held up his right forearm to show a series of puckered scars. "How I got these. Be particularly careful of that tongue though. If'n they weasel it down your throat, it'll suffocate you. At the same time, they can lock their teeth over your mouth. No way to free yourself from that kiss o' death. They just lap up any blood they can get. That's why they call the black ones their war-bats. They have been breeding them for war for the past twenty years. Why we are raising so many pigs. Before that they only had a few gyrlocks that were fertile at most. Found they needed fresh kill to make them breed. And then, did they ever breed! That's why some of them left the caverns here and live in caves throughout the land. The only way the Pitters could protect themselves was with these whistles."

"Have you any more of those whistles?" Sur Sceaf inquired.

"You mean you don't have any?" Donny scrunched his face in disbelief. "How in Joa's name, did you get through them then?"

"We are warriors, and, no, we don't have any whistles," Sur Sceaf explained, "This is the first we've encountered the war-bats underground or as we've been calling them, were-bats. We could sure use some of those flutes if you have them."

"Follow me." Donny went to a cabinet next to the cave wall, which had several wooden boxes of the metal whistles. Donny reached into an open box and started passing out the flutes to Sur Sceaf's twelver and Brekka's twelver.

As Sur Sceaf examined the flute-like instrument, he said, "So the gyrlocks below are not the only ones. You said there are other camps?"

Donny looked at him for a long moment. "Yes, but not many. Just escapees."

Freyxus said, with her usual curiosity. "So, if we just blow on these, the gyrlocks retreat."

Donny nodded, "That's right, lady. They can't stand the noise, but we never use them on the fruit-eaters. The fruit-eaters are gentler and smarter. They take word commands."

Freyxus appeared fascinated. "What kind of commands?"

"Fly north. Fly south. Carry. Rest.'

"I've watched and listened to them getting trained whenever I feed them."

"Very interesting," Sur Sceaf said. "I saw these larger brown drogs actually carry a man. Otherwise, I wouldn't have believed it."

Donny looked up at him with an exhausted look on his face. Sur Sceaf had no idea how long the man had been working. "They also carry supplies, weapons, and even small livestock."

"How do you summon them?" Verushka asked.

"The Pitters use different commands for different groups of bats, 'Hobb,' is one of the three strongest fliers. 'Jill,' is the call used to summon several of the females, which they use to spot runaways in the night. 'Molly,' is the call they use for the white smaller fruit collectors when they want them to follow the drogs in foraging so as to glean. Fact is, those 'Mollys' can strip an orchard in a night, while the farmers are none the wiser for it. It's what the Pitters call double-dipping, and why the tax collectors demand that every orchard be registered."

"Why do they call it double-dipping?" Starkwulf asked.

Donny winced in thought. "It's a government trick. They don't ever strip the fruit until right after taxation. That's often why the rdokian mountain folk get blamed for stealing. In any case, just use the right call, and the drogs will come to do your bidding."

Sur Sceaf considered they must be similar to the wyrm-kats and had human seed code implanted in them for such a high level of intelligence. They were simply another variety of trans-humans. Else, why the human hands, feet, and pronounced forehead.

"Will they come to anyone's bidding?"

"They are always eager to do your bidding, because they know it means they get a special treat. Usually peaches or plums, but paw paws are their favorite. We have called them in before, and they always come. You say *'Ride up'* if you want to go to the surface, but I do not know how to command them to any particular place for I don't know any particular place like the commissars do."

Freyxus asked, "Has anyone ever tried to take them away from the bastion besides the commissars?"

"Usually only some of the red and orange-clad commissars, and a few black-clad priests and Hryre Seath use them. They often go for great distances. My friend Tom Tom, reported that he stole rides several times and to exotic places as far as the drowned lands. Said he rode most of the night. I heard Overseers talking about how the commissar, Linconkudder, just returned from a trip to Charleston to give orders for the legions there to march north and delivered medicine to stop the plague before it spreads. They also said, before that, Linconkudder was in Gettisbuhr, then came back by horse disguised as Hryre Seath so the emperor could ride back here on his personal drog."

"That explains why Hryre Seath got here before Brekka and Wilona," Va-Eyra observed.

"Sometimes, the drogs don't return for days, but several work shifts ago, I overheard the chief overseer say to Scolopendra, the commissar in charge of all the caverns, that they were real curious about a group of women camped out on the hill above the Big Springs. I suppose they were spying on them, only they couldn't set foot on what they called the kings' mound, on account of the great fear of heathen wraiths. So guess that's why they sent out a flight of drogs to grab the one they thought was the leader. Whitest person I've ever laid eyes on, and we get pretty white down here with no sunlight."

Without warning, a trembler struck. Debris fell from the cavern above and the brown were-bats all stirred with a network of screeches and screams. Some flew off and then re-jostled and fought for perch space once again.

Donny's eyes widened with fear. Brekka calmed him with a hand to the shoulder. "That explosion was Lord Arundel up above, striking with the boom sticks again. He's attempting to breach the Pitters sealed tunnels, which is why it was so important to get you out of the big cavern."

"So that's what's happening up there," Donny said. "They never tell us much. We play dumb, and just catch and patch what we can."

Freyxus looked Donny square on. "The explosions are probably the only way for us to breach those sealed compartments. Should also keep the commissars from knowing we are here. Wouldn't you say?"

"Not likely," Donny said scratching his close shaven head. "You could bomb them until the chickens stop laying, and you wouldn't make a dent in their command center. It was built to take a lot more abuse than anything this generation has. Tom told me it was built by the Amerikans to resist aerial attacks from their flying machines; also heard that from the overseer. And what you probably need to know, is they can practically see everywhere."

"What?" Sur Sceaf said, stepping forward believing he had misheard. "How can they see everywhere?"

"When I's young, it took a long time for me to figure that all out, but they knew any time I was slackin' in my work." He pointed up to an object on the tunnel walls. "See those cans up 'er on them walls. Those are their eyes. Probably gawking at us right now. That is lest you're keeping them distracted with all that bombing above. But the fact is, they may not be watching on this shift. Most of the guards be sleepin' during these hours. Then they'd never 'spect you comin from below. I didn't even know you could do that. Knew they had those square elevator tables down below, for taking us out in the sun and for depositing troops, but those require a special password to even operate."

"So they've possibly been watching us all this time?" Freyxus exclaimed. "Aren't you afraid of what they might do to you?"

"Not anymore, miss. I'm numb now. Have been ever since las' year. I'm no better than a plough ox, never had much of a life like I heard Tom Tom talkin' bout. My childhood wif my family is the only time I reckon I was ever truly alive. This place, as you can see, is nothing more than a livin grave. If it t'wern't for my pa who was a schoolmaster and taught me readin', writin' and 'rithmetic early on, I'd be as ignorant as the others. Most of them don't have any home-learnin' at all. Tom Tom said it was a good thing to know book learnin', but I ain't never found much use for it down here. Fact is I sometimes feel like I'm two men in one body. Like sometimes I talk like my pa, and sometimes I talk like the folks down here."

Brekka knitted her brows. "But surely, blasts that make the rocks shake at this level must be making some impression on those commissars." Brekka took off her helm and wiped the dust and grit from her neck with her swan scarf. "Sort of cracking their armor. Don't you think?"

"Yeah, it don't make no difference to them." Donny shook his head. "They're sealed tighter than a box turtle in that chamber. Not likely your men above are having much of an impact on them either. Save it might keep them from looking down here at us." He smiled a vacant smile, like that of a man when he's too exhausted to face the next problem. "But like I said, Miss, I know a way in."

Brekka seemed to remember something. "They had the same far-seer eyes in a can in the citadel. I know what to do. Hold your torch up, Freyxus."

As Freyxus held her torch up, Brekka reached into the center of her shield, the metal transmuted, then as she turned the iridium side towards the far-seer cans on the cavern wall, one by one a glob of light issued from the shield and a loud pop followed by sparks trailed down the cavern walls like hot dripping wax.

"Now that is a curious weapon you have there, lady." Donny's eyes were wide open. "That settles that, they can't see us anymore, but we best be watching. They'll send Pitter police down here with their shock sticks to punish us, and they have that sickening yellow smoke, too."

"Smoke?" Sur Sceaf asked. "What kind of smoke?"

"Saw it used once, when we tried to break out of here, because they wouldn't allow us to eat meat anymore. Said they had to have the meat for their war-bats and legions fighting in the hills." He shook his head at the memory. "That's when they took my friend Tom Tom Hardy away. It was seven winters ago. Tom Tom organized us to try and make a break, so we could flee to the rdokian mountain folk for help. The commissars have always feared the rdokians for their wild fierceness and unpredictable attacks. Tom said, even if the mountain folk would sooner cut your hand off than shake it, they were a hell of a lot nicer than any Pitters, and would give you a fair shake at life, if'n we were to 'scape here. But I can 'member that dread day like it was yesterday. As we approached the commissars' chamber they shot out that sickening yellow smoke at us. Tom Tom said it was a poison gas. Next thing I knew, we woke up back in our level, and no more Tom Tom. You see the gas makes you sleep. You can't breathe it without sleeping."

"So how do we get into the emperor's chamber without them gassing us?" Sur Sceaf asked.

"I saw the gas coming out of a green pipe, and when I went up for my sun day, I noticed the green pipe went into a large black tank up above on the quarry wall. If your man up above could cut that pipe off, they would have no means of smoke-gassing us, cause that's their only source."

Sur Sceaf was confused. "How in hell's name, do we get a message to Arundel to cut the green pipe? Anybody got any ideas?"

"It's plain to see, one of you is going to have to fly out of here and tell him," Donny said, his dark sunken eyes making him look even more ghoulish against his doughy skin in the torch light as another series of explosions went off above.

Something in Donny's speech signaled to Sur Sceaf that this man was to be trusted and that his dullness came from a life of hopeless drudgery underground, rather than a weakness of wit.

Sur Sceaf looked around before asking, "Then why haven't you ever tried escaping by way of the drogs?"

"I give it some thought, but after our first attempt they said they would cut a foot off if we tried again, and we didn't know where to flee to once Tom Tom was gone. You see, Tom Tom was a Dominiker's son."

"Hold on a moment. They put Dominiker children down here?"

Donny nodded, "Like all Dominiker children who are disobedient, they get sent here, cause they'd be killed in the regular labor camps. Tom was ashamed that his pa had become a Dominiker and that he had to leave and shun his Hickoryan friends. Nevertheless, he knew lots more freedom than we were ever accustomed to. He even knew where the mountain folk lived. Knew the mountain witches, cause his mother was the daughter of one. He even formed a trading link with them and the ghost market. He used to smuggle piglets, chickens, and rabbits out of here to build up a supply of gold solidus. But if we escaped now, we wouldn't even be able to find our old homes. We'd be lost wif out Tom."

"What more can you tell us about getting into the emperor?" Brekka inquired.

Donny lifted his hanging jaw to speak. Tom Tom told us about the strange people; the ones that live in the command center and cannot be approached by anyone except the emperor, Katus, and a few special commissars like Scolapendra. And he said the people of Angrar are guarded by hellish beasts that could rip a pig apart like a cat rips a rat asunder. They called them Tyfons."

"Tyfon!" Sur Sceaf repeated. "We've already dealt with their kind."

Donny said, "I wouldn't know. Tom said they are larger than four bears, have claws like a badger, and a head that's sheer muscle. Not to mention teeth that could smash a boulder, and one hell of a howling hunger to boot. Beware! Cause he told me they were made from ancient beasts, called Bone Crushers. And said these monsters were equal to ten bears in strength."

"And how do we pass them?"

"Don't know." Donny shrugged. "Never seen 'em! Do know that one of the other shifts was called to remove a dead one the other day. They said it took their whole shift to cut it up and take the meat to the gyrlocks. And little chuck said the beast was enormous. Freakiest thing was they found a man's hand in its stomach."

"If it's any consolation," Freyxus said, "Sur Sceaf, I have several beast stoppers in my pack. Combined with yours, I'll bet we could knock them out."

Brekka said, "Good thinking. Hold on to them. It sounds like we're going to need them soon enough. Get some out and put them in my pack."

"As you wish." The tall blond procured them from her rucksack.

Va-Eyra inquired, "Don, did they say what the beast died of?"

"Name's Donny, Miss." He shrugged his shoulders. "Don't know. Chuck said a witch killed it."

Sur Sceaf chuckled, looked over at Va-Eyra, "Witchy woman."

She smiled, and Starkwulf said, "Maybe you should be the one to ride out of here on the bat broom."

"You don't want to know what I'd do with that broom if I had one now." She scowled. "Probably be swatting some smart asses."

Donny scrunched his face with a confused look.

But Sur Sceaf contemplated Donny's words. Something in the way Freyxus looked, struck him that she was the one to send up. "Freyxus, do you want to be our champion? How do you feel about bats?"

The tall blond shook her silken hair as if to rid it of something nasty, "Normally they give me the damned creeps, but I'll do anything for the welfare of Syrdom, my lord and King."

"Alright Donny," Sur Sceaf said. "Fetch Freyxus one of those drogs down here; and Freyxus, be careful to avoid the archers above. They won't know it's you until you signal to them. For Freya's sake, they won't be expecting any were-bats at midday either, so hopefully you'll be alright."

Freyxus finished placing the beast stoppers in Brekka's pack. She stood tall and looked like she was breathing deep while looking up at the ceiling, no doubt to build her courage to take flight on bat wings.

Donny walked over to a side chamber covered by the strange membranous film they had seen before, and came back out with a hand full of fruits. He called out, 'Hobb.' No sooner had he shouted than three sturdy brown batmen appeared hovering above them. Mighty gusts of wind hit the warriors. Soon one landed. Sur Sceaf could see it stood about eight feet tall, muscular, and sleek as a race horse on nettle.

The stocky ox-like man ordered, "*Land*," and soon the other two landed. They looked like men with a fox's face and settled on man-like feet with hooks on their heels. They wrapped themselves in a beautiful mahogany cape of wings crisscrossed over their chests.

Donny touched the first one that landed and motioned with a quick limp hand upward to the others, who flew back to their camp on the ceiling. Va was compelled to take the Were-Kats a ways off, as Scratch was showing very aggressive posturing, and snarling.

The winged beast stood two heads higher than Donny, showed absolutely no aggression, but utterly dwarfed Freyxus, when its wings spread out it looked utterly formidable.

Freyxus approached the drog donny called Hobb with hidden trepidation. "Is there anything I shouldn't do or anything that would possibly spook this beast."

Donny frowned. "Only thing occurs to me is dogs. Seems a commissar got thrown off when a pack of dogs treed 'em. Otherwise, Hobb here is gentle as a lamb. 'Specially when he knows there's a treat in store for him."

"It doesn't have a saddle. How do I mount?"

"You become one with him. Put your feet here at the base of the wing. Sort of like a leather stirrup and put your arms around his neck and hold on to his fur. It doesn't hurt him, and he doesn't seem to mind either."

Freyxus followed his instructions. The soft fur of the creature enveloped her in warmth like her mother's fox fur coat. A memory she had repressed percolated up through cracks in her soul. A memory of her mother wearing that very coat on the day the Pitter legion overcame the settlements in the white forest of Zamora. She remembered the blood soaked coat and the Pitter spear sticking through her mother's back. Horrors echoed in her mind as she thought about the horrible treatment she and her people received in the colosseum of frisco after their capture. She remembered all the flesh hunts and animal contests of the arena, and the obscene disregard for human life in the decadent circus where she had to witness men, women, and children, none too few relatives, torn by the teeth of beasts, the death screams of which still haunted her mind and invaded her sleep. Nor were those men, women, and children strangers to her in any way. In fact, many were her childhood playmates, kith and kin. With Freya's help, she had managed to triumph over overwhelming odds and certain death, much to the chagrin of her Pitter tormenters. Surely, she could ride this winged beast that seemed so strong, yet so gentle, like a well-seasoned horse.

"What's it like?" Brekka asked. "Are you alright? Are you sitting comfortably, Freyxus? Is this doable for you?"

"It feels strange," she said. "But definitely doable." She glanced at Sur Sceaf. "This I do for you, my king. I don't want you to forget it."

Sur Sceaf smiled warmly at her. "I have every confidence that you will succeed. You are, after all, your father's daughter. The blood of the Great Aethelstan be with you."

"And the blood be with you!"

Suddenly, from the corner of her eye she caught sight of Ruhm approaching. "Damn, lady, you do us proud! Not one in a thousand would be so daring."

His smile warmed her heart, but before she could answer, Donny instructed. "When you are ready to go, touch his right ear and say '*ride up*.' You can steer by saying '*left, right,*' or the four directions, then '*ride up*' or '*ride down*'." He looked with a childlike expression in his brown eyes and said, "Have you got it?"

"I've got it," Freyxus said. She took a tighter grip on the thick fur of his chest with one hand and touched his right ear with the other. "*Ride Up*." She felt his frame arch and bow under her before launching into the air. The drog's enormous wings expanded and grabbed air like a sail drinks wind. As they lifted off the ground, she felt the same sensation she once felt leaping from a ledge into the wind of a grassy hillock of Zamora. It also reminded her of her pony ride when her father, Aethelstan plopped her on the back of Wind Striker, her first fjord pony.

She had ridden the fjord with ease. It was second nature to her. It had been a fated event. It was shortly after her eighth birthday when she had gone to the training camp where her father was instructing young bloods in horsemanship. She was intrigued, and insisted on joining him as he put the boys through their rigorous training. So her Fa had a full sized mare saddled for her, and from that day on, she proudly rode at her father's side. By age fifteen she already knew she would become a lady knight, and had heard about her cousin twice removed, named Brekka, who had been given the first designation of lady knight since the days of the famous sword toting Lady Myra-El.

Eighteen of her twenty brothers had ridden off to war with her father along with the rest of the men above age fourteen, leaving Zamora for the Isle of Ilkchild where the Pitters were expected to attack. But contrary to their intelligence, an unexpected legion of Vardropi dropped into their virtually defenseless settlement. The rest of her family, two younger brothers and eighteen sisters, the youngest who was only two years of age, had been taken captive with her to the colosseum. After she had won her freedom from the colosseum she made her way to Stonyford, only to learn from her Brother Stanfax that her father had been given the death-eagle by a Vardropi leader in the now legendary battle of the ceiba grove where it is said he walked the crow post.

As her winged steed gracefully flew through the large cavern, she realized that what drove her to survive everything was her planning of the wrake and vengeance she would wreak on the bastards who had killed her family in Zamora and in the Frisco Colosseum. Now was the great day of that vengeance. She recalled the prophecy of Elrus that Woon would send aid on the wings of darkness.

The lift and the swoosh of the wings was both exhilarating and terrifying. Swift horse rides, diving from towering cliffs into pools of clear mountain water flashed through her mind, but nothing was comparable to this pleasure of being above the powers of the ground. Nothing had ever been this stirring to her blood. Unless it was the first time she laid eyes on the young Custus Ruhm Lee. Not only was he the handsomest Young Blood she had ever seen, but sheer masculinity oozed from every part of his well-built body. *Oh Ruhm, will you ever take serious notice of me? Or will I always be hidden in the shadow of Brekka.* She had seen him rock Brekka in his arms, and each time she wished it had been her.

She cuddled up to the beast and surprisingly felt as if they were one. Despite the initial terror, every feeling inside was uplifting and joyful.

As the drog climbed on the wind, she looked down on Sur Sceaf, his men, and her fellow lady knights as though they were mere toy soldiers and dolls below her. Her soft ride carried her some four plough lengths through the eerie light of the great chamber and then into a wide dark hole that became total, pitch darkness. She was only conscious of the steady swoosh of the wings grabbing for air and the constant sensation of lift and wind on her face. Careful not to cling too tightly around the hobb's neck, she looked up and saw the stars. They were brilliant gems against a velvet dark backdrop. According to her calculations it must be late morning, but who can know when underground? In the caverns she had no concept of what time it really was without consulting the water clock, nor could she guess how many hours had passed beneath the earth.

She listened to the rhythmic swoosh of the wings, until first twilight appeared above and then suddenly, she was launched out into the brilliant sunlight of early morning and marveled that in the dark tube they had come up through, she could see the stars, yet here above the ground, it was already bright dawn.

Looking down, she saw as far afield as Bender's Woods and the sprawling Hospitaler camp with its tidy rows of tents, horse corrals and busy nurses in their grey frocks. To her left bulged the kings' mound with all its dolmans and menhirs arranged in circular orders. In the green lap of Big Springs the Cerulean ballooners were readying their multicolored balloons for launching. Upon the promontory ranged the fyrds, calvary, and dog soldiers up and ready for action. Below in the enormous stone bastion, she saw the glorious spread of Arundel's armies in their various formations, arranged throughout the fortress in full battle array. Just like Sur Sceaf's Twelver, they resembled moving toy soldiers below her. A trumpet blasted, and Syr Folk archers ran along the walls like fast scurrying squirrels. She knew instantly that the archers perceived her as a threat. "*Fly up*," she commanded as the leathery wings of the Horse-Bat scooped up the air and pulled them ever higher. "*Wings away, my mighty air-horse! Wings away!*"

"*Up, Hobb*," she ordered. Instantly with a soft chortle, the drog lifted her above the clouds, its warm eyes studying her for further direction. She wondered if these creatures were capable of speech like the wyrm-kats, but every indication was that they were mute to human speech.

Below, through the white haze of the clouds, she saw the vast and colorful quilt of farmsteads, forests, and pastureland. In the village called pikeside, she noticed a young boy asleep on a hill overlooking a grassy pasture. What a sight it would be if he were to awake and look up.

Here in the light, the mere sensation of flight was both breathtaking and thrilling. She had to suck in air and could not refrain from yelling for joy at the sheer pleasure of airborne freedom, and the feel of her long blond hair streaming behind her. Hobb chortled with what she took to be commensurate joy.

The stone bastion grew smaller like some sort of contorted stone box, but everywhere around her were the soft cottony clouds, some swelling to mighty columns of sun brilliant white tree shapes, and others spreading into soft carpets of brilliant snow white sheets, there in the pastures of the sun, the moon, and the stars. And as they passed through a cloud she wondered what a night flight must look like.

"*Right*," she commanded. They circled like a dove in the sky until she saw the swan banner of Arundel emerging from the gate house below and knew Arundel had now been alerted to her presence. She gave a laugh. "Hah, Ary, there you are. My little stool pigeon, it's me Freyxus. I'm not an enemy. Point those arrows at someone else, and let me know when it's safe to land. Here I come. Such a messenger pigeon you have never received before." She giggled, causing the drog to turn his head questioningly to see what she was doing.

"*Down, Hobb*," she ordered, and felt the thrill of dropping through the clouds at arrow speed causing her to swallow her breath. Wind whipped through her hair and the patchwork scenes below grew progressively larger and larger. Once again, she gave the order, "*Right*." Hobb's mighty wings caught air like an umbrella as he circled just beyond what she figured to be an arrow's shot. Slowly she began to descend with alternate commands of "*Down*" and "*Right*."

She could now see the archers take their positions as the swan banner followed Lord Arundel to the top of the bastion wall, and as he looked up, she held her right arm up to the square while holding tight to the fur of her flying fox-horse steed and gave the sign of the dove. Gracefully, Hobb spiraled downward like the circular dance of a falling autumn leaf.

Lord Arundel was working out an alternate plan of attack in the gate house. Although the boom sticks showed little measured effect, he determined to keep the blasts going according to the plan until a more viable plan could be conceived and developed. Long Swan had just voiced his opinion that they should find a way to smoke the enemy out when they were shaken by the warning blast of the trumpets from the bastion walls.

"What now," he exclaimed, before hurriedly running out. He quickly shouted to Redelfis to take charge of the troops inside the courtyard below. He raced up the stairs to the parapet with Yellow Horse directly behind him, holding the swan banner high so that all troops knew the whereabouts of their commander at all times. If that were not enough, then certainly they could all see the black and white checkered clothes that the jester wore.

As Arundel reached the parapet he could see the archers were streaming out to take up their positions along the walls, their bows at the ready.

He looked to the sentries along the guard towers and they were signing, 'Above.' Looking up, he could see what looked like a large brown bird with a silver back circling above like a messenger pigeon before it lands.

As he and Yellow Horse struggled to catch their breath, the commander of his archers, Herewulf, ran to him with eyes wide opened. "Forgive me, my lord," Herewulf cried, "it's one of those were-bats. It flew straight up out of hell before we even had a chance to draw an arrow on it. Since they are not wont to fly in this bright day light, we did not think to guard the skies."

Arundel scanned the skies, and breathed hard before inquiring, "Herewulf, what is that silver thing upon the beast's back? Can you see any better than I?"

Herewulf put his hand over his eyes to shield them from the bright clouds and said, "By the gods, my lord, if my eyes are not tricking me, methinks it's a woman."

Arundel puzzled over it for a few moments. "A woman! I've never known the Pitters to use a woman for anything but breeding. Hryre Seath murdered his sister and bears an open hatred for all women. He would not deign to trust them."

Yellow Horse declared, "Only their papessa was ever capable of wielding power, and that was brief at best, and from then on the emperor is paranoid of any female."

"But what are we seeing here, then?" Herewulf puzzled. "It would be easier to tie a rope of water in a knot than for us to figure this out. To be safe we should shoot."

As Arundel continued to stare at the strange circling were-bat that was slowly descending, Yellow Horse exclaimed, "Look, my lord! That woman has blond hair. Ary, I know of no Pitters with blond hair or much hair at all for that matter. Sure as hell ain't no Hickoryan either. They don't let their women fight. Dominikers are known for shallow wives, but occasionally aspire to political positions. Must be a Dominiker?"

Arundel focused his sight then pondered for a moment. "If my eyes do not deceive me, she wears the silver armor of a lady knight. No Dominiker woman has ever been known to war."

"Probably some sort of demonic trick brought on by the dark elves," Herewulf offered. "Maybe they killed and skinned one of our lady knights and are parading her scalped hide and armor as a trophy. It's not unheard of, you know. Sort of letting us know they have won the battle underground and showing off their trophy like the emperor displayed his sister's brain from the parapet the other day."

"No, she's moving about. She's not dead," Arundel said. "If only my far-seer were here."

"I will send for him, my lord," Herewulf said quickly.

"No, just wait a moment. It looks as though she intends to land. Albeit ever so slowly."

After three more circles, Arundel detected the creature above had descended by another few hundred feet. "I can't tell but it appears she is signing."

"My lord," Herewulf said urgently, "the demon is within range of my best bowman now. Aelfwyn could shoot it down from here in a cinch."

"Patience, my man, for Os sake, have some patience." Arundel continued to shield his eyes and try to make out what was happening. "Signal your men to be ready, but not to fire and to lower their bows." He surveyed the terrain below. All his men were in battle formation and there was no sign of the Pitters.

"It doesn't appear that this is a strategy or some sort of distraction before an attack."

No sooner had he said this than the circling were-bat dropped lower. Now he could plainly discern its features. "By the god's, it's Freyxus. Drop your fire altogether men," Ary shouted. Look, she is giving the swan square with the sign of the dove. Only a Herewardi royal would know the sign of the dove. Stand down!"

Ary quickly returned the sign of the dove. Herewulf gave the signal to stand down for those who could not hear. The bowmen assumed an at-ease stance.

Ary watched as the creature stopped circling and the mighty winged-beast descended to where he stood. He marveled that Freyxus should have such excellent control over the demon that looked a good three heads taller than he.

Herewulf declared, "My lord, watch out, it's about to land."

Yellow Horse said, "It's one of those big brown bats, not the wicked black ones."

Arundel answered, "I suspect they are the Pitter's messengers; the very equivalent of our pigeons."

As the creature landed upon the wall, mighty gusts of wind blew his hair and evaporated the sweat from his face. The creature landed on the wall and retracted its umbrella like wings. It stooped down allowing Freyxus to dismount. She reached into her rucksack, withdrew a hand full of raisins and extended her hand to the tall winged beast. He nibbled until all the raisins were gone. "Thank you Hobb for bringing me here safely."

To Arundel's dismay, the were-bat burbled what seemed to be a pleasured response of some sort.

Freyxus said, "Os-Frith, Lord Arundel, I bear an urgent command to you from your father, the High King."

Arundel was still in shock, as he studied the mahogany-colored beast in awe and wonder. "And this creature is safe?" he asked.

"Absolutely, there are different races of were-bats. The black ones are the Vampyrs and are their War-Bats, the brown ones are their carriers. They call them drogs, and the white ones are fruit-gatherers called fruitys or mollys." She shook her head and smiled big. "My lord, I've got to tell you, you have no idea the joy of flight. For the few minutes I was up there, I was a god-woman being carried across the sky like Holy Mother Freya riding her chariot of flying-cats. It's more exhilarating than battle or anything I've ever experienced. I could float, I could soar, dive, whirl, fly up to great heights, and see as though I was standing atop Mount Elflohana and the clouds were all my pastures. By all the gods I love, I hope to have one of these flying foxes someday."

She reached inside her pocket, pulled out a prune and handed it to the beast as she stood there in what appeared to be utter rapture. Arundel noticed the creature's warm eyes were excited with joy as it handled the plum like a chipmunk, rolling it in its hands, and then nibbling at it delicately with its deer-like mouth.

Yellow Horse's eyes were big with wonder. "Does it have a name?"

Freyxus grinned. "His name is Hobb," she declared, patting the thick mahogany fur on his chest. As though the carrier understood, it bobbed its head.

Arundel said, "I'm eager to hear what's happening below. But that will have to wait. I'm sure you are here on pressing business."

"I am indeed," Freyxus said. "Hear me! For these are the king's words. 'I charge you to find a green pipe running out of a black tank and break it open with a boom stick. Beware of the poison gas it will emit.' I saw the tank upon my descent. It's over there on that quarry shelf." She pointed to the tank perched on the stone ledge to the east.

"It shall be done," Arundel declared. "Herewulf, find Going Snake, take three men with you, and scale that quarry wall to the black tank. Have Going Snake put a boom stick under the green pipe and light a long fuse. Make sure you get the hell out of there before it blows because it could belch poison smoke fumes likely as deadly as our beast stoppers."

"It shall be done, my lord," Herewulf declared before descending down the stairs to carry out his orders.

Freyxus held up her hand. "With your leave, my lord, I shall now return to the high king on the spirits of the wind."

"You have my leave, my lady, but before you go, tell me what's happening below."

"We have made our way up to the eighth level and freed some laborers, who are, even now, guiding us to the emperor's lair. Also, you no longer need to fear the Vampyr bats, as we believe we have poisoned the lot down below."

"Off with you, then, and may the gods be with you." He turned to Yellow Horse with a wide smile. "This, I've gotta see; a flying lady knight on a red air steed."

Arundel and the others watched with great interest as Freyxus re-mounted the flying-fox. After settling herself, she leaned forward, touched his right ear and ordered, "*Rise up*."

Immediately, the huge flying fox unfolded its huge wings like a fan and sprang into the air. Arundel felt the whoosh of air from its great wings as the carrier soared skyward, then spiraled down to disappear into the dark hole in the top of the pyramidal mound.

He turned to yellow horse, who stood with mouth agape, "Can you imagine what benefit these creatures could have for us if we commandeer them?"

"Well, if we do, I want to be the first one to take a ride, and I'd also be leery of holding any picnics under them."

Arundel laughed. "And from the looks of it, we'd have to keep them away from our orchards."

Sur Sceaf looked at the strange little cubicle, the moving room before him, and said, "Now Donny, you say this room will take us directly to the inside of the emperor's chamber?"

"It only holds four, but it will place you right into the kitchen that serves them. You'll likely run into two Pitter guards. Least wise, I ain't ever seen any more than three there at a time. They've trimmed down since the conflict. The others are the kitchen staff gleaned from the surrounding labor camps. Once you leave the kitchen area, you'll come out into the mess hall where the Pitters and the Dominikers sit to take their meals. Directly outside the mess hall, to the north, is the chamber of the Angrar's Special Arch-Envoys. I don't know their names and I've never seen them, but Tom Tom said his parents told him about them. They always remain aloof and make no contact with anyone but Hryre Seath, Katus, and the commissars, with but few exceptions. Where the Arch-Envoys are, is what the Pitters call the control center. To get in there, you must fight the Tyfons. You cannot hope to stop them with metal, blade, or spear. They are too strong, and they guard the entrance to the center, suffering none to pass or repass."

"Then how do the Pitters come and go?"

"I am told that they have the beasts chained and by pressing a button they can restrain the beasts until someone safely passes."

"Have you ever been to the command center before?" Brekka asked.

Sur Sceaf weighed her question, wondering if Donny was giving reliably accurate information.

Donny shook his head. "Never, but Tom Tom passed it once. He said it had big glass windows, but curtains screened it off from his view."

Sur Sceaf felt compelled to ask, "Tell me more of this Tom Tom. How is it he had so much access to the Pitters inner circles?"

"Tom Tom Hardy, son of a Dominiker, was highly favored by Rhoda Eckstein, one of the scientists that worked in the control center. He once told me that he believed Rhoda was secretly working to replace the Pitters with Dominikers. He believed she had gained the favor of Angrar in this, and Tom was unusually bright and found the favor of the Angrar. Seems Rhoda convinced the arch-envoys that the Pitters were too cruel, too rigid, and too difficult to retrain, but it was only what he called a conjecture." He cocked an eyebrow and said, "You know that word."

Sur Sceaf said, "We do."

"Tom Tom told us Arch-Envoys were very disturbed by the new revelations of Katus, and it greatly angered them that the Papessa had been killed. Somehow Katus was giving instructions that were contrary to that of Angrar, and he had gained too much favor with the emperor, so they couldn't overthrow him. Said he had power with the masses of the Pitters and that he claimed to commune face-to-face with the dark elves."

Sur Sceaf declared, "You needn't worry about Katus. We have killed him."

Donny had a look of utter amazement on his face. "That means Tom Tom was right. Katus was *not* immortal."

Brekka said, "This Tom Tom is starting to sound like a very smart man with some very good ideas."

"Smartest man I ever met," Donny agreed. "Rhoda told him he had great promise. Secretly gave him information 'bout how the world was in the days of the early Americans and said folks enjoyed far greater freedoms in those times. According to Tom Tom, she claimed she lived through ten generations of emperors, all of who married their sisters until the scepter of rule came down to Hryre Seath, who was told by Katus that if he would stay a spiritual eunuch, he would be the greatest emperor to ever rule. It wasn't difficult to convince him because he was jealous of his sister's favor with their parents anyway. Seems she always bested him, and he hated her with a murderous passion. But adding to the hatred, the emperor Kittim didn't care for Hryre Seath, who was too effeminate and subject to his frequent nervous fits that often sent him in to seizures writhing on the floor. So Kittim favored his little Papessa. Ever since the death of his sister, Hryre Seath has had a fear of women and homosexuals. That's why he didn't work well with the Vardropi as his parents were wont to do. Rhoda told Tom Tom that La Papessa was to marry her twin, Hryre Seath, at age eight, but when it was time, he killed her with a rock while they were fishing. Ever since, he imagines she's coming back to possess his soul, and had to summon Katus on several occasions to drive away her spirit."

Donny scratched his head and tweaked his lips to one side. He narrowed his eyes, as if concentrating, then said, "Tom Tom was restless; all unsettled. He wanted to set the world right again, but he was only one man and we laborers were of little, to no help. With one will against a universal will he became progressively more disturbed by all the oppression and hypocrisy he saw coming from the Pitters. Hoped to use us to break the might of the Pitters and said the Arch-Envoys were not really that impressive when you got to know them. He even smuggled books in for us to read and taught us like we were Dominikers. Under Rhoda's influence, he began to question the motives of the arch-envoys. One day, he confronted them directly about something or other, and that's all it took for him to lose favor, and so he was banished down below with us for three years of toil for punishment. Good Ol' Tom Tom! He could not be bent to the angrar's will like his parents. No siree!"

Sur Sceaf's curiosity was aroused. "I wonder if he's the same Tom Hardy that leads the Swamp Foxes at Wymouth?"

Donny appeared surprised. "Could be. Ain't nobody seen Tom Tom since we tried busting out of here."

Starkwulf glanced toward the moving room. "When shall we launch the attack, my lord?"

"If the loud blasts keep up, then we'll know Freyxus failed. But if it is a faint blast, it means Freyxus has conveyed my orders and has been successful in her mission."

"What do you mean, if Freyxus fails?" A feminine voice said from behind them.

Brekka turned and embraced Freyxus in a warriors grip. "You're already back!"

Freyxus smiled wide. "By the living gods, Brekka, it was the most beautiful experience of my life."

Sur Sceaf quickly walked over to her and said, "Did you relay the message?"

"I did. And the Lord Arundel is acting on it right away." Her face was ecstatic with joy and he contemplated how that winged ride could affect one so, only to remember Zschamillah's astonishment the first time she sat a horse and felt the glory of riding above the ground.

While they assessed their plan of attack and took stock of their weaponry, Brekka sat at the entrance to the moving room discussing Freyxus' flight while Starkwulf discussed with Donny how the government of freedom and liberty for all would be established after the downfall and destruction of the Pitter empire. "It would be best if you workers stayed here. We don't want to endanger you in the coming fight. When the enemy is defeated, we will come and free you."

Donny's eyes grew wide. "Are you saying all of us, we packers, shall be freed as well?"

Sur Sceaf smiled. "More free than when you were a boy on the farm of your parents in Falling Waters, Firginia."

Donny got a dreamy smile on his face. "Falling Waters, farm, freedom. Like my folks would say, 'Praise Joa'!" He paused for a long moment. "A man could do whatever he wanted. Free to move about at will. Free to say what one thought no matter who takes offense. At least, that's how Tom Tom and Rhoda described it."

Soon a muffled blast was heard. Sur Sceaf called Scratch over and placed a hand on his shoulder. "Scratch, I want you, Chloe, and Mauser to stand guard for us here. Watch the Hickoryan boys and these workers like you do the sheep. Let no harm befall them. We'll come and get you when you are needed."

Scratch's tail showed his pride with its twisting and jerking. "Scratch watch for Fly Men. Scratch protect the sheep. These not sheep!"

"Watch them like little brothers."

"I watch. They not little!"

Sur Sceaf turned to the Lazy Jokers. "I want you to wait here with Scratch until we come for you. Is that clear?"

Charly said, "But we want--"

"I don't have time to discuss this with you, Charly, I need you here with the kats, and to answer any questions these packers have."

Sur Sceaf motioned for all to get battle ready. He, Starkwulf, Va-Eyra, and Brekka determined they would go first, since the moving room only held four persons at a time. Sur Sceaf smiled, "Heruwer, you will bring up the rear. Guard the tunnel entrance, and make sure we are not ambushed from behind. Here we go, swords drawn, everybody ready for the kill. By the gods, I've waited so long for this day."

"Yes, my lord."

Sur Sceaf reached out and pressed the button with an up arrow. The click sounded dead to the touch so he pushed it several more times. Nothing happened.

"What's the matter?" Donny asked.

"The room is not moving. Did I press the wrong button?"

Donny leaned around and said, "Did you press this one?"

"Several times."

"I'll be damned," the ox of a man said. "They knew our plan. They shut power off to this el--e--vator."

Sur Sceaf fired back, "Think Donny, is there any other way to the command center?"

His broad face went dull, "I can't think of...wait a minute! There is one possibility. If we go up Service Tunnel G we can get to a service slider above. It's up one more level. It's where we exchange goods. There's room enough to put two at a time into the kitchen dock. Because they are not expecting any deliveries, no one should be there."

"Cheese weed, Donny!" Sur Sceaf exclaimed, "By all that is holy, what are we waiting for, let's get going."

With Sur Sceaf and Donny in the lead, they quickly raced through the access tunnel where they found another small dimly lit chamber. This chamber appeared to be hand chiseled. Along one wall were empty crates. On the floor were dehydrated spills of mushrooms and an occasional dried prune. Directly ahead was a large metal door approximately six feet wide by three feet high. Next to it was a metallic lever type device.

"This makes it work," Donny said, as he pulled down the lever. The door came down and a metal platform slid out with ease and only the slightest of sound. It was large enough to hold two men on their hands and knees.

Freyxus remarked, "It's like the sliding cutting board in my mother's kitchen."

Brekka said, "I think we could get three ladies in there at a time."

Va said, "And it's made of sturdy thick metal."

Sur Sceaf turned to Donny. "Tell me what can I expect when I get in there?"

Donny drew a hand across his brow. "You will open into a loading dock and directly before you will be the kitchen, and on the other side of the kitchen is the cafeteria. You will have to pass through the swinging doors to get into the kitchen, and there should be no more than two guards on duty. Occasionally there are four."

"What about the cooks and kitchen staff? Are they Pitters or captives?"

"They are all captives. No need to concern yourself with them. They won't resist you."

As the squad crowded around, Sur Sceaf inspected the interior, and then said, "Starkwulf and I will go first. The rest come in the order you are positioned. Heruwer, you and my twelver bring up the rear."

Sur Sceaf caught the look Brekka, Freyxus, and Va-Eyra exchanged with each other. Va-Eyra said, "If there is an ambush, you should not go first, my lord."

Brekka chimed in. "Let the three of us go instead."

Sur Sceaf frowned. "Your concern is noted, but I really need to spearhead this one."

Starkwulf grinned at his wife. "Don't worry Va, I'll take care of your baby brother."

With the others looking on anxiously, Sur Sceaf squeezed into the drawer on his hands and knees only to be pressed even tighter into it by Starkwulf's broad shoulders. He felt the cold metal of the box on his skin through the cracks in his vambraces.

Donny took hold of the lever and asked, "Ready?"

"Ready!" Sur Sceaf and Starkwulf replied in unison.

The box slid easily into the loading dock. It was a large concrete storage room. Along the wall to the left, it was lined with boxes of fruits and vegetables. The two adjacent walls were stocked with crates of produce. To one end, through a door with a glass window was the kitchen, as Donny had said it would be. The smell of cooking pork soup filled the air.

They climbed out of the loader and walked over to the kitchen doors. Through the small glass window, he could see the white-clad cooks going about meal preparations with the *clang* of pans and the *ring* of dishes. There he saw four Pitters sitting lazily at a table playing some sort of game using rocks. Starkwulf joined him and after a moment whispered, "I count twenty-one kitchen staff. None of them look as if they've ever seen the sun or lifted a sword in battle."

As he and Starkwulf stepped to the side of the window, he heard a *clunk* behind him. Turning he observed Brekka's brazen copper hair pop up like a jack-in-a-box, followed by her shield and helm, and then Va-Eyra, and Freyxus in turn. Sur Sceaf held his finger to his mouth in the sign of silence, and motioned for them to wait. In less than ten minutes all of the twenty-eight members of their war party had arrived on the dock where they hugged the wall behind Sur Sceaf.

Suddenly, the door burst open, and a fat cook unsuspectingly stepped inside. Sur Sceaf saw his eye whites show and his fleshy mouth start to form a scream. Instinctively, he struck the man over the back of his head with the pommel of his sword and watched the bald cook fall unconscious to the floor where Brekka and Freyxus dragged him to one side.

Sur Sceaf signed, 'Hard and Fast,' raised his sword high, and with Starkwulf at his side and the others lined in battle formation behind, they thrust through the doors in a stampede. The Pitter guards on the near side of the table sat frozen. Starkwulf severed one's head, and Brekka the other. Sur Sceaf ran his blade through the one on the opposite side of the table so fast it split the Pitter's tongue and came out the back of his head. Va-Eyra hurled her blade through the fourth one's chest as he attempted to stand. All the cooks scampered up against the wall and looked like mice in a corn crib when you flash a sudden light on them. They shook, quivered, and quaked in utter terror.

Sur Sceaf shouted, "We are here to kill Hryre Seath and set you free. We are not here to do you any harm. But if you send up any sort of alarm, be assured, we will kill you on the spot." He studied them for a moment, then said, "Everyone of you, get into the kitchen dock." He pointed and they filed off into the storage room like sheep into a paddock.

As soon as the doors closed behind the kitchen helpers, Starkwulf said, "We better strike fast, my lord. We don't know if they have some other means of warning that we are here."

Ruhm drew close to Brekka. "I'm right here if you need any backing Brekka."

Va-Eyra pressed against Starkwulf and said, "I've got your back, love."

Brekka followed. "And I've got your back, Fa."

Starkwulf and Sur Sceaf exchanged looks. Sur Sceaf commented, "With the ladies at our back, we've got this victory."

CHAPTER 10 :

IS THIS HE WHO CAUSED THE NATIONS TO TREMBLE?

SUR SCEAF'S HEART WAS POUNDING for joy at the thought of ending the life of Hryre Seath and thereby putting a final end to all the misery of the nations. Seared into his memory as clearly as the day it had happened was the time the Pitters had tortured him at the bottom of a pit and entombed him there in hopes of making him their eternal slave in the after life. Now the day of vengeance was at hand. The anticipation of finally collecting the long overdue debt ran like a streak of raw fury through his entire being.

They sprinted through the empty cafeteria, then down the corridor in the direction of the control center. They turned a corner and ran into a rat pack of Pitters charging with spears. At least they looked like spears, but, in reality, were some sort of dragon's breath. He shouted, "Shields!" just in time to be met by a wall of flames like a blast from a steel furnace that singed his beard and the hair of his head sticking out from beneath his helm. At his side, Starkwulf was putting out a fire in his own beard, but it appeared they had taken the brunt of the flames, sparing all those behind them the lick of flames.

Brekka grabbed Sur Sceaf by his breastplate and shouted, "Let me to the fore, Fa. My shield will turn the tide in our favor."

"Be careful!" Sur Sceaf ordered as he stepped to the side to let her and Ruhm pass.

She squeezed by as Va-Eyra continued to beat out some flames dancing over Starkwulf's surcoat. With shouted curses, the Pitters sent forth another blast, but this time, when it struck Brekka's shield, the flames flew back at them with an intensity that scorched every Pitter in the rat pack like a torch dropped on ants emerging from an ant hill.

Moving forward, Sur Sceaf stepped over the charred and smoldering bodies. On either side of the corridor were glass walls, beyond which Dominikers and Pitters leapt out of their chairs in a state of panic and began scrambling out doors at the opposite end.

On the glass side, there were no doors or access points. Sur Sceaf struck the glass with the butt of his sword so as to break through, but instead of the glass shattering, his heavy sword rebounded as if it had struck pronk. "Try your axe, Brekka."

Brekka stepped back and then with one hammer hurl split the window. When Sur Sceaf tried to retract the axe, it resisted. The glass wall appeared to be some sort of flexible material that trembled like water, but would not shatter and was too strong to pry open.

"This is too slow," Starkwulf declared. "Let's find another way in."

"Forget that!" Sur Sceaf replied quickly. "Let's just make a go for the control center. That's where the emperor operates from."

As they ran down the corridor, another wave of Pitters hit them, this time with slashing swords. Sur Sceaf felt the impact of their charge, then fought like it was his last battle, with Brekka on one side, Starkwulf and Va-Eyra on the other, and the rest of their company, swords flashing, pulled up the rear. In a wolf-rage, up went his thrust with bone splintering force, and Pitter after Pitter was knocked off balance with the bucklers of their impenetrable Syr Folk shields.

A large goose whistle began honking, and red lights flashed over and over on the walls above them. When Sur Sceaf and Brekka were exhausted, they dropped back and were replaced by Verushka and Pata. Freyxus, Ruhm, and Cisne tagged Va-Eyra and Starkwulf, until step-by-step the Pitters, with agonizing screams, fell under foot. The blood made the floors slippery from pierced guts and hacked off arms or legs. Though dangerously slick, they forced their footing before moving on.

After what seemed like hours of stiff fighting, but was actually far less, the corridor grew silent. As Sur Sceaf assessed the damage, he ascertained all had gone fairly well. All had only minor nicks and cuts. Although Verushka was covered in blood, she assured him, none of it was her own. As Sur Sceaf was wiping his blade clean of the gore, small cans all along the corridor opened, emitting slender wisps of the yellowish gas, which

Donny had forewarned them about. Surprisingly, it did no one harm as it swirled around their feet and dissipated into the air.

Freyxus declared, "Thank the gods, Going Snake cut off the supply of the sleeping gas from up above."

As everyone took a breather and relaxed there in the silence, they heard heavy breathing coming from somewhere up ahead.

Va-Eyra frowned. "That's one of the Tyfons. It's unmistakable I heard its breathing on the day one clawed Russell's hand off."

Sur Sceaf signed, 'Go cautiously!' then approached slowly with his detachment following in a narrow phalanx formation. As they rounded a corner, he halted suddenly. Ahead of him stood two monstrous hairy beasts who had the appearance of giant wolverines and mouths full of teeth. Iron collars circled their thick necks from which emanated heavy chains that disappeared into a hole in the wall. Even standing on four feet, the monsters stood taller than three large draft horses atop one another. They had claws like sickles, and teeth that were bone crushing in their thickness protruding from a large, muscled wolverine-like head. Their black eyes bore a ferocity that was beyond demonic and made a grass beast seem like a ground hog. He had never seen anything this horrific before; they were much larger than the tyfons they had fought out on the surface. Fear and terror shot through him. He took a deep breath, forced himself to calm and silently prayed, *Ullr give me strength.*

Va-Eyra whispered, "The beast stoppers. We need the beast stoppers."

Brekka said, "Hurry Fa, get them."

The Beasts strained at the end of their tethers making their enormous chains.

"Stand back, everyone." Quickly, he swung the pack around from his back to his front, pulled out a beast stopper, jerked the cord to activate it, and hurled it at the feet of the menacing bone crushers. Green smoke filled the air and an acrid odor tortured their nostrils. Seconds later the tyfons emitted a bellicose roar that made his heart skip a beat. Quickly, he grabbed another beast stopper, pulled the string and hurled it. Then without waiting, did likewise to a third. As the smoke billowed towards them they were forced to back away from the wall of death. Through the smoke a loud *thud* was heard. The floor shook and the halls rang, followed by a rattle of chains and a second large *thud.*

After a moment of tense anticipation, Freyxus said, "I think we got them, my lord."

Starkwulf declared, "I think we need to wait until the smoke clears to be certain."

Brekka was concerned, "They surely know we are here. So why is there no response?"

"Methinks, they either believe we are a diversion, or it's as Donny believes, it is impossible to get into the control center."

Sur Sceaf waited for a good quarter of an hour as the greenish smoke was slowly drawn off by a whirring vent in the hallway. While they waited they discussed a strategy. Brekka had suggested using the beast stoppers to kill them all. Since there were numerous unknown variables, Sur Sceaf defined their mission as one of capturing the leadership and bringing them to public justice. The oppressed people of these lands needed to see the emperor die a justly administered death. They mutually agreed that they would attempt to preserve the scientists, Hryre Seath, and as many of the commissars as possible to put on trial and display them for their war crimes.

Once the smoke cleared, and it was safe to move in again, Sur Sceaf and Starkwulf peered around the corner and spied the heap of beast flesh before them. The massive giants had attempted to escape the smoke and headed for the doors, but they now lay dead on their sides with their enormous black tongues lolling out.

They made their way behind the beasts to the two metal doors, on either side of which were the flexible glass windows stretching for fifty feet. The room was brightly lit. They caught a clear glimpse of the emperor standing in front of the priests, the commissars, and members of the Ennead atop a platform overlooking tiers of seats. Before they could identify the others in the room, solid iron gates slid down the windows blocking their view.

"Damn, it's like grabbing a rooster by the tail feathers and having him get away." He inspected the doors, but they had no handles. He stuck his sword in the crack between them, exerted great force, but the doors would not budge. Sur Sceaf lunged his body against it, and it was like striking a solid wall of iron. There, just beyond those doors, the enemy was at his fingertips, and yet he was powerless to get to them.

He was so frustrated that he and Starkwulf climbed atop the fallen tyfons and at the count of three hurled themselves together. The doors would not give, neither would they move.

He sucked in a deep breath, closed his eyes, and took his mind to a quiet place he had often gone as a young blood on the Unequa Stream at Lake DiAhman. He pictured the calmness of the silent stream. As he went into an altered state, a vision came to him of using the boom sticks and stacking the dead Pitters against the door to increase the impact.

He opened his eyes to see his compeers all staring at him. The first thing he said was, "Hurry! Give me all the boom sticks you have on you."

Starkwulf gave him one, Brekka gave him three, and Veru had ten. "That should be enough."

Hryre Seath was fast losing confidence that the end of his enemies was at hand. He was shocked that the Syr Folk could make it this close to him. He had been assured by Ish and Vardrop that they were snug as a clam in its shell, and virtually untouchable. Now he was making eye contact with the heathen king on the other side of the plexiglass.

"There must be a traitor among us. None of the doors above have been breached though they continue to try. None of the caverns below have any access to the outside world except through the silo doors below. How else could they have found their way in here from the bottom of the caverns to the command center without someone punching in the code and letting them in?" His suspicion immediately considered the dominikers. *Damned humans can't be trusted this close.* Then he considered Rhoda; always the advocate for the humans.

Vardrop stood atop the assembly by the control panel. "I just think these Syr Folk are a hell of a lot more resourceful than you give them credit for. Who could have betrayed us? No one is foolish enough to risk his life."

Hryre Seath said, "Worshipful, my suspicion is that it was Rhoda Eckstein. Katus did not take to her, and you have seen how she warbles like a cuckoo bird for the laborers."

Rhoda shot to her feet. "By Angrar, I have done nothing but serve the cause for hundreds of years, and lately I have been busy reverse engineering this plague. I resent even the implication that I might be involved in some sort of conspiracy when I don't even leave the laboratories or my room for anything, but my work."

"Then why did Katus warn me that it was your plan to replace the Pitters with dominikers?"

Ish shook her head. "Katus was a superstitious bone counter. The reason we have brought in so many dominikers is because the other nations have grown weary of your harsh methods, and if we are ever to win them over we need a softer hand now. And how would Rhoda have betrayed us, seeing as she stood right here with us the whole time?"

"She had to have given one of the packers the code for the elevators to the silos."

Ish was affronted. She declared in an angry tone that gave him pause. "How dare you! Rhoda does not have the codes. No one has them but us, the arch-envoys. Are you saying we betrayed our own cause?"

Hryre Seath realized his suspicions had gone too far. "Certainly not, Holy Ones, but how did they get in here?" He looked at the screen on the control panel and saw the activity in the corridor just beyond the control center. The Syr Folk were busy stacking bodies over some dynamite at the door.

Vardrop chose to ignore the outside corridor and looked instead at the white-clad scientists. "That should not be our concern now. They're here, they've breached our under chambers, they've overcome our gas defenses, and killed the master tyfons. Hryre Seath, your Pitter troops have miserably failed us. Even though we have all the advanced technology, these Wood Lords have still managed to defeat us time after time. Our only hope lies in reverse engineering of the plague they set on us so as to kill them." He turned to Rhoda and asked, "Is that mutated plague ready yet?"

"Not yet, your Holiness," Rhoda replied from behind her heavy walnut desk. "It shouldn't take much longer." She bowed and left the room.

"Then go and make it happen." Turning to Hryre Seath, Vardrop said, "Send your lieutenant and get these dominikers to show us where they've stored the grains. I have the feeling we the core may be hunkered down here for a long time, and I don't want the Pitter legions plundering our stockpiles, nor can I bear the thought of them feasting on our flesh when the going gets tough."

The scientists began making their way out towards the laboratories, while the Dominikers made their way to the storage units. The military awaited further orders. But Hryre Seath was not comfortable with the enemy being this close. "The enemy is at our core. What do we do?"

Vardrop leaned forward and pressed a few buttons on his panel before declaring, "The wood lords have been blasting away at us all night. This bunker was built by my generation of Americans. It's designed to take far greater beatings than anything these primitive heathens can deliver."

Hryre Seath caught a look of doubt crossing Ish's pale wrinkled face, and for the first time he saw what he thought was fear on a god's face as she declared in a low voice, "I don't know, Most Holy One. Those doors were designed to withstand a massive blast from above, but perhaps the designers did not consider a direct explosion only a few inches away. And it looks to me that's what they are up to right now. It also concerns me that you are considering bringing legions into this level."

Hryre Seath glanced at the Syr Folk, amazed at their energy and determination. He saw the herewardi king and the red-headed lady knight with all her she-devils. He was enraged that he had gotten so close to pickling her brain and making her his servant through all the eternities. He couldn't help but feel doubt in his god. Here the most Exalted Arch-Envoys of Angrar were, as trapped as he, and the direction of the battle was not looking well by any standard. Hryre Seath eyed the large walnut desk of Rhoda's.

"Don't fret yourself. The legions are only a measure to check these medieval baboons. Then they will be sent back above. I just pressed the panel buttons to release the young tyfons loose on the plains to keep the Syr Folk at bay. I'm not thinking the blast of a few sticks of dynamite can have much of an impact on this place."

Hryre Seath was nervous. He saw the determination in the faces of the Syr Folk. "If it's alright with you, Most Supreme Holiness, I'm going to get under the shield of Rhoda's desk until that blast they're setting goes off."

The commissars filed off with the military to lead only the most trusted and proven elite legionnaires in.

Hryre Seath swallowed hard. "Most Holy God, Angrar, I must confess, I have my doubts that those doors will hold back the enemy. Forgive me for being so brazen, but so far none of our plans have stopped the progress of the swan-lords, and I grow more fearful of my life by the moment."

"Oh, you of little faith," Vardrop hissed. "I took you under our wing and exalted you above the nations of the land and now you don't have the will or guts to be an emperor when the time calls for it. I don't think you should concern yourself over this small handful of medieval troops. They are no match for our advanced technology. In a few days, Rhoda will have a plague that wipes them all out."

"Forgive me again, your holiness. I did not wish to be unfaithful. How can I prove that I am still worthy to be your emperor?"

"By staying here in the control center with us to witness the truth of our divine protection."

"I will stay, worshipful. Only let my lack of faith have the comfort of sheltering beneath Rhoda's desk until after the blast. You know how we of the rat's blood are driven to find the security of confined spaces."

"Very well, if that's what you have to do, but immediately after the blast, I want you to divert the legionnaires into the cafeteria area, and get these damned pests under control so that we can launch the plague on them."

Sur Sceaf declared, "We need to do this quickly before they can escape. Strike hard and fast before they figure out a way to stop us." He placed the boom sticks directly against the control center's unyielding doors, turned to his warriors and said, "Drag those Pitter bodies over to here."

Soon they had twelve dead Pitters stacked against the door. He took out the last boom stick from his pocket. "At the count of three I want every one of you to head back to the kitchen dock with the cooks and stay there. Get into a fetal position in turtle-phalanx form and wait until the blast is over. Then as soon as we hear the blast, we'll charge back in here. Beware, they're gathering their troops to assail us. Get it?"

"Got it," they answered in unison.

As his compeers ran in the direction of the kitchen, Sur Sceaf carefully lit the fuse of the boom sticks, taking one last glance at the iron wall before him, then turned and raced after his comrades. When he reached the kitchen dock, he hurriedly huddled under the phalanx with his friends, shouted to the cooks, "Duck low and brace for impact. Stand away from the door."

When they looked confused, he showed them with gestures how to cover their heads. Not even sure they understood, but at least they got down into a huddle.

It seemed an eternity, but as he counted, it was eight seconds. A deafening explosion sent debris flying through the dock. The dust was so thick that it was like being in a smokehouse and nothing, in any direction was the least bit discernible. Ears rang and they struggled to decipher the usual sounds through the confusion. The cooks were all coughing, giving some sense of orientation. Sur Sceaf's ears were still ringing too loud to talk to them or discern if anyone was harmed. His chest felt congested, and he reached into his pocket to pull out a kerchief to breathe through. He stood up, took the kerchief away briefly and shouted through the ringing, "Stand to phalanx! And sound your name off."

The first voice coughed out like it was coming out of a deep tunnel, "Starkwulf," then followed "Va-Eyra," a choking "Brekka" came out, and then one by one, each member of the twenty-eight gave their name. Groans and coughing could be heard coming from the cooks, but their conditions were not ascertainable.

As soon as the dust cleared enough to move, Sur Sceaf said, "Move in phalanx form to the control center." He looked and moved for the first landmark he could recognize, which was the kitchen door. Once they made it to the kitchen door, he realized it was just the door frame. The doors had been blown to pieces. He shouted one last command at the cooks. "Stay where you are."

He knew the corridor was to the right, so he said, "Double file and hold to the hips of the person in front of you."

There was so much debris in the corridor mixed with slime from the pulverized bodies of the slain Pitters that it felt like walking through a gravelly, muddy stream. The sounds started sounding like they should, they were no longer muffled. They inched along ever so slowly. Sur Sceaf felt the grime-ridden wall to his right with his elbow to keep his proper bearings. The dust grew thicker in the hall, and everyone was hacking so much that he had to stop to choke out, "Use your handkerchiefs and swan scarfs."

After waiting for a few moments he could make out the same red lights blinking in the hallway and heard the same persistent and irritating *'honk, honk, honk.'* Finally, he got to the place he knew was near the control center and spoke through his kerchief, "Can you feel the doors, Starkwulf?" He coughed repeatedly, having taken in more than a mouthful of the choking dust.

A muffled, "It's here!" came through a kerchief. "They've been blown off their hinges."

Pleased that his vision had been proven correct, Sur Sceaf shouted, "Shields up. Enter doorway, two by two." He joined Starkwulf at the entrance and the two went shoulder to shoulder, shield to shield, through the threshold. Groans and curses were heard at the far end of the control center. Then, a loud *clunk* was followed by a *whirring* sound. Bit by bit, the air began to move and visibility rapidly improved. The fans had kicked in.

Sur Sceaf could now make out a pile of black clothed bodies against one of the half walls at the front of the amphitheater. Some of the seats directly before the doors were leveled. Several dead khaki-clad bodies laid lifeless across the remaining seats, and papers were strewn all about the amphitheater. The side doors were all blown off. The heavy doors were still intact but blown more than halfway up the amphitheater where they hung over the upper tier seating.

Starkwulf stood gazing over the blast scene. "Hryre Seath is not among these bodies. He has to be here, there was no time to flee. I'm telling you he's in here somewhere."

"But where? All I see is wreckage and splintered desks. There doesn't appear to be any place he could hide.

Ruhm suggested, "Perhaps we should send for Chloe and have her sniff them out.

He lowered the kerchief and said loudly, "Brekka, you and Va-Eyra take the lady knights and pursue those fleeing dominikers."

Brekka saluted. "My lord, may we have General Lee to accompany us."

Freyxus' face lit up.

Interesting, he thought, before turning to Ruhm. "What do you think, Ruhm?"

"I'd be delighted, my lord."

Brekka, with Ruhm at her side, and the rest of the lady knights close behind, raced down the side hallway until they reached a closed door. Above the door had been stenciled the words LABORATORY 6Q, AUTHORIZED PERSONNEL ONLY.

Ruhm inquired, "Does anyone know what that means?"

"They had one in the Poisoned Lands. It's where the scientists perform their works of darkness." Brekka replied.

"Do you think it's safe to enter?"

Brekka tested the knob. The door opened slightly. "It's unlocked."

"That could mean ambush!"

Freyxus said, "It could also mean they feel safe."

"Whatever, we have to get in there," Brekka declared moving over the threshold with sword drawn.

Ruhm hissed, "I claim the right to enter first, just in case it is an ambush."

Brekka saw the determination in his eyes and found herself thrilled he insisted on protecting her and her sisters at his own expense. She nodded approval and pulled aside for him. She ordered swords drawn and shields up.

Ruhm plunged through the door, followed immediately by Brekka and the sword-maidens. Seeing no imminent threat, Brekka and Ruhm halted midway across the large chamber.

Freyxus said, "Doesn't look like an ambush to me."

The room was filled with tables with strange apparati and numerous vials and flasks. At the far end, white-clad scientists and dominikers with swords at their sides cowered against the wall.

Ruhm ordered, "You have ten seconds to lay down those arms."

The bulk of dominikers threw down their clanging swords, but three older dominikers with significantly more decorations on their blue sur coats charged toward them with raised swords. Brekka slew one only to turn and see Ruhm had killed the other two. The rest of the dominikers bowed down, resigned to their fate as Ruhm raised his sword in preparation for beheading them.

Brekka shouted, "No, no, stop. There shall be no more slaying. These are humans who have surrendered. We spare all who submit to our will."

"The scientists, yes, but the dominikers are ever deceitful. Do you know how much they have robbed my people of? They would have killed us if we had not overpowered them, and I for one will never forgive."

Verushka interjected, "I agree with Ruhm. These people have participated in all the Pitter atrocities. Did you not share the log of Ben Hori with us in council? It said that it was the dominikers who raped all the quant women during your dog team journey last winter in the wild lands of the north."

Brekka looked at the still bowing Dominikers in their handsome uniforms. "For the gods' sake, Veruskha, these Dominikers are no more than fifteen or seventeen winters of age."

She gave Brekka a bold look, "As were many of our fallen."

Ruhm emphasized "And as were the ones that so ruthlessly raped the quants and destroyed their settlements."

Brekka considered their arguments. She understood their justifiable rage, but she had dedicated her life to creation, not destruction. She took a deep breath before declaring, "No, there shall be no slaying. These Dominikers are no different than the Growlings in the Poisoned Lands. We not only made those Growlings loyal allies, but we took away their diseased faces and skin. If Dominiker minds have been poisoned by Pitter doctrines, we can cleanse them as well."

She noted her Fa-Sis, Va-Eyra did not look convinced, arguing, "If Crooked Jack or Elfbeard were alive, they would tell you that when you wound your prey, you must hunt it down and kill it. Dominikers are not like the Growlings, they were not born into ignorane and servitude, they made conscious decisions to join with evil and subjugate their fellow humans. I am tired of mercy for these filthy curs. I am surprised I have carried on sparing thim thus far. But seeing this once holy monument put to such evil use, I am finished with mercy."

"I understand, Fa-Sis. But in the name of the Council of Women, I invoke the right to exert my power by reason of the Ur Fyr in me and in the name of Ullr it shall be done."

Va frowned as she asked, "I have not checked. How do I know you have that authority?"

Before Brekka could give answer, Freyxus spoke up, "It was granted her by the Roufytrof, that we lady knights may answer the same purpose as the Council of Women during all military campaigns outside of Herewardi realms."

Va sighed. "In that case I yield to your authority in the name of Ullr the merciful."

The Dominikers shot troubled glances up at them from time to time, while the scientists remained clustered at the end of the long room awaiting their fate.

After Brekka and Ruhm had darted out the door in pursuit of the blue uniformed Dominikers and the white-clad scientists, Sur Sceaf slew a Dominiker brazen enough to come at him wielding a blade, then spinning about, he dropped a charging Pitter dressed in the usual khaki uniform. At the same time Starkwulf severed an arm from one of the black-clad priests, who was lying on the ground and attempting an upward thrust at Sur Sceaf's groin with a dirk.

In the pile of black robed priests before them, most were either dead or soon to be dead, and offered no resistance to Syr Folk blades other than upheld hands or legs. One-by-one Sur Sceaf and Starkwulf first gave a lethal stab to the two remaining priests then, together, tossed the bodies to the side. Sur Sceaf took stock, looked around and posed the question, "Do you hear that?"

Starkwulf nodded, "Sounds like it's coming from that big desk up in the corner."

Sur Sceaf and Starkwulf exchanged looks before both came to the same conclusion. While Sur Sceaf's twelvers cleaned their weapons, he and Starkwulf slowly climbed up the tiered amphitheater until they reached the upper platform. To their left the control panel with its mysterious lights and screens seemed intact. To their right was a large walnut desk. As they stood silently, Sur Sceaf heard the sound of muffled coughing and signed for Starkwulf to approach from the right while he approached from the left. At his signal they tapped the top of the desk with the tips of their swords.

Sur Sceaf ordered, "Crawl out of there or die on the spot." His heart swelled with anticipation. *Could this be the long sought-after prize? Is the Dark Emperor under there?*

Slowly, a disheveled Hryre Seath crawled out with his crushed mitre still clinging to his head and covered in fine dust. He was still coughing and choking while raising his arm to shield himself from an expected blow.

"Yeoh Wah!" Sur Sceaf shouted in triumph, and the sound echoed down the corridor, letting Brekka, Ruhm, and Va-Eyra know they had apprehended the emperor.

"Please! Show mercy, oh Mighty Swan Lord. Show me mercy!" the emperor pleaded.

As Hryre Seath knelt in supplication, Starkwulf quickly bound the emperor's hands behind his back with some leather thongs. Together they jerked him up to his feet. Suddenly they were rushed from the side by two wounded Pitter guards, their short swords raised for the kill. Starkwulf shouted, "Watch out!" He turned in a flash to bring down one attacker, while Sur Sceaf brought down the other with a swift and lethal upper thrust. Hryre Seath had fallen back to the floor, cowering with his forehead pressed against the hard cement.

Starkwulf ordered, "It is not befitting for an emperor to squirm. Get up, you worm," The disdain clearly accentuating his command.

When the emperor refused to rise on his own, they took him by his arms and dragged him like a carpet bag towards what had previously looked like choir seating and plunked him down on a step like a sack of rotted potatoes.

As Sur Sceaf removed his helm to wipe away the sweat, dust, and grit from his brow, Brekka, Ruhm, and Va-Eyra led a group of white clad scientists through the door. They numbered five, and were followed by ten young Dominikers bound and led in by Senora Pata. The rest of the lady knights brought up the rear.

"Returned so soon, I see you captured the scientists," Sur Sceaf said. Turning to the lady knights he commanded, "Pata, get the wyrm-kats and bring them here. Then, Freyxus, you ride Hobb up to the top. Tell Lord Arundel the day belongs to us, and to start the mop up. As soon as I find the means of unsealing the caverns, have him flood them with his fyrds. And this is my order which alters not nor will it change. *Suffer no Pitter to live.*"

Brekka swiftly interjected, "My lord, I remind you of our discussions about sparing the Dominikers."

"Thank you, my dear," Sur Sceaf said as he turned back to Freyxus and commanded, "Inform Lord Arundel that he is to spare any Dominikers who sue for peace; otherwise treat them as enemy combatants and render them their just due."

Freyxus saluted, signed for Cisne and Pata to go with her, and they were off in a flash. The very air reverberated with victory.

As Sur Sceaf held Hryre Seath by his scrawny arm, he ordered him up, and this time as the emperor clumsily clamored back to his feet, Sur Sceaf could see he was a nothing, a coward, he was an unman and no warrior at all.

"What shall come of me?" Hryre Seath whined in his self-pity.

As Sur Sceaf looked him square on, he noticed almost mouse rather than rat-like features, buck teeth, long pointed nose, beady dark eyes devoid of any humanity. For all his posturing and threats, he seemed a very weak man. In fact, Hryre Seath looked more like a buffoon with his crushed and dusty mitre still clinging to his head, and the purple robes appeared as ridiculous and pretentious as a pig in a silk dress.

"Is it not obvious? You shall know the iron of death. That is what shall come. For your dark deeds in the Ea-Urth shall die with you, that no child may ever again be deprived of her parents, and that faith, reason, and tolerance might increase in the Ea-Urth, forevermore. We are a religiously tolerant people, but your religion is incompatible with humanity. Be gone from Middle Ea-Urth to the cursed realms of the Muspuli."

"You speak of faith, what do you Herewardi know of faith or religion, with all your damned harlots and your worship of your fallen barbaric gods! And you dared to send that squirming dog of a virgin into my realms to torment me. The seed of the woman, I think not. She's nothing more than a demonic witch under the control of my sister's evil spirit."

"And for that insolence you shall pay dearly, for that witch shall surely slay you." Sur Sceaf felt the comedy of the moment more than anything else and half choked, half laughed. He almost cried that such a weakling had somehow been put in possession of so much power and had ruined so much of humanity. "It does not appear your three gods who are one are really gods after all. Perhaps you have come to learn that our twelve gods are truly one. Is it within your comprehension to understand that if your three gods can be one then why not twelve of our gods be one, or even a hundred of our gods? The words of your blind seer, Katus, were from the dark elves, and have all gone down into the dust with him, Puppet that he was. But you know all too well that we would have allowed you, as we allow all beliefs, to co-exist with us, but you would not suffer any form of tolerance or equality to exist, nor did the long dark train of emperors before you. When you are gone, the age of religiosity will have died, and the new age of faith and reason, whatever that faith may be, will reign. Because faith, whether true or false, is man's ultimate birthright in middle earth, to tease out for himself alone and grant each man his own form of enchantment along the march for truth, in our case, the Osatru."

Starkwulf placed the tip of his blade under Hryre Seath's chin. "And where are your gods hiding now, Hryre Seath?" he taunted.

Hryre Seath's face grew sullen, his ashen skin even more willow-grey from the dust that coated it. His eyes reflected defeat and the futility of further struggle seemed to have finally hit him. He shifted his gaze towards the large control panel with lots of buttons on top.

Sur Sceaf smiled. "Starkwulf, I'll tend the prisoner. Check under that panel. I suspect the rat-gods are hiding thereabouts."

Starkwulf's eyes gleamed as he walked over behind the desk, leaned over, and said, "Alright, come out of there now."

Two fragile aged figures in dusty blue embroidered robes, slowly emerged, one female and one male. Each of the gaunt figures feebly crawled out from under the desk. Their clean shaven skulls showed their disdain for the natural look the Syr Folk preferred. At a nod from Sur Sceaf, Starkwulf helped them to their feet.

"Ish and Vardrop, I presume."

CHAPTER 11 :
THE ARCH-ENVOYS AND THEIR FALSE GODS

SUR SCEAF AND BREKKA INTERROGATED the scientists who had placed themselves in the position of gods over their Transhuman creations of Pitters and Vardropi had for the past six hundred years, imposed their oppressive doctrine on the nations they conquered.

The aged crone in blue said sarcastically, "The Wood Lords, we must needs presume? Finally, we meet face to face. Have you any inkling of the powers we could place in your hands?"

"You have nothing to offer me," Sur Sceaf declared matter of factly, "nor can you have any hope of tempting me into sparing your wretched lives. Even if you were capable of tempting me, my gods would never sanction anything short of your death by iron. Nor would I incur the wrath of all the innocents slain by your actions. Nay, for their blood cries out from the ground for wrake and vengeance. So mote it be."

Verushka returned to the control center from the top door with a team of equally aged white-clad scientists in their dotage, and herded them into the seating just above Sur Sceaf and Starkwulf.

Sur Sceaf nodded his approval at her, then studied the two figures who had called them wood lords. They were so old that they looked infantile. Their big eyes with dark eye shadows, their large almost bald heads with wisps of hair, spindly necks, and wrinkled skin, which looked as though they had never seen a day of sunlight, put him in mind of newly hatched crows.

The frail man with hunched back broke the silent expectation the rest of the scientists sat in. "I am proud to be Doctor James Vardrop, the Creator of Operation Angrar, and I am sure my assistant and significant other, Doctor Afeerah Ish is ever bit as proud of our accomplishments."

Sur Sceaf sneered, "Vardrop and Ish. Your names are as bitter as wormwood in my mouth." He turned to Brekka, and said, as he pointed to the two authors of all they'd come to loath over the centuries, "Can you believe these are the maggots who have made the nations to tremble? Seeing them naked and powerless makes me want to laugh, but instead, I know I shall weep for how they have oppressed all the Nations of Panygyrus and brought them under their soul crushing, systemic cruelty for these past five-hundred years. These are the ones who deliberately committed genocide on a scale unparalleled in history for the sole purpose of *homogenization, standardization, and globalism.* They advocated concepts that are the blueprint of all dehumanization and call for the crushing of the human spirit so as to enslave mankind. It has greatly offended the gods of many nations. To that ideal they made lives bitter under the yoke of oppression and extended the life of the evil generation who placed technology above humankind, as all of Loki's kin are wont to do."

"Also, Fa, let us not forget these are the ones who waged war on us during the day of our Baldurean glory and have never ceased pursuing us. And, like the black wolf, have ever followed us in an attempt to swallow the man child of our holy blood line."

Va declared, "Lady Brekka, you speak a great truth."

Brekka intoned, "My lord, indeed, their actions have earned them the same fate as Gloomulah in the poison lands. After all, it is they who first tossed the misseltwig at our longfathers near this very spot, nigh six hundred years ago."

Ish's ashen complexion flushed. "When you say Gloomulah, do you mean Doctor Elli-Termis Gloomley?" she asked in a soft quavering voice.

"We knew her as Gloomulah," Brekka said, sword drawn and in hand. "A wicked Harridan Hag fit only for the company of Hellheim. She was the Destroyer of Children in secret places! It is she whom I personally wrestled to her death and brought an end to her evil rule. She, like you was under the influence of the evil muspili and she, like you probably could never even entertain the thought that she was being manipulated by dark spiritual forces beyond her or your comprehension. It is so evident that the dark elves have thoroughly blinded your kind." She flourished her sword in front of their beady eyes. "It was this very wave blade that drank her black blood, as it will likely soon drink yours."

Sur Sceaf interjected in a soft but commanding tone, "There will be time for this later, my dear."

Ish replied, "I see this mighty lion, though born toothless, has now come of age to be known as the Syr Folk." She shot a glance at Vardrop.

Brekka drew a long breath before sheathing her blade, then staring at them with disdain, declared, "By the gods, it is all I can do to not slay you two as well as the emperor here on the spot. But Syr Folk law demands you be brought before the people and your fate pronounced by the king. Not to vindicate you, but to record the acts and deeds of the sword of righteousness for posterity's sake."

As soon as the remaining doors lining the pyramidal mound sprung open, Arundel ordered his Fyrds and a heavily armed calvacade of Red Men to mount and ride into the caverns with torches lit, swords, and tomohawks drawn. It was not long before they came to the charging Pitter legions afoot. The twang of bow strings and the whirring of tomahawks met the onslaught.

Their war horses plunged into the Pitter ranks and trampled the enemy forces beneath their hooves until the grey dust of the cavern floor ran with coursing rivulets of blood. Lord Arundel's forces had the advantage of coming from the high ground, and the immense forces ran over the legionnaires like army ants in a termite mound. By the third rotation of the phalanxes, the few legionnaires that remained turned tail and fled into the lower levels. Red lights rotated and flashed from the cavern walls as Ary drove his cavalry to the lower caverns in pursuit. Suddenly, from the next level down came a thunderous roar, whereupon Arundel signed a halt. In the next instant a large herd of bone crushers came storming in their direction, too tightly packed to count, even if they'd had the luxury of time. Having anticipated just such an encounter, he had his men in the first line seize their longbows and nock their arrows, to which they had secured Cerulean beast stoppers. Upon Ary's signal, each of them pulled the fuse and shot their arrows down the cavern at the approaching stampede.

By the time the shine in the monsters' large eyes was seen, the smoke of the beast stoppers turned the caverns into a wall of thick green smoke, but not before Ary spotted several of the huge beasts with Pitter limbs sticking out of their bone crushing mouths.

Uffa, who had maneuvered himself close to Ary, removed his Amadou Fedora to wipe the sweat from his brow. "Should I alert Mendaka and Xarela that the bone crushers may be storming out the doors in the hollows?"

Ary noted the resemblance of his nephew to Alfheah, then declared, "They've been briefed on what to expect. They'll be prepared."

"Fa-Bro?"

"What is it, lad?"

"What do I do with all this energy I'm feeling right now? It's eating me alive."

Ary smiled at the Beetle. "If you wish to be a great warrior, you must learn the strength of calmness. When one waits, one must relax entirely, and soar on the wings of your expectations. Then, at the right moment, the eagle drops on its prey from the sky. Now, calm yourself, and as soon as that smoke is dissipated we go forth slaying and to slay, if any Pitters remain. Return to your position on the left flank and ride steady."

The boy gave him an almost worshipful look before riding off.

Once the air cleared from the tunnel, the dirt road lay strewn with the hulking bodies of the giant beasts. Ary signed for his men to follow. Redelfis rode up to his side, and as they made their way through the still-twitching giants, their tongues lying in the dust, he inquired, "My lord, these legionnaires must have wives and children somewhere in these caverns. After all, there was no other place for them to go."

Ary knitted his brow. "Of course, they do. That thought has haunted me since before we entered these caverns. I don't even like stumping on baby rats when I find their nest, let alone something that's going to look human, but by the gods it is our sworn responsibility to extinguish the Pitter abomination out of the Ea-Urth and that duty falls to our generation."

Redelfis declared, "I don't know if I can kill a child, even one of rat seed. I just don't think I can."

"My blood brother, I do not require that of you. But, as for me, it is a duty I have sworn to the Roufytrof. I am pledged to destroy the abominable seed forever. You may withhold your hand, but I must slay."

Yellow Horse rode up still dressed in his checkered jester's uniform, with his face freshly painted for war and dark deeds. "My lord, it is time we slay the brood rats and their kits. Nits make lice! Not one of them shall escape my tomahawk. Therefore, I delight in this day, for I shall avenge my people who were slain at Frink Glen. Now is the great day that my parents and tribe shall witness my 'hawk drink the foul blood of their slayers, and the thunder beings shall dance in the heavens for it."

Ary nodded. "Yes, let us get to the dark deed, in which I take no pride, but which the gods require must be done, for it is no work of theirs, and we cannot ask them to do it if we ourselves refuse it."

Ary's forces rode two more levels down the spiral road until they came upon a large side chamber blocked by furniture, wood, canvas tarps and some boulders. "This it is," the jester exclaimed. "We have found the rats' nest."

Ary ordered the barricade torched. As the fire touched the canvas, the flames began to consume it while they waited. Redelfis cleared his throat of the billowing smoke. "My lord, the merciful thing would be to fill their chambers with smoke from the beast stoppers."

Yellow Horse jerked the reins, turning his steed around. "Redelfis, you astound me. Mercy is only for the merciful. These hell-rats destroyed my people and set me on a course of misery for most of my life. As the great Chief Onamingo declared, 'It will be blood for blood. Nothing but blood will bring atonement under the eyes of the Manitous.' And by the gods, only blood for blood alone will reset the balance of life."

Ary coughed and nodded his head. "Both of you are right, I can see it must be so. You have my permission to stand down should you wish Redelfis and as for you Yellow Horse, you may drink the sweet blood of vengeance. All others prepare your 'hawks and blades and trample the seed of these hell-rats with your hooves of steel."

"So mote it be!" Yellow Horse flared his nostrils, swung his tomahawk above his head and goaded his horse to a prance. "Remember men of Syr Folk," he shouted, "do not leave so much as a suckling infant to live so far as the curse be found!"

After a full night of stacking Pitter bodies outside the bastion for burning, Ruhm and his men bathed and soaked in the cleansing waters of what Brekka once told him was her ancestral homeland, Othala, as it was formerly named. According to Brekka, these waters were holy, and she had said that sacred serpents would lick one's wounds, both of the body and the heart and relieve one of any psychic burdens. Whether the waters, the serpent licks, or the ale his men were passing around, Ruhm's heart was indeed eased of so many burdens. The fierce countenance of the herewardi wizard who had picked him up out of blindness seemed to stare out of the clouds at him.

As he took a deep draught of ale, he laid back against a sun-warmed limestone away from the bantering and teasing of his overly playful officers. He reminisced on the time when he was but a nineteen-year-old youth. He and Brekka had attended a picnic at Wallenwood's Church near a place called Sassia Wood. They had remained long after the end of the picnic, splaying their fingers together in a contest of strength.

At first, he had been confident he would easily defeat her, but when it became apparent that he could not, and that she was indeed a match, he pulled her close and kissed her instead. Both of their hands relaxed into an endearing grip, and the kiss was not only returned, but lasted for some time, until the owners of the woods Earl and Carla Higgins made their way down by lamplight to extinguish the campfires.

Earl, once a Hickoryan Skipper on the Chesapeake, called out, "Looks like the makings of a marriage between the two youngin's, Carla. What do you think?"

Carla doused one of the campfires with water from a bucket. "If not, it's likely to be the start of one of the largest firestorms we'll ever see, an ant in an ant lion's pit."

The two of them shared a laugh. "How about it, Young Lee? Do Carla and I see marriage garlands in the making, or is you caught in the ant lion's pit?"

"Oh Earl, I've asked her, but she won't give up her culture, and I'm sure not gonna mine, but you're dead on right, I can't get out of the pit."

Earl scrunched his lips. "Well, my boy, I know what your problem is. It's the same as your daddy and his daddy before him. It's plain clear to see. Pride! Now I've lived with Karl Throckmorton long enough to be taught Herewardi ways, and I've lived among the Herewardi long enough, to know they are a good people to the core. Trouble is, like I said, you have too much pride, and your traditions have infected you with One-ism. It's a disease not found in any of the Herewardi lands. You got to get over thinking there's only one person for you, or you'll die at the bottom of that pit."

Carla chuckled. "At least, if you ever want to put your ring on that pretty girl's finger. She's Herewardi to the core."

Brekka winked at Carla.

Loosestrife dripped water on his face, wrenching him out of the pleasant memory. He smacked Loosestrife on his naked calf, hard enough to send him scrambling for balance. It was true. He was infected with One-ism and pride. When it came to Brekka, it would never work. He wondered why he hadn't realized that sooner, why it had taken so long to realize such a fundamental truth. His whole culture was infected with the belief in One-ism. One god, one sun, one wife.

Except for the shuffle of the troops determining which Scientists needed medical treatment, everything was silent. Sur Sceaf took a deep breath and said, "We shall deal with your judgment later. Right now, I need to know, which control unscals the doors above?"

A crackling voice of one of the Scientists behind him said, "I can show you where that is."

Vardrop turned and barked, "Not yet Rhoda. We should try negotiating first."

The wrinkled old lady faced him square on. "Can you not see, Doctor Vardrop? These are the true humans. Not the twisted half-humans we made in our labs nor the façade of humanity you created in the Dominikers."

Sur Sceaf lifted his eyebrows and motioned for the old lady to draw near. "Please, come down and show me, Rhoda."

The white coated, aged figure led them to the busy looking panel of lights and screens. After pressing a few buttons, she turned, and said in her age-strained voice, "All doors are open. I have lived since the dawn of your Forefather's defeat until the setting of your victory here today. You might be surprised at the number of us Scientists that have secretly hoped for your victory. And now we joyfully surrender our ship to you, Captain."

Sur Sceaf smiled. "Thank you ma'am. As the King of the Syr Folk, I thank you. I am pleased to find there are people of honor and common sense among a race that we now come to call the Evil Generation."

The feeble old Scientist said, "We know your race well, and a nobler King and Ring Lord has never existed in all the span of my life. You are of the Old Race. For centuries, I have longed for this day. When once again humanity would reassert itself into individual tribes above this monstrosity I so unwillingly was forced to serve and obey. Desire has failed me, but you are the best looking specimen of a man with a pure heart that ever walked the Earth. I hope your seed increases and that the Free Enterprise that you practice makes all nations to prosper as you Herewardi have."

CHAPTER 12 :
THE END OF TYRANNY

GOING SNAKE AND XARELA HAD relieved Ruhm and his cavalry at false dawn, and were busily stacking more bodies of Legionnaires, Pitter women and children on the far lip of the landing, ready to be doused in whale oil and ignited by the all-consuming flames of the Dragon's Breath.

Sur Sceaf had granted the request of the Hickoryan Tramps to clear the area of the slain Bone Crushers in exchange for the meat. They proposed keeping the best cuts for themselves, and feeding the offal and scraps to their hogs. Scores of Tramps had just begun their labors when, clad only in a loincloth, Sur Sceaf arose from his bed inside the Red Pfalz Command Tent, stiff from his battle the day before. To his displeasure, he found it took more time to recover at the edge of fifty-seven winters than when he was younger and in his prime. He slipped on some moccasins, grabbed soap and a towel, and carrying his clothes with him, walked out in the quiet pre-dawn through the dewy grasses and mint patches along the way where only the morning guard was awake.

Campfires smoldered to ashes as the crow of the cock broke the absolute stillness of the predawn. Only the Star of Earendil had shown bright against the darkened Eastern sky. As he made his way towards the Big Springs reflecting on the success of Lord Arundel's thorough purging of the Legions, the ashes of the numerous and enormous bonfires consumed the remains of a once terrible foe, never to rise again.

Despite this total victory in the heart of Pitterdom, battles still raged in the South Lands. At the last reports, Il-Alim, Ehira and the various groups of Hickoryan Freedom Fighters were busy quickly tightening the noose. In Charleston, the former capitol of the Hickoryans, Barmachmud, the Commissar of the Charleston Zonga and Flar-dah labor camps, had barricaded himself inside his Zonga, but according to Il-Alim, he and his Legionnaires had been greatly weakened by the two Moonth siege. Il-Alim was planning the final attack within a fortnight. At Big Springs, White Moose and his Mufsiks held the remaining group of ruling commissars, those favored by Hryre Seath including the Master of Cages, Horquenada, the Slayer of the White Goddess, Wilona God's kin.

Not all of Sur Sceaf's allies and commanders had agreed with his order that these commissars not be immediately slain, but, as he had explained, he wanted as many people as possible to gather and witness the end of tyranny. Once the inquisition was concluded, and the sentence of death passed, these commissars would suffer an ignominious public death, that justice may be seen to be served.

But that was in the future. Now, he welcomed the fresh morning breeze that was gradually carrying away the stench in a dark cloud to the northern sky. He passed the Ceruleans' deflated balloons arranged in tidy rows, the corrals of Sharaka ponies, and the coke fires used to inflate the balloons. The vast array of tipis and white tents reminded him of his youth when the Herewardi and Sharaka would celebrate their brotherhood together in great feasts, contests, and games in preparation of the Great War. A feeling of joy ran through him that this long friendship would now continue under the skies of peace.

At the edge of the pool he circled until he found a suitable place for the king's ritual bath. A quick look around showed him that he was all alone; everyone else asleep from the exertions of a battle well fought and won. He laid his bundle of clothing on a nearby stone.

Kneeling on a large flat limestone shelf, he splashed water until his body was dripping wet, and then soaped down. The moon was a bare sliver in the western sky, while the Morning Star shone brighter than he had ever remembered seeing it before, causing him to wonder if their victory had somehow increased its magnitude. The end to this long war seemed to have renewed the entire world and imbued it with a fresh face.

But as for him, he still felt the demonic influences of the heightened warrior spirit that had been required during war. For almost four years his entire focus had been on wreaking blood and destruction on the enemy, and though he had accepted these demons as helpful hitchhikers when he'd put on the dark cloak of war, it was now time to rid himself altogether of them. It was time for the dark passengers to return to Hellheim and the Nether Realms.

As the first rays of dawn pierced over the Eastern skyline, he looked up the large hill to the southeast of the Elf Waters--the place the Hickoryans called Tor-Ili--where two pillars from the Era of Os still proudly stood in the Home Land anciently called Orthala. The Ur-Fyr burned bright in his chest that this victory had served to create a Middle Ea-Urth reborn unto a marvelous reawakening. Still, he was very aware that the defeat of the enemy was only the first step toward eliminating the Pitter indoctrination of Latin and Lies. It would not be a short road to the realization of the new concepts of liberty and freedom for all, and all the remains of the Roman Cult of Vardrop were purged from the land and minds of the people through the higher teachings.

Suddenly, he heard the voice of the Great Chief Onamingo as clearly as though the Old Sachem was standing there beside him. *"Surrey, my son, there is a time to be a Red Chief, which you have performed admirably well, but now it is time to become the White Chief, to shepherd a lasting peace and harmony among the Nations."*

Smiling at the sagacious prompting of his esteemed Father-in-law through the veil of the Spirit World, he eased himself into the crystal clear spring until he was fully immersed in its healing waters. The water was cold but bracing, and prickled his skin, as if snake tongues were dancing over his skin from head to toe. These Elven Waters were well-known to be filled with healing serpents since the days of Os-Syr-Hrus and long before. In truth, as he held his breath beneath the surface, it was as if all the demons of war were being drawn out of him and displaced with the forces of light. As the first rays of the Sun skimmed the surface of the water, he felt rejuvenated.

Precisely as the Sun rose on its saffron wings, he rose from the water facing the East whereby he lifted his arms in a Swan Swear and spoke in the Folk Tongue, "I greet you, oh green-eyed Howrus, and I call upon thee, oh Heavenly Mother Freya, to give of your breast and feed us from the sky. Oh, bright and shining Baldur, drive the shadows from my heart, and cleanse my soul of all that is toxic and dark. Never have the things which the Elves hate—wickedness, falsehood, and oath breaking—been done by me. I now call on mighty Tyranus to lend me his sword that I may cleave good from evil and light from darkness, and do the will of the Great God in all the Nations of Panygyrus. Almighty All Father Odhin, King of Gods, cleanse me of all influences of the Dark Elves that blind mortal men, so that I may once again rejoice in Life. Oh King of the East, rise and show me the way to judge wisely, as it is done above. Almighty Ullr, grant me thy tender mercies with which to govern my people. Oh, Master of the Ur, impart the Elf Fire unto me that I may know the righteous course of the Heavens and the eternities. So mote it be."

A quiet, penetrating whisper seemed to envelope him. *"Well done thou good and faithful Son. Thou hast been a True Steward over a few things, and, now, I shall make thee Lord over many, until the day when thou shalt take thy seat on the right hand of the Gods in the Halls of the Celestial Dragoon of Val-Ullr where all thy Ancestors and Posterity shall meet."*

The Ur Fyr burned in his chest as bright as the rising Sun. He felt invigorated and more alive than he had ever felt before. Climbing out of the water, he stood on the flat limestone and dried himself with a towel. A golden trout swam swiftly by chasing a minnow. Lark song spilled through the air, followed by a chorus of song sparrows in the nearby verge. He dressed into a clean loincloth before slipping into his Elven undergarments made of finest white silk embossed in golden runes over each chakra, the privilege of an anointed King. He thought about what points he should make at the Inquisition scheduled for High Noon.

Looking up at the crest of the Kings' Mound, he noted what appeared to be a dolman adjacent to an interesting arrangement of stone henges almost directly between the dolman and the pillars he'd viewed earlier, nestled in a grouping of feathery Ancient Yews. The brilliant Hickoryan Young Blood, Charly Duke, had marked the place as Ili-Tor on his map, but he had also heard the Jokers say Tor-Ili. Charly told him the locals feared to go near the place, as it was the burial grounds of the King-Race and guarded by vicious Wights that would pursue you to your grave if you violated the treasures they guarded. Unfortunately, he would be too busy to explore the curious and intriguing arrangement of stones today.

Still, he thought maybe he could explore it on the morrow, and made a mental note to have Long Swan tell him the meaning of such a name, and why the locals had legends of Heathen Gold buried there. He rolled up his towel and sodden loincloth and headed back to his tent to prepare for the Inquisition of Vardrop, Ish, and the Emperor Hryre Seath.

As he walked through the tent door, he found it brimming with his closest comrades and family members. It took only a few steps forward to feel that the tent was imbued with a new spirit. His Blood Brother, Mendaka shot him a silent nod of approval and a wide smile. Yellow Horse, the Jester, stood in front of the camp stove breaking eggs on a griddle over the cooking fire. On the table sat plump newly baked breads and the famous Quailor pretzels made in the image of the Herewardi Knot. Sur Sceaf's personal cook, Hogor, sat in the corner, munching something resembling husk bread.

Sur Sceaf tossed his towel into the corner and asked, "What's the occasion?"

Hogor grinned. "It is good news. Yellow Horse is taking Brimhilde to wife! I'm going to make him some mock duck cooked in a thin wine and serve my last barrels of rye-wolf to celebrate the evening. So, in return, he volunteered to make breakfast for us this morning."

"Well, what do you know? The confirmed monogamous is taking on another wife. When's it going to happen?"

Yellow Horse glanced his way. "As soon as Elisheba arrives from the Omala, I'll need her approval."

Sur Sceaf marked that though the Jester was dressed in his usual black and white harlequin suit, he appeared even more comical in Hogor's white hat and oversized apron. As he flipped the sizzling eggs, he declared, "The Firginia people called Dunkards from the Hospitaler Camp, made and gifted these breads for you."

Hogor said, "They were even here before I got the cook stoves going; made it a point to get them here from Bender's Woods before breakfast."

His sister, Va-Eyra, handed him a krug of the High Desert Ale and said, "I also have good news for the King."

"And that would be?"

"Just got a Harrier in this morning; the King's Flowers are leaving the Omala today and should arrive here in a Moonth."

He felt a surge in his loins and a thrill in his heart. "My Bride-Covey is coming that soon? Who will drink a symbel with me?"

Starkwulf raised his mug to him with a nod of his head. "I will drink a Symbel with the King, who is also a lonely husband."

Everyone in the tent eagerly chimed in, "We will drink a Symbel with the King."

Lord Arundel said with a fox's grin, "As soon as we have krugs in hand, we will drink a Symbel with thee."

Laughing, Mendaka rose to fill the krugs with High Desert Ale. He then filled the gilded Memory Cup Horn before passing it to Redelfis.

At first, Redelfis appeared startled before collecting his wits. He took several gulps before declaring, "I wish to sing the honor of Rabinbrot, the Rdokian guerilla that assisted me in the siege of Gettisbuhr. He was not only a brave Warrior, but he also deflected many an arrow from my back. I would have you all drink to our eternal friendship."

"Here, here," came a chorus of voices and exultations before the toast was drunk in hearty gulps. Mendaka then filled the Bragging Cup to the brim until the foam dripped down the horn. As he stepped forward to hand it to Starkwulf, Va-Eyra nudged him and said in mock disgust, "You would have to give this Cup to the biggest liar in the entire Syr Folk army, wouldn't you?"

Starkwulf shot her a devilish glance before lifting the horn in the air for all to see. "Before I give my brag, I request that all you Young Bloods here come stand around me and hold out your krugs for a refill. The fact of the matter is, when I took the siege alongside Arundel, I got speared so many times I was mistaken for a porcupine. Once I take a drink from the Bragging Cup, ale will spill from all these holes in my body!"

As he drank, a roar of laughter filled the tent, along with shouted accolades.

Sur Sceaf called out, "Well done, my good and faithful friends. You have set the mood for our breakfast fest. Now, let us pass around the Cups for all to give their contributions while we eat, brag, and boast."

After an hour of flyting and boasting the Memory Cup was empty, and the Bragging Cup ended up in Going Snake's hand. "I take great pride in being the last to drink of the Bragging Cup, which I note is nearly empty." He took a swallow before holding the cup upside down. "It may be the ale speaking, but I wish to boast that I will take one hundred wives before I turn forty winters and even that would not equal my first wife."

Yellow Horse snorted loudly. "Well, that may be so, but they will have to be fat, blind, deaf, and insane!"

"Ha," Going Snake retorted. "I dare you to say that to my wives."

A wave of laughter followed before Sur Sceaf raised his refilled krug. "Let us drink to the gods and our great victory. Let us also beseech them to aid our brothers still fighting the fast fading shadow of the empire in the South Lands."

All present drank deeply.

"And now," Sur Sceaf continued, "Let us drink to Yellow Horse, who prepared this fine breakfast to celebrate his marriage proposal to the wise and merciful warrioress, Brimhilde. I feel confident Elisheba will confirm this choice with open arms."

The table breathed the delicious scents of eggs, bacon, and buttered grits mingled with the aromas of hot bread and those delectable pretzels of the Dunkards.

Once again all drank. Many then called for a refill while Long Swan took up his silver lyre. After strumming a few notes, he began to play the Herewardi Hymn, "My Kinsmen Slain," a song about the struggle between good and evil that continues beyond the grave into the Realm of Spirits and the stars of the heavens.

As the soft music wafted over the tables, Sur Sceaf said, "After filling my plate three times, I must say I no longer know the real Yellow Horse." He glanced directly at the jester standing near the cook stove. "It wonders me, are you Jester? General? Or Cook?"

The wily Red Man offered a cunning grin in return. "That depends on what advantage is due which, my lord," Yellow Horse replied, wrapping hazelnut dough around the wooden sticks and carefully placing them over the cook fire for the traditional after breakfast treat.

"Well, to me, Yellow Horse, you are all three in one. First, the greatest and wisest Jester I have ever known, and secondly, a dear friend, and last, but not least, you have proven a great General and true Counselor to my son, the Lord Arundel. You have done much to further the cause of Syrdom, and from the taste of those eggs, your cooking ain't too bad, either."

Redelfis chimed in. "And, although he is my constant antagonist and often leaves me in a fury, I must concede it is true what you say about him."

"That is because the left eye knows what the right does not see," Yellow Horse returned with a grin.

"Ah, another riddle from the Jester," Redelfis retorted. "But I am learning."

Yellow Horse turned solemn. "My lord, you say you do not know me, but I know you. You are the eagle that spread his mighty wings over a little Red Boy in the smoking ashes of Frink Glen, and who nurtured me all my life long. You are the man I have come to know and revere as my Father, and though we share no blood, we share much Spirit."

The words from the normally reticent Jester wove tendrils of deep affection around Sur Sceaf's heart. "And yet, at age fifteen Winters, you put off your Herewardi name of Ashchild."

"Because I owed it to my Sharaka Father, Bear Rider, to keep the name he gave me alive. To this day I cannot remember anything about my life before Frink Glen. From henceforth I shall be known as Ashchild Yellow Horse. I vaguely remember my Mother made breakfast for me that morning, and then the screaming in the camp as people ducked and dived to avoid arrows falling from the sky like a Summer hail storm. But I don't remember anything before that day about my Father, my Mother, or my life. All I know is what you and Mendaka told me about my family."

Long Swan ceased strumming to say, "Sometimes, the Gods steal our memories and hold them as treasures to return to us when we die. Otherwise we might never escape their power."

Mendaka spoke up. "Originally, you were to be my adopted Son, but Little Doe said that your Mother, Raven Song, told her when you were born that when you were older, she was going to send you to live with a Herewardi family where you would be taught both the ways of the Herewardi and the Sharaka. It seems your Grandmother on your Mother's side had been Herewardi. At first, you were sent to the house of Muryh the Builder. But when you and Arundel became Blood Brothers, it seemed logical the two of you be raised under Sur Sceaf's wing."

Yellow Horse nodded. "I will always be grateful to Muryh and his Bride-Covey, but I'm glad I was raised in your house, Sur Sceaf. Not only was it more fun, but it was far more stimulating. Muryh's household didn't allow me the wild freedom of expression I needed to be who I truly am."

Sur Sceaf said, "Your parents were dear friends of mine. It pleased me to honor your Mother's plan for you, that you be educated. You more than fulfilled our hopes for you."

Yellow Horse smiled. "Mendaka was just telling me some of the antics you, Father, and he used to get into as Young Bloods."

Sur Sceaf shot a sharp glance over at Mendaka, who was tying down some packs with a devilish grin on his face, pretending to not hear the conversation.

Sur Sceaf said, "Some stories are better left to sleep."

"You mean like when you and Father tied a rattler's rattle on a large king snake and dropped it into Prancing Rabbit's tent, and she came running out naked and screaming."

"Alright, we were young, foolish, and filled with the lust of King May. What can I say! Let it all be out in the open. The King. Has. Sins. And although I'm getting long of tooth, I only ask that the Gods allow me the joys of a woman in my bed until my last days."

Redelfis intoned, "So Yellow Horse may I simply call you Horse's Ash from here on."

After the laughter died down, Yellow Horse chided, "Oh, my Brother, you do learn the Jester's gild way too fast."

Lord Arundel raised his krug with froth running over the sides and declared enthusiastically, "I second Father's declaration. This would be a miserable world without our women."

Laughter roared from one end of the tent to the other. From the corner of his eye, Sur Sceaf caught a glimpse of a grey horse arriving outside the tent door.

Yellow Horse waited for quiet, and then continued, "Mendaka meant no harm, such tales help me put a face on my Father. I'd like to think I got some of my Trickster blood from my parents."

"Your Father was tricky as a fox in battle. You can be proud of Bear Rider. Your Mother, on the other hand, was a gentle, quiet spirit, but you have much of her looks. One of the last things your Father ever told me was that in an effort to raise a great Warrior to withstand the Pitters and their allies, he had your Mother feed you wolf hearts. When you join them at the Council Fire in the Sky, you will find they are very proud of their Son."

A call came from the door. Redelfis rose from his seat and opened one of the flaps. There stood a lean Herewardi youth with a sharp nose, ruddy of complexion, a long curly blond mane of hair, and a prominent brow suing for an audience. He carried bulging saddlebags as well as several dispatch tubes.

Arundel looked up. "Ah, yes, Ilklif." The Youth had been a faithful Silver harrier back on the Isle and close to the spitting image of Ilkchild, his Father.

"Please come in, join us for breakfast, and give us the letters from our dear wives we have so yearned for." Arundel said.

"Thank you, my lord," Ilklif said as he placed the saddlebags and dispatch tubes on Long Swan's portable scribing table. "This may be the last full breakfast I get for several weeks, but the news of our victory has energized me enough that I had to hear it firsthand from your lips."

Arundel smiled. "I will proudly declare it to you now that after so many centuries of struggle we can finally say; we have made an end to tyranny with only a weak shadow remaining in the South Lands."

"Soon to be erased by the bright Sun of a New Day," Va-Eyra added.

Ilklif raised his arms high in the sign of the Swan. "Praise the Gods! I knew it when on the journey here. Beginning at Roanoke, I saw the Triskelions burning on the mountain tops and thought surely the Arrival of the Gods is at hand."

Arundel smiled. "I know you just got here, but I had Wyth pack you some treats for the trail back, and if you stay a spell, the hazel-nut bread will be ready for butter and honey. I pray the gods speed and guard your journey back. You shouldn't have any problem, if you stick to the trails we've outlined on the revised map Flammalf prepared for you."

As Arundel said the words, Sur Sceaf was immediately seized by the thought that now that the Pitter Masters were no more, there would be a lot more lawlessness and robber bands in some parts of the Mid Lands vying for dictatorial rights in hopes of forming their minor fiefdoms, oppressing innocent folk, setting up outlandish toll roads, extorting and robbing the weaker travellers. It would be up to Governor Khem to establish law and dominion over those wild parts. History had always shown that when a vacuum was created, lawlessness rushed in to occupy the void.

Ilklif said, "Let me get this straight, just to confirm, I am to swiftly ride with the letters and dispatches, as addressed, first to Khem of Ophir, then to the Bastion at Omala, from which pigeons will be sent with the messages to the Citadel in the Poisoned Lands, the letters to Kanarus' Lair, Fort Rock, Witan Jewell. And from Witan Jewell the messages will be sent thence to Urford, and across the Aurvandilean Sea to the Roufytrof at Godeselle. And after my messages are dispatched I may begin my long journey back to Moon Door and see my Fiancé, Faebrekka, Daughter of Duv-Ba."

"There's just one more thing," Sur Sceaf said.

"What is that, my king?" Ilklif said with expectant eyes.

"I want you to take Huwe and Wil with you."

He frowned, "But my lord, they will only slow me down, and it's been nearly nine Moonths since I saw Fair Faebrekka."

"I empathize with you, my boy. You have no idea how I miss my wives. I know Huwe and Wil shall slow you down, but the messages you carry are going to light the Syr Folk with untold joy. Their cautiousness will not slow you down as much as a robber's arrow. These men are expert fighters and keen woodsmen who will spot any signs of danger far afore hand. I need you to get through alive with the news that we have won the day. I want you to report to each station along your journey back to the Isle of Ilkchild, tell every friend your news. I will be sending out Silver harriers two by two every fortnight with updates and status reports until we have fully secured life and liberty under law from one end of Panygyrus to the other. This is the dawning of the New Age of the Marriage of Faith and Reason."

"You can bet I'll get the message spread, even though wahelas, dog men, or grizzlies should bar the way."

"Well said," Arundel demanded. "Now, take a place at the table and eat your fill. Yellow Horse has prepared us a victory feast. Unfortunately, you have missed a fine Symbel, which is why Starkwulf is still leaking like a sieve."

Laughter burst free. Even Long Swan struck a wrong note while laughing.

Sur Sceaf picked up a piece of bacon Mendaka proffered and was savoring its rich flavor when El Yid showed up at the door. Without bidding, the tall lean figure glided through the tent door like a pirate's saber, bowed at the neck and said, "I beg an entrance to your table already, my lord."

Relishing his distinct Jywdish dialect, so similar to Yid's Father, the Rabbi Amschel, Sur Sceaf motioned for him to sit. "Let Dancing Saber be seated." The Brothers in the tent clapped. "You did a great job at Nu-Yalk and Balmor. We salute you as a Brother of the blade."

El Yid smiled as he came to the table, eying the hot breads. "My lord, did you ever think to see such a day?"

"Not so soon, Yid. Never did I think to see it so soon as now." He smiled. "Please, don't stand. Sit and eat with us." Noting how lean El Yid looked under his black cape, Sur Sceaf decided he could surely take on some extra poundage without any harm. In fact, he could almost hear his Sister Ruth, Yid's Mother, urging him to eat.

"I'll sit and savor some of that hot bread and pretzels, but I'll have to pass on the bacon. It's not kosher."

"Sometimes I forget you are even a Jywd," Arundel said, as he drank from a fresh krug of dark ale.

"It's no problem. Sometimes I forget it myself, and believe me, bacon is the ultimate temptation. It used to drive my Father mad when mom made it for us kids."

Redelfis moved over to give Yid room on the bench. "It sounds like it was quite a dilemma growing up with a Jwydic Father and a Herewardi Mother."

"Not so much. I was taught to embrace both worlds, but when I reached manhood, and with my Mother's blessing, I chose to live as a Jywd in honor of my Father, but that in no way kept me from honoring my colorful Herewardi heritage."

Sur Sceaf said, "Well, I don't know many Jywds as dedicated to their faith as you are, Yid. It pleases me when any man honors his ancestors."

"My Father taught me that we Jywds are a chosen people and must keep the law of our God, El Shadai, and so it will be with me and my house, evermore. For Abraham was true to his God and that is the God on whom I call for my protection." He paused to drizzle the honey over his golden brioche. "You can see, we each have been chosen by our own tribal Gods, and as a member of the Syr Folk Confederation we now get to celebrate our wonderful differences with each other. It's the one point upon which we all can unite. "

"The mere fact that you are true to Abraham's God, Yid, is why I have appointed you a high and holy calling."

"Why ever do you say that, my lord?" El Yid asked with raised eyebrows. "Methinks you have something up your sleeve, and I wonder if I will survive it."

Va-Eyra laughed out loud. "He always has something up those sleeves, Yid. You should know that by now. Surely, Ruthie warned you?"

Arundel arose to fetch another full krug from the barrel and placed it in front of Yid. "Come on Yid, Sur Sceaf had our lives mapped out when we were but toddlers. It's his way. Drink with us, and hear what Commission he has doomed you with."

"I am the master of crypsis," Starkwulf offered, "but in matters of the mind, Sur Sceaf is even more cryptic. You'll think he's a mile away, but believe me, he's leading you by your *peyos* right where he wants you to be."

Sur Sceaf smiled at Va, acknowledged Starkwulf's remark with a half-nod, and then turned to Yid, "I want you to be the Lord of the new State of Jywdah that I am proposing to establish in Nu-Yalk."

Yid turned pale. "Why me, my lord? I've been as happy as a Sea Otter in Godeselle. I've come to love the Sea above all and, besides, Sol-Om-On is twice the Jywd I am."

"It troubles me that the Jywds have no real home land of their own, so I have considered the merits of both you and Sunchild. He may be twice the Jywd you are, but he's half as flexible as you are. The City-State of Nu-Yalk has large Jywdic populations, who have for the past five hundred years been made to serve their Pitter taskmasters. They have been served Latin and Lies for far too long. They will have need of higher and more flexible teachings, such as only you may render. Rabbi Amschel and I have been communing on this point. He has appointed Jesse ben David and his wife as your Councilors. Use Sunchild to be the Commander of your land army. You will be able to raise the Nu-Yalkers' consciousness to the concepts of freedom and self-determination within the Panygyric Confederation as planned. You will be dealing with two contentious populations. The Yengish are witch hunters and stone throwers, while the Jywds wish to silence them. I'm convinced, you alone, can help them transition into this wondrous world we are shaping. Besides, there are many Dominikers in that place, and only you will be able to discern whether they are to be shown mercy or the sword."

"I mean no disrespect, my lord, but Sunchild is content staying on land. In my heart, I truly believe Sunchild could serve you better in this capacity. We all know how brilliant he is."

"I am well aware of Sunchild's many gifts. He's a man without equal, but he has a blind side for absolute justice and in this case we need a merciful judge. If Sunchild had his way, he'd put every Dominiker to the sword, and some day their descendants would rise up and be a thorn in our sides again. I don't want that. But you are slicker than butter on grease, and you will be able to lubricate the friction between Jywd and Dominiker, because choosing harmony over confrontation is simply your nature. Let me be even more direct. I want you, Lord Yid, when I convene the Constitutional Convention, to be sitting as the Lord of Nu-Yalk."

As he looked around the table, Sur Sceaf noticed more looks of approval rather than looks of doubt.

"I know this is a great honor. I would never reject a Commission from you, my lord and King. I just hope I can match your expectations. You know those Nu-Yalk Jywds are not like our Jywds in the West. They will have their own stiff-necked ideas. They will claim they are older, more orthodox, and therefore superior. I've seen it in the Salmalhuer Jywds. From what my Father, the Rabbi, has told me, they are more like outlandish folk than Jywds. You are correct that they have been tainted by their long exposure to the Pitter's Latinate teachings and their imposed subservience. The transition from bondage to freedom will be most difficult. God only knows what vengeance they will want me to impose on their Dominikers oppressors."

Sur Sceaf held his mug up for Hogar to refill. "I am sure they will be different, just as these Hickoryans in Firginia are not like the ones on the Isle of Ilkchild, but there are too many Dominikers in Nu-Yalk to allow them all to be killed, and such an influx of immigrants in any other sector of Panygyrus would lead to conflict on a grander scale, whereas it can be done in Nu-Yalk, if you will be both peoples' surety. You, alone, are capable of operating from such a paradoxical place and balancing the needs of both. Your Seed Code will give you that power. Appoint Sol-Om-On on your council, along with Jesse and his wife, and the four of you, I am sure, can build a marvelous City-State. I've proven Jesse's wife, and she will insure the others will not bulldog you."

El Yid pinched his Royale, dithering a little. "I will accept, my lord." Then as a curious change came over his voice, he added, "Of course, Sur Sceaf, best of Kings, Pyrsyrus brought his wives with him. His wives wouldn't hear of Pyrsyrus swanning around on the Sea without them. Sure would be a lot easier, if I could do likewise, and come home to the comfort of a woman's touch every night."

Sur Sceaf smiled his understanding. "We are all, of this self same mind now. Surely, you didn't think I would ever deprive you of their sweet company. I'll send to Omala for your wives. And of course, you know that's going to raise even more issues for your cousin Jywds of Nu-Yalk to have to deal with. If it suits you, you can have a Sea Palace like Pyrsyrus to rule from. Just park it in the Bay of Huttston, until they get used to the idea that their Governor has many wives and that your children have many Mothers."

El Yid teased, "Frankly, if you ask me, it's like pulling a bad tooth out of a child's mouth. It's better if it's done all at once, so that the kid doesn't have too much time to protest. It wouldn't hurt to bring in some Jywds from Va-Gedulah to help govern and be examples of our new society."

"I'll send for a migration party of Jywds under Rabbi Amschel's advisement to assist you. Be assured, I'll make it so. I really need this to happen."

"And so it shall be, my lord." Yid took the final drink, set his mug down, and said, "And with your permission, I go to prepare my men for this new assignment."

As he exited, he passed a green-clad Beetle who had just arrived. The young messenger stood at Sur Sceaf's shoulder awaiting permission to speak. Sur Sceaf forked in some grits before looking up. "Yes, what is it Here-Arundel?" he asked after swallowing.

"My king, Ruhm Lee begs an audience with you before the judgment of the Emperor is sealed."

"Let him enter." Sur Sceaf glanced across the table at Arundel, who lifted a questioning eyebrow, and the Green-Beetle went out to relay the message.

Seconds later, Ruhm came into the tent with his Eagle Owl, Uhu, on his shoulder, saluted, and knelt. He stood up, then reached into his pocket, pulled out a piece of paper and handed it to Sur Sceaf.

"What's this for?" Sur Sceaf asked.

"It's a bill for fifty two chickens from Charly Duke's Hickoryan Uncle, the poultry farmer."

"Why give it to me?" Sur Sceaf furrowed his brow. "That's what Quarter Masters are for."

"It would seem, while guarding the outer perimeter, Scratch, Mouser, and Chloe couldn't resist a night hunt in the good farmer's chicken coup, which, of course, scared the hell out of him and his boys, especially when Scratch said, 'Sur Sceaf Top Cat. Sur Sceaf pay'."

The tent roared with laughter. Sur Sceaf shook his head and said, "The Ketten deserve a feast of celebration, too. I'll gladly pay the bill."

"Chester also asked that he be paid in gold solidus. Said he'd been gasping for a fag for three months, but his wife wouldn't let him have any of those paper-wrapped tobacco sticks, what some folks are now calling Virginia cigarettes." He grinned. "She's also forbidden him from bushin' it." He imitated tipping a bottle to his lips. "He doesn't want her to know he's been paid in solidus, 'cause he's planning to tell her the chickens got replaced at no cost."

Sur Sceaf laughed. "I think we can honor that, even though I suspect ol' Chester is gouging us a wee bit."

Ruhm grinned again, but didn't deny it. "My king," he said sobering, "I have sought to speak with Brekka, and she is nowhere to be found. I was hoping you might know where she is before the Inquisition is set at High Noon."

"She's gone up to the Kings' Mound along with her Lady Knights to fast and pray and offer up her vows and oblations."

Yellow Horse approached with a bit of bacon dangling between finger and thumb. The owl's eyes brightened and she eagerly stretched forth her neck to snatch the morsel. Ruhm waited until she resettled herself before asking, "Did I hear aright, Brekka is to be the Executioner today?"

Sur Sceaf regarded Ruhm silently. The young General appeared careworn, almost frazzled in fact. He considered the shenanigans with lovers Ruhm had embroiled himself in the Shenandoah, and as he contemplated the consequences, the Ur Fyr witnessed to him that Ruhm was now being melted in the Crucible of the Gods. He actually felt a tang of pity for him. He would have felt compassion were it not for the fact that this man would be transmuted into something purer than his antics would lead one to believe. The Gods would not lead anyone through this process that did not have a pure heart at their core. Still, he couldn't help but feel sorry for the torment the man must surely have to endure, but nothing good is born without pain or testing or proofing and the best gold must pass through the alchemy of the flames that the Norn Sisters would surely demand.

"You probably won't see her before the executions."

"Executions!" Ruhm blurted out. "That's why I've come. My people are talking. We are for the executions, but we've seen how you've shown mercy to the Dominikers and the Huskers, and fear you may grant the Emperor some sort of mercy as well."

"You may give your people the assurance that the Emperor will die by blood and iron at the hand of a Maiden. This has been prophesied from the beginning."

Ruhm appeared puzzled. "Doesn't Herewardi Law require a trial by jury and judge?"

"If there was a Constitution and a judicial system set up, there would be a trial, but for now all operates under King Law, and I am the King, and as King, I am duty-bound to uphold the vows all the Syr Folk have made, whereby we swore they would die by blood and iron. Judgment has been passed that Hryre Seath, Ish, Vardrop, and all their most terrible servants shall die in the full rays of the Noon Day Sun on Sur Day of next week. Last night I ordered runners dispatched in all four directions to announce the upcoming Executions and that all are invited to witness the end of Tyranny."

"I'm very glad to hear that is your judgment and will reassure my people. But is it absolutely required that the execution be by a Maiden's hand, for, if not, I'll gladly volunteer to take Brekka's place. I don't think she should soil her hands with the polluted blood of these vermin."

"I respect your desire to preserve my Daughter from any more bloodshed." Sur Sceaf offered Uhu a piece of egg, and the owl swiftly took it in her beak. "Now, here is why you cannot be the Executioner. Prophesy says Brekka, as Lady Life, shall be the one to slay them and end their works of darkness and vile deeds in the land. Suffer it to be so, that all prophesy may be fulfilled. Do you have a problem with that, Ruhm?"

"Not at all, my lord. I understand now. Better that they should die, and free the earth of their kind than to have a lengthy trial that frustrates the people whose trust we must now earn. I just felt Brekka had seen more than enough blood and destruction, but she is a Daughter of your Gods, and I understand she must answer to those ends."

Sur Sceaf gave another piece of egg to Uhu, feeling her beak against his fingers as she gently took it. "I hope you understand Ruhm that some matters have already been written in the Stars. Better the peoples of this land get started on the right foot with no encumbrances of the past blocking their progress. We are building a new world of balance between faith and reason, and we wish for all nations to understand that women are to play a major role in that world. Brekka is the one appointed to deliver us that new paradigm. Now, I pray you suffer it to be so, that the glory she deserves can be hers."

Ruhm grinned, glanced around, and then said with conviction, "So mote it be!"

CHAPTER 13 :
THE INQUISITION

THE TIME FOR JUDGMENT WAS at hand. The water clock showed a few minutes before High Noon as Sur Sceaf exited his tent dressed in the formal attire of the Herewardi Gentry—full length cordovan leather coat, a blousy white shirt and matching loosely tied cravat. He scorned to don the clothing of a Warrior any longer. Along with the emerald and golden eye of Howrus affixed to his tunic, his dark cherry-red sash denoted the Royal Blood Line he proudly bore, and of course, he wore the Sacred Signet Ring denoting his Kingship, the Hring of Hrus.

The Senior Officers of the Syr Folk forces were already gathering on the Landing near the Tree of Death next to the Altar of Angrar, a site chosen deliberately to symbolize the victory of the Syr Folk over the Empire and its bloody tyranny.

Sur Sceaf took no particular delight in executions, but the hand of justice had long been stayed, and this day would fulfill all vows of vengeance sworn to his ring. Once his hands were washed of this final duty of war, he would be free to enjoy a normal life in the arms of his wives, in his gardens, among his pigeons, and in his barns and fields. He wished that his Bride Covey could arrive in time to join him for the coming week of celebration, triumph, and thanksgiving to their Forefathers and the Gods.

The sky above was a brilliant blue with but one silver cloud directly overhead. Herewardi tradition required that significant procedures affecting all the people be conducted under the noon day sun, which practice had come to be referred to as 'under the Eye of Howrus', and this event would be no different. The combined sweet and acrid scents of burning flesh and stinking Pitter clothing filled the air, and it didn't take long for murders of crows and gyres of buzzards to gather in the clear sky above.

Other than the Syr Folk Officers who were allowed to attend the Inquisition, none other were permitted to pass or repass on the Landing. Although those camped on the Promontory had a clear view of the Landing, they could not hear the proceedings. The official transcript of the Scribes would be published and promulgated to all through the ministrations of the Silver harriers and Green beetles streaming back and forth through the gathered masses.

Most of the attendees wore traditional military regalia, while others dressed in the attire of their office. Brekka arrived in her full battle dress of silver armor over white silk decorated with gold and silver cups that ran from her codpiece to her knees. She had even decided to wear her Swan Helm with its soaring wings, the distinctive badge of the first Lady Knight since the era of Myra-El.

Mendaka had chosen his Shamanic attire of white buckskin tunic with a bone pipe breastplate covering his bare chest, along with fringed leggings. He carried the traditional medicine crook of the Sharaka Tribe and had painted his face the colors of spiritual potency—red, black and white.

Arundel was clad in his red fyrd commander's attire. Both Chise and Zoot were dressed in beaded buckskin war shirts, buckskin pants and impressive eagle-feathered war bonnets. Kanarus chose to attend in the traditional garb of a green knight. Dr. Walter Shanks, dressed in the traditional homespun black attire and hat, representing the Quailor non-combatants--Hospitalers, drovers, teamsters and culinary workers.

Long Swan, in his capacity of Prothonotary Scribe and Law Speaker, was to be the presiding judge. In his brilliant white robe, Long Swan appeared heaven-sent. The golden runes on the brim of his deep hood shone in the saffron Sunlight like the flames of the Corona.

In accordance to the Laws of the Inquisition as laid down by the first Syr Folk Chief Justice, Chief Onamingo, anyone in attendance had the right to ask questions. All questions and answers were to be recorded and entered into the Historical Record of the Syr Folk. Jesse ben David

and his wife, Devorah, had been chosen to transcribe every spoken word
for Posterity.

When all were assembled, Long Swan took his station next to the Altar
with the Tree of Death on his left. He raised the symbol of his authority,
the long swan staff with its Swan-winged Serpents climbing toward the
pine cone finial cap. Heimdal trumpeted the formal commencement of
the inquiry into the rationale for the actions and deeds of the offenders.

As the sound of the horn blast faded, four Zamoran Fyrd members,
each having lost upwards of twenty family members to the Pitters in
former days, escorted the sixteen elderly and fragile white-clad Scientists-
-men and women alike--to the Altar. Studying their faces, Sur Sceaf saw a
variety of expressions—some displayed openness, others resignation, and
still others, pride. In his hand he held the stone of judgment. If the stone
lit up the accused would live. If it did not light up the accused would die.

Long Swan signaled Heimdal once again, and four Kanichens
prodded the Emperor and the Arch Envoys to join the others. The
Emperor was arrayed in a soiled purple robe and crumpled miter, and
appeared furtive and fearful.

How ironic, Sur Sceaf thought, *that Hryre Seath has not prepared
himself for death. But how could he, when the one true God he believed
favored him as his Anointed One, was little more than an illusion. The
Emperor has been left to free-fall into a spiritual Abyss.*

Ish and Vardrop, however, remained stoic and unmoved. Since last
he saw them, they seemed to have shriveled and shrunk, as though dying
from a rapidly accelerating wasting disease.

Seven Mufsiks in white knee-length lava-lavas with knives at their
sides herded the seven remaining Commissars in their orange robes
to a spot ten yards from the Scientists. Most registered fear, but the
hunch-backed Horquenada glared his defiance, reminding Sur Sceaf of
a cornered wolverine.

Long Swan waved his scepter from East to West and West to East again,
invoking the Spirit of Howrus. As he did so, Sur Sceaf found himself pondering
the Ancient Lore of the Herewardi, especially the writings of Arundel the
Second, who declared that the Prophet Elrus was not only a Prophet, Seer and
Revelator, but that he had also been one of the few Seers who were a Time
Diver. As such, he had the capability of diving into the roots of the past or
soaring into the heights of the future. He possessed total awareness.

It had been said that on one of his journeys into the spirit realms, he had enlisted the spirits of great ancestral armies of the past. Upon his return to the flesh, he announced that *"those who are for us are far greater than those who are against us."* Thus, Sur Sceaf concluded that the Ancestral Elves would be coming to aid him in these final days. Invoking the Spirit of Howrus, as Long Swan had just done, would secure just such aid.

"Vardrop, Ish and Hryre Seath, this is an Inquisition," Long Swan declared. "I, in no way, wish to convey to you that this is in anywise a court of due process, which would grant you the right to legal representation or advocacy. This Tribunal falls under King's Law. Your sentence has been long decided by the governing bodies of the Herewardi Roufytrof, and sustained by the Council of Chiefs of the Sharaka and the Society of Ephrata of the Quailor as well as the Sanhedrin of the Jywds and the Congress of Virginia. It was determined by all bodies that there had been too many martyrdoms and too many innocents slain to show you any form of mercy or compromise. In addition, when the Council of Women consulted the Norn Sisters, they received unanimous confirmation that you shall suffer death by iron and blood, and this is to be administered by the hand of the Seed of the Woman. Therefore, the Warriors of all three tribes, as well as their allies and fellows have sworn a sacred oath never to sheath their swords until the worms scour the flesh of your bodies and drink the last drop of your blood. For your atrocities and abominations, which you brought against the Nations of Panygyrus, you deserve no less." Long Swan then stretched forth his scepter toward the Commissars. "As the evil hands of the Emperor, you Commissars deserve no less. And as for you, Horquenada, the Goddess Freya has reserved a death of your own design, for you are the slayer of so many of the Baldurean Race whom the Gods especially love."

Sur Sceaf caught the satisfied nod of Kanarus' head.

"By Tyranus, so mote it be!" Starkwulf cried out. Va-Eyra's cry of "Here, here!" was echoed by many in attendance.

Long Swan waited for the shouts to fade into silence before continuing, "As for you Scientists, you will be pleased to hear that those of you who swear fealty to the Panygyric Confederation and work in aid of shaping a better world will be spared death unless the Stone of Judgment should indicate otherwise. Think not to deceive the Gods.

Those who refuse to swear by the King's Ring shall be thrice killed, by drowning, strangulation, and the cutting of the throat."

The majority of the Scientists appeared elated, but Sur Sceaf perceived a look of derision sent his way by a tiny, wispy man in the front row.

Jesse and Devorah were diligently writing.

Long Swan continued, "The sole purpose of this inquiry is to permit you to present your rationale to our Posterity.

"Hryre Seath, it has become obvious that you were little more than a tool of these Arch-Envoys here before us. This in nowise excuses your crimes against humanity and the evil deeds you wrought throughout Middle Ea-Urth. We will not be hearing your report, which has already been written in blood and by the lash from your evil minions who have already met their fatefrom one end of this land to the other, who has already met their Fate at the edge of our blades."

Suddenly, the gyre of vultures circling above became so dense that the Sun only shone through the center, like a pillar of light focused on the proceedings. Sur Sceaf took this as a sign that the Valkyrie were leading off his fallen Warriors. It was comforting to him that some would be going to Valhalla, some to Vanaheim, and others to Alfheim, and many to the Halls of Val Ullr, while some others went to their rest in Hell, each according to their deeds and thoughts in the flesh.

Long Swan pointed his scepter at the Arch-Envoys and intoned, "I call upon the gods to witness these proceedings. Vardrop and Ish, one or both of you may begin."

Vardrop shot Long Swan a look of disdain, wet his thin purple lips, and began, "At the end of the last era, at a time when you Herewardi were little more than a secret communal ancestral cult of intellectuals who focused on the restoration of ancient lore, martial arts and self-sufficiency—and had even begun to reveal your Heathen Roots to the other Nations—Ish and I were Scientists, who practiced the politics of peace."

When Vardrop paused for breath, Long Swan interjected, "Let me remind all those in attendance that it is permitted to ask questions or make comments during the testimony."

"In that case," Brekka declared, "I wish it to be entered into the record that the truth of the matter is that Drs. Ish and Vardrop practiced the politics of a false peace, what you called Pax Pittorum."

Vardrop shot her a sharp glance. "Have it your way. I shall proceed." He cleared his throat. "Much of this I already declared to you in the Control Center when you captured us."

Long Swan stated emphatically, "Suffer it to be so that history has a proper accounting of it all. If you do not give your account we shall give posterity our account for you."

Vardrop nodded. "In those days while some of your Forefathers hoarded gold, erected their great structures, and worked for a strong agricultural base, others began to promulgate false hopes of what they called 'good government'—freedom of thought, press, culture, and religion. At that time, Ish and I were employed in New York with full governmental support of our research. At first, we worked in a genetics lab with ordinary citizens desiring improved offspring, but it soon became apparent that these people for the most part only wanted male children with great athleticism and above average intelligence. Eugenics turned into an eating frenzy. People who had been approved for the procedures were soon superseded by those with bigger wallets or political clout. We knew such gene splicings would have no good ending, and neither did we see much real gain from it."

Dr. Shanks appeared appalled as he remarked, "Of course, you achieved little in the way of positive results. Without character development and moral science your Seed Code wash could have left little benefit."

Ish responded, "An astute observation, Master Quailor."

Sur Sceaf was astonished to catch a sweet look passing over her wrinkled face. He suspected she must have been a dark beauty in her prime.

"It was at this time that Dr. Vardrop and I became involved in another government funded operation in the New York prison system. Officials wanted us to develop a way to decriminalize the prison population through genome manipulation. We hoped to turn them away from crime to become productive citizens. Both of these programs ultimately turned out to be flawed. No matter what we tried, the inmates' criminal thinking errors proved too big a barrier to overcome, and their criminal tendencies had too great of a genetic penetrance. We had to change their genes or seed code as you say."

"In point of fact,' Vardrop amplified, "once they were released, instead of turning into law abiding citizens, most used their new abilities to perpetuate even more deviant crimes. We were left with the conclusion that the world was irreparably broken, and we could see that the New World Order had failed to deliver on its promises of world peace, and, in fact, was fast plunging us into a horrible dystopia of worse and greater conflicts."

Mendaka spoke up. "Why in the world would you twist the forces of nature so perversely? The Manitous scorn such devilry."

Vardrop offered him a patronizing smile, which only served to render his wrinkled countenance more grotesque. "We had seen how all mankind was torn by race and religion in endless irresolvable conflicts. We set out to build a new civilization based on reason alone and to make the world one race only. Imagine what could be accomplished with a homogeneous population across the whole globe."

Brekka shook her head. "It disgusts me that you are defending the indefensible. The very fact that you countenance the manipulation of the Seed Code is enough to condemn you in my eyes."

"On the contrary, I'm explaining the thinking of our generation," Ish declared in a quavering voice. "We were, and are, pioneers on the frontiers of science. Some of our colleagues labored to create artificial humans using mechanics and electronics, mere Robots, but we preferred pushing the boundaries of natural science. In fact, we were in a race with many other Nations. You see, we were catching up to Russkaya, Cathaya, and Arapia; the three great powers on the other side of the globe. All three had homogenized their population into one religion, and standardized their populations into one race. Then, each one declared war on the others in one monstrous blood bath, which nearly obliterated the peoples of Africa and turned the continent into a satellite of Arapia. Even though the war established the peoples of Arapia as the most populous, none of those three powers was able to prevail over the other entirely. They simply exhausted one another until they amassed enough energy to enter war again." Ish's voice cracked and was becoming progressively weaker until she was forced to stop.

Vardrop put a reassuring hand on her shoulder. "My dear, allow me to elaborate for you."

Ish appeared grateful as Vardrop took over the narrative. "The Recombining Labs at Big Sur were originally created to genetically engineer tropical and sub-tropical plants to exist in cold climes and were administered by a New Zealand firm with ostensibly no connection with the American Department of Defense. But in reality, specialists from the military were combining jaguar genes with those of humans to create Trans-Human cats, which, by the way, you have not shunned to use, as we noticed you have them amongst your ranks. These were intended to aid the Special Operations units, particularly in the wars raging in South America.

"Our enemies across the ocean had already developed monsters and giants, which no one could safely control. Animals whose Seed Code we secretly procured, like the giant beasts from Russkaya, which you saw guarding our door."

Ruhm called out, "You mean the Bone Crushers?"

"Yes, the Tyfons," Vardrop said proudly. "They took us centuries to reproduce. You must admit they are a splendid genetic engineering feat. Though they were our enemy, I have great admiration for the Russkies and their Scientists. Before the Earth Changes, particularly the meteor showers, wreaked such havoc on the Eurasian and African continents, the Russian geneticists were leagues ahead of us."

"Such rationale sickens me," Brekka stated emphatically. "Did your generation have no concept of boundaries? Did you not understand what is holy and what is sacred and ought not have been tampered with? Couldn't you separate the light from the darkness? And why couldn't you see the evil you wrought in the Nations has merely been the workings of the Dark Elves manipulating you?"

Dr. Vardrop casually declared, "We did not start out with the purpose of harming mankind, and we know nothing of the workings of Dark Elves. We are grounded in science, not in the superstitious. We believe that the concept of Dark Elves was simply a Pitter concoction which they had adopted from their contact with your Herewardi beliefs, and we just used it to our advantage." Doctor Vardrop paused for breath. "As we were concluding our work in New York, we received an invitation from the world renowned geneticist, Dr. Elli-Termis Gloomley, Professor of Biogenesis at Harvard to combine our research teams. We took our research and development team down to New Mexico and joined her at the acclaimed Citadel."

Brekka leaned over to whisper to Sur Sceaf, "New Mexico must have been the original name of the Poisoned Lands."

He nodded. "Flammelf is already working on a project to catalogue and correlate the original names to add to the revised maps of Panygyrus."

"We are eternally indebted to Dr. Gloomley for her research," Ish explained. "At the time she was working on creating a soldier race, but only to serve the Citadel and surrounding area. She was also working on a servant race of minimal intelligence, great endurance and physicality. Sadly, her creation turned against her and became uncontrollable. Enough of them escaped that they became a pervasive menace, forcing her to construct a wall around the Citadel compound."

Once again, Brekka spoke up. "Yes, we saw the evil fruits of her research and that of her Under-Queen, Yggep, who created even more abominable monstrosities, such as the Chimpanapes, Skinwalkers, Creeps and Snucky Punks; created mostly from aborted fetuses or the evil science of *womb tampering*."

"Precisely," Vardrop declared. "Her thesis was flawed, in that she did not create proper control in her Trans-Humans. Nor did she graft in genes for loyalty and obedience. Ish and I knew we could do better with rat genes and wolf genes. And, on a far grander scale than that of Dr. Gloomley."

Sur Sceaf was disgusted by the look of pride that crossed Vardrop's wizened face. His stomach churned at the lack of insight into the damage this man had wrought in the Ea-Urth.

Ish amplified, "Dr. Gloomley disparaged us. Swore we didn't need creatures with more than minimum intelligence for fear that they would overwhelm us, and if control was needed, that could be achieved by applied pharmaceuticals."

Brekka leaned into him and whispered, "Those damn noogs and the chemically castrating agents used on the Grodor and the Blacks at Wymouth."

"Let me remind you our goals were far loftier," Ish claimed without a bit of irony in her voice, "We planned to build an absolutely obedient and vicious army in order to create a Utopia free of the manifest disharmonies of the New World Order."

Sur Sceaf realized that what he had perceived as a sweet look before was actually the flower behind which the adder was poised to strike.

"With little warning, the Earth Changes began, as if some master wizard had put it all into motion, first with climate destabilization, then massive flooding, earthquakes, solar flares, and, finally, prolific meteor showers. For Gloomley and her people, the Citadel, being far underground and able to withstand these powerful forces, was the safest place on Earth, but Vardrop and I were convinced that the only way to remake the world was to return to our labs in New York where we immediately set to creating the Pitters and Vardropi from the surviving prison populations we knew so well and had already groomed with the faith of Angrar."

"Initially," Vardrop continued, "we had recombined genetics to mix bat Seed Code with human Seed Code so as to replace the need for human fruit gatherers. It was a small step to mix human Seed Code with vampire bat Seed Code to get a race of aerial warriors, the Gyrlocks, thanks in large to Dr. Rosenberg." He indicated a tiny man standing in the first row of scientists.

Dr. Rosenberg bowed and declared in a voice filled with pride, "However, it took so long to build them until we discovered that allowing them to hunt live food was what stimulated their breeding instincts, an anomaly that we only discovered in the past thirty years, much to the chagrin of the local farmers and ranchers, who were forced to barn their livestock. Then we were able to build a viable population that was finally large enough to be effective against our enemies."

Smirking, Vardop waved Rosenberg to silence. "My dear Ish and I had already grafted wolf and rat genes into the prison populations up in New York to make the prisoners into unquestioning followers-- reformed, religious, loyal, and vicious. Just like the ancient Romans I so admire. You will know them as the Pitters and Vardropi. Once we had aerial warriors, we were ready to put the capstone on our plans to subdue the whole of Panygyrus. This was not without precedent, of course. After all, the American government was already controlling populations through the drinking water and cleverly administered pharmaceuticals designed to produce mass submission to authority."

A woman Scientist with unexpectedly kind eyes stepped forward and addressed Long Swan, "My dear Wood Lord, if you would kindly permit me to speak?"

Long Swan nodded. "Please state your name and say your piece."

"I am Dr. Rhoda Eckstein, Director of Social Sciences. I relish this opportunity to say what I was forbidden to say for the past five hundred years. As you can see, we are no better off than the world we condemned so self-righteously. In fact, I believe we have made it far worse. We Scientists were inflated with our own narcissistic beliefs, even more so than the Evil Generation. Believe me, Wood Lord, I rue the day I ever joined this team, and not a day passed that I didn't try to return my colleagues to a more sane and humane philosophy."

Long Swan exhaled. "Unfortunately, Rhoda, dictatorships are not wont to hear opposing views."

"Too late I, too, found that to be so." With a sigh, she resumed her place amongst her colleagues in white.

Ruhm cleared his throat and requested the floor. After a motion from Long Swan, he asked, "Tell us more about your creation of the Vardropi and Pitters. When I breed my horses, I select for temperament and disposition. Is that what you are talking about here?"

Dr. Vardrop looked pleased. "In a way, you are correct. We took the selection process much further in what we call a genetic splice, or grafting, which is done by injecting the genes into the prison population. We formed a prison ministry to indoctrinate the transhumans with our dogma. They had no idea they were serving our designs. Thus, with their rigid fanaticism, they would be our pliable crusaders, and thus one by one we planned to erase the historic religions of the world. Once everyone was of one religion, we could do away with religion altogether, as there would only be one to eliminate rather than a thousand fanatical cults."

Ruhm shook his head. "It astounds me that you persist in arguing what you did was admirable and in the service of mankind. How can you be proud of contradicting the very nature of humanity?"

Sur Sceaf noted that Ish was obviously taken aback by the question. "Of course, we're proud of all that we did. Even before the Earth Changes, the world was broken, and could not be fixed under the systems in place! But, after the Earth Changes caused the collapse of civilizations and destroyed the Ruling Oligarchy of the New World Order, there were not enough executive authority or oversight organizations to prevent us from creating the scaffolding of a better world. We saw that if we wanted to create a happy people, all we needed to do was eliminate all the unhappy ones. We saw it as a positive to eliminate the world's ills, and we sought to rid all disruptive differences, the two most prevalent being race and, as I already mentioned, religion. Our primary goal was to create a standardized society with no points for contention. There would be one government, one religion and one leader. To that end, we established the Pitter Empire; and to control them, we created the belief in one God we called Angrar, named after our research program. Once we destroyed all religions and homogenized all races, we would have ended the Pitters ourselves, as they were only our means to an end."

Hryre Seath lunged forward before being restrained by powerful arms of Starkwulf. As he struggled to break loose, he arched his body menacingly toward his two superiors. "Katus was correct when he repeated the warning of the Dark Elves that you never had our best interest at heart. In fact you actually favored the Dominikers, didn't you? I should have listened to Katus when he argued that you were little more than pretentious crow bait, and when he urged me to commit you to the crow cages. You are not God's chosen envoys. I see it all now. You sprang from the same race as these Heathens we have defeated from one end of the land to the other."

Starkwulf sneered at the red-faced Emperor. "You could never defeat the Herewardi. Our Gods would not have suffered such nor would they have forsaken us."

Starkwulf gestured to one of the guards to restrain Hryre Seath before turning to Ish once again. "This is where you made your critical mistake, thinking you had subdued us with your tortures and brutality. I, myself, bear the wounds of three wives sent to their graves with their lungs pulled out by the brutal hands of your emissaries, and my children left as food for the fowl of the air. Although you sent me into the bowels of Hell, I rose up even more determined to obtain my just vengeance. And I am far from alone in vowing Godly retribution. As you see, we have reversed the blows of death from the Sea of Aurvandilea in the West to the Sea of Aegir in the East."

Ish scrunched her wrinkled lips and said, "You have me there. But if I may explain? After the Herewardi were driven to the Umpqua, it only required an administration using the Dominikers and a small military presence to keep all other peoples in submission. Our Commissars had the power to nullify any effective resistance. Their acts and words were final. After a hundred years of having our own way, the sheer power of manipulating the future became addictive, and we found we could not move into phase three, The Age of Reason, because we loved the power phase far too much. You will see. It will happen to you too."

Vardrop shot her a corrective glance. "Once again, methinks you reveal too much, my dear."

Ish surrendered a smile, which was little more than a grotesque twisting of her parchment thin lips. She responded in a cracking voice, "And once again what difference does it make now?"

Starkwulf continued his interrogation, his nostrils flaring and the look of an eagle in his eye as if he was ready to pounce on Vardrop any moment. The shadow of the Wose was in his expression. "Even though you knew you were betraying your own plans? It sickens me that you continued to oppress the Nations."

Dr. Vardrop looked as if he had just sucked a sour pickle. "It's one thing *to see your sins,* and an entirely different thing to turn from them. We loved playing god; establishing the one and only True Church. And even though we had fellow Scientists that disagreed with the process, we silenced them by saying we had to endure the dictatorship of religiosity before we could move into the next phases, but we knew the truth. There would never be a self-willed exit out of the dictatorship phase; particularly after we worked out the formulae of extending our lives. That alone was an opiate, for, as Dr. Gloomley always spoke, *'no one wants to die'.*"

"You have deceived and used me." Hryre Seath cried out once again. "I believed all that you told me. You promised you would crush all our enemies and make me the Divine Emperor like the Caesars of Old. But now I see all you spoke was lies."

"Surely," Dr. Vardrop said, "you of all people cannot complain of the privileges we bestowed upon you. After all, you are a sister killer, and that was the first step of your downfall. Once you broke obedience and conspired with Katus to obey what you called the Dark Elves over the Angrar, you were soon to be erased from our plans."

Hryre Seath winced. "If it were in my power, I would kill both of you right now. I should have followed Katus when he said the Dark Elves would exalt us. Not the Angrar." A genuine expression of terror spread across Hryre Seath's face as he appeared to have some sort of epiphany. "Where?" There was a long silence. "Where will I go when I die? I thought you were God." The Emperor wept like a child. "Will the Dark Elves be able to save me?"

It was apparent to Sur Sceaf that Hryre Seath was nothing more than a programmed true-believer, a mere emotionally retarded puppet, who believed the cruel joke Vardrop and Ish had perpetuated in the Ea-Urth, what Vardrop called a biological robot. To his surprise, a sense of pity arose in his chest for the fallen Emperor. How ironic that he had any humanity in him at all, for now it was to be his undoing.

"I have a question," Arundel spoke up, his voice and his words deliberately measured. "Why did you choose to give up on the government of the Amerikans? Why not continue to build on it?"

"Because we determined that there was no soil for liberty or Constitutionalism to grow. The system became too corrupt to repair. The Americans were already one step from dictatorship due to extreme executive overreach which had effectively nullified the Constitution. The American government had completely departed from the moorings of a democratic republic, and the leaders had become mere puppets of powerful corporate entities. For years corporate lust for power and money infected all the leadership. All progress was bled off to other Nations, which was followed by religious and racist revivals that plunged us further behind the other Nations. Reluctantly, we deduced that our noble goals would be much more benevolent than the tyrannical measures we saw as inevitable. Of course, in the beginning, we needed to keep a tight rein and a tyrannical hand over the ignorant masses. That's why we were forced to create one religion and one race that would ultimately consume all others. With race and religion unified, we combined the cannibalistic consumptive forces of Yengish capitalism and what we call Marxism, which allowed us to subdue practically the entire continent of North America under one government. Don't you see how brilliant all this was? It was our Manifest Destiny that we had to create the One God that would end all other Gods before we could set up the perfect Utopian society."

Mendaka interjected, "And who got to decide which race was going to be the selected one?"

"It was strictly my choice," Dr. Vardrop said proudly. "And being from New York, I chose the people I was most familiar with. I then resolved to transform these chosen people into my proud Dominikers."

"You arrogant bastards!" Ruhm bursted out, "You crushed and enslaved entire populations that had existed for generations; that had created rich and diverse cultures full of beauty and expression. Do you even know how many beautiful Races and Tribes you blotted out of existence? What you did to the Black Race alone was a crime against all humanity and will never be forgiven," he spat in the dirt, "And all this in the name of a made-up god! No more than a paper, blood-drenched god at that."

Ish was angry at his words. "Master Hickoryan, you mustn't judge our chickens before they had a chance to fully hatch. We were just about to end the dictatorship of religiosity and create a perfected race from the remaining Dominikers. We would have delivered an orderly and homogeneous world into their hands if you Syr Folk hadn't intervened and knocked the hen off the nest and then attempted to bastardize all the eggs by granting sovereignty to every tribe, race, and kindred under the stars."

Mendaka's dark eyes shot fire through his war paint. "Why were you so hell-bent on destroying the Red Man, the Herewardi, and the Quailors? We are little different than the Dominikers."

"It was simple." Ish gave a creepy smile out of her crepe skinned face as she pretended to brush lint from her uniform. "The Red Man could not be subjugated, no matter how hard we tried. They were too fiercely independent. As for the Herewardi, well, they were the antithesis of all we stood for with their many wives, their many Gods, their war-like spirits. We could never accept their belief in Royal Blood and their deep mysteries which they religiously guarded. They too could not be controlled. Now, as for the Quailors, they would have perpetuated the psychosis of warring religious beliefs, and we would eventually have been plunged once again into the world we so abhorred. Except for accelerating our timelines for a homogeneous population and the recent surge in our promotion of the Dominikers, we have never departed from our mission to achieve a glorious perfection."

Sur Sceaf breathed hard in disgust before declaring, "The word perfection sticks in my craw. It's such a lifeless word. We seek wholeness, not perfection. The very concept of perfection is dehumanizing. We Herewardi do not believe in concentrating the productiveness of the many into the hands of a few. Your selfish Dominiker capitalism be damned. Our way is to promote free enterprise where all have a shot at improving their lot, and no government or corporation is allowed to rig the system in favor of the few."

Doctor Vardrop countered, "But you Herewardi have your Royalty; your precious Blood Line. That has the potential for concentrating the wealth in the hands of a few, does it not?"

"It is true that our Royalty is based upon a Blood Line, not built on the exploitation of underlings such as you created, but free men governed by strict laws through the Holy Council of the Roufytrof. In our system Royal Blood is never allowed to triumph over merit. It is an ancient contract with our people. That is why we made it our mission to uncover Mount Heredom, build our holy Temple, and crouch as a lion atop it as a guardian of peace, and an aggressive protector of other weaker Nations and peoples who become the victims of the forces of evil and the avarice that the Dark Elves have set to work in this world."

"Dark Elves," Vardrop scoffed. "I know of no such things. Come now, I know the Herewardi to be astute philosophers. Do you really believe such fables?"

"I marvel that you do not, for they pre-date you by eons. Our wise men tell us that they have destroyed many other worlds, but Odhin has decreed they shall not prevail here."

"Oh, your God, Odhin. No doubt no more than a mere contrivance like our God, Angrar."

A murmur of anger ran through the attendees. Sur Sceaf shook his head. "I advise you not to tempt the Gods, for they do not suffer themselves to be mocked!" He no sooner finished than a ball of lightning travelled along the parapet and struck a crow cage, blowing it into hundreds of pieces. A look of pure terror crossed Vardrop's face, while Ish cowered in disbelief.

Long Swan raised his scepter, indicating that he reclaimed the floor in his official capacity. "Fortunately for you, the Gods have left your condemnation in our hands. As their mouthpiece, I now pronounce that condemnation. You called your vision of the New World a dream. In the name of Odhin, I declare it to be a nightmare. The Lore Masters have taught us that in the Pearl State of Amerika, true freedoms, liberty and equality prevailed, and would have continued to unveil one of the greatest forms of government ever begotten, but the Holy Grail of government was shattered when the Republic was crushed to form a Criminal Union bent on devouring its own citizens and sent rape-apes to rampage throughout the Southlands and the lands of the Red Men to the West in order to commit cultural genocide in the name of gain.

"Crony capitalism emerged and began allowing sinister intruding populations into the healthy body, thus infecting all free government and cultures. This was promoted and aided by your false priesthood of academia and your prostituted press, which tolerated no diversity of opinions, demonizing and marginalizing all who advocated for the principles of free trade, freedom of information, and the glory of Tribalism. The government became like an entity turning on its own fetus in the womb, spying on its citizenry, stripping the healthy citizens of their ability to defend themselves, and forbidding all forms of free thinking and expression with your insane political correctness, warped concepts of social justice, and that greatest of evils that you call Marxism.

"You chose the Dominikers because they are the descendants of the Witch Hunters whose inherent trait was to continue these witch hunts and their stone-throwing. You promoted all forms of fanaticism and control, with no thought to the sacredness of the Original Constitution. Your Pitter Empire only added a heavier and deeper yoke to the Nations of Panygyrus, and was a nightmare to all humanity, causing wars from one end of heaven to the other. Your Seed will be forever blotted from the Ea-Urth. Your story will be told with horror, and you will be known throughout eternity as the depraved megalomaniacs you are." Long Swan turned to glance at Sur Sceaf. "My king, I give you the final word."

Sur Sceaf stared silently at the three accused standing before the backdrop of the blood-stained Altar and the Tree of Death. The crow cages creaked in the wind behind them. "I feel as though I am looking at rogue mongrels that have just slain half of my flock, their shameful faces still covered with the blood of the innocents. I see no spark of conscience in your hearts, nor hear I any remorse in your words. I cannot hope that monsters such as you could be capable of sufficient introspection to own the evil you have committed. Only the thin strand of your breath separates you from the final judgment that the Gods shall soon render under our hands. When we release you from your mortal coils, the hounds of hell shall beset you and feast on your souls forevermore, somewhere in the acid depths of Hellheim. You will not find forgiveness in this world nor the worlds to come, ages without end."

A genuine expression of terror spread across Hryre Seath's face as he appeared to have some sort of epiphany. "Where? Where will I go when I die? I believed in Angrar, and now I know not what to believe." Hryre Seath fell to his knees and besieged, "Please, please, don't let my Sister's goblins have at me. They will surely claw out my eyes and eat my heart. Suffer me not to die."

It was apparent to Sur Sceaf that Hryre Seath was nothing more than a programmed true-believer, a mere puppet, who believed the cruel joke

Vardrop and Ish had perpetuated in the Ea-Urth. To his surprise, a sense of pity arose in his chest for the fallen Emperor. How ironic that he had any humanity in him at all, for now it was to be his undoing.

Sur Sceaf just shook his head. "I cannot tell what will befall you in the next world, but I know you must pay for your crimes, and the gods require every iota of debt you have incurred. It is not a burden I would care to even share."

Yellow Horse sprang forward until he was face-to-face with Hryre Seath. "I can tell you what shall befall you, you rat-faced son-of-a-bitch. You will be bound with the ice cold guts of Katus on a sharp rock from which your back will be burnt and the venom of Nidhogg will drip on your face throughout all the generations of time. And from below, the dragon will come to devour you and, then, finally with one blast from its nostrils, consign you to the Lake of Fire in the Bottomless Abyss."

CHAPTER 14 :
JUDGMENT DAY

I T WAS HIGH NOON. THE SUN'S scorching eye beat down brutally on the Gyrlock images cast on the black iron gates of the Big Springs Bastion. Once again the sky was a clear vivid blue without clouds, save for the by-now familiar silver cloud resembling a giant mirror floating directly overhead.

Brekka stood in the full armor of a Lady Knight with all her Lady Knights behind her, baking in the Sun under their gleaming polished silver. Two ravens with golden eyes kept the host of cawing crows away, by perching atop the Old Dead Oak overlooking the landing. Not even the excessive heat could stop the villagers coming from the far outlying areas of Merry Land and from as far South as Cherokee Firginia. They had all gathered to see the final judgment to be rendered to Hryre Seath and to hear the outcomes of the Panygyric Congress.

The maggots had gorged on so much blood, the air was thick with newly molted flies which covered the ground in blankets of swirling black masses. During the past two weeks since the Inquisition, the Gatherers of the Dead from the Rogue Nations had cast lime in a ragged semi-circle on the Promontory facing the landing as well as the landing itself to deflect most of the offensive odors, but there had been too much bloodshed to possibly mask it all.

To Brekka's left, the Tree of Death from which she had been hung, stood as a witness to the proceedings. Before her was the Pitter Altar

Stone, beyond which gathered the teeming masses of spectators. From the conversations she had heard while making her way through the throng, Brekka deduced that most of the spectators had come for some form of closure. Many simply could not believe the Pitter Empire had come to an end, and sought confirmation with their own eyes. Others were simply there out of morbid curiosity, while most of the Syr Folk forces attended to witness the fruits of their long labors.

She had prepared herself mentally for this event through prayer and meditation. Her Father, Brother and the Command Leadership sat mounted on their white steeds at her right hand, showing their support. Ruhm sat mounted to her left, while his Hickoryan Cavalry was arrayed in their dress greys down below by the Big Springs, along with the masses of Hickoryans, Red Men, Blue Men, Green Men, Jywds, Black Men, and representatives of just about every Nation across the face of Panygyrus. Many had come for the Congressional Convention, and to see the execution of the Emperor, who had ruled over them with the iron fist of tyranny, making them to serve all the days of their lives in bitter bondage until the Gods had granted Brekka the honor of delivering the final death blow to these Oppressors.

She took a deep breath to get her courage up. Instinctively, she glanced over at Ruhm on his grey mount. When her eyes met his, he tipped his hat and gave her the reassuring sign of the dove to go forward in peace. Miraculously, her nerves relaxed like a feather on the breeze.

Behind her, Freyxus led the Lady Knights in a chant: "How is it the mighty are fallen? How is it that tyranny has come to an end? Consider the ways of the Gods, ye peoples of the Ea-Urth. They have broken the yoke of tyranny and established their peoples forever in the Holy Land. Give praise, ye nations and races of the Ea-Urth. For this day the Gods have delivered us from the perverse hand of our oppressor."

Twelve Trumpeters blasted from the top of the parapet. The crowds stirred with a rustle of conversation as they looked on. Beside the altar, muscular Sharaka drummers, dressed only in red loin clothes, beat a solemn dirge on their large red drums. Chise and Zoot flew the Banner of the Flying Sea-Serpent, designated as the new flag of Panygyrus. Quailor Hospitalers stood in their black pants and white shirts or grey dresses with white aprons, clustered to the South like a band of magpies witnessing the final judgment. Iron scraped against iron as the Iron Gates slowly creaked open. Fyrd soldiers in double file, dressed in their red sur coats and bearing both White Horse and Swan Banners paraded out with the three, King-convicted, prisoners. Representative Fyrd Officers from every Fyrd led Hryre Seath forth in his dirty purple robe, with his crumpled mitre still atop his head, and placed him before the Altar.

Brekka took a step forward. *Indeed, how the mighty have fallen,* she thought. The once powerful Emperor was now reduced to a shrunken, beady-eyed rat creature with trembling limbs and an inhuman curvature to his spine.

The peoples shouted, "Boo! Boo! Boo! Death to tyranny. Death to oppression! Death to the bringers of death."

Once, Brekka raised her hand, the throng fell silent. The only sounds she heard were of her own heart beating in her throat, the buzzing of flies and the snorting of nearby horses. Her hands were sweating as they grasped the Labrys, a Lady Knight's weapon symbolizing the Lips of Hrus and the execution of the spoken will of her Longfather. She was refreshed by the wings of her helm as it caught a slight breeze, cooling her face and neck.

Brekka pronounced in a loud, clear voice, "Have you any final words, Hryre Seath?"

Hryre Seath dropped to his knees, beseeching in a quavering voice. "Mercy, Seed of the Woman! Mercy, O revered Daughter of the Wood Lords! Mercy, oh Swan-Maiden and friend of Odhin. Spare my life, I beg you, Virgin of the long line of Hring Lords, spare me and I will serve thee faithfully forever!"

Brekka answered. "Know you not that it is mercy I show to you, Hryre Seath? By Woon, We and Wili, you came from the Dark Realms of Niflheim and are of Loki's kin. There can be no more place in this world for your kind. The Dark Elves weaseled your race into our world through a womb not of Nature's cast. The Gods have a place for you, but it is not here. Now, let me send you back to Niflheim for your correct employ and mayhap, in the endless burnings, your soul can be purged enough to enter some better state than what now awaits you."

"No, no! I beseech. Anything, but death. Know you not that my Sister's goblins will heckle and torment me there for times measureless to man."

Brekka sensed the support of her Lady Knights, as once again Freyxus led them in a chant. "The Gods have struck off the heads of the wicked and brought the mighty low into the dust. Loki's kin can have no place in the realms of man and the worms shall drink their blood."

At a nod from Brekka, the two Fyrd Officers forced Hryre Seath to his feet. As he struggled to free himself, they compelled him face down with his head across the fly-filled altar. Brekka took a deep breath and hefted the Labrys above her head. "In the name of the Syr Folk Confederation, and by all the Holy Gods of Osgard, I pronounce death as final judgment upon you, and lift your head from your shoulders that you die by iron and bleeding. For so it is written and so it shall be done."

She paused momentarily to catch her breath, and then brought her Labyrus down with a clean stroke across the neck of the Emperor. The razor-sharp blade severed his puny neck as easily as one severs off a chicken's head. Hryre Seath's head tumbled to the ground with the blood-drenched mitre still attached, and blood shot in streams and spurts from his neck over the Altar. The crowds threw their hats in the air and roared their approval so loud that all the birds of the surrounding brush took to the air and filled the sky with wings.

At a nod from Brekka, the two Fyrd Officers tossed his body to the side as if he were a sack of trash, much as he had done to his victims in times past.

Horquenada shouted, "You Heathen Witch. Would that I had sent you to your death like that White Witch whose bowels I drew out like a worm from the dirt."

Ruhm guided Spitzer close to within an arm's length of the Commissars, drew his sword and held the top beneath Horquenada's chin. "One more word from you, and I will take your ears and eyes!"

Horquenada's mouth went agape before he managed to shrink back. Ruhm sheathed his sword before offering Brekka a nod of encouragement.

The Lady Knights chanted: "With a strong arm the Gods have brought low the proud, and those who have perverted the laws of nature now speak forevermore only from the dust which shall blow away in the winds of forgetfulness. The blood of the fallen is avenged!"

At a nod from Brekka, two more Officers brought Ish forward. Unlike the Emperor, the Old Woman seemed more resigned to her fate. Brekka announced, "You have been King-convicted, Ish. It is customary to allow the condemned to speak their Swan-Song. Have you anything to say?"

Ish looked up, her face a cobweb of wrinkles, and in her crackly voice declared, "We have sinned a great sin in the Earth all the days of our lives. It is with great regret that I go to the grave. I have unto this day always had a dread fear of death. Though we stretched our years with artificial means beyond what they were intended to be, you can have no idea what torture it is to have the blood of a seventeen year old woman coursing through your veins while having to wear the ugliness of old age like an iron garment."

Brekka replied, "Nature is beautiful in her season, and has intended true beauty to be a passing thing, as its true value lies only in its passing rareness."

"I see that you are the rising of a new and healthier generation, for you have both the blood and the beauty of youth. I know of no God, but I hope I shall find mercy when I shed this mortal coil, for I no longer fear death. No, I do not. But oh, how I fear the grave!"

To her surprise, Brekka felt an inexplicable moment of compassion. "Ish, I only wish you had come to this conclusion so much earlier. Just like Gloomulah, you gave no thought to the pain you allowed your underlings to suffer. You bear sins too great for the wings of mercy to ever cover. I am sorry you die faithless, but there is no place for you and your kind in our new creation. Mother Freya will have no perversity in her worlds, for the boundaries of all Races and Beings was long ago set by the Gods, over which they will suffer none to pass."

The Officers caused Ish to kneel with chest over the bloody altar upon which so many innocents had been sent to their unwarranted deaths. As Brekka lifted her Labyrus, she noticed a trail of tears running down Ish's wrinkled cheek. Stilling herself, Brekka smote off the head of Ish. Once again the crowds shouted their approval. The Officers laid her carcass next to that of the Emperor and rolled her head away with their feet..

A struggling Vardrop was brought to the Altar next. His skinny neck put Brekka in mind of a turtle outside of its shell. She looked him square on and asked dispassionately, "Have you any last words to speak?"

His soulless eyes blazed back defiantly. "You call this civilized? You people are barbarians! You will breed endless misery by permitting the diversity of cultures, religions, and races to have individual sovereignty. Once again you have set the stage for endless war."

"On the contrary, we shall make a Baconian Paradise as was the original intent of our forefathers for this Land. It shall be an Atlantean and Osyrean Kingdom of Glory on Ea-Urth."

"Uncivilized Witch! You've destroyed the beauty of my creation. How can you ever hope to do better than I did?"

Despite his bombastic accusations, she could read the abject fear in his terror-stricken face. "It is as civilized as we are capable of now, but by Os, you shall meet the iron of death and the judgment of bleeding, for the earth thirsts mightily for your blood. This day has long been prophesied by the Seers, Sages, and Shamans of all our peoples. You have brought this upon yourself by all your evil deeds. You have cast yourself as a false-god, imposed your will on the nations of the Ea-Urth against their better interests, and yoked them under diabolical oppression. May the Gods damn you to Hell."

"Prophesied," he hissed out, the wattles on his neck shaking from the force with which he uttered the word. "There are no Gods. There is no prophecy. We were the only Gods this world has ever known. We were the true scientific elite ordained by reason and education to lead the ignorant masses to order and to impose a communism and homogeneity of perfection. To prove it, all you have to do is look at our technology. Witness how much more advanced in technology we are than you. Had we not intervened, the world would have in all likelihood degenerated into savagery, eternally stuck in a downward spiral of religious and racial wars. We were the standard of civilization, and now you have plunged the Earth back into a new barbarism from which it will never again emerge."

Brekka held her axe, still dripping with Ish and Hryre Seath's blood. "Barbarism is the axe the Mother Spirit sends for you. You bred only perversity with your technology. She will have no perversity in her realms. Neither should any man dare to breach the laws of Nature. You have lived a lie, and done much evil in consequence of it, true believer that you are. I have seen the Gods, met the Chief God along with the Sisters of Fate, and I have witnessed all their prophecies fulfilled. I am divinely assured that you must be extinguished from the Ea-Urth, for even your wretched underlings, the Pitters, knew more than you of the Other World to come." Her hand crept down her axe.

The Fyrd Officers forced him to his knees, laid him chest down across the Altar until his cheek was in Hryre Seath's blood, and flies peppered his face. Brekka brought her axe down in one swift blow that snapped and crunched the scrawny neck of Vardrop like a match stick. She struck so hard that sparks flew, and Vardrop's bald head rolled to the ground with eyes wide open. The look of utter fear and terror stared out.

The Lady Knights chanted: "The Gods led and preserved a remnant of us through the years of our unvictories, whereby they shaped and molded us. They established us upon an Isle of the Deep where they strengthened our arms. Under the Seed of the Woman, the battle by day and the terror by night were caused to cease. And from the Gods come great tidings of comfort and joy, and the promise of their return now breaks forth in the East."

As the crowds exulted in celebration, a great relief came over Brekka. From now on she would never need to be a Warrior or executioner again. She breathed out a relieved sigh, laid her Labyrus upon the Altar, and raised her hands in the sign of a Swan. She said, "Beloved Brothers and Sisters, it is finished. The World of Hryre Seath and his minions are dead. The soils of Panygyrus are finally ready for the Seeds of Liberty, Tolerance and Freedom to be sown."

She glanced over at Ruhm, who smiled warmly at her, saluted, and nodded his approval. The crowds of people continued to shout for joy, waiving their hats, and stamping their feet. Hogor put the heads of the enemy on pikes which then Sur Sceaf, Starkwulf, and Va-Eyra planted next to the Tree of Death, like three scarecrows perched in a garden. The blood from their heads trickled down the staves of the pikes to pool in the dust where flies quickly clustered to gorge themselves in its thick syrup.

At an order from Sur Sceaf, the Trumpeters heralded the final executions. Dog Soldiers prodded the orange-clad Commissars to the Altar, whilst the Mufsiks sequestered Horquenada for themselves. As the last notes faded away, Chise, resplendent in his chiefly attire, stepped forward. His voice was strong and exultant. "This day the Manitous have freed the Red Men from their shackles of the Usurpers to once again live our birthright as the freest of all people. It has long been our Manifest Destiny that the Red Man should take up his rightful inheritance as Steward of the whole of Panygyrus, where by our Brother Races may learn our ways of freedom."

On the Promontory the Ceruleans began the Syr-Haka, the sound swelling to thunder as other members of the Syr Folk armies joined in. Two Dog Soldiers led each Commissar in turn to the Altar where Chief Chise slit their throats. Chief Zoot joined his Twin at the Altar in a ritual cry of victory, offering their enemies up to the Thunder Beings. Zoot then ordered a Dog Soldier to pour whale oil over the pile of bodies, and set it alight with a torch passed to him by White Moose.

The Mufsiks in their white lava-lavas disappeared into the fortress with Horquenada, shortly reappearing on the parapet above next to one the arms of the Crow Cages. As the flames leaped into the sky, the black iron arm rotated until the dangling Crow Cage it held was visible. The mechanism lowered the iron coffin toward the landing. The Mufsiks had cut out Horquenada's tongue and stuffed him into the cage without bothering to remove the rotting corpse of its previous victim, its decomposing arms dangling between the bars, and a grimacing smile of death on its face as if it was happy to embrace its tormentor in his final grips of death.

As the iron cage was slowly lowered to a spot halfway down the stone wall, Horquenada shook the bars furiously while shrilling gurgling curses that no one could make out. As if on cue, Kanarus led the shouts of rejoicing from all the people's gathered.

Through the bloody bone fires and smoke of the burning bodies, Brekka's eyes filled with tears at the memory of her dear Sister Wilona. She would miss her all the days of her life, but took comfort in the knowledge that she was now dwelling with her Celestial Family. Brekka reached down and gathered some dust to absorb the blood smeared on her hands. Later she would take a ritual bath to cleanse herself of the blood, and her mind of the horrors and vileness of the last three years.

At her command, the Swan Maidens shook their sistrums and sang, "Justice is rendered. The wicked have fallen. Brekka never has been unveiled by mortal man. She stands with her foot upon the necks of the Sons of Overpowering. The Ea-Urth is cleansed like the Garden of Idunn!

After allowing his people to celebrate and rejoice for several moments, Sur Sceaf dismounted and strode to the edge of the landing to address all the gathered multitudes of people below. Ravens swirled overhead; one came down to rest on Sur Sceaf's shoulder, chortled briefly, and took flight beside its companion on the tree of death. Amid a swirl of comments, he raised his hands for silence. The throng not only consisted of people from the far outlying areas of Merry Land and the Firginias, but also from the mountains and the coasts, from Sylphania, and even the far reaches of the northern woods and Kanada. Instead of going silent, they exuberantly roared with cheers, while the eastern peoples shouted in wave after wave, "Imperioto! Imperioto! Imperioto!"

Brekka cringed, knowing her father despised that title and its meaning, so rooted in the Latin and lies of Vardrop and Ish as it was.

Sur Sceaf stretched out his arms for silence, until, with the last few shouts, the crowd went quiet.

"People of the Firginias and Merry Land, its Sister Kingdom, and those of you from the far north, the days of emperors are no more. Although I know you meant to do me praise, please, I ask of you to let that word, *Imperioto*, and all other latin lies, die in this land. It is from the evil days of the romish cult, from a day when great evil and darkness spread its wings across the Ea-Urth like the disease of the dark elves who spawned it. It was a time when the ancient landmarks of freedom and humanity were drowned in a sea of blood, torture, and religious darkness that blotted out the golden laws of old. It was a time when elven knowledge was utterly squelched. We will begin rebirthing these golden laws. I warn you, our governance will be such as you have not been used to. The burden for any free peoples shifts to your own shoulders. As to whether your dreams become a reality or not, is up to you. Expect equality of all races, religions, and peoples, but never expect equality of merit or wealth, for such has never been the design of nature, who cannot err. Your future lies solely in your own hands, as well as the responsibility for your own actions."

The crowds roared with cheers.

"Now is the great day of freedom, home rule, and self-government, a day in which you shall reap the fruits of your own labors, and reclaim your lands with dignity. It is a day when you must strive for the greatest moral science you are capable of, until moral progress has made us all free. We will now be governed not only by law, but also by the ur-fyr that burns in every heart. Those of you who have somehow managed to follow a spiritual faith are free to worship where and how you wish."

White Moose and the Mufsiks raised a shout. Talks-As-He-Walks shook his medicine staff and loudly proclaimed, "The day of the red man has returned!"

Behind Sur Sceaf, the dog soldiers, the sharaka, and the apaches all trilled their approval. Sur Sceaf turned to his blood-brother, Mendaka, and the two shared a smile before Sur Sceaf signaled his intention to continue.

"After the panygyric congress convenes, the laws of the land will be promulgated to you all. And every man, woman, and child will be free to govern themselves without the burden of heavy taxes, tithes, and involuntary servitude. There will no longer be any such thing as property tax or income tax. Those things are from the past, and were designed by the dark elves and enemies of mankind to enslave you. We must now learn tolerance, even of intolerance, for the freedom which knowledge confers can only be learned in stages. Rejoice, for after years of strife, grief, and tribulation, a new day has come to us all."

The crowds went wild with cheers from every corner of the springs and bastion. The women danced with bells and crotales on their hands and feet, and the trumpeters blew their bronze lurs, carnyces, and trumpets. The two guardian ravens took flight into the dark clouds of an approaching thunder storm that appeared like a dark giant approaching out of the west. With claps of lighting and the roaring thunder of mighty Tyranus, a cool wisp of air poured in to quench the heat of the day. It was as if the god of justice had personally come to cleanse the final blood and filth from the land. As the torrential rains poured down, the crowds reluctantly ran for the shelter of their tents.

The cleansing thunderstorm, the likes of which no one had ever remembered seeing, continued throughout the afternoon hours in a heavy downpour. Periodically, fantastic flashes of lightning ripped through the skies. Loud claps of thunder seemed to tear the fabric of the old world apart. The thorough downpour washed the altar and the dead oak clean of all the blood and gore. In the darkness of the storm, the frightful faces of the three king-convicted tyrants flashed like the remnants of a now passing nightmare. Someone had planted a wet Hickoryan banner with a red blood rood against a white background which flew near the scarecrows on the pikes. In the ferocious wind, Brekka read the black writing beneath: ***Thus Ever To Tyrants***. She had been told by Ruhm, it was a motto dear to the Firginians.

Toward twilight, the storm passed as abruptly as it had approached. Brekka exulted in the cool freshness of the air. The sense of wet leaves and damp earth replaced the stench of war. She suddenly felt reborn and more vitally alive than she could remember since she had left the isle. It came to her suddenly, that she was now free to express her love to Ruhm and accept his love in return. She could scarcely wait to be with him. Delicious temptations danced through her mind.

She stood outside her tent watching the peoples as they quietly and reverently poured out of their shelters. At first they were subdued by the cleansing of the storm, and then spontaneously pockets of festivities, dance, and singing began again throughout the camps. The air smelled of fresh ozone. People traded goods freely, shared tales of the many battles and feats of the brave men and women who had fought in the long years, and drank more spirits than most were accustomed to.

She was happy most people were celebratory, but the Herewardi had one more solemn duty to perform this night. She summoned the lady knights from the tent, and together they joined the solemn torch-lit procession led by Long Swan, Sur Sceaf, and Arundel to the garden of heroes in Pikeside.

Under the sliver of a moon, the sign of the virgin, the graveyard was well-lit with torches and lanterns. The funerary assistants from the rogue nations had been working day and night to lay out rows of upright stones over the graves of the Syr Folk fallen. Several of the stones bore runic writing telling of the heroic deeds of the fallen soldiers. Under the direction of Long Swan they circled the graveyard with torches and sang funeral dirges, while laying feathery yew wreaths on the graves of their honored dead. Platforms were erected in the Sharaka portion of the burial grounds, upon which laid fallen braves wrapped in buffalo hides. Mendaka led the chants for the traveling spirits to return to the council fires in the sky. The Hickoryans had their graves to the south, but were going to honor their dead on the third day, a custom going back to their god, Jehoshua Hammaschiach, the Christ.

Brekka was deeply grieved as she surveyed the anonymous graves. She had known many of those now gone forever. Her throat tightened so that she could no longer speak, and tears ran down her cheeks. Her chest felt like it would implode as she reviewed the faces of the fallen in her head, while hundreds of memories of her former days with the sleeping heroes paraded through her mind. There was not a man or lady knight that did not weep aloud. She adjusted a wreath over one of the graves and gradually separated herself from the throng.

She pulled her cape over her head, grabbed a lantern and made her way up the path to the hill through the dark of the windswept night. As she climbed the mound, she could hear the voices of the fallen braves and warriors coming through the soughing yews. She knew in her being they were grateful for their own sacrifice they had offered, and were being led on their way by the valkyrie and shamans to the summer lands behind the veil into the other world. Upon reaching Tor Ili, she prayed and gave thanks to the gods, praising them for the victory.

Whilst she sat in the wood atop the hill in silent prayer, rejoicing in life, a tingle of energy rose from the Ea-Urth and entered her body through her feet. From the sky above, she felt energy flowing down through her, and all the energy converged around her. A light burst overhead, and two glorious elven beings appeared through cloven skies in a column of glistening essence that poured down out of heaven like a shower of stardust. The elven lords, for each bore a crown, rolled down a brilliantly white sheet from above that unfurled like a scroll before her. One of the lords of light commanded her, "Daughter of Hereward, Heir of Widukind, look and behold!"

As she obeyed, a large body of men and women appeared on the sheet before her, and addressed her by name as if they were present, but she knew by their attire that they were from former times.

"Brekka," a tall white-haired man said, "we are the founding-fathers of the Amerikans. We have waited long in the heavens for this day when the seed of the woman would set the world aright again. We established a kingdom of life, liberty, and religious tolerance, such as you are now engaged in building up, but our republic was flawed because of allowing slavery and the mistreatment and displacement of our red brethren."

Another man in gentlemanly attire and red-streaked grey hair tied back in a knot stepped forward and said, "Not a hundred years had passed before the heavens wept. In the name of wars of aggression, a tyrant rose up and pitted brother against brother, that wealth might be gotten by blood, land stolen from the indigenes, and all constitutional restraints were ignored by evil and designing men posing as saints, presidents, reformers, and deliverers. In the name of the union they claimed they had to destroy the republic, and they blinded the people with their flattering words. Powerful and greedy men banded together to consolidate power in entities they called trusts, and claimed they were working in the interests of all mankind, but, in reality, their schemes were no less than the egg of tyranny, thus rendering all of our labors and the constitution we drafted, null and void. Once again, the forces of greed and avarice united to yoke the spirit of man under the march of the elitist imperialism of romish origins."

A third bespectacled man stepped forth and said, "We strictly charge you to never allow anyone to violate any of the tenants of the constitution you are now forming, and to build the freest people and greatest civilization the world will ever know, so that the wounds of this land shall be forever healed and reversed, so that we who labored so long with hopes of true freedom may finally take our rest in peace.

"May all the kindreds, nations, tongues, and peoples of the earth rejoice in the laws you will give them. We strictly charge you to get it right this time. No slavery. No oppression of workers. Keep clear walls between commerce, church, and government. Suffer no private entity with the goal of profit to own or control public resources. The land, the forests, the waters, and the minerals belong to the people, not to corporations. Beware of the anti-race, those who would strip mankind of their personal diversity and identity so as to make you a slave to the state instead of being connected to your true and natural identities, for they only wish to create their high strangeness so as to oppress you."

As the bespectacled figure finished, the sheet faded and rolled back up into the heavens, leaving only the two glorious figures of the elven lords hovering just above the ground.

One elf pointed up to heaven, and the other pointed down to the earth. "*As above, so below,*" they said in unison.

One of the shimmering elves looked down. "The earth upon which thou now standest is holy, and the place where the temple is ordained to be built. For I declare, this is the mount heredom your generations have sought. Here lived the god-kings of old."

Both lords gave the sign of the swan and rose into the heavens like flaming arrows followed by a clap of thunder and an explosion of lightning that ripped across the sky like the hurled bolts of Tyranus, leaving Brekka to ponder the strange happenings of the night in the ancient yew grove atop Mount Heredom.

THE END

AUTHOR BIOGRAPHY

Russ Howard was born in the north end of the Shenandoah Valley. He grew to manhood in rural West Virginia, where the mountaineer culture conveyed to Russ a sense of fierce independence, which is a running theme in his books. In his youth his first passion was for the animals he kept, an assortment of creatures from owls and pigeons to chipmunks and foxes. As he entered adolescence he developed an obsession for running and became an accomplished cross-country and track athlete.

His education spanned across international borders. He attended four major universities in three states and for a number of years he lived abroad as a student in various german cities as well as Kitzbuhl, Austria. During his stint there he learned to love and appreciate the german tongue and culture.

He is greatly influenced by English literature, Germanic, Keltic, and Slavic mythology. He is an admirer of the operatic genius Richard Wagner, the political innovator and democratic theorist Thomas Jefferson, and reveres J.R.R. Tolkien as the greatest modern story-teller. Russ's spiritual philosophies have been condensed from sources of mysticism and kabballah. He especially praises the works of Rudolph Steiner, Bruno Bettelheim, and Martin Buber.

Most of his life he worked as a mental health investigator, and a marriage, family and child therapist. Now Russ lives with his wife Kathryn, a dancer, in Roseburg, Oregon. He spends his time as an avid gardener, small-scale farmer, and shepherd.

Thank you for reading *The Evil Ennead.* I hope that you fell in love with the heroes, hated the villains and laughed with the jesters.

If you liked the book, please leave a review for this book on whatever platform you purchased it. Every review gives me renewed vigor to carry on with the stories of Panygyrus, and leads other readers to enjoy the fantastic world you have come to love.
Thanks again, Russ L. Howard

The Evil Ennead is the tenth book in the eleven book series, *The King of Three Bloods,* which follows the many trials and tribulations faced by the freedom-loving Syr Folk. If you enjoyed this, the tenth installment, you are humbly, though excitedly, invited to continue your journey with all the many colorful characters in book eleven, *Rebirth of the Elven-Gods.*

Be sure to check out

TheKingofThreeBloods.com

for future book releases, articles by and about the author